SECRET SINS

SECRET SINS

Secret Sins

Kate Charles

LARGE PRINT
Oxford

First published in Great Britain 2007
by
Allison & Busby Limited

Published in Large Print 2008 by ISIS Publishing Ltd.,
7 Centremead, Osney Mead, Oxford OX2 0ES
by arrangement with
Allison & Busby Limited

British Library Cataloguing in Publication Data
Charles, Kate
   Secret sins. – Large print ed.
   1. Women clergy – England – London – Fiction
   2. Murder – Investigation – Fiction
   3. Detective and mystery stories
   4. Large type books
   I. Title
   823.9'14 [F]

ISBN 978–0–7531–8092–1 (hb)
ISBN 978–0–7531–8093–8 (pb)

Printed and bound in Great Britain by
T. J. International Ltd., Padstow, Cornwall

For the world's greatest fan, Laurel Anderson

Acknowledgements

As ever, this book would not have been possible without the encouragement, advice and expertise of many people. Among them are Suzanne Clackson, Deborah Crombie, the Revd. Dr. Joan Crossley, the Rt. Revd. Christopher Herbert, Ann Hinrichs, Gianna Lombardi-Roberts, Marcia Talley, Margaret Anne Tibbs, and Mel Thompson, as well as my wonderful agent, Dot Lumley, and my two splendid editors, Susie Dunlop and Barbara Peters. Heartfelt thanks to all of them.

CHAPTER
ONE

Callie Anson first met Morag Hamilton at a Mothers' Union meeting. Jane Stanford, the vicar's wife, was very much in charge of the Mothers' Union at All Saints' Church, Paddington, and as the lowly curate, Callie was deliberately keeping a low profile, sitting in the back row as Jane introduced the speaker. Callie's thoughts were elsewhere: certainly not on the woman who was to demonstrate how to make festive Christmas decorations out of yogurt pots and ribbon, with the assistance of scissors and a glue gun. The Mothers' Union was not an institution which held much appeal for her in any case, but she knew that Jane would take as much offence if she were not there as she would if Callie were to try to take too prominent a role in its operation. The safest option, she had long since discovered, was literally to take a back seat.

As the correct use of the glue gun was explained, Callie's attention wandered still further, to the woman sitting nearest to her in the back row. She didn't recall having seen her before, though she wasn't exactly a striking or memorable type: late middle-aged, small, compact, neatly put together, with capable-looking hands folded over a black handbag on a tartan-clad lap.

Her grey hair was short and tidy, if not stylish, and her eyes were concealed behind spectacles, their frames unfashionably large.

What did seem out of place to Callie in the midst of the well-groomed London ladies was the woman's complexion, her cheeks ruddy with small broken blood vessels, as if she had spent much of her life out of doors and in a less genteel and rarefied climate than the soft rains of Paddington, Bayswater and Hyde Park.

Callie spoke to her at the earliest opportunity, as soon as the speaker had finished and the applause had died away. There was a discreet rush in the direction of the tea urn, but the woman hesitated for just a moment, and Callie turned to her.

"Hello," she said, extending her hand. "I don't think we've met. I'm the curate, Callie Anson."

The woman took her hand in a firm grip. "Morag Hamilton," she said, her strong Scottish burr as much an indicator of her origins as her un-English name. "I'm new here."

"It's good to meet you, Morag. And good to have you with us. Do you live in the parish?"

"Yes, that's right. Just round the corner, in fact." Morag indicated the direction with a tilt of her head.

"Oh, we're neighbours, then," Callie said, raising her eyes to the ceiling. "I live in the flat upstairs."

"Over the shop." Morag smiled. "That's something I know a bit about myself. My husband was the village doctor, and we lived above the surgery."

"In Scotland?" Callie ventured.

"That's right. In the Highlands," she amplified. "Gartenbridge. Not far from Aviemore. Do you know it?"

Callie shook her head. "No. I've been to Edinburgh once or twice, but that's as far as I've been in Scotland."

Morag gave a brisk laugh. "Edinburgh's so far south, it hardly counts as Scotland at all!"

"I understand the Highlands are very beautiful."

"Oh, there's nothing so lovely on earth." Morag's eyes looked over Callie's shoulder, as if focusing on something far away, and her face softened. "You really should go, you know. Go for a week, and you'll never want to come back."

Callie felt a prickle of curiosity. If the Highlands were so perfect, what was Morag Hamilton doing in London? Might her husband have retired and taken a fancy to city life? As she thought how to phrase the question diplomatically, she was forestalled by Jane Stanford, who was proprietorially steering the speaker towards the refreshments. "Callie, it looks as if Mrs. Barton could use a hand with pouring the tea," she said sharply, her brows drawn together in disapproval at the curate's failure to read her mind. "I would help, of course, but I must look after our speaker."

"Yes, of course, Jane." Callie smiled an apology at Morag Hamilton, who quirked an understanding eyebrow in Jane's direction. That endeared her to Callie, who decided on the spot that she liked the Scottish newcomer. "I'll see you later, Mrs. Hamilton," she promised as she made a move. "Do come this way and have a cup of tea and a mince pie."

"Please, call me Morag," insisted the other woman. "And it would be very nice to see you again."

Rachel Norton woke gradually, and not because it was yet daylight. The only source of light was from the ensuite bathroom, glowing faintly round the top and side of the stripped pine door. These Victorian houses had many charms, but period features came with a price — and that included doors which didn't quite fit in their frames and single-glazed sash windows which admitted the chill winds of winter without putting up a great deal of fight.

Half awake, Rachel couldn't quite decide whether her sleep had been disturbed by noises from the bathroom, or by the baby's movements. Under the duvet, she ran her hands over the great mound of her belly, still not used to the shape she had assumed over the last months. Yes, the baby was kicking, all right. She shifted a bit, trying to find a more comfortable position. Most of the time now she slept on her back; anything else was just too awkward.

The cracks of light round the bathroom door morphed into a rectangle as Trevor came through, clad in his running shorts, a grey tee shirt and his expensive state-of-the-art trainers. His iPod was strapped round his upper arm in a holster.

"Morning," Rachel murmured.

"Oh, love." Trevor came to the side of the bed and leaned over, kissing her forehead. "I hope I didn't wake you — I was trying to be quiet."

"The baby was kicking."

4

Trevor gave a fond chuckle and patted the duvet above the mound. "He'll be a football player. Mark my words, Rache."

"You're so sure it's a boy." Rachel's protest was perfunctory and half-hearted, oft-repeated. The scans had been noncommittal on the subject, but Trevor was unfazed.

"It's got to be. A beautiful blond boy." Trevor lifted a lock of the thick blonde hair spread on Rachel's pillow and fingered it lovingly, then patted his own close-cropped fair head. "Couldn't be anything else."

Rachel changed the subject. "What time is it?"

"Seven. As usual. You know I always run at seven."

Like clockwork, she reflected. You could set your watch by Trevor's timekeeping. A run along the canal at seven — winter or summer, dark or light — , home for a shower and a quick breakfast, and at his desk by half-past eight.

Trevor was much happier these days, since he no longer had to commute into the City. His office was at the other end of the corridor, in the large bay-fronted room at the front of the house. When they'd bought the house, six months ago, Rachel had fancied that room for their bedroom, but Trevor had been adamant. "I'll spend more time in the office than the bedroom — we both will, for that matter. Makes sense to use the biggest room. Space for all the computers and filing cabinets. And good light." She hadn't really argued. It *was* a big house, and their bedroom at the back was perfectly adequate in size. And they'd taken the small bedroom next to it, knocked it through and fitted it out

5

as an ensuite, still leaving another bedroom to use as the nursery.

They'd come a long way from the scruffy, cramped flat in Stoke Newington that they'd shared for a few years before their marriage, and where they'd started their married life a scant year ago. Trevor was an IT genius — she'd always told him so, and eventually he'd carried through with the threat he always made when his boss hacked him off. He'd told him where to put his job, and had started up on his own as an independent IT consultant. Some — many — of his old clients had followed him; it hadn't taken long for word of mouth to bring others, and now the business was flourishing. They'd bought the Victorian semi in Paddington — with the canal close by for the daily run — and left Stoke Newington behind forever.

Rachel, too, had quit her job — as a bookkeeper in the same City firm where Trevor had worked, and where they had met. Trevor had insisted that she could do his books instead. After all, with the business growing like it was, he needed a good bookkeeper. She didn't miss the commute, she admitted to herself, but she *did* miss her co-workers, her mates. She'd been working there since she left school, and those people were almost like family to her. The congenial coffee breaks, the confidences shared over sandwiches at lunchtimes, the drinks at the corner pub after work: those things were undervalued at the time, barely thought of when she'd agreed to pack in the job. Now, when she no longer had them, she valued them fiercely with a nostalgia she'd never expected in herself.

6

And now, with the baby on the way, Trevor didn't want her to work at all. "We don't need the money," he said often. "You can be a stay-at-home mum."

"But your books . . ."

"I can hire a bookkeeper," Trevor had stated grandly. "I'll advertise."

The baby kicked her again, even more violently than before. Rachel flinched and rubbed her stomach.

"I'm off, then." Trevor leaned over and kissed her lightly on the lips. "See you in a bit. There's no rush for you to get up, love. Take your time."

"Have fun," she called after him.

"Running isn't supposed to be fun," Trevor reminded her as he slipped his iPod earphones into his ears and pushed the play button. With a wave over his shoulder he disappeared down the corridor, already breaking into a trot.

Rachel waited until she heard the front door close, then struggled into a sitting position and reached under the bed for her laptop. Propping it up awkwardly on her bump, she opened it, logged into the wireless network, and checked her e-mail.

Neville Stewart had scarcely seen his friend Mark Lombardi for weeks. They'd run across each other occasionally at the police station, once or twice sharing a meal in the canteen, but it seemed as if the old days of bachelor evenings together at the pub had come to an end.

There had been no row; they hadn't changed their pattern by design. It just happened that the station's

7

two most confirmed bachelors had developed relationships at the same time, and things had changed.

Today, though, Neville was feeling restless, missing
the old camaraderie he and Mark had shared.

There was an underlying reason for his restlessness,
one he didn't want to think about too closely.

Triona.

He was sick of the status quo, tired of the way things
seemed to have stalled out. Going nowhere: that was
their relationship. Why was she so stubborn?

They had met up again a couple of months ago, nine
years after a brief but intense affair which had scarred
them both. The magic, Neville realised at once, was still
there. Triona affected him as no other woman had ever
done, before or since.

He had invited her out to dinner; she had accepted.

He had gone to pick her up at her flat — her posh
flat in a warehouse conversion overlooking the river.

They'd never made it to dinner. They hadn't made it
any further than her bedroom.

Turning over the papers on his desk without really
looking at them, Neville recalled that night with a
complex mixture of burning longing, self-pity, and
anger.

It had been as good as ever. Better. Triona had
matured, was now a grown woman who knew what she
wanted and knew how to give pleasure, without losing
any of her raw animal energy. He knew her so well,
recalled every detail of her body, yet she was a stranger
to him, a source of unexpected delight.

That night had been the best, most memorable one of Neville's life. He hadn't wanted it to end. He'd assumed, naturally enough, that it would be just the first of many such nights to come.

In the morning, lying with Triona in his arms, her head pillowed on his chest, he'd looked round her bedroom. "It's a great flat," he said, playing with a curled strand of her long black hair. When he'd first known Triona, her hair had been shorter, wild and curly with a life all its own. Now she'd grown it out, wearing it in a neat and elegant knot by day. That night, though, he'd freed it from its constraints; it had sprung back into its curly ways, untamed and uncivilised. "Do you own it? I don't suppose you'll want to move back to my scruffy old place. It would make more sense for me to move in here."

Triona twisted round to stare at him, her dark blue eyes abruptly losing their drowsy look. "What on earth are you talking about?"

"My flat. It's the same old place in Shepherd's Bush. No nicer than it used to be, and not very convenient for your job in the City. This will be a bit of a commute for me, but . . ."

He tailed off at the look on her face. "Don't be daft, Neville." Triona sat up and wrapped the duvet round her. "Neither one of us is moving anywhere."

"But . . ." He reached for her; she jerked away.

"It happened," she said crisply. "It just happened. Okay? And I enjoyed it. I won't pretend that I didn't. But it was a one-off. Don't make the mistake of thinking that we're back together. Not in any sense of the word."

Eventually she relented, just a tiny bit. "If you want me back," she said, "you'll have to prove it. You'll have to woo me. No more shagging. We'll forget all the water under the bridge, and pretend we've only just met for the first time."

"But we shagged the day after we met," Neville pointed out. "You moved in a few days later."

A smile tugged at the corner of her mouth. "Perhaps we're not the world's best example," she admitted. "But this time it will be different, Neville. If you want a relationship, it has to be on my terms. And my terms are simple. In a word, courtship."

She'd meant it, too. And he'd been bending over backwards to do it her way. Dinner dates, flowers, the whole bit.

And after weeks of this game, Neville was sick of it. Sick of the artificiality, sick of the frustration. They were going nowhere.

Last night he'd confronted her about it. After dinner — admittedly a nice, romantic evening — he'd pressed her to take things a step further. "Let me stay the night," he'd begged. "Don't you think we've waited long enough?"

Triona had been firm, though. "No way, Neville. You just don't get it, do you?"

He'd asked her the question which for him summed everything up. "Do you want to be with me or not?"

She'd lowered her eyes, turned her head away. "That's not really the point."

It seemed to Neville that it was exactly the point. He wanted to be with her. *With* her — in her bed, in her arms. God, how he wanted it. But he was tired of playing games. Enough was enough.

Tonight, he decided, he wouldn't be available. And maybe not tomorrow night either. Let her stew.

He picked up his phone and rang Mark Lombardi.

Jane Stanford had always put great stock in Christmas, busy time that it was for her husband Brian, and tried to make it special for her family.

On a vicar's stipend there had never been a great deal of spare cash for splashing out on the trimmings, so Jane had to plan carefully, putting aside small sums of money through the year and using her creativity to make that money go as far as possible. Fresh trees were increasingly expensive; some years ago she'd obtained a very good-quality artificial one at a church jumble sale, and had fashioned some decorations for it herself. She'd knit a set of crib figures out of bits of left-over wool, and the wreath for the front door of the vicarage was trimmed with a recycled bow from an ancient flower arrangement and some pine cones she'd found in the park. On Stir-up Sunday she'd made her own Christmas pudding, and the Christmas cake, laced with brandy from a generous parishioner, had been maturing in the larder for even longer than that.

Their parishioners were very generous, Jane acknowledged, especially at Christmas time, providing enough bottles to get the Stanfords through the first few months of a new year. That was how she thought of them: *their* parishioners, rather than Brian's. She was a partner in Brian's ministry, proud of her calling as a vicar's wife, smug in her feelings of superiority to those modern clergy wives who scorned their proper place at the heart of the parish and instead took up jobs outside the home. Or even, in this day and age, went for ordination themselves.

That, inevitably, reminded Jane of Callie Anson, her husband's curate. Why Brian hadn't been given a nice young man as a curate was beyond Jane. Up till now the curates had always been young men: some more pleasant than others, some brighter or more capable, but always men. The nicer ones Jane had treated almost like members of her family, like older brothers to the twins, inviting them to meals and sometimes even doing their laundry. But much as she'd tried, she just couldn't warm to Callie Anson.

It wasn't that she was jealous of Callie — not exactly. She didn't think that Callie was a wanton temptress, trying to steal her husband away from her. Though, Jane knew, such things were not unknown with vicars and female curates: she'd read one or two accounts in the papers. Proximity fostered intimacy, and when people were thrown together in the course of their jobs, day in and day out, sharing confidences ... Well, anything could happen. It was human nature. Not that she didn't trust Brian, of course.

Brian had suggested that they might invite Callie to join them for Christmas lunch. That, as far as Jane was concerned, was out of the question. "She has her own family," she'd pointed out. "Her mother lives in

Kensington, doesn't she? And isn't there a brother? Why would she want to come to us? Christmas is a family time."

"I just thought it would be nice to offer," Brian had said mildly. "I don't think she gets on all that well with her mother. And when Tom was the curate, you invited him for Christmas at least twice."

"That was different," stated Jane, though she wasn't able to explain why. And this year things were going to be different enough as it was.

For the first time, the boys would be coming home for Christmas, back from their first term at Oxford. Jane and Brian had visited them once during the term, taking them out for a meal, but Charlie and Simon hadn't yet been home.

So their homecoming would be special, and Jane was determined that this Christmas would be the best ever for the Stanford family, with no curates or other hangers-on to spoil it.

On this particular evening, Jane was feeling even less charitable towards Callie Anson than usual: Brian, having received two tickets to a posh pre-Christmas charity concert, had opted to take his curate rather than his wife. Jane felt she'd done a very good job of masking her disappointment from him; she'd even managed, with a semblance of cheerfulness, to tell him to have an enjoyable evening.

"You're sure you don't mind?" Brian had said at the last minute — far too late to have done anything about it if she'd said yes.

"I'll enjoy an evening in by myself," Jane had assured him.

She'd had a scrappy supper of leftovers; she'd listened to *The Archers*. She'd checked the telly listings and not found anything remotely appealing, then had picked up her library book and tried to immerse herself in it.

But she couldn't get the picture out of her mind: Brian, enjoying himself with Callie Anson. Listening to the concert, eating the lovely food at the livery company reception, chatting to interesting and important people. Brian would be introducing Callie to them, showing her off. Callie, with her shiny brown bob and her attractive figure, probably wearing a brand new frock.

Deliberately she switched her mind to thoughts of Christmas. Christmas, and the boys.

Dropping her library book, which wasn't that good anyway, she got up and went to the telephone. On impulse she dialled Simon's mobile number. A chat with him was just what she needed to cheer her up. Mothers were not supposed to have favourites, especially when it came to twins, and Jane didn't — not really. She adored both her boys. But Simon was the one who was temperamentally more similar to her, of all people on earth the quickest to understand her moods and most likely to say just the right thing.

"Mum?" said Simon when he heard her voice. He sounded surprised. And was it her imagination that he didn't sound pleased?

"Hello, darling. I just wanted to say hello."

"Umm . . . Mum. Could I ring you back later?"

Her maternal antennae twitched, sensitive to the tiniest signal. "Is everything all right?"

"Fine. I'm just . . . This isn't a good time. Okay?"

"It's not important," she assured him. "Don't bother ringing back."

"Okay, then. Bye, Mum." He hung up.

Jane stood for a moment, staring at the receiver in her hand. What on earth was wrong?

Charlie would know. He and his twin brother had always been extraordinarily close. Jane rang his number. He answered after a couple of rings.

Sensitive now, she asked him, "Is this a good time for you? I'm not disturbing you, am I?"

Charlie laughed. "I'm working on an essay. So I'm delighted at the interruption, Mum. What's up?"

How could she put it? "I was just . . . wondering about Simon," she began. "I rang him just now, and he . . . Well, I just wondered if something was wrong."

"Oh," said Charlie. "I expect he's with Ellie. Not wanting to be disturbed, if you understand me."

"Ellie?"

There was a brief silence on the other end. "Hasn't he . . . ?" Charlie began. "Oh, bother."

"Who is Ellie?" Jane heard a squeak in her voice as she said the name, tasting it in her mouth, knowing instinctively that it would become familiar to her.

"He said he was going to tell you. Weeks ago, Mum. I thought he had done."

"Tell me what?" Now her voice was calm, deliberately so.

"About Ellie." Charlie sighed. "His girlfriend."

"Girlfriend?"

"He met her during Freshers Week. They started going out straightaway. And they've been inseparable ever since. He spends all his time with her — I've barely seen him for weeks." Charlie sighed again. "I really thought he'd told you, Mum."

"No," she said. She played with the phone wire, unkinking a twist in the spiral cord. "But why, Charlie? Why didn't he tell me?"

Charlie spoke slowly, as though choosing his words with care. "Maybe he thought you'd be jealous."

"Jealous?" Jane gave a laugh which sounded forced to her own ears. "Why would I be jealous? Simon's always had girlfriends. Both of you have, all through school." And they had: it was only natural. Her sons were good-looking, red-blooded boys. Of course they'd had girlfriends.

"Girlfriends, yes." Charlie cleared his throat. "Ellie's different, Mum. It's . . . serious."

"But he's only known her for a few weeks."

Charlie gave a dry chuckle. "You've always told us that as soon as you met Dad, you knew he was the one."

"Yes, but —" Trust Charlie to remember that and throw it back at her now.

"Ellie's the one, Mum." His voice was gentle, as if breaking bad news to a child. "Believe me. She's the one."

Neville and Mark met for dinner at a Chinese buffet not far from the station. "This worked out well," Mark said as they sat down facing each other across a red tablecloth. "Callie is out tonight. Out with her boss, the vicar. Some posh do."

"You'd better keep an eye on that sort of thing," Neville warned, grinning. "She'll throw you over for the boss."

Mark smiled. "I'm not too worried. He's married."

"And you think that will stop him?"

"Also middle-aged and not exactly a catch. Callie has better taste than that — or at least I like to think so."

Neville suppressed a small twinge of jealousy. "So — things are going well, then?"

"Yes and no." Mark fiddled with his chopsticks. "Callie's great. I really, really . . ." He swallowed. "Well."

"Don't tell me. It's the family thing."

Mark sighed. "Always the family thing."

"They don't like her?"

He didn't look at Neville. "They haven't met her. They don't even know about her."

"Good God, man." Neville shook his head. "How long are you going to wait till you tell them, then? Maybe when you send out the wedding invitations?"

Mark stood and moved towards the buffet table. "We're a long way from that, Nev."

Neville followed. "Just tell them. Bloody get it over with, man. You've been seeing her for months. If you think there's any future in it, you're going to have to tell them."

"I'd like to think there's a future." He took a plate and regarded the choice of starters, then helped himself to some prawn crackers, a spring roll, and a spoonful of seaweed. "In fact, I can't imagine my future without her."

Neville heaped his plate with sticky ribs and added a few fried wontons, banishing a momentary mental vision of Triona. "Then you don't have any choice."

"I know. I know." Mark went back to the table and for a moment he picked at the seaweed with his chopsticks, looking thoughtful.

"I don't know how you can eat that bloody grass," said Neville, picking up a rib with his fingers.

"It's good. Just a bit hard to eat, is all."

Neville, chewing on a rib, was incapable of speech for a moment.

Mark thought out loud. "My sister," he said. "Maybe I could talk to my sister. She might be sympathetic. She might have ideas about how to tell Mum. *Nostra mamma.*"

Around the rib, Neville asked, "Is your sister married?"

"Oh, yes. She's been married for years. She's older than me," he added. "Eight years older. Nearly nine."

"And she did what your parents wanted her to?" Neville lifted an ironic eyebrow. "Married an Italian and had lots of bambinos?"

"*Bambini,*" Mark corrected him automatically. "Only two, as it happens. Serena's had a lot of problems with her pregnancies — just like my mum. She's had several miscarriages and that sort of thing."

Neville made a face. "Too much information."

"Sorry. You did ask."

He put down the chewed bone and picked up another rib. "These things are almost more trouble than they're worth," he grumbled. Like women, he was about to add. That, though, might lead him down a path where he definitely did not want to go. It was all very well for Mark — those Mediterranean types always wore their hearts on their sleeves anyway — but he didn't want to talk about his romantic woes to anyone. Not even Mark. And he wasn't going to talk to Triona. Not tonight. Maybe never.

CHAPTER
TWO

It was several days before Callie found the time to pay a call on Morag Hamilton. Afterwards she wasn't quite sure what had impelled her to juggle her schedule, find out Morag's address, and turn up unannounced on her doorstep. Whatever it was, though, she was glad that she did.

The corners of Morag's eyes crinkled with pleasure at the sight of her. "What a nice surprise," she said, opening the door wide. "Come in and have a cup of tea, my dear. I've just put the kettle on."

"That would be lovely." Callie followed her into the flat.

The parish of All Saints', Bayswater, was full of very elegant old houses which had been converted into flats. This, however, was not one of them. It was part of a purpose-built block, stuck incongruously between two Georgian mansions, and had been put up in the 1960s — one of the low points of British architecture. At that time it must have been the height of modernity, but now it was tiredly dated, stark and ugly. Morag had seemingly done her best with it, filling it with homely furniture and covering the walls with soft watercolours of what Callie assumed were Scottish scenes. There was a realistic gas fire burning in the blocky modern fireplace, and an assortment of framed photographs ranged on top of an old upright piano against one wall. A tall bookcase held a varied collection of recent paperback novels mixed with leatherbound classics: Dickens, Scott, Robert Louis Stevenson. Callie followed her usual procedure when visiting a parishioner for the first time: she looked at the books, then at the photographs, for clues about the owner's interests, history and family.

There were clues aplenty here, but Morag was back quickly with the tea.

"Sorry," said Callie, caught in the act of examining the photos. "I was just being nosy."

Morag didn't seem to mind. "Not at all. There's nothing secret about them."

"Your family?" Callie said encouragingly.

"Aye."

"And you have a dog!" Callie picked up a photo of a sturdy tan-coloured Cairn terrier, standing against a background of mountains and heather, staring beady-eyed into the camera.

"*Had* a dog." Morag's voice was matter-of-fact, but Callie detected strong emotion behind the words. "Macduff. Best dog there ever was."

"Oh. He's . . ."

"Gone. Over six months now. Sixteen, he was. A good age for a dog. But . . ."

There was nothing perfunctory about Callie's response; her rush of empathy was immediate and sincere. "Oh, I'm so sorry. You must miss him dreadfully."

"I do."

"I have a dog," Callie confided on impulse. "A cocker spaniel — black and white. Bella. I haven't had her for very long, but I just can't imagine losing her."

Morag sighed, and her eyes were misty. "It comes with the territory, I'm afraid. Their lives are cruelly short." She picked up another photo, of a sandy-haired man with wire-rimmed spectacles. "Donald, my husband. We were married for nearly forty years. He died a few months before Macduff. And I'm ashamed to say that of the two, I probably miss Macduff a bit more. But then, I spent more time with Macduff than I did with Donald. He was a doctor — worked all the hours God gave, and then some."

"So you're on your own now?"

"Yes, I'm on my own." Morag replaced the photo on top of the piano and moved to the tea tray. "Do you take sugar, my dear?"

"No sugar." Callie sat down across from Morag in a shabby but comfortable chair as Morag poured the tea. She was more curious than ever: why had Morag Hamilton moved to London? "You said you haven't lived here long?" she probed.

"Not long at all." She handed Callie a cup. "I scarcely know a soul. It isn't . . . well, it isn't like Scotland. People aren't all that friendly, are they? They don't go out of their way."

"We try to be friendly at All Saints'," Callie said defensively.

Morag picked up a plate of shortbread biscuits and extended it towards Callie. "Aye. And I appreciate it. Quite a few people have spoken to me after services and so on. But you're the first person who's come to call."

Callie felt ashamed on behalf of her congregation, not to mention her vicar. When she'd mentioned Morag Hamilton to Brian, at their weekly staff meeting, he'd looked vague. "I think I know who you mean," he'd said. "Small woman? Grey hair? Go and see her, by all means, when you have a chance."

At least, she told herself wryly, she had Brian's blessing. He didn't like it when he felt she was doing things behind his back.

"I have a confession to make," Morag said as Callie crunched into the shortbread.

Oh, dear, Callie thought, automatically assigning the word an upper-case C in her mind. She'd never heard anyone's Confession, and as a deacon, not yet priested, she wasn't authorised to do so. "If you want the Sacrament of Confession, you'll have to see Father Brian, I'm afraid," she apologised. "I'm just a deacon."

Morag laughed. "Not that sort of confession!"

Flustered, Callie said, "Oh, well, then."

"I've never been much of a churchgoer," Morag went on. "I've tried to be a good person, but I never really had the time or the inclination to spend all of my time in church."

"Mm," Callie said, not sure what else was required of her.

"But when I moved to London, and ended up with All Saints' just round the corner, it seemed to me that it would be a good way to meet people."

Callie could contain her curiosity no longer. "Why *did* you move to London?" she blurted. "If you didn't know anyone here?"

"Oh, I didn't say I didn't know anyone," Morag said, lifting her eyebrows as her mouth twisted in an ironic smile. "I said that I was on my own. And I am. But my son and his family live not far from here. St. John's Wood, just up the road."

"Your son!" Callie sprayed biscuit crumbs in her lap.

"Angus." Morag put down her tea cup and went to the piano, selecting a photo which she placed on the table in front of Callie. "And that's my granddaughter Alex, and his wife, Jilly."

Callie picked up the photo and studied it. No casual snapshot: it was a studio portrait, and a very expensive one at that. The man — Angus — stood in the centre, a detail which Callie found interesting. He didn't look very tall, and had dark hair which receded sharply from his forehead, though he seemed surprisingly young in spite of that. He was wearing a well-cut suit, almost certainly bespoke, and a colourful silk tie of the sort currently favoured by newsreaders. His heavy-lidded eyes stared straight at the camera, almost in challenge.

Jilly, the woman, was on his right. If you looked up "trophy wife" in the dictionary, thought Callie, her picture would be there. She was blonde, she was young. She was beautiful, in a sleek, well-maintained way. Her dress wasn't exactly revealing, but it didn't conceal a

24

great deal either: a body which was no stranger to the gym and the tanning bed. Her gaze at the camera was coy, with half a glance directed at her husband.

The child, Alex, on the left, was a different matter entirely. Even though she was looking at the camera, no doubt at the photographer's command, it was an unwilling eye contact, almost detached from it and the other people in the frame. Her eyes were saying, as clearly as if she were speaking the words, "I don't want to be here, and none of this has anything to do with me."

No one would have called her a beautiful child, but she was certainly arresting, in spite of her efforts to fade into the background. Her hair was frizzy rather than curly, and she had a wide mouth, stretched into a pro-forma smile and revealing a brace on her teeth. Those expressive eyes, though, were large and fringed with luxuriant lashes.

"How old is Alex?" Callie asked. "Is this a recent photo?"

"Aye, it's quite recent. She's twelve."

That explained part of it: Callie remembered twelve as a particularly difficult age.

"Poor wee bairn," Morag said, her voice soft. "She's not grown into her face yet. You may not think it to look at her, but I do believe she'll be a beauty one day. Like her mother. She's a lot like her mother."

Callie couldn't imagine Alex ever looking anything like the glamorous woman in the photo. "Like Jilly?" she blurted.

Morag made a noise in the back of her throat. "Surely you can't think Jilly is her mother? And Jilly is a painted doll, not a real beauty."

"Jilly is her stepmother, then." That, too, explained a great deal.

"Aye." It was as if she didn't trust herself to say any more than that.

"Why isn't she with her mother?" Callie knew it wasn't her business, but there was something about this girl, merely glimpsed in a photo, which had touched her.

Morag shrugged and looked at her watch. "That's a long story, my dear. One I don't have time to tell you today — I have an appointment in a wee while. But if you come back another day, I'll tell you all about Alex."

Callie finished her tea and rose to go, knowing that she would be back.

The high heels echoed in the hospital corridor, clip-clopping briskly away from the room. Frances Cherry, hospital chaplain, listened to their retreat for a moment, her attention never leaving the elderly woman in the bed beside her. The woman was distressed, and not just because she knew she was dying. "I don't want her having it," Irene Godfrey choked. "Not a penny."

"She's your only relative?"

"She's a monster! I haven't seen her for years. The only reason she came was to make sure she was getting my house and my money."

Frances didn't doubt that the woman was right: the niece's demeanour had been anything but affectionate.

She'd been called in very early in the morning because her aunt didn't have long to live, but she'd been business-like, brisk. She had offered to ring her solicitor right away, to have him visit the hospital immediately and get everything in writing. A proper will. "It will all come to me anyway," she'd said, "but it would be much easier if we had it all tied up ahead of time."

Irene Godfrey had refused, the niece had gone. Angry footsteps, clip-clopping down the corridor.

"She hates cats! She always has done," the old woman sobbed. "When she was a child, and her mum brought her to visit, she kicked Snowball! I caught her doing it once. How could anyone be so cruel? Snowball was a defenceless animal."

"And now you think . . ."

"I think that as soon as I'm gone, the first thing she'll do is have Fluffy and George put down. I can't let that happen." She squeezed Frances' hand with surprising strength.

"Then who . . .?"

"My friend Maisie. She'd look after Fluffy and George," said the woman. "She loves them. I know I can trust her." She struggled to sit up. "I need to make a will," she said urgently. "Now, before it's too late."

Frances was inclined to believe she was right. She also felt that unless the will were done properly and with great care the niece would use every means in her power to overturn it, and could quite possibly succeed. "Do you have a solicitor?" she asked.

"No. I've never needed one before." Tears welled in the woman's eyes. "Can't you find one for me? Now?"

There was a clock on the bedside table, though Frances wasn't sure why: time had ceased to mean anything to Irene Godfrey. An hourglass would have been more appropriate, she thought, with its sands rapidly running out. It was, Frances saw, the wee hours of the morning. Just gone six. Profoundly dark outside. No self-respecting solicitor would be out of his comfortable bed yet, let alone welcome a phone call from someone he'd never met.

But she didn't know how much time they had. How long could she afford to wait?

She stroked Irene Godfrey's hand and said a silent prayer. The answer came to her almost immediately. "Triona," Frances breathed with gratitude.

Triona might not be happy about it, but she would come.

Two hours later, the deed was done. Triona O'Neil, exuding professional competence, had drawn up a simple will and had called in a couple of nurses to witness Irene Godfrey's signature. And a few minutes after that, her mind at rest, the old woman had closed her eyes and slipped away. Frances had said a prayer, then as the hospital mechanisms for reclaiming a bed for the next patient went into operation, she took Triona to the hospital cafe.

"Come on," she said. "I'll buy you a cup of coffee. Even a sticky bun, if you like. You've earned it."

"You look knackered," said Triona bluntly. "How long have you been here?"

Frances shook her head. "Oh, a few hours. I don't usually work nights, but I was called in. Mrs. Godfrey asked for me, and the nurses knew she didn't have long."

She might not look very wonderful, Frances was aware, but Triona herself looked worse than Frances would have expected, even given the earliness of the hour. Her hair was as tidy and professional-looking as usual, brushed back into a knot, but her eyes were shadowed, with blue smudges beneath them, telling of more than just an hour or two of missed sleep.

They went back a long way together, did Frances and Triona, though they'd lost touch for a number of years. Frances still found it difficult to equate this elegant and mature woman with the passionate young firebrand Triona had once been. She must, Frances calculated, be a bit over thirty. In her prime, from Frances' perspective of approaching fifty.

Frances reiterated her apologies for the early call. "I was really desperate," she said. "I didn't know what else to do. The poor old thing was dreadfully upset. And if you'd seen the niece . . ."

Triona waved her hand. "Don't worry about it. You didn't wake me, if that's what's bothering you."

"Are you okay?" she asked impulsively.

"Fine." Triona turned her head away.

They had reached the cafe, crowded with hospital personnel grabbing something to eat or drink in between various duties. Frances scanned the room and spotted a table about to be vacated. "Why don't you sit there," she suggested, "and I'll join the queue. What would you like? Coffee? Tea?"

"Coffee, please."

In a few minutes she was back at the table with a tray: coffee and bacon rolls. "I thought we ought to have something to eat," she said. "A bit of breakfast." Frances didn't usually succumb to the lure of bacon rolls, but the smell of the bacon had been too tempting to resist on an empty stomach.

"Thanks."

"You do eat bacon, don't you? Heather, my daughter, has become a vegan. She'd probably never speak to me again if she saw me tucking into this."

"How is Heather?" Triona took a plate and a mug from the tray and arranged them in front of her.

"Fine, as far as I can tell. You know she's married? And they're coming for Christmas. So it won't be long now."

"Yes, I remember you telling me."

"I'm looking forward to it," Frances said.

She *was* looking forward to it, but that was only part of the truth. Part of her was dreading Christmas. She and Graham were due to meet their new son-in-law, an ageing American dropout — with a ponytail — called Zack, who had managed to turn Heather into a self-righteous eschewer of any animal-derived product. It would be nut roast for Christmas this year.

"Graham is well?" Triona asked.

"Yes, fine. Busy as always."

"And how is Leo?"

Her dear friend, Leo Jackson. Frances gave an involuntary sigh. "I think he's as well as could be expected."

"You know I don't read newspapers. But I'm aware that they have a short attention span — they must have forgotten about him by now."

"Pretty much." Frances took a fortifying sip of coffee. "He's dropped out of sight, and the press have moved on to their next victim."

Triona raised an eyebrow. "Gone into hiding, has he?"

"Not exactly. He did at first, of course — the Bishop sent him off to a monastery. For reflection and counselling. But being Leo, he soon got fed up with that. Wanted action, not contemplation." She smiled, picturing him: a giant of a man, always on the move. "So he volunteered to go to the Caribbean. Hurricane relief work. The last I heard from him, he was helping to rebuild a church that was flattened."

She missed him terribly. He'd been a part of her life for years, a friend who was always there — there with a word of encouragement, a hug. Through the difficult years of waiting — and fighting — for the right of women to be ordained as priests, he had been a rock and a constant support. And recently, as well, they'd been through such a lot together. Their bond of friendship was an extraordinarily strong one. She thought about the number of times they'd been together here in the cafe, drinking coffee and talking. An odd couple, she knew they must have appeared: Leo so large and so black, towering over the petite redhead.

31

Neither conformed to the stereotype most people attached to the Anglican priesthood.

Suddenly there was a lump in her throat. If he'd been there now, he would have noticed. "Frannie, pet," he would have said in his booming, lilting voice, leaning across the table in concern, covering her small white hand with his large dark one. "Whatever's the matter? You can tell Leo."

Instead, though, it was Triona across from her. And Triona was the one who wasn't quite right. Her very white skin was even paler than usual, and there was an unhealthy sheen on her forehead and upper lip. She swallowed hard, then took a sip of coffee. Her eyes widened, her hand went to her mouth. "Excuse me," she said faintly from behind her hand, rising to her feet. "I'll be right back." Her head swivelled round. "Where's the loo?"

Frances took charge. "It's this way," she said, abandoning her breakfast and guiding Triona towards the ladies' room.

"Sorry. You don't need to . . ."

Frances waited by the row of basins, listening to the unmistakable sound of retching. Uncontrollable, gut-wrenching. She remembered how it felt, and instinctively she knew what was wrong with Triona.

Eventually Triona emerged, looking sheepish and wrung-out. "Sorry," she murmured. "I'm so sorry to ruin your breakfast."

Frances was ready with a damp paper towel to wipe her friend's face. "Nothing to be sorry about. You can't help it."

"I think it was the smell of the bacon that did it. And I shouldn't have drunk that coffee."

"Probably so. When I was expecting Heather, I couldn't touch coffee."

Triona swallowed hard, and averted her eyes. "You know, then," she said in a flat voice.

"It's pretty obvious to anyone who's ever been pregnant. Morning sickness is wretched." Frances was shorter than Triona, and couldn't really put her arm around the other woman's shoulders, so she rubbed her arm instead. "Would you like to talk about it?" she suggested.

"No." She swallowed again. "Yes. But not here. And not in the cafe."

"No food smells," Frances agreed. She had worked at the hospital for years, and knew its every corner intimately. There were a few consultation rooms, where doctors took families to give them bad news in private, and one was quite nearby. She led Triona there and sat her down, then took a seat next to her. Sometimes, she knew, it was easier to say difficult things if you didn't have to look at someone face-to-face.

"It just started a few days ago, maybe a week," Triona said. "But it's been horrible." She clasped her hands together in her lap.

"The father?" Frances suggested gently.

Triona almost spat the name. "Neville. The bastard."

"Neville *Stewart*? Detective Inspector Neville Stewart?" She was astonished, and couldn't help showing it.

"That's the one."

"But . . ." Frances thought back, trying to remember. Triona had mentioned that she'd known Neville Stewart, a long time ago.

Neville Stewart. Frances supposed that some women — perhaps many women — might consider him attractive, with his slightly boyish looks and his trim body, though she couldn't see it herself. He'd never bothered turning on his Irish charm with her, of course; she'd hardly even seen him smile. Well, she acknowledged to herself, there was no accounting for taste.

"I'll start at the beginning, shall I?" Triona's voice was sounding more Irish than usual.

"That would probably help."

Triona positioned her body so that she was facing the window rather than Frances. "I met Neville Stewart years ago. Nearly ten years back."

"About the time you and I lost touch," Frances realised.

"Yes. And he was probably the main reason. When we were together, living together, there wasn't time for anything else in my life."

"Were you together for a long time?"

"Three months. A lifetime. Take your pick." Triona closed her eyes. "God, I loved him. I was crazy in love with him. And he . . . I don't think he knows the meaning of the word 'love'." She swallowed, stopped. There was a long silence.

"Did he leave you after three months?" Frances prompted eventually.

"No, I left *him*. I moved out."

"I don't understand," admitted Frances.

Triona's hands twisted together, then sprang apart in a dramatic gesture. "I wanted him to marry me, see? But he was terrified of commitment. So I thought I'd shock him into doing something. I moved out. I was so sure he'd come after me. Find me and . . . something. Whatever. But he didn't. He never tried to find me. He just bloody let me go."

Frances still didn't understand; this seemed to her to be a very perverse way to get someone to marry you, and it also seemed like water long since under the bridge. She waited for Triona to continue.

"I married someone else after a few months. Someone from work — a solicitor from the firm where I was doing my articles. I didn't love him," she added bluntly. "I never loved him. I married him to spite bloody Neville Stewart. I hoped that Irish bastard would lay awake at night and think about what he was missing, what he'd passed up."

"And did he?"

Triona gave a short, bitter laugh. "He did not. He didn't even know I was married! How's that for an irony? I went through six years of a bad marriage to spite him, and he never even knew it."

That still didn't explain how she was now carrying his child. Frances was good at waiting and listening; she folded her hands in her lap.

Getting up restlessly and moving to the window, Triona went on. "And then he walked back into my life. Or me into his — I suppose it depends on the way you look at it. That day when you . . ." She paused delicately, as if unwilling to remind Frances of something she would rather forget. "I hadn't seen him since I left him. Nine years, almost to the day."

Frances observed the tension in her back, heard the pain in her voice.

"I'd been hating him for nine years. Hating him as passionately as I'd loved him. But when I saw the bastard again, I realised that the love was still there, too. Always had been. You can't just stop loving someone because you want to, can you?"

"I suppose not."

"He was still a free agent. I'd shed my husband a few years ago. It wouldn't have been professionally ethical for us to see each other until your business was all sorted out. But after that . . . he invited me to dinner. And being a fool, I said yes."

"So you're back together."

"I wish it were that simple." Again the bitter laugh, as Triona wrapped her arms round herself and leaned her forehead against the glass of the window. It had just started to rain; fat drops hit the glass and rolled slowly down, leaving beaded tracks. "We slept together. Just the once. Once, which turned out to be enough." She rubbed her stomach. "He wanted to move in, straightaway. Start where we'd left off. But I . . . said no."

"You didn't want to get back together?"

"I wanted it more than anything." Triona began drumming her fingers on the window in rhythm with the rain. "But on my terms, not his. I told him he'd have to make an effort. Win me over, woo me."

"And has he done that?"

Triona shot her a look over her shoulder. "Oh, he was brilliant. For a few weeks, at least. Flowers, romantic meals in expensive restaurants, evenings at the theatre. Every night when he wasn't on duty. I was beginning to feel sorry for him — he was spending so much money on me, and I knew he couldn't really afford it. I was about to give in, let him move in with me."

It was all in the past tense, Frances noticed, then she realised what must have happened. "But when he found out you were pregnant . . ." she blurted. The old story.

Triona turned to look at her, lifting her chin defiantly. "He doesn't know," she stated.

"Then what . . ."

"I was feeling a little . . . peculiar. Started having this wretched morning sickness. So one morning, about a week ago, I did the test. Peed on the strip, turned it blue: pregnant." Triona closed her eyes. "I was going to tell him that night. Tell him I was having his baby. But then . . ." She swallowed. "He didn't call me. Not that night, or the next. And I haven't heard from him since. The bastard."

"But he doesn't know." Frances tried to defend him. "Maybe he's been working hard, on an important case."

"That's what I told myself the first day or two. But after that? He has a telephone — more than one. And a mobile. His fingers aren't broken, as far as I know. If he were just busy, he could call me and tell me so. No, he's decided that he doesn't want to see me any more, and is taking the coward's way out."

"Why don't you call *him*? See what's the matter? I'm sure that once you tell him about the baby —"

Triona cut angrily across her words. "That's just the point. I'm not telling him. I *can't* tell him. I won't have him marrying me out of pity. Or bloody duty." She paused, tempering the tone of her voice. "You have to understand about Neville and me. Our relationship was always . . . volatile. Up and down. The good times were fantastic, brilliant. The bad times were bloody awful. And if he married me because he was backed into a corner — not because he wanted to more than anything in the world — our life together would be hell. He'd resent me, he'd hate me. And I'd end up hating him as well. What kind of a family would that be to bring a child into? It wouldn't be fair on any of us."

Frances rose and went to her, taking her hands and squeezing them. "Then what are you going to do?" she said softly.

"Oh, I won't be getting rid of it, if that's what you think." Triona blinked hard, as if to dispel tears. "I've always been pro-choice, and defended a woman's right to do what she likes with her own body. As you know. In spite of what the Holy Father says. But when it comes to my own baby . . . well, I just couldn't." She lost the fight against the tears; they trickled down her cheeks like the rain on the window. "I'll have this baby. Without Neville bloody Stewart. And if I'm lucky, he'll never find out about it."

Detective Inspector Neville Stewart was bored. It seemed like weeks since he'd had a decent case to get his teeth into. Car theft, muggings, burglary, petty drug stuff: it was all too tedious for words. They hardly ever caught the perps, and it didn't make all that much difference when they did — they'd be back on the streets, doing it again, before you could say "Crown Prosecution Service". What he needed was a good murder. Something that would give him a buzz, get his brain cells going. Something that would take up his long, lonely evenings.

And paperwork was making him crazy. Every little petty crime spawned a mountain of paper. He hadn't joined the police to push bits of paper round his desk.

Glaring balefully at his heaped in-tray, then at the rain streaking down the window, wishing — as he occasionally did — that he hadn't given up smoking, Neville pushed his chair back from his desk and went in search of coffee.

In the corridor outside of his office, he ran into Detective Sergeant Sid Cowley, going the other way. Cowley was wearing an overcoat, carrying a brolly.

"Hey, Sid. What's up?"

Cowley paused. "Hi, Guv. I'm just off on a case."

"Anything interesting?" As if, thought Neville.

"Doubt it." Cowley shrugged. "Missing person. Bloke goes jogging. Doesn't come home. Wife panics." He shrugged again. "He's probably just buggered off somewhere to keep dry. By the time I get there, he'll likely be tucked up at home, taking a hot shower after getting a bollocking from the wife."

Neville made a snap decision. "Hold on a second, Sid. I'll come with you. Let me get my coat."

"It's not really a job for a DI."

"Don't want me cramping your style, eh, Sid?" Neville slapped the sergeant's shoulder. "Just in case the wife is . . . dishy? Or desperate."

"Bugger off," Cowley growled. "With all due respect, Guv."

Must have hit a nerve, Neville thought complacently as he grabbed his raincoat. He could read Sid Cowley like a book, when it came to women.

This case might not be anything exciting. It might be over before they got there. But at least it would get him out of the bloody station.

CHAPTER
THREE

The wife *was* dishy. She was young, she was very pretty, she was blonde. And if Neville wasn't mistaken, her hair colour was natural, not out of a bottle. Not pale: that sort of deep corn colour which is very difficult to achieve artificially.

She was also heavily pregnant.

That, thought Neville, might just put Sid Cowley off.

And she was on the verge of being hysterical.

"Trevor is never late," she told them as she showed them into the downstairs lounge of the substantial Victorian semi. "I always say you could set your watch by Trevor. I tease him about that."

He would let Sid deal with this, Neville decided; after all, it was Sid's case. He'd just come along for the ride.

Cowley was taking out his notebook. "Let's start at the beginning, Mrs . . . err . . ."

"Norton. Rachel Norton." She wrapped her arms round her distended belly.

The lounge was clean, almost sterile; it had the air of a room which was seldom used. The three-piece suite fit the space perfectly, as though it had been bought for it, and looked as if it had never been sat on.

This was not a social visit, and coffee was not offered. Rachel Norton gestured for the two policeman to sit on the sofa.

Cowley looked at the notes he'd made earlier, on the phone. "So, Mrs. Norton. You say that your husband, Mr. Trevor Norton, went jogging at seven a.m."

"He always does. Every day. Rain or shine." Today was definitely a case of the former: the rain was slapping aggressively against the front bay window, streaming down it in great runnels. She looked at the window and gave an involuntary shiver, hugging her shoulders.

"And when did you expect him back?"

"He's always back by eight. He has a quick shower, gets dressed, eats a bowl of cereal. He's always at his desk by half past eight."

Cowley blinked, looked confused. "So he works . . .?"

"Here. At home. Didn't I say? He runs his own business at home."

"What sort of work does he do, Mrs. Norton?" Neville interjected. Cowley narrowed his eyes at him, warning him to back off.

"IT. Computer consultancy." She couldn't keep the pride out of her voice. "Trevor is a genius with computers. It was about a year ago that he decided to start up on his own. He's done *very* well."

"Does he work entirely at home, then?" Cowley picked up the thread. "Or does he go out sometimes?"

"Oh, he spends quite a bit of time out of the office. It's part of the job, see. He has to be where the computers are. When someone has a problem or something. They call him, and he goes."

"Maybe he had an appointment," suggested Cowley. "Or something urgent came up. Does he carry a mobile when he jogs?"

Rachel Norton shook her head. "No. He doesn't carry his mobile. He wouldn't let anything disturb his running. All he takes is his iPod."

Neville watched Sid Cowley's face; sure enough, a look of envy flashed across it. Neville knew that Sid was lusting after an iPod, but hadn't yet managed to save enough spare cash to buy one. He'd told Sid more than once, with all the self-righteousness of an ex-smoker, that if he gave up his two-pack-a-day habit, it wouldn't take long for him to be sporting those distinctive white earphones.

Come to think of it, Neville realised with a shock, Sid hadn't lit up once since he'd been with him this morning. He hadn't smoked in the car, and he hadn't asked Mrs. Norton if he could smoke in the house — that was usually the first thing he did. And on closer scrutiny, Neville could see that Sid was chewing gum. Bloody hell — was he really quitting?

"What sort of iPod does he have?" Cowley asked.

Rachel Norton furrowed her brow, looked at him oddly. "I'm not sure. The latest model, I suppose. Does it matter?"

"I was just curious," he mumbled, then got back on track. "So you can't think where he might have gone."

"He's *never* been late like this." She inspected her watch. "It's nearly eleven o'clock. He should have been home three hours ago. *Three hours.*"

Three hours was nothing in their world. If he'd been in charge, thought Neville, he would have cut things short right now, made some soothing noises to the lady and told her to let them know if he came home and otherwise call them again tomorrow morning if he still hadn't turned up. Trevor Norton was a grown man: if he wanted to slope off for a few hours, get away from the pregnant wife, then it was scarcely any business of theirs.

But Neville wasn't in charge, and he didn't say a word. Sid, evidently, had different ideas. Either he was trying to impress the guv with his conscientious approach, or he fancied Rachel Norton in spite of her grotesquely distended shape. Or maybe, like Neville himself, he was bored and had nothing better — or more interesting — to do.

"Does your husband have a diary?" Cowley asked. "On his desk, perhaps?"

She shook her head. "Not a paper diary as such. It's on his computer. And on his PDA, of course."

"Could we have a look?"

"Yes, of course." Rachel Norton led them back into the entrance hall and up a flight of stairs. She had to hold onto the banister, virtually pulling herself up. "Sorry," she said at the top of the stairs, drawing a ragged breath. "I'm not moving very fast these days."

Cowley looked her up and down. "Trevor's happy about the baby, is he?"

"Delighted," she said, smiling. "He can't wait."

Neville knew what Sid was getting at: the same thought had occurred to him. Maybe Trevor couldn't cope with approaching fatherhood. Maybe it had all been too much for him, and he'd done a runner.

The room at the front of the house, above the lounge, was an office, fitted out with modern Ikea-style office furniture and equipped with all the latest technology. There were two sleek flat screens which Neville assumed must be computers, though they bore scant resemblance to the ugly hunk of beige plastic on his desk at the station. A printer was recognisable, but there were all sorts of other gadgets and gizmos which spoke nothing to him of their functions.

And there was a telephone, which began ringing almost on cue as they entered the room.

Rachel Norton's hand fluttered to her throat; she reached for the phone. "Hello?" she breathed in a voice whose tremulousness might have been attributable to her recent climb, but somehow Neville didn't think so.

He watched her carefully as she listened to the voice on the other end. "No," she replied, sighing. "No, Trevor isn't here. I don't — I'm sorry, I can't — Yes, I'll —"

In the meanwhile, Cowley was taking advantage of the interruption to remove the chewing gum from his mouth, wrap it in a bit of tissue, dispose of it in a nearby wastepaper bin, and pop in a fresh piece.

Rachel put the phone down and turned to Cowley, biting her lip. "That was one of Trevor's clients. Trevor was supposed to be with him to sort out his configuration. At ten. He hasn't heard from him. He tried Trevor's mobile, but it was switched off." She took a deep breath. "Doesn't that prove that something's terribly wrong? Trevor would never let one of his clients down."

Cowley eyed the computer screens. "Could we see his diary, Mrs. Norton?"

She sat down in front of one of the displays and tapped a key. The screen saver disappeared, replaced by icons and a blue desktop.

"He left his computer on?" Cowley asked.

"Trevor always leaves them running," she said over her shoulder as she clicked on an icon. "He says it's better for machines which are in regular use. All that switching on and off just wears them out."

A calendar page appeared on the screen, replicating a page in a desk diary. "Here's today," she said. "The appointment at ten. And another at two in the afternoon." She pointed to the screen. "And at four, he's taking me to the antenatal clinic."

It still, thought Neville, didn't mean that Trevor Norton hadn't intended to disappear.

He picked up the only ornament on the desk, a silver-framed photo of Rachel Norton in a traditional white wedding gown. Slim, beautiful, radiant. "How long have you been married, then?"

"Nearly a year. We married right after Christmas last year." She gulped, rubbing her bump. "We'd been together for a few years, and Trevor was ready to start a family. We both were. So we decided to get married. Lovely wedding, it was."

Cowley scribbled a few things in his notebook, then snapped it shut. "Well, thank you, Mrs. Norton," he said. "Please do ring and let us know if your husband comes home."

"*If?*" she demanded, twisting in the chair to look up at him. "And what if he doesn't? What then?"

A few minutes later they were back at the car, anxious to get out of the rain. "What do you make of it, Guv?" Cowley asked as he slid behind the wheel.

Neville shrugged. "I still think he might have gone somewhere to get dry, when the rain started pelting down. Or maybe he's done a runner."

"With a wife like that? He'd have to be mad." Cowley put the key in the ignition, but before turning it, he wrapped his gum in tissue, put it in the ash tray, and got out a fresh piece.

"Maybe he's got cold feet about the baby. Wouldn't be the first time that happened."

Cowley nodded thoughtfully. "Yeah, I suppose."

"A baby sounds good in the abstract. Then his wife gets big as a house. You know what I mean?"

"Maybe he's even found someone else." Cowley turned the key and the car engine sputtered reluctantly to life. "I don't suppose he and his wife are doing much shagging these days, and maybe he's gone somewhere else for it. Can't blame him for that, Guv. Not really."

"If he doesn't turn up in twenty-four hours, I think I'd start looking at that possibility. If I were you, that is," he added. "And it was my case."

"The computer," Cowley said sagely. "There might be e-mails or something. People can be really stupid about what they leave on their computers."

"Or he might come home in the next five minutes."

"Or not. No smoke without fire, Guv."

Neville saw his opening, and went for it. "Speaking of smoke, Sid . . ."

"Yeah?" His voice was defensive.

"Did I notice the absence of something this morning?"

Cowley kept his eyes on the traffic in front of them. "Okay. I'm trying to quit."

"So what I said about the iPod made sense, did it?" Neville couldn't help gloating. "In two, three weeks you'll have saved enough dosh to buy one."

"That's part of it," Cowley admitted. "But the truth is, Guv . . . Have you ever heard of findagain.co.uk?"

"Huh? What's that?"

"It's a web site. Helps you track down people you went to school with," Cowley explained. "So you can meet up with them again."

Neville snorted contemptuously. "I can't imagine anything worse! One of the best things about leaving Ireland was knowing I'd never have to lay eyes on any of those clowns from school as long as I lived. Anyway, what does that have to do with the price of fags?"

"Well," Cowley explained with a touch of defensiveness, "I signed up. And found this girl — a girl I fancied like crazy when I was at school. She never had the time of day for me then, but now . . . well, it's going great."

"Ah. A girl." Sid always had some girl or other in the picture, but it had never stopped him from smoking before. Maybe this one required a larger than usual outlay of cash. That was something Neville could relate to: Triona, with her fondness for posh restaurants and the bloody theatre, had nearly bankrupted him, before he'd decided that enough was enough. "Expensive, is she?"

"No, it's not that." The traffic light in front of them turned to amber and Sid put his foot on the brake. "She hates smoking. She says that . . . that kissing me is like licking an ash tray. She says that if I don't quit . . ."

"Oh, well." Poor Sid, he thought. Bloody woman had him by the short and curlies. He knew what that was like. Not good. Not good at all. "Well, Sid. I hope she's worth it," Neville said, shaking his head. "I hope she's bloody worth it."

Mark Lombardi didn't see much of his sister these days. Not nearly enough, given the fact that she had been like a second mother to him for the first decade of his life. Serena had been eight when Mark was born; with their mother working all the hours God gave at La Venezia, the family restaurant, Serena had been the one there in the evenings to help with homework and tuck him into bed.

Now, though, she worked every bit as hard as their mother at the restaurant, which meant that lunchtimes and evenings were impossible. If Mark wanted to see Serena, he usually had to make a point of visiting her in the morning.

When Serena's children were younger, Mark had done his own share of babysitting in the evenings. But now Angelina was at university, and Chiara was twelve — an age when she considered it a grave insult to have a babysitter, even if it was her adored uncle Marco.

Serena had married young, at eighteen. It was exactly what the family — *la famiglia* — had wanted. His mother would never have admitted it, but Mark had always suspected that it had been carefully planned from the beginning. Guiseppe di Stefano, son of a friend of Mark's mother's sister, had come from Italy to attend university in London. He'd been given a job at the restaurant — washing dishes, mostly — to help him earn money for his fees. As a family connection, he'd even been invited to move into the spare room as a long-term guest.

The inevitable had happened; proximity had worked its magic. Serena had fallen hard for Joe, as he was soon called, and they'd married immediately after he finished his degree.

Now they lived just round the corner from the restaurant in Clerkenwell. That was convenient for Serena, of course, but also convenient for Joe, who lectured at the University of London in nearby Bloomsbury.

It wasn't very far from Mark, either. He had left home a few years earlier and had moved into a flat off High Holborn, sharing with a chap who worked in the City. His mother had been dismayed and distraught: why should he leave home? And to live with a stranger at that, when he could be surrounded by his loving family? Looked after — and fed — by his loving mother? It was unnatural. Incomprehensible. Italian men stayed at home with their mothers until they married and were passed over into the care of their wives. That was the way it was supposed to work.

He hadn't really expected that much drama. But even if he'd anticipated it, Mark still would have made the effort. It was essential to him to have his own space, even if that space was shared with a virtual stranger. The flatmate — Geoff — was the price he'd had to pay; he never could have afforded the flat on his own. They got on just fine, with no conflict, and in fact seldom saw each other. Geoff worked long hours and so did Mark, and these days when Mark wasn't working, he was seeing Callie.

Callie. He was thinking about her as he ate his cornflakes; he thought about her most of the time, when he didn't have other things he had to give his attention to. Often even when he did.

What was he going to do about Callie?

Part of the problem with Callie, of course, was her profession. She was ordained in the Church of England. A deacon. Not a priest yet, but she would be in a few months' time. And that, though he hated to admit it to himself, was an issue for him.

Not the Church of England bit; he was okay with that. His parents — his mother in particular — would find that very difficult. For them there was only one Church, and it wasn't the Church of England.

For Mark, though, the issue was her priesthood. He'd grown up in the Church, suitably in awe of Father Luigi and Father Giovanni and Father Giorgio and all of the other priests who kept their flock on the straight and narrow. They were different — set apart. Not like real people, with flesh-and-blood needs and desires. His mother had fostered that idealised view of the priesthood, and it went very deep into his psyche.

Yet Callie *was* made of flesh and blood: very desirable flesh at that. She was attractive, warm, and — yes — sexy.

Under other circumstances . . .

But she was nearly a priest. She had standards to uphold, a whole way of life that set her apart. It would be wrong to push her into a physical relationship. Not when he wasn't in a position to offer her anything in the way of commitment.

It was too soon for that. His parents didn't even know she existed.

Christmas was approaching, with all its family demands. And he'd want to see Callie as much as possible over Christmas. He couldn't go on like this, concealing her existence from *la famiglia.*

The time had come, he realised, to talk to Serena. She was sensible and sympathetic. She wouldn't freak out like his mother would. She would know how to handle it, how best to broach the subject with Mamma.

He would see her now, on his way to work. Now, before he lost his nerve.

Serena di Stefano was as unlike their mother as it was possible to be, apart from having inherited her unfortunate tendency to miscarry. While Grazia Lombardi was small and dark, conforming to the stereotypical image of Italian women, Serena had inherited the genetic characteristics of some long-ago Venetian ancestor: like a true Venetian, she was tall, beautiful, and possessed of a glorious mane of reddish-gold hair. (Considering that their father, too, was dark and not above middling height, there were always the inevitable family jokes about the milkman or *il postino*.) And while Grazia Lombardi was excitable, Serena's temperament lived up to her name. Whether her name had been bestowed because even as a newborn infant she had displayed a sanguine and calm nature, or she had simply grown into the name, was a moot point. Her serenity was deep-rooted; she was unflappable in the most trying circumstances, from domestic upheavals to crises in the kitchen of La Venezia. When Grazia Lombardi lost her head, Serena di Stefano could always be counted upon to keep hers.

She greeted her brother with a kiss on both cheeks and a smile which reached her eyes. "Come in, Marco. There's fresh coffee."

The coffee was made the Italian way, in a tiny pot on the hob, rich and dark and served black in a cup the size of a doll's tea cup. A thimbleful of pure caffeine. Mark accepted it gratefully.

They settled down at the kitchen table; in this household, as in their parents', the kitchen was indeed the heart of the home, where day-to-day living and significant family moments alike transpired.

"How is everything?" Mark asked.

"Things are mad at the restaurant."

"Christmas, I suppose. Works parties?"

She nodded. "It gets worse every year. Starts earlier and earlier — this year we began before the beginning of December. Every lunchtime, every evening. We're fully booked. If this trend keeps up, in a few years' time, we'll be serving Christmas lunches during the summer holidays, just to get them all in."

Mark laughed. "How is Mamma coping?"

Serena's anwering laugh was rueful. "Need you ask?"

"She thrives on it," Mark reminded her.

"Oh, absolutely. Without it, she'd just sit round and . . . get old. The excitement keeps her young."

Observing the wrinkles at the corners of Serena's eyes when she smiled, Mark suddenly realised that his sister herself was no longer young. She'd turned forty that year. Middle-aged, no matter how you looked at it. And he wasn't that many years behind: it was a sobering thought.

"How is Joe?" he asked automatically, after a bracing sip of coffee.

"Joe is . . . Joe. Works long hours, especially coming up to the end of term. He says he has lots of marking to do. And he says he can't work at home, with Chiara making so much racket. She's been practising her lines for the school nativity play."

"I thought she was going to be the Virgin Mary."

Serena nodded. "She is. A great honour, of course. Mamma's over the moon."

"Since when does the Virgin Mary have lines?" Mark demanded. "I thought she just sat about and looked . . . you know. Happy about giving birth to the Son of God."

"Don't forget the Annunciation," Serena smiled. "You know. When the angel lays it all on her, all the 'Ave Maria' stuff. 'Be it unto me according to thy word,' Mary says. And later on, the Visitation to Elizabeth. That's when she says the Magnificat. 'My soul doth magnify the Lord.' Then there's Mary's soliloquy at the manger."

"Huh?" Mark put his cup down. "I know I'm no Biblical scholar, but I don't remember Mary's soliloquy."

Serena lifted her eyebrows. "Poetic license, from what I understand. The teacher fancies herself a bit of a playwright. Anyway, it gives Chiara quite a few lines to learn." She added, "You *are* coming, aren't you?"

"It's in the diary," he assured her. "I wouldn't miss it for anything. Especially now that I know about the soliloquy."

She picked up the coffee pot and held it invitingly over his cup. "More coffee?"

Mark stole a glance at the clock on the wall; he really needed to get round to the reason for his visit, so he could go on to work. "Yes, okay. I'll have another drop."

After refilling her own cup, Serena opened a packet of biscotti and dumped them on a plate. "Have one," she urged. "I really bought them for Angelina — they're her favourites."

"When is she coming home?"

A momentary shadow, so fleeting that Mark thought he might have imagined it, crossed Serena's face. "I'm not quite sure. Her term ends next weekend. But she says she isn't coming home until a few days before Christmas. Probably not in time for Chiara's play."

"Oh, well. I'm sure she'll make it if she can."

Now there was no doubt about Serena's expression: she was not happy. "That's not all there is to it," she said slowly.

Mark couldn't imagine what she meant. Angelina was an intelligent and sensible girl, not one to cause unnecessary worry or concern to her parents.

"She has a new boyfriend," Serena blurted.

That was hardly surprising. In addition to being intelligent and sensible, she was also a very pretty girl, and she was almost twenty years old, in her second year at university. The surprising thing was that this hadn't happened years ago. "So, what's the problem?" As he said it, Mark knew, with a hollow feeling in his stomach, exactly what the problem was. "He's not Italian," he said slowly.

"No. He's not Italian. He isn't even English. He's . . . well, he's from Hong Kong. Chinese. And she's bringing him home for Christmas."

Brave girl, thought Mark. She must know how that would go down.

Serena traced the pattern on the tablecloth with her finger. "It doesn't matter to *me*. As long as she's happy, I don't mind whether he's Italian or . . . or a Red Indian."

"But Joe minds," he guessed.

"Joe has gone spare. *Pazzo*. Raging round the house, carrying on." She shook her head. "Well, he's her father. There's always been something special between them."

"It doesn't mean she's going to marry this . . . Chinese bloke," Mark pointed out. "It's her first boyfriend. Not necessarily serious."

"She wouldn't bring him home if it wasn't serious," Serena stated. "She must know how her father would feel about it. And," she added, "Joe was *my* first boyfriend. Papa was Mamma's first boyfriend."

Yes, they took relationships seriously in this family, Mark reflected. That was part of the problem. Part of *his* problem. "What about . . . Mamma?" he asked. "Have you told her yet?"

Serena sighed. "No. Not yet. I'm still trying to figure out how to break it to her. You know what she'll say. What she always says. '*Mogli e buoi dei paesi tuoi.*' "

It was a common phrase in the household, poetic in Italian if prosaic in English, meaning that spouses and cows should always come from your own country. "Yeah," Mark groaned. "That's what she'll say, all right."

"Maybe I'll tell Papa, and let him do the deed. But that would be the coward's way out."

"Well," said Mark, "it sounds like it's going to be an interesting Christmas." He drained his coffee cup and stood up. Today was not the day to burden Serena with *his* problem. That would have to wait for another time.

It was a Friday: Callie's day off. She hadn't made plans for the day, hoping that perhaps Marco's schedule would allow them to spend some time together. But he would be tied up till evening, he'd told her on Thursday night.

The rain was pitching down, which meant a brisk — and brief — walk along the edge of Hyde Park with Bella. Even so, Bella was drenched, and had to be towelled off and brushed. Then Callie took the sort of long, restorative bubble bath which wasn't usually possible on the other six days of the week. After that she dressed in jeans and a colourful stripey jumper — no dog collar on a Friday.

While soaking in the bath, she'd considered going out to buy a few Christmas decorations for the flat. Maybe even a tree and some fairy lights. But this wasn't really the sort of weather which was conducive to the holiday spirit. And besides, it would be nice if she and Marco could do that together. It would be fun to put up the tree and decorate it with him, whereas by herself it would be just another chore.

Just another chore. That brought her thoughts, inevitably, to her mother. During the last weeks of her developing relationship with Marco, she had rather neglected her mother, and this was a niggling source of guilt. Laura Anson was supremely skilled at sensing guilt, and exploiting it to the full.

She really should go to see her mother.

Callie went through to her study, sat down in the desk chair, and stared at the phone. Summoning up her courage for the deed.

The phone rang — a stay of execution. "Thank you, God," she breathed, reaching for it.

"Hi, Sis," said her brother's voice.

"Peter!"

"Long time, no see."

It hadn't been *that* long — no more than a few days; spending time with her brother was a pleasure rather than a duty, and as they both had flexible schedules, they usually managed to get together at least once a week. Peter was a freelance musician; when he worked it was usually in the evenings, so often he dropped by during the day for a cup of tea or a bite of lunch.

"You were here for lunch on Monday," she reminded him.

"What are you up to now? It's your day off, isn't it?"

Callie sighed. "Actually, I was steeling myself. To go and see Mum this afternoon. I was just about to ring her."

"I'll go with you," he offered. "It's always easier for both of us that way."

"Oh, that would be great." It was true: their mother couldn't aim at two targets simultaneously.

"Why don't we have lunch first?" Peter suggested. "My treat," he added grandly. "McDonald's."

"Surely you could stretch to Prêt à Manger. After all the meals I've given you."

He chuckled, unrepentant. "Better yet, how about Pizza Express?"

"Sounds good."

"In about an hour? The one in the Earl's Court Road? That's the closest one to Mum's, I think."

Callie looked at her watch. "That should work. I'll give Mum a ring."

"See you, then." In a provocative voice he added, "I have something interesting to tell you."

Oh, no, thought Callie. He must have a new boyfriend. Another doomed relationship.

When it came to his love life, Peter was both a romantic and an optimist: an attractive but dangerous combination. He embarked on each new relationship with enthusiasm, certain that this one would be *the* one. And the inevitable disappointments never got him down for long. Through it all, Callie was his confidante, his sounding board, rejoicing with him and then consoling him. She wasn't sure that she was up to it today.

Sure enough, Peter was more than usually ebullient, waiting for her just inside Pizza Express, out of the rain. It wasn't like Peter to be early — not for anything.

She may as well get it over with, Callie decided. "What's this all about?" she asked as they were shown to their table.

"All in good time, Sis."

The waiter hovered. "Would you like something to drink?"

Peter raised an eyebrow at Callie. "We're on with Mum?"

"Yes. At half-past two."

He turned back to the waiter. "Then yes. Definitely. A bottle of house red."

"A whole bottle of wine at lunch?" Callie protested half-heartedly.

"I may even order a second bottle. It's Mum, remember."

Their mother. A bitter woman who blamed her husband for dying on her. A woman who never approved of anything that either of her children did. Who was always complaining that they didn't visit her enough, yet seemed to find their visits tiresome and inconvenient. Who was still, in spite of all the evidence, trying to find a nice girl for her son to marry.

Callie held out her glass as soon as the bottle arrived.

Peter was looking at the menu. "I think I'll have the American Hot. Or the Hot American, as I like to call it." He grinned. "I live in hope."

"I can't resist the Veneziana," Callie said with an answering smile.

"Funny you should say that." Peter put the menu down on the table and clinked glasses with her. "It reminds me of what I wanted to tell you."

"It does?"

"You'll never guess where I had lunch yesterday."

Callie shook her head.

"La Venezia. In Camberwell." He took a sip of wine, watching her reaction over the rim of the glass.

She stared at him, aghast. "Peter! You didn't!"

"I did. And I must say, the food was divine."

Marco's family's restaurant. In spite of her repeated hints, Marco had never taken her there. She was beginning be paranoid about it, to think that there was some reason he didn't want her to meet his family. "But . . ." she sputtered.

Peter was hugely pleased with himself. "It wasn't easy getting in, mind. The place was packed. All those grim works Christmas lunches — crackers and silly paper crowns. But I flirted with one of the waiters, and he found me a little table in the corner."

She groaned aloud: worse and worse.

"And then someone different came to take my order. A woman, and she seemed to be in charge. I reckon she was Marco's sister. About the right age, I think. And she was a bit like Marco round the nose and mouth — a family resemblance."

"Oh, Peter." Callie closed her eyes, burning with embarrassment.

"Don't worry, Sis. I didn't identify myself. I didn't say, 'By the way, my sister is shagging your brother.'"

Her eyes flew open. "I'm not. How many times do I have to tell you?"

Peter grinned wickedly. "I thought I'd trick you into admitting it. It was worth a try."

"But I'm *not*. Don't you think I'd tell you if I were?"

"Well, I don't know what's wrong with you, then. He's absolutely gorgeous. If he were playing for the other side, I'd . . . well, it wouldn't take me long to get him into bed." He took a gulp of his wine. "Are you sure he's *not*, Sis? That might explain why nothing's happened yet."

Callie didn't want to discuss it. The fact was that Marco hadn't in any way pressed her to go to bed with him, and she wasn't sure how she would react if he did. Not that she didn't want to, but it wasn't like they were engaged or anything close to it. Not like it had been with Adam. Still . . . "He's not gay," she stated in a voice meant to discourage any further exploration of the matter.

"Pity," said Peter reflectively.

Peter approved of Marco Lombardi — approved enthusiastically. That, as far as Callie was concerned, was a big plus in Marco's favour. Peter had never approved of Adam, her ex-fiancé. He'd never thought that Adam was good enough for her, and events had proved him right.

She was dying to ask him about Marco's sister: what she looked like, what she'd said. Whether his parents had also been present, and whether he'd had any conversation with them.

But she wasn't going to give Peter the satisfaction. Pressing her lips together, she glared across the table at his smirking face. She'd never tried to interfere in any of his relationships, and she didn't know why he felt he had the right to involve himself in hers.

Still, she knew that she wouldn't be able to stay cross with him for very long. She never could, and apart from anything else, this afternoon they would have to be united in facing a common enemy.

CHAPTER
FOUR

Neville was scheduled to have the whole weekend off. He'd been looking forward to it for weeks, planning to spend it with Triona. The idea had been for them to get right out of London, leaving on Friday evening and driving to a cosy country pub with log fires — a pub which offered bed and breakfast and exceptional food. A romantic weekend in the country, doing . . . whatever one did in the country. Neville hadn't been too clear in his mind on how they'd actually spend their time, apart from sitting in front of a log fire with a pint of Guinness. With any luck, he'd be able to get Triona into bed. Two days, two nights. Surely the log fires and the country air would work their magic, and he'd break down her resistance. That was the most cherished part of his plan, the heart of it all.

All gone up the spout, now. He hadn't called her; he wouldn't call her. She was out of his life, and he was better off without her.

And the weekend stretched in front of him in all its emptiness.

Neville woke early, in spite of his resolution to have a lie-in. He turned his face to the pillow in the still-dark room, trying to go back to sleep.

Maybe he'd have a wander round Shepherd's Bush Market later on. He'd always enjoyed doing that on a Saturday morning: just seeing the variety of things on offer and the even wider variety of people buying and selling. And for later there was always the pub. His local, where they knew how to pull Guinness to perfection. If he wanted to, he could drink till he was legless; he'd have the whole of Sunday to sleep it off.

Or maybe he'd find himself a girl. One who wasn't interested in a meaningful relationship or being bloody wooed with champagne and roses. He still had his black book; he still knew a few girls like that. He didn't have to spend the weekend alone if he didn't want to.

But it all became academic when, just before seven, the phone went.

"Guv?" said the voice of Sid Cowley.

"It's my day off," Neville growled. "In case you didn't remember."

"Forget about that, Guv." Cowley paused. "That bloke yesterday? The one who didn't come home from his morning run?"

"Yeah. What about him?"

"Some dog walker, out early. He saw something odd and gave us a call on his mobile."

"And?" Neville thought he could see where this was leading, and he didn't like it much.

"We're not sure it's him yet, but . . . it looks like our blokes have just pulled Trevor Norton out of the canal."

"Bloody hell," said Neville.

While Callie had Friday as her day off, her vicar Brian took Saturdays. That meant that Callie had to do Morning Prayer on her own.

It had been a fairly late evening. They hadn't gone out, but Marco had brought a DVD of a recent film, and after dinner, cooked by him, they'd curled up on the sofa and watched it. He hadn't left till nearly midnight.

This was more or less the pattern of their evenings now, unless Marco had to work or Callie had a meeting or a special service. When both of them were free, he would come to her flat — never the other way round, as he had a flatmate in residence. Sometimes they would have a takeaway; more often one or the other of them would cook a meal. Of the two, Marco was the better cook — not surprisingly, given his family heritage — and he seemed to enjoy cooking for her, arriving on her doorstep with a bag of goodies. His meals could be elaborate affairs, taking a long time to prepare and a corresponding amount of time to eat.

Callie had set her alarm for the latest possible moment. No time for a leisurely bath this morning. A quick shower would have to suffice, and afterwards as she struggled into her clerical shirt, she talked to Bella, who sat watching her with liquid brown eyes. "No time for a walk now, darling," she said. "But I promise I'll come back right after Morning Prayer. We can have a nice long walk then." She parted the bedroom curtains and peered out. "It's not raining," she added. "Not like yesterday. So that's all right."

Bella didn't say anything, but Callie fancied that her expression was one of approval.

The Reverend Brian Stanford, vicar of All Saints', liked a lie in on his day off. Ordinarily his wife Jane did as well, but this morning she'd been awake early. For a while she stayed in bed, then she got up and quickly pulled on her dressing gown — the Victorian vicarage was draughty and inefficiently heated. She moved as quietly as possible, so as not to disturb Brian's sleep.

Jane went out into the corridor, to the first floor landing. There was a window there, and if you stood at a certain angle and pulled back the curtain a bit, you could get a glimpse of the church. Sometimes it soothed Jane to look at the church, solid and Victorian, comforting in its bulk and in what it stood for.

You could also see the church hall, and the side door which provided access to the curate's upstairs flat. As Jane stood there, that door flew open and Callie rushed out, her cassock flapping behind her, and sprinted towards the church.

Late again, thought Jane, with a little grimace of disapproval. She didn't have her watch on, but the clock on the church tower indicated that the curate was cutting it as close as possible.

Not surprising, really, given how late it had been when that young man had left the flat last night. The church clock had been inching towards midnight.

Jane wasn't usually up at midnight, and she was not consciously keeping tabs on the comings and goings from the curate's flat. But lately she hadn't been sleeping very well, and she would often find herself creeping to this window during the night, seeking the comfort of the church's proximity.

Last night was not the first time she'd seen the young man. She'd caught glimpses of him before, indistinct in the dim glow of the street lights; once she'd seen him arriving in daylight and had had a better look at him. Slim, with curly dark hair.

She wondered who he was: not a member of their congregation, that was for sure. Jane prided herself on her comprehensive knowledge of the congregation, and no one new ever escaped her notice. She wondered whether Brian knew about him. Had his curate confided in him?

It had only been a few months since the break-up of her engagement to Adam Masters; she wasn't wasting any time, Jane reflected sourly.

Young people today seemed to be like that: jumping straight from one relationship into another. Not, Jane told herself, that Callie was so very young. She was all of thirty. But she seemed to Jane to be of a completely different generation to herself and Brian, who now inhabited the far side of forty.

And her own son Simon? Would his relationship with this Ellie person be a short-lived one? Charlie seemed to think not, and his twin knew him better than anyone. Jane hoped that Charlie, in this instance, was wrong.

Not that she was jealous, as Charlie had suggested. That was ridiculous: why on earth would she be jealous of her son's girlfriend? No, it was just that Simon was too young. Just eighteen — far too young to entangle himself with a girl.

Entangle? What did that mean these days? Jane supposed, from the way Charlie had talked about it, that it meant they were sleeping together. Having sex, to be blunt. Young people seemed to do that at the drop of a hat nowadays, though her boys hadn't been brought up that way. If that were the case, she hoped that Simon knew enough to be careful. Accidents could happen, and Jane was not ready to be a grandmother.

She hadn't told Brian about Simon and Ellie. There just hadn't been a good time. And somehow it seemed to her that to discuss it with Brian would lend to the relationship more importance than it merited — would, in some way, almost make it more concrete. He might feel that it was his responsibility to have a man-to-man talk with Simon, as a father and — even worse — as a priest. That would be awful — excruciatingly embarrassing for all of them. If she ignored it, the whole thing might go away, and Brian need never be the wiser about it.

Besides, today was the last day of Oxford's Michaelmas Term. Tomorrow the boys would be home, and perhaps the weeks of separation from Ellie during the holidays would cool Simon's ardour a bit, give him some perspective.

Tomorrow! Jane could hardly wait.

Chilled, she crept back to bed. As she slipped in next to Brian, he turned onto his back and stretched his arms above his head. "Oh, I've slept well," he said. "What time is it?"

"Just gone eight."

"Janey." He shifted to face her, his voice wheedling. "You wouldn't like to bring me some breakfast in bed, would you?"

Breakfast in bed? It *was* something he had always enjoyed, as a special treat. But it hadn't always been the first thing on his mind, waking up with his wife on his day off. Well, thought Jane acidly, this must mean they were well and truly middle-aged.

"All right, then. In a minute," she acquiesced. "But first, there was something I was wondering about?"

"What's that?" he murmured, only half paying attention.

"Did you know that Callie Anson has a new man in her life? Has she told you about him?"

"What?" Now Brian was listening.

Morning Prayer didn't generally attract much of a congregation; there were even times when Callie was on her own. This morning, though, there were three others in the stalls, and Callie noted that one of them was Morag Hamilton.

After the brief service, Morag lingered behind the others as Callie said goodbye to them at the door. "I was just wondering if you had a wee bit of time this morning," she said diffidently, when it was her turn. "I hate to bother you . . ."

Callie looked into her face and saw that it was troubled. "No bother at all," she said immediately. "I need to walk my dog right now, but perhaps if you fancy some exercise . . ."

"That would be splendid." Morag's smile was grateful. "I don't get enough exercise as it is."

"Come along with me, then. We'll collect Bella and take her to the park."

By the time that Neville got to the canal, the crime scene tape was up and the SOCOs had arrived. So had Sid Cowley, who stood with his hands shoved in the pockets of his leather jacket — the rain had given way to a damp December chill, the sort that sat on your shoulders and seeped through to the bone. Cowley looked morose as his jaws worked on a piece of nicotine gum. "Evans has been here," he said, referring to their Detective Superintendent. "Didn't stay long, but he's putting you in charge. It's not my case any more."

Fair enough: a Detective Sergeant could look into a missing person, but when a dead body was involved, a more senior officer was called for. Still, Neville felt sorry for Cowley. "Never mind, chum," he muttered. "I'll be the one with the headaches, then."

"Headaches, for sure, Guv." Cowley gave him a grim smile. "As crime scenes go, this one isn't the greatest. We don't even know that it *is* the crime scene. He could have gone in anywhere along the canal."

Neville watched the white-suited SOCOs in action, going about their business — taking photos, crawling on their hands and knees looking for evidence. "He drowned, I suppose?" he asked the sergeant.

"The doc said so. Water in the lungs. Won't know for sure till he gets him on the slab, of course."

Something didn't quite add up, as far as Neville was concerned. "Are we sure it's a crime?" he demanded. "How do we know that he didn't lose his footing in that wretched rain, and just fall in?"

"He's been bashed on the head," Cowley stated matter-of-factly. "Before he went into the water. I saw him — it wasn't an accident. I didn't need the pathologist to tell me that. Neither did Evans. That's why he's put you in charge."

"Bloody hell." He glanced at the bank of the canal, where a sheet concealed what was left of the victim. "And are we sure it's our man? Trevor Norton?"

Cowley took the gum out of his mouth, wrapped it in tissue, and popped a fresh piece before replying. "He's not carrying any ID, if that's what you mean, Guv. But he fits the description. White male, late twenties. Wearing running gear. Expensive trainers."

"And the iPod?" Neville asked, remembering Cowley's covetous expression the day before.

"No iPod." Cowley gave a sage nod. "I know it's your case now, Guv. But if I was in charge, that's what I'd be looking for. I think the poor bugger was killed for his iPod."

Morag made a fuss over Bella, which endeared her to Callie. "I do miss Macduff," the older woman confided. "He was such a grand little dog. Small dog, big heart."

"Would you think about getting another dog?" Callie suggested. "Lots of people in London have dogs. And we're so close to Hyde Park."

72

Morag walked along the pavement beside Callie, looking straight ahead. "When Macduff died, I thought I'd never get another dog," she stated, her words visible as soft puffs of mist in the cold morning air. "Too much . . . pain. Losing him. Then, lately, I started thinking about how much company it would be to have one."

"Well, then." Callie was enthusiastic. "I'm sure you could get a rescue dog. Or if you wanted one like Macduff — he was a Cairn, wasn't he? There must be breeders somewhere. I could look on the internet."

"No." Morag shook her head. "No, it wouldn't be fair to the dog."

"But like I said. It's not a big deal to have a dog in London. And you're at home most of the time, aren't you?"

Morag stopped; Callie, pulling on Bella's lead, stopped as well and swung round to face her.

At last Morag turned towards Callie, and Callie could see that there were tears in the other woman's eyes — tears which began to spill over and trickle down her weathered cheeks. "Oh, I'm sorry," Callie said, stricken. "I didn't mean to bully you or anything."

"I've been to the doctor," Morag said, so quietly that Callie strained to hear. "That's why it wouldn't be fair to get a dog. I . . ." Her voice caught on a sob. "I have cancer."

It was a part of his job that Neville hated: breaking the bad news to family members. But now that he was in charge of the case, it was up to him to tell Rachel Norton about the body in the canal. And it couldn't be put off, either; once he'd done everything he could at the crime scene, and the body had been removed to the mortuary, he would need to escort Rachel Norton, as next of kin, to provide formal identification.

"God, Sid," he said as they approached the Victorian semi. "Times like this, I wish I still smoked. I could use a fag right now."

"Me, too, Guv," Cowley stated glumly. "It's been —" He consulted his watch. "It's been thirty-seven hours and twenty-two minutes since my last fag."

"But who's counting, eh?" Neville sighed. "What if she goes into labour or something? We need to get a woman FLO here right away."

They had reached the Nortons' home. Just before Neville pushed the bell, he and Cowley looked at each other and said the name together. "Yolanda Fish."

"Ring her on your mobile," Neville directed. "Get her to meet us at the mortuary, if it's humanly possible."

He waited with his finger hovering over the bell, glad of even a brief reprieve, until Cowley had done as he'd been told, and nodded in confirmation. "Yes," he said. "She'll be there."

"Thank God for that," Neville muttered, giving the bell a savage push.

It didn't take long for Rachel Norton to answer the door. It was almost as if she'd been waiting just the other side of it since they'd taken their leave of her nearly twenty-four hours earlier. Her eyes were shadowed, and looked huge in her pale face. She moistened her lips with her tongue. "Come in," she said in a voice that was already heavy with tears, stepping to one side to allow them through.

Once again they followed her into the sterile lounge. Neville declined her offer of a seat, preferring to deliver the news standing up. But he gestured for her to sit down.

Obediently she sat, looking from Neville to Cowley. She opened her mouth as if to say something, then shut it again and sighed.

"Mrs. Norton," Neville began. God, how he hated doing this. "I'm afraid we may have some bad news for you."

Morag Hamilton shivered and pulled her coat closer. "Do you mind if we keep walking?" she said. "It's awfully cold this morning."

Callie's impulse was to give Morag a hug, but her body language discouraged it. Instead she fell into step beside her, heading towards Hyde Park. "When did you . . . when did you find out about the cancer?" she asked awkwardly.

"Yesterday. The consultant rang with the test results. I'd suspected for a while, of course. You do, don't you? If you know your own body. Especially if," Morag added with an ironic smile, "you've spent most of your life married to a doctor."

"What . . . what did he say?" She didn't want to pry, didn't want to press her with questions that Morag wouldn't want to answer. Questions like "What sort of cancer is it?" or "Have they caught it in time?" or "How long are they giving you?" Better to let Morag take the lead, and tell her only as much as she wanted her to know.

"Actually, my consultant is a she," Morag corrected her.

Callie felt foolish: she, of all people, should know better than to make assumptions about professions and gender. She glanced at Morag and caught another shiver. "Listen, if you'd rather go to a caff and warm up with a coffee —"

"I'm all right." She smiled. "Wee Bella wouldn't be best pleased with that. Look at her — she's having a grand time."

The worst ones, thought Neville, were the ones who screamed and shouted and refused to believe what they were being told. Rachel Norton wasn't like that. She sat very still, her arms wrapped round her huge belly, and shook with silent sobs.

He stood awkwardly, wishing like anything that Yolanda Fish were there. Sid Cowley, in his new subordinate role, wasn't proving very useful. It was if he had opted out: your case now, Guv. You deal with it.

Neville caught Cowley's eye and mouthed the word "tea".

Cowley appeared grateful for the chance to escape; he headed for the back of the house.

To Neville the room seemed stuffy and overheated, its radiator chugging away efficiently. After the damp chill outside, it was like a hothouse in there. Neville felt a trickle of sweat down the middle of his back. He closed his eyes, unable to bear the sight of Rachel

Norton's distorted face. Her eyes were screwed up, her mouth twisted. She wasn't having the baby right here on the spot, was she?

After what seemed like an age, Sid Cowley returned with an inexpertly assembled tea tray and put it down on the coffee table. At least he'd remembered the sugar. Neville poured the tea into an incongruous Homer Simpson mug and spooned in three sugars.

Rachel Norton just looked at him, still saying nothing. She made no effort to take the mug from him when he held it out to her, forcing Neville to kneel beside her and wrap her hands round it, guiding it to her mouth. "Drink it," he ordered. "It will do you good."

She complied with a sip, then grimaced. "I hate sweet tea."

"It's good for shock."

"Too hot. Too sweet." Rachel's words caught in her throat. Another gush of tears followed. "Trevor likes . . . liked . . . two sugars."

There was nothing to say to that.

"His favourite mug," Rachel added, swallowing hard. "Homer Simpson. His hero."

On the mug, the round-bellied man with yellow skin and three hairs on the top of his head held up a can of beer. "Everything's better with Duff," it proclaimed.

"There's a chance that it's treatable," Morag said in her matter-of-fact way. "They're not making any promises, of course, but it isn't totally hopeless."

"That's good," Callie said, feeling utterly inadequate.

"But the treatment won't be pleasant. Lots of drugs with nasty side-effects."

Bella trotted on ahead of them through the park, ecstatic to be there, not minding the cold. Callie wished that her ordination training had provided a course on the right thing to say in moments like this; as it was, she had to feel her way through it, relying on common sense and empathy — and on God. "Isn't it lucky that your son is nearby. Your family. They'll help you through it, Morag."

The older woman's laugh was loud, but totally without mirth. "Angus? You must be joking."

Yolanda Fish had not always been in the police force. For more than twenty years she had been a midwife. Then, after the notorious murder of black teenager Stephen Lawrence and the enquiry which followed, the Metropolitan Police had made an active effort to recruit minorities and train them as Family Liaison Officers in accordance with the enquiry's formal recommendations. Yolanda's husband Eli, a career policeman, had learned about the initiative and had encouraged her to apply.

Ready for a mid-life career change, she'd never looked back. "It was either this or the Church," she often quipped. "And I don't look good in black."

The job fitted her like a glove. She had all the necessary qualities in abundance: compassion, tact, common sense. Yolanda was, in the true sense of the word, a wise woman, and a caring one. Her maturity and experience brought an extra dimension as well.

Yolanda's greatest sorrow was that she and Eli had not been blessed with children. In her earlier career, all of those babies she'd helped to bring into the world had been the outlet for her maternal instincts. Now she lavished her nurturing skills on those with whom she worked, including her police colleagues, who regarded her as something of a mother figure. And because she was not ambitious for promotion — was content to remain a Detective Constable and to do her job as well as she could — she was not perceived as a threat to anyone else's dreams of advancement. She was, as a result of these factors, held in high regard by everyone who knew her.

So Neville Stewart smiled — with pleasure as well as relief — when they arrived at the mortuary and spotted Yolanda waiting for them as promised.

It would have been difficult to miss her. A tall dark-skinned woman with a statuesque figure and a head full of tiny braids, she held herself upright, and she gloried in bright colours. Today she was wearing a vibrant shade of turquoise, everything co-ordinated from her trousers and jumper down to the dangly earrings and chunky necklace.

With a discreet smile at the two officers, she moved quickly to Rachel Norton's side. "Oh, lovie," she crooned. "The baby. When is it due?"

"Christmas Eve." Rachel's lip trembled; her eyes welled with tears. "Trevor . . . he said it would be the best Christmas present ever. And now Trevor . . . oh, God." She looked around her, as though suddenly realising where she was and why she was there. It seemed to Neville that she was coming out of her earlier state of blank shock, almost like waking from sleep.

Yolanda's capable arm encircled the young woman's shoulder. "Oh, lovie. Lovie."

"I can't bear it," Rachel sobbed. "I can't do it."

"You can, lovie. It will be difficult, but you can do it." Yolanda gave her shoulder a squeeze. "For Trevor."

It was quickly accomplished. They went into an inner room; the face was exposed; Rachel gave a nod, then buried her head in Yolanda's neck. No words were necessary.

Now the postmortem could take place, and they'd have a better idea of what they were dealing with.

At this point, the one thing that they knew for sure was that Trevor Norton had not died of natural causes.

Alex Hamilton came home from school to an empty flat. That was nothing new, at least not in the months they'd lived in London: her father worked long hours, and her stepmother lived her own life. The most Alex could expect in the way of nurturing was a selection of ready meals in the fridge; Jilly didn't cook at the best of times, not for herself or Alex's dad, and certainly not for Alex, who, she often said, was not her child.

Alex wasn't particularly hungry, anyway. She seldom was: food wasn't important to her, and as a result she was thin as a rail, subsisting on crisps and sweets at school, and foraging in the evenings. The ready meals were easy to prepare in the microwave, and if she didn't fancy one of those she could always eat a bowl of cereal or a piece of toast.

What *was* important to Alex was her computer, her lifeline to the world. Her dad had got it for her, and she didn't know what she would have done without it.

Dumping her rucksack just inside the front door, shedding her coat and tossing it over the nearest chair in the sitting room — Jilly would tear a strip off her for that later on, but she didn't care — Alex headed for her bedroom. She shut the door behind her, even though there was no one else in the flat.

The computer was on, but the screen was password-protected. Just in case, though Alex reckoned that Jilly, even if she were interested enough in her step-daughter to look at her computer, was too stupid to have the first idea of how to use it. Dumb as a box of rocks, that was Jilly. Dad certainly hadn't married her for her brains: Alex knew that much.

Quite frankly, Alex didn't know why he *had* married her. Yes, she was beautiful, but not *that* beautiful. Not if you scraped all that make-up off. Certainly not as beautiful as Alex's mum. Compared to her mum, Jilly was a painted doll. She'd overheard Granny saying that to Granddad once, and it had stuck in her mind. A silly, vain doll. And stupid, stupid, stupid.

Alex tapped her password in and looked eagerly at the screen. Two new e-mails! She would look at the one from Kirsty first.

Kirsty was her best friend — her very best friend in all the world, and had been for as long as she could remember. They were only a few weeks apart in age, and had grown up together in Gartenbridge. Constant companions, they'd always been in the same class at school, and during school holidays they'd played together every day, exploring the countryside and sharing the worlds of their imaginations.

Alex missed Kirsty desperately. Almost as much as she missed her mum, though in a different way. Her longing for her mum was a deep chasm, walled off in her mind, too painful to be approached except in the dead of night, in the worst of nightmares. The absence of Kirsty she lived on a day-to-day basis.

There was no one like Kirsty at her new school. No one she could imagine as a soul-mate, as a companion. They were all so sophisticated, so sure of themselves. So snobbish. She held herself aloof from all of them, knowing that they found her odd and unapproachable. She didn't look like them, all well-groomed and clothes-conscious. And she didn't talk like them, either. They mocked her accent behind her back, making sure that she could overhear them.

Alex didn't care — that's what she told herself. She didn't want any of them as friends. Through the magic of electronics, she still had Kirsty.

At first, in those horrible few weeks after the move, they'd e-mailed each other at least a dozen times a day. Alex had poured it all out to Kirsty, all of her agony, and Kirsty had responded with the comfort Alex needed so badly. It wouldn't be for long, she'd assured Alex. Alex's dad was sure to get tired of boring, stupid Jilly. He'd realise what a mistake he'd made, and before

Alex knew it they'd be back in Scotland. Back in Gartenbridge, with everything the way it used to be.

The frequency of the e-mails had tailed off gradually, as had their emphasis. Kirsty now kept Alex up-to-date with what was going on at school and in the village, filling her in on things that had changed, were changing. The corner shop where they'd bought sweets after school had closed down. One of their favourite teachers was getting married and wouldn't be returning for the next term. The people who had bought Alex's old house had painted it yellow.

Yellow! Her least favourite colour. It must look terrible. Alex didn't like to think about anything changing, didn't want to imagine anyone else living in *her* house. The only house she'd ever known, the house of her happy childhood. A few months ago. A million years ago.

Still less did she want to think about Kirsty changing. Yet there were hints in recent e-mails. Kirsty's periods had started; Alex hadn't yet reached that milestone on the road to being a grown-up. And more and more of Kirsty's chatter now centred round Ewan Fraser, a boy whom they'd both once despised, with his sticky-out ears and his freckles. According to Kirsty, he had improved vastly in recent months. He'd started hanging round, walking home from school with her. Ewan Fraser! It made Alex gag, just thinking about it.

Kirsty with a boyfriend — unthinkable. How they'd laughed at the girls in the next form, mooning round after boys.

And yet Alex herself had a secret — one she had shared with no one, not even with Kirsty. *She* had a boyfriend. A boyfriend!

She hugged herself with the deliciousness of the secret.

Jack — he hadn't yet told her his other name — was very good-looking, not like that sad Ewan Fraser. He was funny, he was nice.

Not that they'd actually met face-to-face. Not yet, anyway. So far she'd only seen his photo. But there was no rush. He was her friend, her confidant, someone she could pour her heart out to. She would meet him eventually.

And for now, there was an e-mail waiting from him. Smiling, as she hadn't smiled in months, exposing her hated tooth brace, Alex clicked to open it.

CHAPTER
FIVE

Much as Neville hated to admit that Sid Cowley was right, he was inclined to think that Sid had hit the nail on the head when he said that Trevor Norton was probably killed for his iPod.

Just one of those senseless crimes — in the wrong place at the wrong time. They'd seen it over and over again. Some poor sod goes for a drink at his local on a Saturday night, finds himself in the middle of a fight, and ends up on a slab. Or a mum takes her kid out in the pushchair, just like she's done a hundred times, and some tanked-up wanker's car jumps the curb and kills them both.

Death. Out of nowhere, unpredictable. And for no good reason at all. It could just as easily have been the next bloke with an iPod — they were everywhere these days — and it would have been some other poor woman crying her eyes out instead of Rachel Norton, not much more than days away from having the dead man's baby.

He and Sid talked about it on their way back to the Nortons' house, after the postmortem. The results had been much as expected: Trevor Norton had drowned, but only after being hit on the head with a blunt instrument.

There was no reason to suspect that it had been anything other than a random crime, and that was going to make it a pig to solve. Trevor Norton could have been killed by anyone, and they could now be just about anywhere. Unless the samples taken at the postmortem revealed some unexpected DNA, or the blunt instrument turned up, or the murder had been filmed on a CCTV camera, there might be nothing to link the killer to the crime apart from that iPod. One iPod in a city full of iPods, anonymous and untraceable. Needle-in-a-haystack stuff.

Yet all possibilities had to be explored, and that included a thorough search of the Nortons' house.

And asking Rachel Norton a lot of questions. Questions she understandably wouldn't want to answer right now. Neville knew that they'd have to contend not only with Rachel in her bewilderment, but with Yolanda Fish in protective mode, like a mother hen with a chick.

Mark Lombardi had just finished his lunch in the police canteen and was on his way back to his desk when his mobile vibrated in his pocket.

Callie! he thought, smiling. But as he pulled it out, he saw on the display that it was his sister.

He punched the button to accept the call. "*Pronto. Ciao*, Serena."

"Marco! Sorry to bother you." There was a great deal of background noise — cutlery, crockery, people talking. "Can you hear me all right?"

"No bother. I can hear you fine. What's up?"

She sighed audibly into the phone. "I need to ask you a huge favour, Marco."

"What?"

"Are you busy tonight?"

That didn't sound good. He'd promised Callie that this evening he would bring over all the ingredients to teach her how to make fresh pasta from scratch. "I have plans," he said cautiously.

"You know I wouldn't ask this if I weren't desperate, but can you cancel them?"

"Go on," he said. Babysitting? It wouldn't be the first time he'd been asked at the last minute to look after his niece Chiara.

"I told you how busy we are with all of these special Christmas parties."

"Yes."

"Well, one of the students who waits tables for us came in this lunch time with a terrible cold. It was putting everyone off — you just can't have someone blowing their nose over the food and sneezing on the customers."

Mark thought he could see where this was going, and it wasn't babysitting.

"So I sent her home," Serena went on. "And I've been on the phone ever since, trying to find someone else."

He had reached his desk. Closing his eyes, Mark mentally let go of the alluring image he'd been carrying round with him all morning: himself and Callie in the close quarters of her kitchen, both up to their elbows in pasta dough. Callie, with a smudge of flour on her cheek . . . "Let me guess. You want me to wait tables tonight."

His sister's voice was pleading. "We're fully booked. We just can't be short-staffed. Not tonight. If you could . . ."

"Yes, all right," he said, trying not to sound grudging about it.

Now her sigh was one of relief. "Marco, you're a star. Really."

"Yeah, yeah."

"I'll owe you one," she acknowledged. "Can you be here by six? Or better yet, half five? All the tables will have to be laid after the lunch crowd goes, and the crackers —"

"I'll be there. Worry not, *mia sorella*."

Yolanda opened the door to Neville Stewart and Sid Cowley reluctantly. She was a police officer; she knew they were doing their job, and that it couldn't wait. But her instincts to defend Rachel, to keep them away from her, were strong, intensified ten-fold by Rachel's pregnancy.

There was a paradox at the heart of Yolanda's job as Family Liaison Officer, and it was one which she was usually able to embrace without much difficulty. Her role in a murder enquiry was as the human face of the police, nurturing the bereaved and keeping them informed of the progress of the case. She was to be there for them, on their side, more like a social worker or a priest than an officer of the law.

And yet . . . Yet it remained an undeniable fact that most murder victims were killed by someone they knew. In many cases, of course, by someone within their family. And that meant that the people Yolanda was looking after were also often suspects themselves. Sometimes one of the people whom she plied with cups of tea and comforted in their grief turned out to be a murderer. As a police officer, she had to be aware of that possibility, and to be open to it. At times she'd had to exploit her position of trust within a family to come up with something that would help to solve the crime, something to which the investigating officers would not have access — a few words uttered in extremity, an insight into family dynamics. And she had no problem with this; it was part of the job, even if it meant that a bit of her had to remain detached from the people she was trying to help.

But Rachel Norton was different. Rachel was totally vulnerable, and utterly alone. She had no one but Yolanda to look after her. Her parents, she told Yolanda, were on holiday in Greece. Her sister lived in Leicester and had a family of her own to worry about, and besides, they'd never been close. She didn't get on well enough with Trevor's family to want them around, and since leaving work she didn't really have any friends she felt she could call upon.

So Yolanda felt even more protective than usual, with the wholeheartedness that made her so good at her job. Eli wasn't going to be seeing much of her over the next few days, she knew, whether they caught the killer right away or not.

"You're not going to be hard on her now, are you?" she said severely to the two officers at the door. "She's had a great shock. She's very fragile." It wouldn't do any good to ask them to wait till tomorrow.

"We're not totally insensitive, you know." Neville stepped past her with Cowley in his wake. "But there are a few things we have to ask her, so we can get on with what we have to do."

Rachel was in the lounge; she hadn't moved since Yolanda had left her to answer the door. She sat in the middle of the sofa, hunched forward, her head down. Yolanda resumed her position at her side and took one of her hands as the two policemen settled into the chairs.

"Mrs. Norton," said Neville. "I know this is difficult for you. But I'm sure that you want to help us catch the person who did this."

She nodded, her face concealed from Yolanda's scrutiny by a curtain of loose blond hair. With her free hand, Yolanda smoothed the hair back and tucked it behind Rachel's ear to afford herself a clear view of her charge's expression.

"Mrs. Norton, did your husband have any enemies?"

"Enemies?" She sat up straight, startled. "But he was mugged! You should be out on the street looking for a mugger instead of wasting your time asking me such ridiculous questions!"

"We have to ask," put in Cowley, who had taken out his notebook.

"Did he have any enemies?" repeated Neville. "Say, any business rivals?"

She shook her head decisively. "No. Nothing like that. He was respected. By his clients. By everyone."

Neville drummed his fingers on the arm of the chair. "So you can't think of anyone who would have wanted to kill him."

"Of course not."

"All right, Mrs. Norton." Neville looked across at Sid Cowley, who was scribbling away. "Now I have to ask you something that could be very upsetting."

Yolanda could feel the tension in Rachel's body as she tightened the grip on her hand; she shot a warning glance at Neville. "Easy, now."

"We can't discount any possibility at this point, so we have to ask some difficult questions. Don't take it personally." Yolanda felt the words were directed as much towards her as to Rachel.

Neville shifted in his chair. "Was Trevor . . . um, I mean . . ." He cleared his throat. "Is it possible that there were . . . any other women in his life?"

Rachel's reaction was not what Yolanda would have expected: anger, indignation, "how dare you". No, Rachel slumped over and the tears began again. "You just don't understand, do you?" she sobbed.

"Don't understand what?"

She swallowed hard, reached for a tissue, and dabbed at her eyes. "That Trevor . . . he loved me more than anything. That there was never anyone else for him. Never. I was the first woman in his life. The only one." She blew her nose. "I don't suppose you've ever loved anyone like that, Inspector. I can't expect you to understand."

Neville, observed Yolanda, looked uncomfortable at that. He didn't seem able to bring himself to make eye contact. "And . . . and the baby?" he asked. "Trevor was happy about the baby?"

"Over the moon. I've already told you that."

"Was it . . . planned?"

Rachel glared at him. "That isn't really any of your business, Inspector. But . . . yes. We'd been trying for a while. And it finally happened." She gulped. "As I said, Trevor was . . . thrilled. He couldn't have been happier." She turned and addressed her next words to Yolanda, gripping her hand. "It was like he finally had everything he'd ever wanted. Me. His own business. Success. This house. And now the baby."

Neville rose, followed by Cowley. "If it's all right with you, Mrs. Norton, we need to have a look round the house. We may need to call in some other officers to conduct a thorough search."

"Whatever for?" She released Yolanda's hand and struggled to her feet to face the two policemen. "Trevor wasn't killed here. Why on earth should you need to do that? Haven't you done enough, with your . . . your nasty insinuations? Why do you have to invade my home as well?" Now the anger that Yolanda had expected earlier was definitely there.

"Mrs. Norton," Neville said, and the Irish lilt in his voice was all the more evident as he spoke formally. "We have procedures. We can't discount anything yet. We want to find the person who killed your husband. I'm sure that's what you want, as well."

"Yes, but . . ."

"We can do this with your permission. Or we can go to the magistrate and get a warrant. It's up to you. But I'm sure that you understand why we have to do this."

Rachel's shoulders slumped; she covered her face with her hands. "Yes. All right."

"And Trevor's computer," Neville went on. "We'll need to take it away."

She lifted her head sharply. "Why?"

"It's routine. We'll need to examine the files, the hard drive."

"We'll give you a receipt for it," Cowley put in. "You'll have it back soon."

Yolanda watched them leave the room. She put her arms round Rachel's shoulders, shaking now with silent tears. "There, there," she crooned. "Yolanda's here to look after you, lovie. Yolanda's here."

Saturdays were problematical for Callie. Most people enjoyed Saturdays as days off, but Callie was always very much on duty, especially with Brian unavailable. And Saturday nights were even more difficult, with Sunday morning just over the horizon. This Sunday was worse than usual: she was scheduled to preach, and she hadn't yet finished writing her sermon.

So although she was disappointed when Marco rang her on her mobile to say that he wouldn't be able to see her that evening, a part of her was relieved. That would give her time to finish her sermon, even to polish it a bit. And it would give her some space to think.

Sitting in front of her computer, trying to come up with some fresh insights about Advent — the period of waiting, of expectation — she kept seeing the face of Morag Hamilton floating between her and the screen.

Morag was waiting, but not in expectation. In dread, and in loneliness.

Callie knew what it was to feel loneliness: in those dreadful weeks after her fiancé Adam had told her that he'd found someone else, she had lived through enough loneliness to last her a lifetime. But she had never faced the sort of ordeal that awaited Morag Hamilton: painful medical treatments with horrible side effects, and no guarantee at the end of the day that they would prolong her life by more than a few weeks or months.

And she, Callie, was involved. Like it or not, she was involved. It was something that none of her courses at theological college had prepared her for. She couldn't just deal with her flock in a detached way, listening to their problems yet remaining unmoved by them. Already she had discovered that ministry meant entering into their pain, living it with them. Walking with them in places she would prefer not to walk, holding their hands.

It was a privilege; it was a responsibility so awesome that she wasn't sure she was capable of carrying it out. Certainly not without God's help.

It was also something that brought with it its own kind of loneliness. She was the recipient — the guardian — of people's inmost secrets, of their fears and their guilt as well as their joys, and that in itself was a huge weight, a burden almost too great to bear. These things were not to be shared or discussed with anyone else. Not even with Brian. Not even with Marco.

She often wished that it were possible to use Marco as a sounding board when she had a particularly burdensome problem to deal with. He was wise, he was caring; he, too, had a job which involved listening to people and feeling their pain.

In fact, she sometimes thought, their jobs weren't all that different from each other. Marco didn't talk about his job much, but she'd gathered from what he did say that a Family Liaison Officer was in a unique position within the police force. Other CID officers' responsibility for a case finished, for all intents and purposes, when they handed it over to the Crown Prosecution Service, but as an FLO his contact with the people in his care was more open-ended, lasting up till the trial and beyond. At any given time he could be involved with a number of families on different levels, providing ongoing contact and support. Once Marco had said to her that their jobs were very similar, except that he worked for the Metropolitan Police, and she worked for God. When he'd said it, she'd found it very amusing, yet there was a great deal of truth in that flippant statement.

Neville was glad to get out of the Nortons' house, and judging from the way his jaws were working on that piece of nicotine chewing gum, so was Sid Cowley. They'd called in a PC to carry the computer away, to take it to those mysterious experts whose task it was to dissect its hard drive, to find not only the things which were evident but the bits of data which had been trashed over the life of the machine. Trevor Norton might have been an IT expert, but Neville was willing to bet that even he had things on his computer which he would never have dreamed would be retrievable.

"Not that it will amount to anything," he grumbled to Cowley. A cursory examination of Trevor Norton's e-mails hadn't revealed anything exciting or shocking. It was pretty much all business, and above-board business at that. No crooked dealing, no obvious enemies. No evidence of a secret girlfriend or mistress, at least not in the e-mails. "Though I suppose if there *was* another woman, he wouldn't have been stupid enough to leave anything where his wife could see it," he allowed. "She did the books, after all. She had access to his computer."

"Barking up the wrong tree," muttered Cowley.

Neville was sure that he was right, that this crime would turn out to be completely unrelated to Trevor Norton's personal life. Still, they had to go through the motions. Leaving no stone unturned — that was what it was all about. At the end of the day, if they were called to account and had to answer any questions about the enquiry, they would be able to say that they had investigated every possibility, likely or not.

And you never knew. Cowley could be wrong. Neville hoped that he was — at least it would give them somewhere to start, someone to talk to. Something to do other than twiddling their thumbs while they waited for the DNA results to come in.

In spite of the distractions, Callie managed to finish her sermon. She printed it out, read through it, pencilled in a few corrections and improvements.

Dinner time, she realised as she saw Bella sitting patiently by her empty food bowl. Callie filled the bowl and Bella accepted it without hesitation, her whole body wagging with gratitude.

Callie herself didn't have much of an appetite, but knew she'd need to eat something. The fridge yielded up a few leftovers: half a portion of lasagne, a bit of chicken, a container of soup. Though it wouldn't be on a par with Marco's home-made pasta, it would do, with the help of her trusty microwave.

She ate at the kitchen table, closely observed by Bella. Then she washed up and went back through into the sitting room.

The fireplace still held the remains of last night's fire. If Marco had been here tonight as planned, he would have cleaned it out and built a new fire; though she felt chilled in the high-ceilinged room, Callie couldn't be bothered. Instead she took the throw from the back of the sofa and wrapped herself in it, settling down in front of the television.

She consulted the listings and found nothing of interest. When, she wondered, had Saturday night television become so tedious? The hundred best something-or-others, a cringe-making reality show, a programme promising an evening of caterwauling talentless teenagers, and a tired old film which she'd already seen and hadn't particularly enjoyed the first time round.

Bella jumped up beside her on the sofa and snuggled close. "Oh, Bella," Callie murmured. "What did I ever do without you?"

The black-and-white cocker spaniel, Callie had discovered, was a wonderful listener, and a discreet one. That was just what she needed this evening; she couldn't get Morag Hamilton out of her mind. "Let me tell you about Morag and her family," she said, scratching behind Bella's floppy ears.

The story, as Morag had related it to her, was a fascinating — if distressing — one. And at the centre of it all was Angus, Morag's only child.

Angus Hamilton had, in spite of his parents' best efforts, grown up as something of a young tearaway. He'd hung out with a fairly rough crowd, inasmuch as was possible in a town in the Highlands of Scotland, and had had a few minor scrapes with the law: under-age drinking, fighting, damage to property. He'd left school at sixteen without any qualifications and seemed set on a course to waste his young life.

It was, needless to say, a cause of great concern for his parents, especially with his father's position as the town's doctor.

Then Angus had fallen under the spell of a woman who was several years his senior: Harriet Campbell, who ran the local pub. "I can't say Donald and I were over the moon about that at first," Morag had confessed. "But we were proved wrong."

Harriet had teaching qualifications. In fact, she'd left Gartenbridge some years earlier and had been teaching in Edinburgh when her publican parents were killed in an accident when on holiday in Spain. A sense of responsibility to them had brought her back to Gartenbridge to take over the family business.

The pub had never been so popular; the young men — and not a few of the older ones as well — hung round the place like bees round a honey pot, and not just for the drink. Harriet Campbell was beautiful, vivacious, sexy. Every young man's dream.

But Harriet had seen something in Angus — something no one else had seen. The school teacher in her recognised his quick mind, his facility with numbers, and told him bluntly that he was wasting his life.

He listened to her as he had not listened to his parents. With her encouragement and help, he buckled down to study, to gain the qualifications he had scorned a few years earlier. Basic qualifications, followed by more study and advanced accountancy training.

Harriet Campbell had been the making of Angus Hamilton. Of that his mother had no doubt. "Without her," she'd told Callie, "he'd still be in Gartenbridge. Or more likely in prison. He was that out of control."

Instead he was in London, the Chief Financial Officer of a major firm in the City. Married to Jilly.

"But what happened in between?" Callie had wanted to know. "And what about Harriet?" She remembered the haunting face in the photo: young Alex, in whom her grandmother Morag saw the promise of her mother's beauty. A mother who wasn't Jilly. "Is Alex Harriet's daughter, then?"

What had begun as a mentoring relationship had inevitably developed into something more complex. It had happened when Angus was impossibly young, just barely nineteen. Harriet, then twenty-five, had fallen pregnant. A hasty wedding had followed.

"Donald and I weren't so thrilled at first, of course," Morag told her. "Angus was so young — we thought he couldn't cope with it. But we were wrong. Having a family made him grow up. He and Harriet were so much in love — they adored each other. And when Alex came along, they were such a happy family."

Callie had reached that point in recounting Morag's story to Bella when the dog stirred restlessly, jumped off the sofa, and went to the door at the top of the stairs.

"Do you have to go out, then?" Callie asked.

Bella wagged her tail.

It was the one downside of having a dog and living upstairs: she couldn't just open the door and let Bella out into a garden. Callie had to put a coat on, get Bella's lead. She ought to change from her slippers into shoes, but she wasn't planning to go far.

The temperature had fallen even further; Callie's breath came out in frosty puffs. Unfortunately, though, Bella didn't seem to feel the cold, and took her time in finding the perfect spot to do her business.

"Hurry up," Callie muttered, hugging herself. She hadn't put on her gloves and her hands were freezing. So were her feet, clad in her fuzzy slippers.

"Hi, Cal," said a voice in the darkness.

Callie jumped, her heart pounding. She spun round, yanking on Bella's lead.

There was only one person who called her Cal.

Adam.

It was anything but cold in La Venezia. Mark was sweating from the heat of the kitchen; even the main part of the restaurant was overly warm, a function of all the bodies packed in round every single table. No one was complaining, though; a good time was being had by all, judging by the noise level.

"More wine!" A man, his face already flushed with what he had consumed, waved in Mark's direction and held up an empty bottle. He was wearing the red paper crown from his cracker, slightly askew. "More of the same."

"Yes, sir. Another bottle of house red."

"Make it two bottles," roared the man. "Save yourself another trip. The night is young."

Mark sneaked a look at his watch. Unfortunately the man was right: it was barely gone eight. The night was young, and already he was exhausted.

No wonder he'd opted out of the family business, and gone into the police instead. Police work, even at its most demanding, was a doddle compared to this.

Serena sailed past him, balancing a tray laden with several plates of steaming ravioli — their mother's speciality, and one of the restaurant's signature dishes. She caught him looking at his watch and smiled at him over her shoulder. "Cheer up, Marco. In a few hours it will all be over."

"What are you doing here?" Callie blurted. Her heart was pounding — from surprise, she told herself. She would have reacted that way to anyone appearing out of the dark and startling her like that.

"I'm taking a walk," said Adam Masters, the man she'd been meant to marry. "Finishing up a sermon. I needed to clear my head, get some fresh air." He leaned over and scratched Bella's ears. "Is he yours? Or are you just dog-sitting for someone?"

"She," Callie corrected him automatically. Bella was wagging her tail in ecstasy — the traitor. "She's mine."

"I didn't know you had a dog."

Callie bit back a retort. There were a lot of things that Adam didn't know about her these days, and there was no reason why he should. It was now three months since he'd dumped her; they had both moved on. "Her name is Bella," she said.

He stamped his feet, one after the other. "It's jolly cold tonight," he said. "Aren't you going to invite me in for a hot drink?"

That had been the farthest thing from her mind. She thought quickly about the state of the flat: had she done the washing up? Was the sitting room a mess? "All right," she said grudgingly.

"I don't think I've seen your flat." Adam's voice was friendly, conversational. Matter-of-fact. He followed her up the stairs; she was conscious of her fuzzy and somewhat dilapidated pink slippers.

"It's nothing as grand as yours," she said, remembering the elegant Georgian ground-floor flat

102

where Adam lived. She'd been there exactly once, for a disastrous meal with Adam and Pippa, his new fiancée. "But it suits us."

"Us?"

"Me and Bella," she said coldly. Once inside the flat, she unclipped Bella's lead and then shrugged out of her coat.

Fortunately the sitting room was reasonably tidy, though the throw in which she'd been wrapped had been abandoned on the floor. She picked it up, folded it and returned it to the back of the sofa. "What would you like, Adam? Coffee? Tea?"

"You know that I never drink coffee in the evening," he said in a teasing sort of voice.

I know nothing about you, she wanted to say. Perhaps I never did. "Tea, then."

"Tea would be brilliant. Lapsang, if you have it."

She didn't have it. Lapsang had always been Adam's tea of choice; Callie used to enjoy it as well, but since their break-up she hadn't touched it. If she had her way, she never would again: that tarry, smoky taste would always bring back Adam and their cosy evenings together. "No Lapsang. English Breakfast, Lady Grey, or ordinary."

"Ordinary will do."

Thankfully, he didn't follow her into the kitchen. Without being asked, he flopped down on the sofa and patted the seat beside him. The perfidious Bella jumped up next to him and leaned against him as he stroked her.

Had it really been an accident, his running into her in the dark like that? Callie wondered as she made the tea. If she hadn't been out there, would he have rung the bell? But why? And where was the lovely Pippa?

She might as well ask; after all, she had nothing to lose. Not any more. "Where's Pippa?" she asked brightly as she set a mug of tea on the table beside him. "Doesn't she usually come at the weekend?"

Adam shrugged, smiling. "Not this weekend. She's with her mum, making wedding plans. The dress, all that sort of thing."

In spite of herself, Callie felt her heart constrict. She sank into an armchair and forced herself to look at him, stretching her mouth into a semblance of a smile. "You've set a date, then? Some time in the spring?" When she and Adam had been engaged, they hadn't planned to marry until after their first year as curates, probably next autumn. But she would lay money on Pippa getting him to the altar before that.

He shook his head, seeming bemused. "Actually, Cal, it's later this month. Right after Christmas."

"Christmas!"

"There isn't any good reason to wait any longer than that."

"But what about Pippa's job?" She was, Callie knew, an infant school teacher.

"She's told them that she'll be leaving at the end of this term." Adam reached for his mug of tea. "I'm sure she'll be able to do some supply teaching in London, at first. And she shouldn't have any trouble finding a full-time job. Eventually."

104

Callie took a sip of her tea; it was scalding hot.

"Anyway," said Adam, as though this were any normal conversation, "the wedding is on the twenty-eighth. Holy Innocents Day. You'll come, won't you, Cal?"

The last of the merrymakers had departed, and so had the hired staff; the doors of La Venezia were locked, with only the family remaining. While Serena and her father laid the tables in the restaurant, refilling salt shakers and putting out Christmas crackers, Mark helped his mother in the kitchen, making sure that everything was tidy and in its place. It was, she always said, the only way to run a restaurant: you couldn't leave at night until the place was ready to open for business on the following day. That was sensible, but it meant long and tiring nights.

Before disposing of the last of the cooked pasta, Grazia Lombardi stopped and looked at her son. "Have you eaten anything, Marco?"

Mark thought back. He'd had a sausage roll and chips for lunch, a good many hours ago. Later he'd had a biscuit with a cup of tea. And tonight he'd grabbed a couple of breadsticks at one point. "Not much," he admitted.

"Ah, you must eat."

"Don't worry, Mamma." It was half-hearted, as Mark realised how hungry he was. He also knew that his words would fall on deaf ears.

She set about her task with the speed and efficiency which enabled her to run the kitchen of a popular restaurant. A frying pan, a bit of chopped pancetta, some cream, an egg: in a few minutes she set a plate of spaghetti carbonara in front of him. "*Mangi*," she commanded.

He obeyed. It was delicious, he was ravenous, and before long the plate was empty. "*Grazie, Mamma*," he said meekly.

As he was eating, she'd washed up the frying pan and put everything away. He washed the plate and cutlery while she made a pot of coffee as their reward for a job well done.

No one, thought Mark, made coffee like his mother, not even Serena: it was thick as syrup, flavourful and strong. He'd watched her doing it countless times; he'd asked her to show him how, and had tried to emulate her method. Somehow, though, it never tasted the same. She had a magic touch when it came to coffee. It was nothing like the stuff that came out of a machine, the stuff they served the customers. The customers didn't know any better; they didn't know what they were missing.

She poured it into diminutive cups and handed one to Mark. He sniffed it, closing his eyes with pleasure before indulging in one tiny, reviving sip. "Mmm, Mamma. Wonderful."

It was at that moment that she pounced. "So, Marco," she said. "We haven't seen so much of you lately."

He knew it was true: before Callie, he'd been much more inclined to drop into the restaurant of an evening — if not to help out, at least to indulge in the pleasures of his mother's cooking. Caught off guard, he fell back on the usual lame excuse. "I've been very busy at work, Mamma."

Grazia Lombardi wasn't buying it. She looked intently at her son. "Marco," she said. "Tell me the truth. *Veramente, hai una ragazza?* Do you have a girlfriend?"

CHAPTER
SIX

Yolanda Fish had not gone home on Saturday night. She wanted to be there, on hand, if Rachel needed her for anything.

The GP had called in, and had offered Rachel a sedative. Rachel had refused; she didn't want to take anything that might have an effect on her baby. Yolanda approved of that decision, but she was not without her own bag of tricks. In her years as a midwife, she had developed a home-brewed potion which would ensure a night of sound sleep to an expectant mother without any danger whatever to the baby. It was basically warm milk infused with a few herbs; a quick trip to the corner shop provided her with all the ingredients she had needed, and Rachel had taken it trustfully, without a word of protest.

There was no guest room at the Nortons' house; it was as if they didn't expect — or wish — ever to have guests. So Yolanda had dragged sofa cushions into the nursery and fashioned herself a makeshift bed in the room adjacent to Rachel's. It made a surprisingly comfortable resting place and she slept well.

But she was instantly awake when, in the hours before dawn, the telephone rang. It was a cordless phone; she had removed it from Rachel's bedroom and put it on the floor next to her instead, trying to anticipate and deflect anything which might disturb Rachel's sleep.

Yolanda reached for the phone, punched the button to accept the call, and put it to her ear. "Hello?"

"Rache?" The voice was a soft whisper, so quiet that she couldn't determine the speaker's sex.

"No. She's sleeping. Can I give her a message?"

There was an audible click, followed by a dial tone.

Shrugging, Yolanda put the phone back on the floor and settled back onto her home-made bed. But sleep now eluded her. She turned on a light and checked her watch: it was barely six in the morning.

Thoughtfully she picked up the phone again and rang 1471; the caller's number had been withheld.

Once again Jane woke early, this time with a huge sense of anticipation. Today her boys were coming home, for the first time in two months.

If it had been any day but Sunday, she would have insisted that she and Brian drive to Oxford to collect them. As it was, the boys were taking one of the frequent coaches which ran between Oxford and London. They would be home in time for lunch.

She'd been to the butchers and had obtained a beautiful joint of beef, always the boys' favourite. It would be a proper Sunday lunch today, cutting no corners and sparing no expense. Beef and Yorkshire pudding, roast potatoes and plenty of veg, and to finish off, a gooey trifle, already made and in the fridge.

Jane didn't know how she was going to get through the morning service, or at least how she would manage to keep her mind on higher things. Advent: anticipation. At least that was apt.

Not surprisingly, Callie hadn't slept very well.

Adam! How dared he turn up like that, as if there were nothing unusual about it, and then have the bare-faced nerve to invite her to his wedding?

She wished she had been quick-witted enough for a scathing reply. Instead she had swallowed a mouthful of scalding tea, rendering her incapable of any speech at all.

And when she'd finally been able to speak, it had been a mild-mannered acquiescence. Pusillanimous! Yes, she would come if she could. Coward! How could she be so weak, so spineless? Why couldn't she have just told him to drop dead?

Her thoughts had run along these lines for what seemed like hours before she finally fell asleep, and then her dreams had been troubled — as they hadn't been for weeks — by Adam's presence in them. Bloody Adam, even invading her dreams like that. She didn't want to dream about Adam. She didn't want anything to do with him. She certainly didn't want to go to his wedding to the perfect Pippa, slim and blonde and beautiful.

And the thing she definitely didn't want to think about was the way Adam's proximity had affected her. In spite of herself, she'd felt that old tug of sexual attraction; at the back of her mind she'd wanted him to take her in his arms the way he used to, and put behind them everything that had happened in the meantime. Pippa, especially, but even Marco. Oh, how could her body be so treacherous?

So when she woke, with Bella snuggled against her for mutual warmth, she made a conscious effort to banish him from her mind. "What a waste of time," she said aloud to Bella. "He's just not worth it, you know. Peter's always said so."

Bella showed no inclination to leave the bed, no immediate need to go outside. Gratefully, Callie stroked Bella's glossy coat, switching mental gears. Before Adam's unwelcome intrusion, she'd been preoccupied with something else, had been telling Bella about it. "I'll finish telling you about Morag, shall I?" she suggested.

She'd left off at the point where Angus and Harriet were married and, with baby Alex, living as a happy family.

Angus had a good job. A high tech software company had opened a headquarters just outside Gartenbridge, and with his newly-obtained qualifications in accountancy, he'd had no trouble getting a job with them. He was keen and had real aptitude; within several years he had progressed up the ladder to a position near the top in the financial end of the company.

Harriet, meanwhile, had given up the pub. She'd sold it to keen incomers, and with the proceeds she had opened a small bookshop in Gartenbridge. It had been her lifelong dream to run a bookshop; with her enthusiasm and energy she had made a moderate

111

success of it, combining it creatively with motherhood as Alex grew from a happy baby to a well-adjusted girl.

And then Jilly had entered their lives.

They had met her at a dinner party. Dinner parties were a rarity in the somewhat limited social scene of Gartenbridge. This dinner party was an exceptional one, the highlight of the social calendar.

Morag and her husband Donald had been there as well, so her account of it was as an eye-witness.

The host was the Managing Director of the software firm which employed Angus. Although he was a man of mature years, as befitted his exalted position, he was in possession of a trophy wife, a great many years his junior.

And his trophy wife had an old school friend visiting from London.

Jilly Greaves.

Morag had described the evening vividly. Harriet in her red dress: a dress which was not new by any means, but which accentuated her womanly figure and her colouring, bringing out the rich auburn highlights of her hair and complementing her dark eyes. And Jilly, pale as a snow queen in ice blue. Angus had entered with Harriet on his arm, proud to be the husband of such a striking woman. But Jilly had sat beside him at dinner, hanging on his every word, admiring him with her wide blue eyes. By the time the evening was over, Angus was clearly smitten. Harriet practically had to drag him away from the party, and Morag could only imagine what had been said between them behind closed doors.

After that, it had all happened very quickly.

Jilly's visit had lasted a week, long enough for several more encounters — accidental or not — between her and Angus. By the end of the week, Angus had declared his determination to Harriet to divorce her and marry Jilly Greaves.

But Jilly had no intention of relocating to Scotland. London was where she had always lived, where she belonged. Where her family lived: the centre of her universe.

Her father had pulled a few strings, and before long Angus Hamilton had been offered a plum job in the City as Chief Financial Officer of a large and prestigious company.

In the time it took for the divorce to become final, Jilly and her mother had planned a spectacular wedding. It took place at the church in St. John's Wood, with the reception at Lord's Cricket Ground.

Morag was ashamed to admit to Callie that she and Donald had gone to the wedding, had come all the way down from Scotland for it. At the time it had seemed to them that no matter how much they disapproved of the marriage, Angus was their only son and it wouldn't be right if his family were not represented at such a momentous occasion. Jilly's family and friends had certainly been out in force. Alex had been an extremely reluctant bridesmaid, in company with Jilly's two nieces and a vast number of her friends. And in the midst of them, Jilly herself, radiant in a dress which must have cost the earth. Triumphant.

The wedding had happened the past spring. Since then, so much had changed for Morag. The death of her husband, the loss of her dog. The uprooting, at Angus' insistence, from her home and her resettlement in London.

That, she told Callie with some bitterness, was the greatest irony of all. Angus had been adamant that the move was for her own good. She would be close to them, her only remaining family.

But since she'd been in London, she had seen them no more than a few times. They were busy: Angus' job was demanding and required long hours, and Jilly had her own family to occupy her. Whenever Morag suggested getting together, they had an excuse at the ready.

They wouldn't even let her see Alex.

And this week, when she had needed them more than she'd ever needed her family, facing the diagnosis and then the knowledge that she had a virulent disease which could well kill her, they hadn't wanted to know.

She had repeatedly tried telephoning their home, getting only their call minder, leaving messages. They hadn't returned her calls. Then she had taken the extraordinary step of ringing Angus at work.

He had been cold, said Morag. Angry, even. "Mother, you must know that I'm a busy man," he'd told her. "I don't take personal calls at work."

"But I need to talk to you," she'd said, trying not to plead. "It's important. I'm not well, Angus. I need your support."

Astonishingly, he had then told her that it would be best in future if she made an appointment in advance to talk to him. "But you'll have to do it through Jilly," he said. "She keeps the family diary. If it's important enough, I'm sure we can fit you in. Give her a ring in a day or two, leave a message, and she'll get back to you."

"No wonder," Callie told Bella, "the poor woman is in a state."

Mark, waking early, was furious with himself. His mother had given him the perfect opportunity. She had asked the question, opened the door.

And he had wimped out.

There was no other way of looking at it. Cowardice had overcome him.

"No," he'd said. No girlfriend. "I'm just quite busy at work, that's all."

Apart from anything else, it was a betrayal of Callie. Like St. Peter denying Jesus three times: "I do not know the man."

But his mother had caught him unawares; he hadn't had time to prepare a careful reply. It had been so much easier to take the coward's way out.

How was he going to rectify it now, though? He couldn't very well admit that he hadn't given her a truthful answer. That would only make matters worse.

Why couldn't he have just told her the truth? Why hadn't he looked his mother in the eye and said, "Yes, I have a girlfriend. But calling her that doesn't do justice to the way I feel about her. I'm pretty sure I've found the person I want to spend the rest of my life with. And no, she's not Italian. But it doesn't matter to me, and it won't matter to you, either, once you've met her. She's wonderful — you'll see."

Instead, to his horror, he'd heard himself promising to make amends for being too busy for his family. At his mother's urging, he'd agreed to join them for a familial Sunday. Today.

Sunday lunchtime was the one time during the week when La Venezia was closed for business, reopening for the dinner trade. On Sunday morning the family would meet up at the Italian church in Clerkenwell for Mass, then squeeze into the Lombardi home for an elaborate and extended lunch, cooked by Mamma. No one else was even allowed into the kitchen: producing Sunday lunch for *la famiglia* was Mamma's chief joy of the week.

Mark had missed the last few Sundays. Now he had to make up for it. And he had halfway promised Callie that today they'd get a Christmas tree for her flat and decorate it. After the way he'd let her down last night, he couldn't bear to disappoint her today.

But he'd promised Mamma.

If only he could clone himself and be in two places at once.

He raised his head and looked at the clock. Mass started at ten and it was already past nine. He'd better get a move on or he'd be late.

Already, though, he could hear his flatmate in the bathroom, taking a shower. And Geoff took very long showers. He'd missed his chance. You snooze, you lose. Mark groaned and turned his face into his pillow.

116

When Alex woke on Sunday morning, she was as usual clutching Buster Bear.

Buster, in spite of her name, was a girl bear. Alex had had her for as long as she could remember — even longer than that, in fact. Buster, she knew, had been a present from Granny and Granddad, when she had been a baby. And every year for Christmas, Mum had made a new frock for Buster. Last year's frock was getting a bit tatty.

Clinging desperately to the receding memory of a dream in which she and Mum and Dad were on holiday together, Alex resisted waking up for as long as she could. The smell of coffee was trickling round the door. That meant Dad and Jilly were up.

And it was Sunday! Alex's least favourite day of the week. Even worse than school days.

Sunday meant that she would be dragged to spend the afternoon with stupid Jilly's stupid family. Living with Jilly was bad enough, but to be expected to spend time with her awful family . . .

Jilly's mother was just as dumb as she was, only older. Likewise Jilly's sister Melanie. Not a brain cell between the two of them. At least they ignored Alex, just like Jilly did. Jilly's dad was even worse: he patronised Alex, and teased her about the brace on her teeth. The very worst of all, though, were Jilly's two nieces. Infinitely worse than the rest — even worse than the girls at school.

They *were* both at her school, in fact, but thankfully not in her year. Beatrice was a year older than Alex;

117

Georgina — named after Jilly's dad and clearly his favourite — was a year younger. They were both blonde and pretty, in that same vapid way as the women of the family, and very conscious of their looks, their clothes.

Butter wouldn't melt in their mouths during the family Sunday lunch. They were polite and knew their place. After lunch, though, they would be dismissed. "Girls, why don't you go and play in your rooms? And take Alex with you." That was when the torture began.

They were relentless; they were naturally cruel. They had a fine instinct for the most effective ways to wound Alex. Once they had exhausted the preliminaries — her frizzy hair, her tooth brace, her skinny body, her ugly clothes, the funny way she talked — they would get down to business, working in tandem.

"You know that Aunt Jilly hates you," Beatrice would begin. "She wishes you didn't have to live with them. Why *do* you have to live with them?"

"It's because her mum doesn't want her," Georgina would say, addressing Beatrice rather than Alex. "Her real mum hates her too."

"That's not true," Alex couldn't stop herself from saying. "Not true! My mum loves me!"

"Or maybe her mum is dead."

"She's not dead!"

"I'll bet she is, and they just haven't told you. She's dead. Maybe she topped herself. Or maybe she's run off with another man. Or even another woman. Your mother's a lezzie."

"A lezzie! Her mother's a lezzie!"

"She's not!"

118

"I'll bet your mum is as ugly as you are. That's why your dad left her."

"Her mum's old. Old and ugly. Aunt Jilly told me."

On and on it would go, Alex trying hard not to cry, not to give them the satisfaction of knowing how deeply they were hurting her.

Every Sunday it was the same.

Alex squeezed Buster. "I won't go," she whispered fiercely. "I won't." She said it every week; every week she was overruled and taken against her will.

Today she was determined that it would be different. She had something important to do: something that would be best accomplished if she were alone in the flat. If resistance didn't work — and by now she knew that it didn't — then she'd have to try another tactic.

She curled into a ball and waited for what she knew would eventually happen.

Her dad tapped on the door of her room. "Alex? Alex, lassie? Are you up? Do you not want a wee bit of breakfast?"

Alex didn't respond, and after a minute he opened the door a crack. "Alex?"

She moaned, then spoke in a soft, pained voice. "Dad, I don't feel well at all. My tummy hurts."

After the parish Eucharist, Jane did something that was rare for her: she went home straightaway, without lingering to chat with anyone. Usually she would be fussing over the urn, overseeing the serving of the post-service coffee. She would be making arrangements about the flower rota or the next Mothers' Union meeting; she would be available for a discreet conversation with someone who didn't want to approach the vicar directly but who knew that a word with Jane was every bit as efficacious.

Today, though, there were other things on her mind. She wanted to make sure that today's lunch was absolutely perfect in every way.

Usually they ate in the kitchen, the warmest room in the draughty and under-heated house; today they would have a festive family Sunday lunch in the dining room, and Jane needed not only to lay the table but also to put the radiator on in good time. Then there were the veg to get ready: carrots, sprouts and cauliflower, as well as roast potatoes and roasted parsnips. Not to mention the batter for the Yorkshire pudding.

Everything was timed for lunch at half-past one — half an hour later than usual, to allow a little extra time in case the boys were delayed.

When Brian got home from church, he came into the kitchen to find her. "Anything I can do to help, Janey? Peel some potatoes or lay the table?"

"Do you seriously think I haven't done the potatoes yet?" she snapped at him, uncharacteristically. "Everything is under control."

Brian recoiled. "Sorry, Janey. Just trying to be helpful."

"I'm sorry," she relented. "I just want everything to be right."

"It's only the boys," he pointed out to her.

But when the doorbell rang, twenty minutes later, it wasn't only the boys standing on the doorstep.

120

After Mass, which he'd made by the skin of his teeth, Mark slipped out of the church and switched on his mobile. Callie would still be at church, but he could leave a message for her.

"I'm not sure what time I'll be able to get to you," he said, quietly in case his mother should sneak up behind him and overhear. "I'll be there as soon as I can." It was vague, but it was the best he could do at the moment.

Jane opened the door, her face split side to side by a welcoming smile. "Charlie! Simon!"

Charlie was carrying a large and ancient suitcase — an old one of Brian's — which he dropped in order to hug her. "Mum. Oh, Mum. It's so good to be home."

Simon had a duffel bag slung over his shoulder. And next to him was a girl, also with a suitcase. She stood close to Simon, almost as if for protection.

Before stepping forward to embrace his mother, Simon cleared his throat and spoke, his voice both tender and proud. "Mum, this is Ellie."

As soon as Dad and Jilly were out of the flat, Alex went scrounging for food, her tummy ache having mysteriously vanished. In fact, she was rather hungry. She ate a bowl of cereal, then washed the bowl and spoon and put them away so no one would be the wiser. Then she ate a banana from the fruit bowl and buried the peel at the bottom of the kitchen bin. This was unusual behaviour for her; ordinarily she would have just left her dirty dishes on the table, with the blackening banana peel draped over them.

One thing you could say about Jilly: she was house-proud. Of course there was a cleaning lady who came in most days, but Jilly enjoyed housework and took pride in keeping things just right. It provided an ongoing source of conflict with Alex, who had grown up with her mother's oft-repeated sentiment that only dull women had immaculate homes. Alex's mum had had better things to do than worry about cleaning, and Alex wasn't much bothered either. In fact, once she knew that her careless untidiness wound Jilly up, she began to exercise it deliberately. Her rucksack dumped by the front door, shoes left in the sitting room, dirty clothes strewn next to the hamper rather than in it. Guerilla warfare, that's what it was.

"How do you do, Mrs. Stanford?" said Ellie. At least, thought Jane, the girl was polite. Someone had brought her up right.

Apart from that, she had little else to commend her. She was an ordinary-looking girl, neither particularly pretty nor especially plain. Jane, in her nocturnal imaginings, had pictured some sort of *femme fatale*, a siren of such outstanding beauty that Simon couldn't help but be ensnared by her. Red hair, Jane had conjured up, profuse and curling round an artfully made-up face, and a voluptuous figure, bursting out of a skimpy dress.

Ellie was not in the least voluptuous; she was, in fact, more on the skinny side, even bulked up by a padded anorak above her jeansclad legs. Her hair was brown and straight and long, without any style to it, and she appeared to be wearing no make-up at all.

"How nice to meet you," Jane said automatically in the split second it took her to assess the girl. "Do come in."

"We thought we'd surprise you," Simon was saying. "We didn't think you'd mind."

We, thought Jane. Simon was part of a *we*.

"If it's okay, Ellie will stay for a few days," he went on. "Before she goes to her parents'."

"You're very welcome," said Jane.

The girl smiled. "If it's no trouble, Mrs. Stanford."

"No trouble at all. The spare room is made up." That, thought Jane, should make her position perfectly clear.

She intercepted a look between them: raised eyebrows on Simon's part, Ellie's lips compressed.

So they *were* sleeping together. Well, what they did in Oxford was out of her control, but under her roof it was a different story.

Simon let it go, sliding the duffel bag off his shoulder and dumping it on the floor. "Where's Dad?"

"He's in the sitting room with the Sunday papers."

"Some things don't change," grinned Charlie.

Alex's most treasured possession — even more treasured than Buster — was a locket, which she wore round her neck at all times, even when she was sleeping; she only took it off in the bath. The locket had belonged to her other gran, her mum's mum, who had died before she was born. In it was a tiny photo of Alex's mum, taken when she was about the age Alex was now. Her mum had given it to Alex on her tenth birthday, and she'd worn it ever since. It was a source of huge comfort to Alex, not least because of the hope it held out that one day she would be as beautiful as her mother. When her mum was twelve, she'd looked a lot like Alex looked now, so that boded well for the future. And wearing the locket made her seem somehow closer to her mum.

Now there was an additional reason for treasuring the locket and wearing it close to her heart. On the other side, opposite the young Harriet's photo, was a photo of Jack.

Jack had sent it to her, attached to an e-mail, a few days ago. Rather than print it out and put it in a frame, where Jilly might spot it if she came into Alex's room to snoop, before printing it she had reduced it to a tiny image on the computer, just the right size to cut out and put in her locket, where no one else would ever see it.

She opened her locket and looked at both photos, kissed each one, and went to her computer. There was work to be done, and she needed to finish it before there was any danger of Dad and Jilly coming back.

After Jane finished the meal preparations and quickly added a chair and place setting, they were seated round the dining table at last: Charlie on one side, Simon and Ellie on the other, and their parents at either end. Brian carved the joint of beef, cooked to

124

perfection just as the boys liked it. He put the choicest slices on a plate which he set down in front of Ellie, the guest in the house. "Help yourself to vegetables," Jane invited, gesturing to the steaming bowls in the middle of the table.

"Thank you, Mrs. Stanford."

"Actually, Mum," Simon said, with a quick sideways glance at his girlfriend, "I think Ellie would rather have an empty plate. She's too polite to say it, but she doesn't eat meat."

"Oh." Stunned, Jane snapped her mouth shut and removed the offending plate, putting it in front of Simon instead.

"I won't have it either, Mum, if you don't mind." He produced an unconvincing laugh. "She's been trying to make a vegetarian out of me as well, and she's succeeding. I haven't had meat for at least a fortnight now."

"But we love vegetables, Mrs. Stanford," Ellie put in quickly. "And these look delicious." She accepted an empty plate from Brian and heaped it with sprouts and cauliflower and carrots.

We.

"Give that meat to me, then, Mum," said Charlie, reaching for the plate. "More for me this way. I'll have theirs, and mine as well."

"Thank goodness for that," Brian said heartily. "I was beginning to think that your mother and I would have to eat it all ourselves."

"No one's going to turn me into a namby-pamby vegetarian," Charlie assured them. "And I could never pass up Mum's roast beef."

Alex knew exactly what she wanted to be when she grew up: a computer-based graphic designer. To that end, she'd asked her father to buy her all of the top-end software now available so that she could get a head start in preparing for that career. She was now quite competent with Photoshop, so she started it up and settled down to work, calling up a photograph of herself which she'd scanned into the computer.

First of all, that tooth brace would have to go. That was easily accomplished, and her smile was now pearly white and unencumbered by metal. She could make her nose a bit smaller, and perhaps her mouth as well. Not a lot she could do with her hair, but she would try her best to de-emphasise its frizziness. She could, though, enhance her flat chest a bit, and add a few pounds so she wasn't quite so skinny.

The trick was to make herself look more attractive, as well as a few years older, without rendering the image unrecognisable. A new, improved Alex, as she wished to appear to her suitor.

No, not Alex: Sasha. That was the name she used in corresponding with Jack. Someone — her mother? — had once told her that Sasha was the Russian nickname for Alexandra, and she thought it sounded far more glamorous and exotic than plain old Alex.

Jack had sent her his photo; he had asked for hers. As soon as it looked as good as she could make it, she would e-mail it to him. With love, from Sasha.

★ ★ ★

126

The day seemed to have gone on forever. Lunch, then an afternoon of board games. Ellie had proved to be brilliant at Scrabble, wiping the rest of them off the board. She'd been almost as good at Monopoly; no one else stood a chance. Eventually, in desperation, Jane had brought out a new jigsaw puzzle which she'd been saving for Christmas, and they'd all clustered round the table, doing their bit, chattering away.

They'd had tea and cake; later, after "Songs of Praise" on the telly, they'd had sandwiches. Fortunately Jane had a packet of cheese in the fridge for Ellie and Simon's. Then another couple of hours on the jigsaw, before it was time for hot milky drinks.

"Simon, would you mind giving me a hand in the kitchen?" Jane requested, hoping for a few minutes alone with her son.

He looked up from the jigsaw, frowning. "In a minute, Mum."

"I'll do it," Charlie said promptly, and followed her into the kitchen. He got the milk out of the fridge while she retrieved the saucepan.

Jane hadn't really formulated what she wanted to say to Simon, and she wasn't sure what to say to Charlie, either. He made it easy for her.

"I suppose you're wondering why Simon didn't let you know that he was bringing Ellie home with him," he said, glugging milk into the saucepan.

"Well, it did come as a bit of a surprise," she admitted.

"He didn't know how to tell you. I asked him if he'd warned you that Ellie was coming, and he said that he thought the easiest thing was just to bring her. Then he wouldn't have to explain anything. She'd just be here, and you'd figure it out."

Jane sighed. "I do wish I'd had a bit of warning. About her not eating meat, for one thing. It made me feel so . . . foolish, when Simon turned his nose up at the roast."

"He's just being silly." Charlie squeezed her shoulder. "Don't take it to heart, Mum. He's in luuuurve." He laughed. "Give him a few months, and he'll be tucking into meat again. This won't last. Trust me."

Jane wished that she could.

After the milky drinks, when everyone else had retired upstairs to their rooms, she lingered in the kitchen, tidying up, taking her time. She put out the boxes of cereal for the morning, laying the table with bowls and spoons. Five bowls, five spoons. An extra chair. She felt keyed up, unwilling for some reason to go up to bed. She knew she wouldn't sleep.

Then weariness settled on her suddenly, like a heavy blanket. She was inexpressibly tired, unsure whether she would even make it up the stairs before she fell asleep.

The house was quiet; she could hear the deep tick-tock of the long-case clock — it had belonged to her grandparents, and was probably the best piece of furniture they owned — as she crept up the stairs and down the long corridor towards their bedroom.

For some reason, she paused for just a moment outside Simon's door.

Jane heard a murmur of voices, then a muffled giggle.

So much for separate rooms, then. But what could she do at this point? She could hardly burst in on them and play the outraged parent. That just wasn't her style, and it would be highly embarrassing for all of them. What if they were . . .

Oh, God.

Sighing, she continued down the corridor. She opened her bedroom door cautiously, expecting the room to be dark and Brian to be snoring away.

But the lights were on and Brian was sitting up in bed, reading a book.

"Oh," said Jane. "I thought you'd be asleep by now."

He put the book aside. "I was waiting for you."

Even in her exhaustion, her heart leapt. Waiting for her. The way he used to do.

"We haven't really had a chance to talk today," Brian said, patting the bed beside him.

"Talk? No, we haven't."

"And there's a lot to talk about." He grinned. "She's a cracking girl, isn't she, Janey?"

"Oh . . . yes. Of course."

If her voice sounded less than enthusiastic, Brian didn't seem to notice. He went on, "Fancy Simon finding a girl like that, and not even telling us. He's a dark horse, that one. Wanted to surprise us, and he certainly did that!"

"She seems very nice," Jane managed.

"She's brilliant," enthused Brian. "What a great addition to the family!"

Jane sank onto the edge of the bed and began untying her shoes. "It's a little soon to be talking like that," she pointed out. "He's only known her five minutes."

"But she's so right for him. You can see it straight away. Sometimes you just *know*. You know?"

She'd known as soon as she met Brian that he was the one for her. But Jane wasn't about to admit that now. "He's so young. They're both young. Far too young to think about anything permanent."

"Oh, don't be such an old wet blanket." Brian tugged playfully on her ponytail, then said in a thoughtful voice, "You know why I think I like her so much?"

"Why?"

"Because she reminds me of you, Janey. When you were young."

Jane closed her eyes; her voice was flat. "Does she, indeed."

CHAPTER
SEVEN

"Callie, I'm so sorry."

She found that she was gripping the phone and consciously relaxed her hand. "I waited for you. All afternoon."

"Yes, I know," said Marco. "I kept thinking I'd be able to get away. But . . . well, it was one thing after another."

"You didn't ring, after you left that message." She hadn't even taken Bella out for a walk, reckoning that he'd be there any minute.

Callie heard him sigh at the other end of the phone. "I'd forgotten to put my phone on the charger. It ran out of juice right after I talked to you."

She bit her tongue to keep back her next retort: doesn't your family own a phone? She would *not* come over all heavy with him, Callie told herself sternly. It wasn't like they'd had firm plans for the afternoon. And not like there was anything . . . firm . . . between them at all. She was beginning to care for him, far more than she'd ever thought she could care for anyone apart from Adam. Up to this point they'd had an easy sort of relationship: they spent a lot of time together, they enjoyed each other's company. When he kissed her, it generated enough heat for her to wish, sometimes, that they could just throw caution to the winds and go for it, but so far she'd managed to restrain herself in that area. And in her more rational moments that was fine with her, after what she'd been through with Adam.

They'd never had a row, never had cross words. Now she felt that they were dangerously close. He'd been inconsiderate, and she was being unreasonable. Not good.

After all, he had every right to spend Sunday afternoon with his family. Or any other time, come to that. She had no claim on him.

These thoughts went through her head in a heartbeat. "Okay," she said.

"Okay . . . what?"

She kept her voice neutral. "Okay anything."

"I'll see you later, all right? This evening?"

"I think it's my turn to cook."

She must not have sounded very enthusiastic; he came back with another suggestion. "No, we'll go out. My treat. All right?"

"Yes, all right." He must be feeling guilty, she told herself.

"See you later, then. Sevenish, I hope. Maybe a bit before." He rang off.

"Men!" Callie threw the phone on the sofa.

Bella looked at her, startled.

"Honestly, Bella. You can't trust any of them. They're all as bad as each other. I don't know why we women bother. I really, really don't." She sat down and hugged the dog, stroking her floppy ears, murmuring, "Take

132

my advice, Bella. Don't ever get involved with a man. They're nothing but trouble."

For a second night, Yolanda Fish had slept on her makeshift bed in Rachel Norton's nursery. Ordinarily she would have gone home by now, but for Yolanda this was not an ordinary case. She felt an exceptional protectiveness towards Rachel, largely because of the baby yet also because the young woman seemed so very alone. No one had come to the house to comfort her or look after her; no one had even phoned, apart from that one mysterious and abortive phone call. And Rachel showed no inclination to ring other people. It bothered Yolanda; there was something unnatural about being so isolated. In the early hours, awake and waiting for sounds from the next room, she vowed to herself to broach the subject with Rachel.

As soon as she heard Rachel stirring, going to the loo, she went downstairs and made tea. She took it straight back up, tapping on the bedroom door with her free hand.

"Come in," Rachel said, and Yolanda complied.

Rachel was sitting up in bed, looking flushed and almost feverish.

"Are you all right, lovie?" Going to her quickly, her old training and instincts coming to the fore, Yolanda put the back of her hand against Rachel's forehead.

"Yes. Fine." She took the cup of tea. "Thanks."

Yolanda sat on the end of the bed and watched as Rachel sipped at the tea.

"If there's anyone you'd like to notify," she said, "I'd be happy to make the phone calls for you. If you don't want to do it yourself."

Rachel looked at her over the rim of the mug and shook her head. "No. There isn't anyone."

"What about your parents?"

"I told you," said Rachel. "They're on holiday."

That seemed a very weak excuse to Yolanda: if something like that had happened to her — if Eli had died in any sort of circumstances, natural or suspicious — she was positive that her parents would have dropped everything and come to be with her. No matter where they were, or what shape they were in themselves. "I'm sure they'd want to know," she said. "At least you could give them the option to come back if they wanted to."

Now Rachel looked down into the mug, not meeting Yolanda's eyes. "If you must know," she said, "I haven't spoken to my parents in years. I just said they were on holiday because that sounded better."

"You haven't spoken to them in *years*?"

Rachel's lip trembled. "My dad . . . well, he was what I suppose you'd call abusive. He hit me . . . a lot. When I was a kid. He'd come home from the pub, all tanked up, and he'd knock me about. And Mum . . . she didn't want to know. I tried to tell her, but she didn't want to know."

"Oh, lovie!"

"As soon as I could, I left home. Came to London. Got a job, met Trevor. End of story. *Now* do you

134

understand why I don't want to contact them? Or my sister?"

Yolanda was appalled, but it did explain a great deal. "Oh, you poor thing."

Rachel shrugged. "A long time ago. Water under the bridge. Besides," she added matter-of-factly, "it's been in the papers, hasn't it? Everyone will know by now."

The papers! Yolanda hadn't thought to check the Sunday papers. Not that they would have had much in them: the body had only been found on Saturday, and the Sunday papers had early deadlines. Today might be a different story. And she supposed that they needed to be braced for enquiries from the press.

Not that this was a spectacularly interesting murder, from the media's point of view. Or the police's, either: the indications were that it was just a sordid mugging gone wrong.

Of course, Yolanda belatedly recalled, the press was big on that sort of thing at the moment. Yob culture, hoodies: they were on their high horse about the societal ills made manifest in the proliferation of street crime by young scofflaws with time on their hands, lack of parental supervision, and no moral fibre. Perhaps they would fasten on this as the latest evidence of a youth-centred society gone mad. Yolanda happened to agree with them, but that was beside the point. She had better be prepared.

In the meantime, she was determined to persevere with Rachel, to get her out of her isolation somehow. "What about the girls you used to work with?" she suggested. "Don't you keep up with any of them?"

Rachel shrugged. "Not really. I'm not part of their world any more." Her voice sounded wistful. "The City seems a long way off."

"Do you miss it? Working with other people, I mean?"

"A bit," she admitted. "It can feel kind of lonely."

"One of the downsides of self-employment, from what I've heard." Yolanda couldn't even imagine how boring it would be, shut up in your own house all day. No one to talk to but your husband. She loved Eli, but she couldn't comprehend living like that.

"It was Trevor's idea," Rachel said. "He didn't *need* other people, see. I was enough for him — that's what he always said. As long as he had me, he didn't need anyone else." She looked down into her tea.

"But that's not very healthy, lovie," Yolanda pointed out, trying not to sound critical of Trevor. "Maybe it worked for him, but . . ."

"He didn't like me going out on my own, either," Rachel blurted, almost involuntarily. "Didn't think it was safe — that's what he said. Especially with the baby on the way." She gulped. "He was . . . very protective of me."

And now she was alone, defenceless. Yolanda wanted to hug her. Yet something started to niggle, deep down. Rachel seemed to need to believe, and to make them — the police — believe, that Trevor had been a saint, and their marriage perfect. But Yolanda knew, from a lifetime of experience, that no marriage was perfect. Even the ones that worked had their grey areas, the murky bits which only the two people involved knew about — and sometimes those grey areas remained unacknowledged, unexplored. What was the truth of this one, beneath the surface?

Neville Stewart was perpetually behind on his paperwork. It wasn't that he was disorganised: it just didn't interest him. Once a case was over, he had no desire to tie up the loose ends. He just wanted to get on to the next thing, the next challenge.

But papers didn't file themselves, and information didn't appear on the computer of its own accord.

So Neville always had a huge backlog of work waiting for him on his desk. He knew it was a failing, and every so often he tackled it, spurred by the burden of guilt or sometimes by boredom. At times it provided an excuse for avoiding something even less interesting to him than the dry bones of dead old cases.

This was one of those times. He had not been gripped, as he'd hoped to be gripped, by the death of Trevor Norton. Random, opportunistic crimes like this one appeared to be were not the sort of thing to get him excited. They were solved — if they were solved at all — by forensic work in the lab, by hard slog on the part of an army of PCs, or sometimes by sheer luck. There was nothing there for a detective with flair and imagination, and that was how he liked to think of himself.

Trevor Norton was no longer alive — no longer running, no longer working at his computer, no longer awaiting the birth of his first child — because he'd been sporting an iPod. Full stop. Cut and dried. No human emotions involved except greed and covetousness. No tangle of motives to be teased out, no complex web of alibis.

The postmortem hadn't turned up anything immediate. Samples had been sent off, of course, but it would be a while before any results were available. According to the coroner, the inquest wouldn't be opened for another day or two. The computer boffins would take their time in retrieving the data from Trevor Norton's hard drive, and it could take days for all of the relevant CCTV footage to be reviewed. House-to-house enquiries were being carried out, round the Nortons' home and all along the route to the place where the body had been found: routine enquiries, unlikely — in Neville's opinion — to turn up anything. He'd left it to Sid Cowley to organise that, and to get on with anything else that could be done at the moment in the Norton case. Which was not much.

He, on the other hand, was dealing with his paper monster. The pile on the end of his desk had grown so large that it was unstable, threatening to slide onto the floor. At the moment there was a kind of geological logic to the piles, like layers of ancient rock which told a story. If the papers ever got out of order, though, he'd be a dead man. It was time for desperate measures.

And it was, as always, a trip down memory lane. An alternative to something even more boring.

He picked up a witness statement form and glanced at it. Willow Tree: the name stopped him in his tracks. It brought back a conversation about names, a conversation in which he'd been tempted to reveal his problematical history with his own name. Willow Tree had been given her name by eco-warrior parents seemingly oblivious to the ridicule it would bring upon her. How could parents do that to a kid?

He conjured up a picture of her. An unconventional young woman, to say the least: carrot-coloured hair gelled into spikes, heavy kohl make-up, a ring through one nostril, and iridescent green fingernails. Underneath it all, though, she was probably a pretty girl. And she'd been a joy as a witness — concise, articulate, co-operative. Intelligent. She'd been upset but not hysterical. He had liked Willow Tree.

And now, thought Neville, now that the case was over . . .

There was no reason why he should not see Willow Tree on a social basis. No reason at all.

She'd given him a mobile number; it was right there on the form. "You can reach me on this number any time," he remembered her saying.

Why not?

He stretched out his hand for the phone and punched in the number.

Monday was the day when Brian Stanford, by long custom, visited those housebound parishioners who wished to receive the Sacrament. When Callie had first come to the parish she had begun accompanying him on his visits, and it was now part of her weekly routine.

All weekend, Callie hadn't been able to stop thinking about Morag. She mentioned it to Brian after Morning Prayer. "I think we ought to call on Morag Hamilton today," she suggested. "She wasn't in church yesterday."

"Morag Hamilton?" He furrowed his brow vaguely. "Remind me."

"I told you about her last week. I've been to see her a couple of times. You said that I should," she added, knowing how sensitive he could be if he thought she was superseding her remit as a curate and flouting his authority over her.

Brian nodded. "Oh, the Scottish woman. Grey hair."

"That's right."

"Is she ill, do you know?" He glanced at his watch, as if he had more important things on his mind, or some pressing engagement awaiting him.

Callie wondered where to begin. "Well, it's a long story," she said. "I saw her on Saturday."

"You can tell me later," Brian stated. "On the way, perhaps."

He was already in motion, already heading home. Maybe, Callie speculated, he was specially hungry this morning and couldn't wait another minute for his breakfast.

In the afternoon, with no results at all from the house-to-house and no other leads, Neville called an informal press conference. He wasn't about to involve Rachel Norton in it — this wasn't that sort of case — but he'd run out of ideas for expanding the investigation, and this just might produce something useful. It couldn't hurt, at any rate.

He distributed photos of the dead man, then made a brief statement.

Trevor Norton had been killed on Friday morning, he stated, while out jogging along the Grand Union Canal, which he did every day at that time. It was known that he'd been wearing an iPod, which was now missing. If anyone had seen Trevor Norton that particular morning, or knew anything else which might be relevant, he would appreciate them ringing a special number.

For good measure, and to exploit the sympathy angle, he added that Mr. Norton left behind a wife who was soon to give birth to their first child. "They'd only been married for a year," he said.

That, he could tell immediately, had been a clever touch: the journalists looked at each other, made tutting noises, and scribbled furiously.

"Do you have any questions?" Neville invited.

"What is Mrs. Norton's Christian name?" came from a man in the corner.

"Rachel."

A smartly-dressed woman raised her hand. "Do you have a statement from Mrs. Norton that we might use?"

"Not at this time." Perhaps, he decided, bringing Rachel into this hadn't been such a brilliant idea; he'd better ring Yolanda and warn her. "Mrs. Norton is, understandably, quite distressed. I would appreciate it if you could respect her privacy."

There was one television camera present, though Neville didn't expect that this would ever make it onto the evening news. The reporter next to the cameraman asked, "Has Mrs. Norton provided a description of the iPod?"

Neville looked at him blankly. He was not a member of the iPod generation; CDs represented the extent of his technological frontiers. Truth to tell, he much preferred LPs, and possessed a treasured collection of traditional Irish music in that ancient format.

Weren't, he wondered, all iPods created equal? White things, with white earphones? He'd have to ask Cowley about that. It *could* be important, he realised: a new and possibly distinctive iPod in some kid's possession could ring a bell that would provide the break to crack this case. "I'll need to get back to you on that," he said.

"Inspector Stewart," pursued the smart-looking woman, "do you have anything to say about this crime as a reflection of the state of the nation's youth? The way they're making the streets of this city a no-go zone for decent citizens going about their business?"

He certainly didn't want to open that can of worms. His boss, Detective Superintendent Evans, wouldn't like him to say anything that reflected badly on the Met's ability to police the streets of London. "We have no information about the perpetrator of this crime," he said firmly. "For all we know, it could have been a pensioner."

It didn't take long for the press to find Rachel Norton. First came a phone call from one of the broadsheets, fielded by Yolanda and turned away gently but firmly. "Mrs. Norton has nothing to say to you at this time," she stated. "If she chooses to issue a statement, I'm sure you'll hear about it."

The tabloids, though, were not likely to take such a genteel approach. The doorbell chimed within an hour of the press conference.

Yolanda put on her most forbidding face, narrowing her eyes at the woman on the short path between the pavement and the house. "Mrs. Norton isn't available," she stated firmly, her breath puffing out into the cold, damp air.

The woman, wrapped in an expensive-looking camel overcoat, didn't look like a journalist; she gave Yolanda a radiant smile. "Actually, it's *you* I wanted to speak to."

That caught Yolanda off guard. "*Me?*"

"I wanted to ask your opinions and feelings about street crime."

"Street crime!"

"And about the yob culture which makes it difficult for law-abiding citizens of this country to go about their business unmolested," the woman added smoothly.

Yolanda couldn't help herself; it was a subject on which she had strong opinions and passionate feelings. "I think," she said, "that there are a lot of parents out there who ought to be locked up."

"You blame the parents, then."

"You see these kids out roaming around at midnight — later than that, even. It's a disgrace. What are their parents thinking about? Do they even know where they are, who they're with, what they get up to?"

The woman nodded in agreement. "Do they even care?"

"People who can't be bothered to keep track of their kids just don't deserve to have them," stated Yolanda with all the passion of her frustrated childlessness.

In the afternoon, Callie went round the parish with Brian. By the time they reached Morag's flat it was tea-time; they were offered tea and home-made shortbread, which neither of them was able to resist.

Callie felt that Morag was a bit constrained, with Brian there, and wasn't particularly forthcoming about any new developments with the family. "I'll be back soon," she promised Morag as they took their leave of her.

It was their last call of the day. Walking briskly back towards the church, Callie reflected that she'd never seen Brian move so fast. It was cold, but there seemed more to his uncharacteristic speed than that.

"Did I tell you," he enlightened her, "that my sons are home? Home for the holidays."

"That's nice. The term's finished, then."

"You'll have to meet them," Brian said, adding, "Simon's brought his girlfriend with him. Ellie. She's a lovely girl."

"I didn't know he had a girlfriend."

"Neither did I." Brian produced an indulgent chuckle. "He surprised us all. But she's a real cracker."

Callie couldn't help wondering whether Jane felt quite the same way.

★ ★ ★

The flat was empty, as usual, when Alex got home from school. She dropped her rucksack just inside of the front door, threw her coat on the floor, and headed straight for her room.

The computer screen was black. Blank! No screen saver, no password prompt. Alex howled in frustration and pushed the restart button.

Nothing happened.

She looked under the desk and saw that the computer was unplugged.

The cleaning lady must have done it. To plug in the hoover. It wouldn't be the first time.

She'd told Jilly a million times to leave her room alone. She'd begged her to tell the cleaning lady. Why couldn't they just follow one simple request?

Alex crawled under the desk and shoved the plug into the power point, then shimmied back out again and punched the restart button. In a moment the screen sprang to life.

E-mail. That was the thing.

Yes! There was a message from Jack.

Eagerly she clicked on it to open it.

"HI SASHA!! LOVED DA PHO2!! SHUD WE GET 2GETHER SOON?!?!??!!"

Alex drew a shuddering breath and hunched over the keyboard to reply.

Climbing the steps to her flat, Callie's thoughts were on Bella; she'd been home at lunchtime to give her a walk, but Bella would be needing another one quite soon. She'd better do it straightaway and get it over with, before it got any darker, and before she'd had a chance to get warm and comfortable. Once that happened, she wouldn't want to go back out.

As she got near the top, she became aware of voices on the other side of the door. Male voices. More than one. What on earth? Loquacious burglars?

The voices stopped by the time she'd opened the door, and two faces were turned towards her. Peter, draped over a chair. And Marco, on the sofa, with Bella on his lap. Tea things — mugs, teapot, biscuit tin — were strewn over the coffee table, and a rather large fir tree leaned precariously in the corner of the room.

Bella wagged her tail but didn't move.

"Hi, Sis," said Peter. "About time you came home. It's a good thing I had a key. I found Marco, here, standing outside in the cold with this whacking great tree, freezing his whatsit off."

"I wasn't expecting you this early," Callie said to Marco, ignoring her brother for the time being. "You said sevenish."

He smiled at her a bit tentatively, as if unsure of the welcome he would receive. "I managed to get away early. I wanted to find a tree," he added. "Your flat's been looking very bare without one."

Callie shook her head, bemused at the pair of them. "I don't suppose anyone's taken Bella out."

"We did," said Peter virtuously. "As soon as we got here, really — she insisted on it. Then we rewarded

146

ourselves with some tea. It's freezing cold out there, you know."

If they'd spared her another trip out into the cold, she would forgive them anything. "I know."

"I was just about to light a fire," Marco put in. "But Bella jumped on my lap, and I couldn't shift her." The dog leaned into his chest, looking blissful as he scratched her ears.

"And we were going to put the tree up, to surprise you," added Peter. "Now we can all do it together. It will be more fun that way."

Callie addressed Marco. "I thought we were going out tonight?"

"And leave me here to look after Bella?" demanded Peter. "Not a chance. I think we'll order in a pizza."

Now she turned her attention to her brother. "What, exactly, are you doing here? Don't you have a home of your own to go to?"

Peter uncurled himself from the chair, came to her, and draped an arm over her shoulder. "Well, you see now, Sis, that's the thing."

She didn't like the sound of that, and she was right to be apprehensive.

He told her — making an amusing story out of it — that the woman in the flat above him had let her bath overflow. Rather badly, in fact: to the extent that his ceiling had fallen down. "Plaster everywhere," he grimaced. "You have no idea of the mess."

Callie could just about imagine; that, though, wasn't what concerned her. "So you're . . ."

"Homeless, at the moment. Hoping to cadge a place to lay my head, to put not too fine a point on it. Throwing myself on your mercy. You wouldn't turn your poor brother out into the streets, would you?" he wheedled.

"But I don't have a spare room," protested Callie. The thought of untidy Peter invading her carefully ordered life . . .

"This sofa pulls out into a bed, doesn't it?"

"Yes, but . . ."

"Sis, you're my only hope," he stated. "I don't have anywhere else to go." He grinned at her. "I'm between boyfriends at the moment, worse luck. And unfortunately I haven't stayed on sufficiently good terms with any of my exes. I suppose I should have been more careful about that."

"What about —" Callie began, but Peter clamped a hand over her mouth.

"Don't even say it," he ordered. "Don't you dare even mention the M word."

Marco, who had been watching this exchange, bemused, from the safety of the sofa, chimed in. "Are you talking about me?"

"No," they both said together as Peter removed his hand.

"Because if you are, it wouldn't work. I have a flatmate, you know. And he wouldn't countenance it."

"I was referring to our mother," Callie said firmly. Even as she said it, she knew it was out of the question. Not in a million years would Peter even contemplate it. And there was no guarantee that Laura Anson would agree. Their mother would complain bitterly about being put upon; even if she said yes and allowed him to move in, she would be on the phone every five minutes to Callie, detailing his latest transgression. A towel on the bathroom floor, a dirty plate left on the table, forbidden food scoffed down. Heinous sins, reported one by one.

"I'll be the perfect guest," Peter declared, his hand sweeping to his heart in a dramatic gesture. "I promise. I won't get in your way. I'll clean up after myself. You won't even know I'm here."

That would be the day. "You'll cook for yourself, then?"

"Well, no," he admitted, then grinned. "But I'll eat whatever you put in front of me. No complaints."

There really was, she saw, not going to be any escape from this one. "Well . . ."

"And I'll walk Bella, even when it's cold," he said quickly. "Resident dog walker." A deal clincher.

Callie gave Marco an apologetic look; he shrugged and shook his head. Wordless communication: they both recognised that if their relationship were going anywhere, it wouldn't do so very easily with Peter Anson in residence.

"How long are we talking about?" she asked. "Days?"

"A few weeks, max. I'll be out of your hair before you know it."

Oh, Lord, she thought. A few weeks — that meant beyond Christmas. But how could she say no?

"Well," Callie said, capitulating, "what kind of a sister would I be to turn my brother out on the streets?"

Peter enveloped her in a bear hug. "Thanks, Sis. You won't regret it."

Callie hoped — against hope — that he was right.

Neville had arranged to meet Willow Tree at a pub near the police station — not the one where he usually went with Mark, but a slightly more up-market one, with a decent menu. He'd give her a good meal, then see where the evening led.

He was a few minutes late leaving work — the coroner had rung to talk about the timing of the inquest — so he walked briskly to the pub. She wasn't waiting outside, but then he wouldn't have expected her to be, in that sort of temperature.

She was leaning against the bar, a pint of Guinness in her hand. "Hi, Inspector Stewart," she said, raising the glass in his direction.

"Call me Neville." He grinned at her approvingly. Guinness! A woman after his own heart. And she was looking a bit more mainstream than the last time they'd met; her orange hair was no longer in spikes, her fingernails were now dark red rather than iridescent green, and she had a discreet jewel in her nose instead of the gold ring. She was rather fanciable, in fact. Under her sheepskin coat, he could glimpse some sort of gauzy ethnic-print blouse, tantalisingly low cut.

He ordered a Guinness; while he was waiting for them to pull it, he turned to her. "Thanks for coming. I hope you didn't have any trouble finding this place."

150

"Not at all. I've been here before, in fact. I work just a few streets away from here, at the health food shop. Planet Earth. Do you know it?"

"No. I'm not a health food sort of bloke," Neville admitted with a grimace.

She smiled at him. "Somehow I didn't think you were."

"And you came anyway. That's a good sign."

"I was . . . intrigued," Willow confessed. "About why you asked me."

It wasn't exactly a question, and Neville didn't answer it directly. He accepted his Guinness from the barman, held it up to inspect it, then clinked it against her glass. "To new beginnings," he said, and drank deeply.

"You're not on duty, then," she observed.

"Not tonight."

"So this isn't an . . . official . . . meeting."

"Good Lord, no." Was that what she thought? That he'd asked her to come so he could question her about a case that had finished months ago? "I thought I'd made it clear that this is very . . . unofficial."

"Just making sure." She sipped at her drink, then licked the foam off her upper lip — an unconscious move which Neville, watching, found extremely sexy. "I didn't know how long I would have to make this drink last."

"As long as you want it to last. There are lots more where that one came from." Neville looked behind the bar at the blackboard with the chalked menu. "Do you fancy ordering some food?" he suggested. "They do a

151

great burger here." As soon as he said it, he remembered that she worked at a health food store, and tried to cover his tracks. "Or I'm sure they do vegetarian food as well," he added. "Tofu, or something like that." That was the extent of his knowledge about vegetarian food; he hoped it didn't sound too ignorant.

Willow laughed. "I'm not a vegetarian, Neville."

"I just thought . . ."

"You thought that someone who works at a health food store must be a vegetarian. Wrong. If I worked in a vet's office, would it make me a dog?" She took a deep gulp from her glass, raising her eyebrows at him. "I happen to love a good burger. Or a nice juicy steak," she added.

This evening was looking more promising all the time. "Let's have steaks, then," Neville said decisively. "Steak and chips."

"Sounds great. Make mine rare."

He gave the order to the barman, then led her to an empty table. "You're a surprising woman, Willow Tree," he said, lifting his glass in her direction.

"Good. I like to keep people on their toes."

There was one more thing — all right, maybe two — that would make his evening complete. "You don't, by any chance, like Irish music, do you?" he ventured.

"Love it," she said promptly. "In fact, I live practically next door to a pub which has the best live Irish music in town. And the best Guinness. Better than any place in Kilburn."

"Where's that, then?" He sounded sceptical.

"Paddy's Place. Just off the Edgware Road. Do you know it?"

Neville couldn't believe there was an Irish pub that he'd never heard of — and so near. "No," he admitted. "I don't know it."

"We could go there after we've eaten, if you like," she suggested.

He settled back in his chair with a contented sigh. Tomorrow might hold all sorts of horrors, but tonight Neville Stewart was a happy man.

CHAPTER
EIGHT

Frances Cherry had had a busy weekend at the hospital, which was overcrowded with victims of cold-weather diseases and even hypothermia. Monday had been no better. Triona O'Neil was never far from her mind, but she'd had no opportunity to do anything about her. She didn't know what she *could* do, in any case, yet the fact that Triona had confided in her had given Frances a sense of responsibility for the other woman.

When it came to the sacrament of confession, or anything like it, Frances was strictly professional in her respect for confidentially. This, though, was different: Triona had talked to her woman-to-woman, friend-to-friend, and not as a priest. That, in Frances' mind, provided her with more leeway.

She had no hesitation in speaking to her husband Graham about the matter. Graham, as a priest himself, was discretion itself, and a useful sounding board. He didn't always tell her what she wanted to hear; that made his advice more rather than less valuable.

It was Tuesday morning before she had a chance to discuss Triona with him. Over their breakfast cereal, she broached the subject in an oblique way. "You remember Detective Inspector Stewart, don't you?"

Graham looked up from his Weetabix, eyebrows raised. "I'm not likely to forget him, am I?"

"I suppose not." She pulled a face.

"He was practically a member of the family for a while. Don't tell me he's back?"

Frances replied with feeling. "No. No."

"Then why are you trying to spoil my breakfast by reminding me about something I'd rather forget?"

She put her spoon down for emphasis. "Well, it's my friend Triona."

"The solicitor," he stated.

"Yes. I was aware, vaguely, that she and Neville Stewart had known each other at some point in the past. But now it seems that they're rather better acquainted than I thought."

"Oh?"

As concisely as she could, Frances outlined the conversation she'd had with Triona a few days before. "I don't know what to do," she finished.

Graham got up, rinsed his cereal bowl, and slotted it in the dishwasher. "I should stay out of it, if I were you. It's nothing to do with you, Fran."

"But she confided in me, and that makes me feel that I ought to do something to help her."

Refilling his coffee mug, he shook his head. "Like what? Ring Inspector Stewart and tell him that the stork is on its way?"

"No, of course not."

Put like that, it sounded ridiculous. It *was* nothing to do with her.

And yet . . .

Yet Triona was her friend; they went back a long way, even though they'd been out of touch for a good many years.

Perhaps just a phone call at this point. She could ring Triona and offer support. Triona, with her famed Irish temper, might tell her to mind her own business; Frances, for the sake of friendship, decided it was a risk she ought to take.

Callie's alarm woke her: time for a shower, a quick cup of tea, and a trip outside with Bella before Morning Prayer.

Shivering, wrapping herself in her dressing gown, she headed for the bathroom, passing through the sitting room. It was a journey she was used to accomplishing without putting a light on.

In the darkness, her shin encountered something hard and painful: the frame of the pull-out sofa bed.

"Ouch!" She hopped out of the way, rubbing her shin, as she remembered.

Peter.

"Sis?" he groaned from the bed. "Wassamatter?"

"I've just ruined my leg." She snapped the light on.

Peter turned and buried his face in the pillow. "That's what you get for being up so early. Serves you right." The words were muffled.

"Don't be ridiculous," Callie snapped. "It's my job. God, remember?"

"Well, maybe you need to rethink your job, then."
Peter rolled onto his back, shading his eyes with his
arm. "In my opinion, if God intended you to be up this
early, he would have made it light."

Callie took a deep breath. He was trying to be
provocative, she told herself. That was just Peter's way.
She would *not* let him draw her into an argument. Not
on his first day as her house guest, for heaven's sake.
"Well," she said in a reasonable voice, "Bella doesn't
care how early it is, or whether it's light or dark. She
has to go outside. And what happened to your promise
to be the one to take her?"

"You must be joking." And with that, Peter pulled
the covers over his head.

Yolanda was wakened by a muffled cry, sounding as
though it came from directly below her. She was out of
her makeshift bed in seconds, stopping to check that
Rachel's room was empty before hurrying down the
stairs, turning lights on as she went.

The cry came again, guiding Yolanda towards the
back of the house. "I'm coming," she called out.

She found Rachel in the kitchen, doubled over,
clinging for dear life to a mop. Her face was pasty, with
a sheen of sweat. Yolanda hurried to her side, prised the
mop out of her grasp, and guided her into a chair.
"What is it, lovie?" Yolanda crooned. "What's the
matter?"

"I think the baby's on the way." The words came out
in a gasp as Rachel clutched her belly. "It hurts."

"There. There." Yolanda stroked her hair, doing calculations in her head: it was possible. Thirty-seven weeks was early, but it was considered borderline full term. "Have you ever had anything like this before?"

Rachel groaned. "Never quite like this. It's never hurt before."

"What on earth were you doing, lovie?"

"Mopping the kitchen floor."

Yolanda didn't bother to ask why. She'd seen it all before: that rush of restless energy in the weeks before giving birth. It was a well-known phenomenon. Nesting, Yolanda always called it. Tidying, cleaning, making ready.

"Let me get you up to your bed," said Yolanda. "Then I'll take a look at you. You're going to be just fine," she added briskly. "Yolanda's here to look after you."

Jane was trying very hard to like Ellie. Simon obviously adored her, Brian thought she was wonderful, and Charlie seemed to accept the fact that she was as good as a member of the family now, so Jane felt it was up to her to make a concerted effort.

Laying the table for breakfast on Tuesday morning, she tried to analyse her feelings. Why was she the odd one out when it came to worshipping at the shrine of Ellie?

It was difficult to put her finger on. There was the shock, of course, at having the girl in her house unexpectedly. And the fact that Simon was so young to be seriously involved with anyone. He still had two and a half years of university ahead of him, plus any qualifications he would need to pursue after that.

Ellie wasn't unpleasant to her, or impolite: rather she was unfailingly cordial. She was a well-brought-up young woman, and always expressed gratitude at the right time — thanking Jane for meals, cups of tea, and other hospitality.

Why, Jane asked herself, did it get under her skin so?

Maybe it was because Ellie *was* so polite. "Thank you, Mrs. Stanford. What a lovely meal." "That was delicious, Mrs. Stanford." It was the way Jane, many years ago, had been taught to speak to her elderly great-aunts. With deference and respect for their advanced age . . .

Perhaps that was it. Ellie made her feel *old*.

She spoke to Jane like someone who had to be placated and indulged. An irrelevance. Someone who was past it, part of an older generation who no longer counted, fit only to be consigned to the rubbish heap of history. Treated with respect, but not engaged with.

Just the way she'd felt about her great-aunts, Jane realised with a jolt. Theirs had been a world so far removed from hers that she'd had nothing to say to them, apart from the pleasantries. There was no level on which she could engage with them. They'd lived through the War, for heaven's sakes — how boring was *that*?

Did Ellie think *she* was boring, because she'd been a child in the sixties, a teenager in the seventies, a young wife in the eighties?

But I'm not old, Jane said to herself plaintively. She wasn't past it. Women in their forties were now considered to be in the prime of their lives. Just look at all the forty-something movie stars: Meg Ryan, Demi Moore, even Julia Roberts. Not to mention Madonna!

With perfect timing born of long practice, she switched the kettle on just as Brian came through the front door from Morning Prayer. He liked his breakfast as soon as he got home, and by the time he was out of his cassock and into the kitchen the tea would be ready to pour.

He came through a few minutes later, holding a letter.

"Oh, the post was early today," Jane remarked as she sloshed milk into two cups.

"Janey . . ." said Brian in a strange voice.

"What is it?" She stopped and looked at him properly: his eyes were wide with shock, as though he'd been poleaxed, and he was extending the letter in a hand which visibly trembled. "Is something wrong? Oh, tell me!"

His words were jerky, disjointed. "No. Not wrong. Far from it. At least for us."

Jane, mystified and concerned, reached for the letter; he held on to it. "Tell me," Jane repeated.

It was a moment before Brian replied. He seemed to pull himself together, licking his lips and clearing his throat. "You remember my Uncle Bernard?"

"Yes." Jane tried to recall what she knew about Uncle Bernard, whom she'd never met. A brother of Brian's late father, he had emigrated when Brian was still a child and had some sort of farm or ranch in Australia. He'd never married, and had never come back to England, even for a visit. They heard from him at Christmas each year, so perhaps this was the annual Christmas card.

"He's dead," Brian said flatly. "He died a month ago."

"Oh! I'm sorry."

Brian waved the letter, a bemused smile creasing his face. "He's left us some money, Janey! Rather a lot of money."

She snatched the letter from his hand and scanned it quickly.

It was a solicitors' letter, written in international legalese, but the gist of it was clear. In his will, Bernard Stanford had left his nephew a hundred and fifty thousand Australian dollars. This, the solicitor believed, was something over sixty thousand pounds sterling. A cheque would follow shortly.

Sixty thousand pounds! Jane realised, after a moment, that she had stopped breathing. Deliberately she took a deep breath, then another. A hard knot of excitement began to form in her stomach.

Making ends meet on a vicar's slender stipend had been Jane's job, and her burden, for a good many years. It was a point of pride with her that — unlike so many clergy wives these days — she had never worked outside of the home. She had supported Brian in his ministry in every possible way; she had brought up two clever boys of whom any mother would be proud. The fact that they were twins meant that expenses always came in twos, which was a continual strain on the budget and a challenge for Jane. When sacrifices were made, they were almost invariably hers: she saw to it that the boys never suffered or felt deprived, and neither did Brian. If she'd had to make do with her old Laura Ashley best dress for more years than she wanted to remember, if she'd clothed herself in other people's cast-offs from church jumble sales, that seemed a small price to pay for the wellbeing of her family.

But now: money! A great deal of money. More money than had passed through her hands in the last three years running.

The knot in her stomach ignited into flame, burning fierce and hot, as the possibilities flashed through her mind. Dreams she had suppressed, hopes she had long ago relinquished, suddenly revived. It wasn't too late, she told herself triumphantly. No, it wasn't too late.

It took over a minute for the sound of his mobile phone's ring tone to penetrate through the deep layers of Neville's slumber. "Oh, God," he moaned, groping for it before he was more than marginally awake. His hand found the phone on the bedside table, his finger found the button, yet his eyes were still screwed shut. "Yes?" he growled into it.

"Guv? Where are you?" Sid Cowley sounded impatient, even agitated.

"I'm . . ." Neville forced his eyes open with some difficulty.

Where the hell *was* he?

A bedroom. Small. Chest of drawers, bedside table, his clothes on the floor. He was in the double bed — alone. He'd never seen this room before — at least not that he could remember. Where was it? How the hell had he got here?

Neville ran a fuzzy tongue over dry lips. "Never mind where I am. What do you want?"

"You're supposed to be at work, Guv."

"Work!" He twisted round and manoeuvred his wrist in front of his face. Yes, he was wearing his watch. And it was past ten o'clock! "Bloody hell," he muttered.

It started to come back to him, vaguely. The Irish pub — a damn good pub, and Willow had been right about the music. And what went better with live Irish music than Guinness? Copious quantities of it. He'd always prided himself on his ability to hold his Guinness — and his facility to out-drink just about anyone. But Willow had proved herself a worthy drinking partner, and had kept up with him pint for pint.

Until . . . what? His memory failed him, petering out at some point just before last orders, when he'd stumped up for a few more pints to tide them over until the music wound down.

"I've been waiting for you," Sid's insistent voice went on. Like a buzzing gnat coming down the phone. "The Coroner's been trying to track you down. And there have been a few . . . developments . . . in the case."

"Developments?" Neville was fully awake now. "Good, or bad?"

"Something good, something ... not so good, probably," Sid said, irritatingly — and no doubt deliberately — obscure. "Anyway, Guv, you'd better get here as soon as you can. Wherever you are," he added with snide emphasis.

"Yeah, yeah. I'll be there soon." That was the best Neville could promise, still clueless as to his current location.

As he reached for his clothes, his head spinning with the effort, he was enlightened on that subject by the arrival of Willow, coming through the door with a large mug in each hand. She was wearing an oversized T-shirt with a Planet Earth logo across the chest, her legs fetchingly bare. "Oh," she said. "Are you awake, then? I brought you some coffee."

"I hope it's strong," Neville stated, reaching for it.

Willow settled herself on the bed next to him and took a sip from her own mug. "As strong as I could make it."

It was indeed strong; Neville discovered with the first gulp that it was also very hot, but he didn't care. The important thing was that the caffeine was doing its work, shooting straight into the bloodstream. Feeling a bit less groggy already, Neville swung his legs over the side of the bed and retrieved his trousers.

"What's the rush?" asked Willow.

"Work. I have to go to work." He turned to fix her with an accusing glare. "Why didn't you wake me? It's after ten!"

Willow smiled. "You were sleeping so peacefully. And so soundly. Like a rock, in fact. I don't think I could

164

have woken you if I tried. And," she added, "I have the morning off. I don't have to be at work till after lunch." She crossed her legs yoga-style, settling back against the headboard.

The crossed legs, and what that position revealed, distracted Neville from getting dressed and raised certain inevitable questions which he felt needed to be answered before he took his leave of her. He sat back down on the bed. "What . . . what happened last night?" he asked awkwardly, his face averted from her.

"I didn't think you'd remember." Willow's voice was matter-of-fact. "You had a lot to drink. We both did. My flat is close to the pub, so we came back here."

"And?" He didn't want to be crude — or ungallant — but he did need to know.

"You're wondering whether we slept together." Willow laughed, sounding amused. "Well, yes, we did sleep in the same bed. It's the only one I have, and I wasn't going to sleep on the sofa just because you were in it. So technically we did sleep together."

"But . . ."

Willow shook her head. "Listen, Neville. There was only one thing you could talk about last night. After you'd had a few pints, that is."

He couldn't imagine what she meant. Had he come on to her, then?

"That girlfriend of yours," she went on. "Triona, is she called? Pretty name. Unusual."

"Triona!" The name exploded from his lips, resounded in his head.

"You talked about her all night. How she's really put you through it, making you jump through hoops for her. How you were sick of it, but you just couldn't get her out of your head. How she's everything you ever wanted in a woman — sexy, beautiful, clever, funny."

"I said *that*?"

"Not exactly the best line to take if you wanted to get me into bed," she said comfortably, laughing. "Most women don't like to hear stuff like that about other women. Puts them off a bit."

Neville was stunned, speechless. He had *never* talked about Triona. Not to anyone. Not ever. She was his private torture, not something to be discussed even with a friend like Mark, let alone with a woman he scarcely knew.

But it wasn't something Willow could have made up. Therefore he must have done it.

"I suppose I'm flattered, in a way," Willow said. "It must mean that you find me approachable. A mate, if nothing else."

It must mean he'd been out of his bloody mind.

She ran a hand through her hair, ruffling it up into wispy red spikes. "Do you want my advice? As a mate?"

Not really, he wanted to say. He didn't want *anyone's* advice, when it came to Triona.

Willow evidently took his silence for assent. "Go after her," she said bluntly. "Get her back. You're crazy in love with her, Neville. You're miserable without her. Why are you being such a wimp about it?"

That stung him to respond at last. "A wimp?" he repeated, outraged.

"Okay, then. Not a wimp. A macho twat. If you can't have things your own way, you'll just take your marbles and go home." The tone of her voice, and her smile, saved the words from being offensively insulting. "Listen, Neville. I'm saying this for your own good," she added. "Trust me. You'll never be happy without her."

"Braxton Hicks contractions," Yolanda pronounced, once she'd got Rachel into bed and checked her over. "That's all it is. Brought on by stress and over-exerting yourself."

Rachel caught her breath sharply, her brow furrowed with pain. In a moment she relaxed and was able to speak. "I've had Braxton Hicks before. This feels different."

"You're getting nearer your time. And you shouldn't have been doing the kitchen floor," Yolanda said, trying to sound stern.

"Sorry."

"You won't try that again, will you?"

"No." Rachel twisted her head and made eye contact. "Thanks, Yolanda," she said. "Really. Thanks for everything. I don't know what I'd have done without you."

"Just doing my job," Yolanda said, almost brusquely. But she couldn't help feeling gratified.

Frances took a break mid-morning, went to her rarely-visited desk, and rang Triona at the office. She was put through by a secretary.

"Hi," she said when Triona came on the line. "I just wanted to see how you were doing."

"Still puking my guts out," Triona said bluntly. "Every few minutes, it seems like. Even in this place full of extraordinarily dim solicitors, someone is going to twig pretty soon."

Frances paused. "And . . . Neville? Have you contacted him?"

"No. I told you. I'm not going to. If I'm lucky, I'll never see the bastard again. And he'll never find out."

"Well," said Frances lamely, aware that nothing she could say would change the mind of her very determined friend, "if you need someone to talk to, you know where to find me."

"Thanks," Triona said. "And thanks for ringing. I do appreciate it."

Sid Cowley was sitting at Neville's desk, drinking coffee and reading the *Globe*. "Good of you to turn up, Guv," he said sarcastically as the desk's owner came in. "Evans will be pleased."

"Evans? Oh, God. What does he have to do with it?" In Neville's experience, anything that involved Detective Superintendent Evans couldn't possibly be good news.

"It's only that he's seen the *Globe* this morning. His secretary showed him."

Cowley held the paper out and Neville snatched it from him. There was probably some coverage of his press conference; what else could it be?

KILLED FOR HIS iPOD, screamed the headline, over a grainy photo of Trevor Norton. Well, that was pretty accurate, if their suspicions were right. Why should Evans get his knickers in a twist over that?

"Read it," said Cowley. "Lilith Noone strikes again."

"In yet another example of yob culture gone mad, young father-to-be Trevor Norton was brutally murdered on Friday by someone who wanted his iPod," Neville read aloud. "Norton, whose wife Rachel is expecting their first child at any minute, was jogging along the Grand Union Canal near his Paddington home when he was waylaid and slain. His body was pulled out of the canal the next day.

"Although iPod murders are not unknown in the US, this is the first slaying in this country which seems definitely linked to the popular digital music player, much sought-after by young people.

"Detective Inspector Neville Stewart, the Chief Investigating Officer, held a press conference yesterday in which he declined to make the connection between this murder and today's rampant and violent youth culture — a culture which, as this slaying demonstrates, makes it increasingly difficult for law-abiding citizens of this country to go about their business unmolested.

"But a Family Liaison Officer at the Nortons' home was not so reticent. DC Yolanda Fish stated, 'I think that there are a lot of parents out there who ought to be locked up. You see these kids out roaming around at midnight — later than that, even. It's a disgrace. What are their parents thinking about? Do they even know where they are, who they're with, what they get up to? People who can't be bothered to keep track of their kids just don't deserve to have them.'

169

"It is a sad consequence of this disgraceful trend that Trevor Norton's child will grow up never knowing his father. Just how long will the police continue to tolerate antisocial behaviour and yobbism on our streets? As this tragic case demonstrates, there is a very thin line indeed between youth culture and lawlessness, even brutal murder."

There was more, in the same vein, but Neville had read enough. "Oh, God," he said feelingly, throwing the paper down on his desk. "I can see why Evans is steaming."

"At least Yolanda is the one he's going to shoot down in flames, not us," observed Cowley with a self-satisfied smirk.

"I agree with her," Neville admitted. "She's absolutely right about these little toe-rags, out on the streets at all hours." Coffee. He needed coffee; heading for the door, he paused to speak over his shoulder. "But you know what, Sid? In this case, I hope she's wrong. I hope we end up proving that Lilith Bloody Noone is totally off-base on this one. Wouldn't it be great if the CCTV cameras picked up a little old lady bashing him over the head?"

"Now, there's the thing," Cowley said. "The good news I mentioned? The CCTV blokes *have* found something. But it's not a little old lady, I'm afraid."

That stopped Neville in his tracks, coffee forgotten.

Callie's mobile rang while she was on her way to visit a parishioner. She saw on the display that it was Mark, and smiled involuntarily. "Marco," she said into the phone. "Hi."

"Good morning, *cara mia*."

Her heart always lifted, and beat a little faster, when he called her that. "What's up?"

"I just wanted to check on how you were getting on. With Peter."

Callie sighed into the phone. "I knew it was a mistake to give in, and I was right."

"He didn't leave you much choice," Mark reminded her. "It was a pretty heavy familial guilt-trip he laid on you. And that's something I should know about." He added, "What's he done?"

"Nothing," she said feelingly. "That's the trouble. He was asleep when I went to say Morning Prayer, and he was asleep when I got back. I had to take Bella out myself."

"But he promised he'd do that for you."

"Exactly," Callie sighed. "And when I got back, he'd finally managed to get himself up. He'd left the sofa bed open, and he'd left his cereal bowl on the kitchen table. Along with the milk and everything else."

"Where was he?"

"In the bath. For the next hour. He used my towel, and dropped it in the middle of the floor. Oh, Marco," she said with emotion, "I don't know how I'm going to survive this. Weeks, he said. Weeks!"

"I wish I could do more to help," Mark commiserated. "But I'll tell you what. I promised I'd take you out last night, and Peter scuppered that. So how about tonight? Shall we go out for a meal?"

"He'll probably want to go with us."

"He's not invited." Mark's voice was firm.

"I hate to think what he'll do to trash my flat while we're out. But yes, Marco. I'd love that."

Callie was still smiling as she slipped her phone back into her bag.

"They've recovered CCTV footage already? That was quick," Neville said. "They'd told us it was going to take days to get through it all."

"They were lucky, apparently. Just happened to look at the right bit."

"You've seen it?"

"Yeah, Guv. I had a butcher's." Cowley, predictably, couldn't resist a needling aside. "While you were sleeping. Or whatever."

Neville ignored it. "And?"

"Just what you'd expect. Bloke in a hoodie."

"They've actually got footage of the murder?" That, thought Neville, would be a bloody miracle. Too good to be true.

"No, not that. But . . . well, Guv, you ought to go and look at it. They'll explain."

A few minutes later he was leaning over a computer while some young whizz kid wielded a mouse. It made Neville feel old — all done on computer these days, and by kids young enough to . . . well, he wasn't going to go there. Scarcely old enough to drive, he amended to himself.

172

"In a few years the computers will do all the work for us," the kid, Danny Duffy, said with earnest enthusiasm. "There are some amazing breakthroughs in CCTV technology already in use in the USA. Face recognition, automatic tracking of suspicious people and unusual behaviour. The computer will even notify us when something's going on."

"Fancy that," said Neville sourly. In a few years, they wouldn't need coppers at all. Just kids with computers. Maybe he should resign now, and beat the rush.

"Anyway, here's what I've found." The kid clicked on a window and a grainy image began to play. "Not too clear, I know. I've enhanced it as much as possible. But the weather must have been pretty foul."

Neville remembered that morning: the rain flinging itself at the window of Rachel Norton's lounge as though it were an unwelcome visitor, demanding entrance. "Yeah. It wasn't very nice."

"Several of the cameras have picked up Trevor Norton. Running. Then — here." Danny Duffy pointed to a figure ambling along the edge of the screen, hands in the pockets of a hooded sweatshirt. "This bloke. You can't see his face because of the hoodie. Unfortunately. But see? He's walking along here. Then out of the picture. And now — here comes Trevor Norton."

Neville leaned forward for a better view as Trevor Norton jogged in on one side of the window and, in a matter of seconds, out of the other.

"The significant thing is that this bloke is the only other person around. No one else. And Trevor

173

disappears before he reaches the next camera. Just plain vanishes. We don't see him again."

Yolanda was in the kitchen making sandwiches for their lunch when Neville rang her on her mobile. "How's it going?" he began.

She glanced at Rachel, who was sitting meekly at the table; perhaps she'd better not mention the false labour. "Fine," she said.

The preliminaries out of the way, Neville got down to business. "Just a few things you need to know."

"Go ahead."

"I'll tell you the bad news first, shall I?" he asked pleasantly.

"Bad news?"

"You haven't seen this morning's *Globe*, have you?" His voice was neutral, but Yolanda's heart plummeted. She'd known she shouldn't be shooting her mouth off to that journalist but she hadn't been able to help herself. Eli always told her that her big mouth would get her in trouble one day.

"No," she admitted. "But I can guess what it says."

"Then I suggest that you take a look at it before you get a call from Evans. Because you *will* get a call. He's seen it, and he's not happy."

"I can imagine." And she could: Evans wasn't a pretty sight at the best of times, but Evans in a towering rage . . . ugly didn't begin to describe it. "Is there some good news, then?" Yolanda asked hopefully.

"Well, I've spoken to the Coroner. He's opening the inquest tomorrow morning." Neville went on to give the details of the time and place. "Do you think she'll want to go?"

"Probably." Again Yolanda glanced over at Rachel, who didn't seem to be paying any attention to the conversation; instead she was studying her fingernails, evidently absorbed in her own thoughts.

"That's not the real good news, though. I've saved that for last," he said.

"Do I need to be sitting down?"

Neville chuckled. "It's not *that* good. Just a start, that's all. The CCTV boffins have found something. A brief shot of someone who's probably our murderer."

"Brilliant!" At that, she noticed, Rachel looked at her, raising her eyebrows.

"Trouble is," he said, "he's wearing one of those hoodies and you can't see his face at all. Some friggin' little toe-rag, just like you said. Jeans and a hoodie."

"Can I tell Rachel?"

"Sure. She needs to know what's going on in the investigation."

Neville rang off and Yolanda turned to Rachel, assured of her full attention. "You have something to tell me? Something important?" Rachel demanded.

Yolanda decided to tell it to her straight, with no preliminaries. "They've found a CCTV image of the bloke who probably killed Trevor."

Rachel's eyes widened; her hand went to her mouth. Then her eyes fluttered shut and, if she had been a character in a Victorian novel, it would have been said of her that she swooned.

In the Stanford household, there was but one topic of conversation at dinner: the money, and how it would be spent.

The boys were most outspoken, and most creative. "Bali," said Simon rapturously. "Don't you fancy a holiday in Bali, Mum?"

"Or Tahiti," Charlie suggested. "We could *all* go. We could have Christmas on the beach."

"We could cruise round the world," Brian said. "I could ask for a sabbatical. I've never had one, you know, so I'm entitled. We could take six months and see the world. Just think of it, Janey," he added. "All those places we've never seen, and never thought we'd ever see."

Ellie was more practical. "You could buy property. Sixty thousand pounds would make a decent down-payment on a little bungalow somewhere, and it would be a great investment. Then you'd have something when it was time for retirement."

"We're not ready to retire just yet," Jane said tartly. It was the first contribution she'd made to the fanciful discussion.

"No, of course not, Mrs. Stanford." Ellie was earnest as she turned to her — and, Jane thought, a bit patronising. "But when that time comes, it's always good to have property."

"Maybe a cottage by the sea," Brian mused. "I've always fancied retiring to the seaside. There's a good High Church tradition on the south coast."

"Or maybe a flat in London," suggested Charlie. "You could rent it out, and be near enough to keep an eye on it. When you retired, you could sell it and make a bundle. Then you could buy your seaside cottage."

"How about a flat in Oxford?" Simon threw out. "We could live there. It would save lots of money. And it would be much more comfortable than living in college."

He didn't, Jane noticed, specify whom he meant by "we". She was certainly not planning to finance a place where her son could sleep with his girlfriend in privacy and comfort.

Charlie changed tack. "How about a new car?"

Brian, with a sheepish grin, made a confession. "I've always fancied a Jaguar."

That elicited a whoop from Simon. "You sly old dog, Dad! And here was me thinking you drove a clapped-out old Escort because you had a sentimental attachment to it!"

"Surely," said Charlie, "a sober black Mercedes would be more in keeping with a respectable clergyman than a flash sports car!"

"A Volvo would be worth considering," Ellie contributed. "They're very reliable cars, and they last for years. My grandparents have one."

No one seemed to notice that Jane didn't put forth any suggestions. It was only much later, after they'd retired to their bedroom, that Brian asked her.

"What do *you* think, Janey? How should we spend the money? A holiday? A car? Or an investment?"

Sixty thousand pounds. Not a fortune to most people — not like winning the lottery — but enough to make a difference in their lives.

"Well," she began. "It would be nice to splash out a bit on Christmas. Give ourselves, and the boys, a really special Christmas to remember."

"But that's only a few hundred, surely." Brian, getting into bed, spread his arms wide. "Think big, Janey. Think big. Isn't there anything you want?"

Jane climbed in beside him. "There is something," she said quietly. "Something we haven't been able to afford."

"Tell me. Whatever it is, you deserve it."

"I want," said Jane, "to have a baby."

CHAPTER
NINE

On Wednesday morning, feeling guilty that she hadn't managed it sooner, Callie went to see Morag Hamilton.

Morag welcomed her warmly. "Coffee?" she suggested. "I'll put the kettle on."

"Great." Callie followed her through to the kitchen and sat down while Morag made the coffee; she couldn't help thinking about her own kitchen and the state it was in. "My brother has moved in with me for a short while," she told Morag.

"That's nice. Or is it? Do you get on with him?"

Callie pulled a face. "Well, I suppose it *should* be nice. We're very close, and I do get on with him — brilliantly, most of the time. When he's not invading my territory."

"Ah." Morag nodded knowingly. "You're used to living on your own, aren't you."

"It's not just that." Restless, Callie got up and paced back and forth, the length of the small kitchen. "To put it bluntly, he's a slob. I'm by no means a clean freak, but — well, it's not a very large flat. There's no spare room, so there's nowhere to contain him. I can't just shut the door on him. He's . . . everywhere. He and his mess."

Morag gave a sympathetic cluck. "How long will this last?"

"Until he gets his ceiling fixed, and that could be weeks." She shuddered, adding, "Or until I kill him. Or kill *myself*. That seems like a distinct possibility at moments. And he's only been with me for a couple of days!"

With a start, Callie realised how self-centred she must sound, and how ridiculous. Morag, in her isolation, would probably welcome an invasion from any number of sloppy and difficult relatives. "I'm sorry," she said contritely. "I'm not here to talk about *me*. How are *you*?"

"Managing." Morag handed Callie a mug, then led her through to the sitting room, where they sat on either side of the cosy gas fire. "Nothing new on the health front. I'm still waiting for an appointment to come through."

"And the family?"

Morag shook her head. "Yesterday afternoon I had a message on my call minder. From Alex."

"Your granddaughter!" Callie glanced over at the family photos on top of the piano.

"It was such bad luck that I was out when she rang." Cupping her hands round the mug, as if for warmth, Morag sighed. "I'd just popped out for a wee while, to the post office. When I rang back, Jilly answered. My daughter-in-law," she amplified, with a grimace.

The "painted doll," Callie remembered. "And?"

"She wouldn't let me speak to Alex. Said she was doing her homework and couldn't be disturbed."

"But that's . . ." Callie didn't know how to finish the sentence. Cruel? Ridiculous? She shrugged.

"Pure spite, I shouldn't wonder," Morag supplied. Tears welled up in her eyes. "Oh, Callie. I'm that worried about wee Alex. She shouldn't be at the mercy of that woman. I just wish there was something I could do."

Neville arrived at the Coroner's court with time to spare; he wasn't going to give Sid Cowley any more cause to needle him.

Cowley, though, was there first. He leaned against the wall outside of the courtroom, smoking a cigarette. "'Morning, Guv."

"Sid! I thought you'd given up!" Neville pointed accusingly at the fag. "And you were doing so well!"

"Yeah, well." Cowley shrugged, not meeting Neville's eyes. "Didn't work out."

Neville remembered Sid's reason for quitting: his old flame from school, the one he'd re-encountered on the internet. "The girl? I thought you said that was going great."

"Not so great after all." Cowley took a long, luxurious drag and blew the smoke out through his nose. "Turned out she had a husband that she hadn't bothered to mention to me."

A rabid and self-righteous ex-smoker himself, Neville nonetheless enjoyed a bit of second-hand smoke when it came his way. Moving surreptitiously closer, he chuckled. "Getting a few scruples in your old age, are you, Sid? I didn't think you'd let a little thing like a husband stand in your way if you really fancied someone."

"Scruples?" Cowley snorted. "Fear, more like. He's about two metres tall, and built like a brick outhouse. Said he'd beat the crap out of me if I came near his wife again. And I believed him."

"Sid, Sid, Sid." Neville shook his head, grinning. "When will you ever learn?"

Cowley changed the subject abruptly. "Listen, Guv. I was wondering about something."

"Yeah?"

"House-to-house hasn't come up with a bloody thing. D'you think there would be any mileage in staging a re-enactment? Say, on Friday morning, a week after the murder?" He gestured with his cigarette. "The bloke jogging by the canal. The iPod. The kid in the hoodie."

Neville wished he'd thought of it himself. "Not a bad idea, Sid. If you can organise the people, I'll get on to the press. You never —" He broke off as Yolanda Fish came round the corner of the corridor, escorting Rachel Norton. So she *had* wanted to come, even though this was nothing more than a formality. Not that he blamed her — in her place, he would have felt the same way.

Rachel was pale, and to Neville's eyes, even larger than she'd been a few days ago. He hoped, fervently, that she wasn't about to have the baby right there and then, in the middle of the Coroner's court.

Jane had rung the GP's office first thing in the morning and made an appointment. It had been quite a few months, if not years, since she'd last been to the GP; she was a very healthy individual who didn't believe in bothering her doctor unnecessarily. Probably the last time she'd gone was to take one of the boys after he'd sustained some sort of sporting injury at school. Charlie, who tended to be a bit clumsy, had once had his wrist broken by a cricket ball, she recalled, and Simon had suffered a great many scrapes and bruises on the rugby pitch.

She'd asked for Dr. Forsythe, who had been their GP for as long as they'd lived in London, only to be told that Dr. Forsythe had retired some eighteen months before. "Dr. Orme has taken over his patients," the receptionist said. "I'll give you an appointment with him."

So Jane sat in the waiting room, unchanged since her last visit save for the name on the sign. There was the usual assortment of patients: an old man coughing in the corner, a younger man rubbing his arm, a hyperactive child who was probably bunking off school by claiming to be deathly ill and was now racing round the waiting room at full tilt while his mother tried to corral him. There was also, Jane noticed, a woman in the middle stages of pregnancy, unconsciously rubbing her bump as she leafed through an old celebrity gossip magazine.

Jane herself had another such magazine in her lap, but her interest in it flagged when she realised it was so ancient that fully half the celebrities featured in it had now split from the partners with whom they were pictured, and for whom they declared undying love. "He's the one I've been looking for all my life," cooed one singing sensation; Jane knew for a fact that she'd recently married someone else, and that there had been at least one other relationship in between. What was the world coming to?

Instead, Jane replayed in her head the scene from the night before. She would never forget the look of astonishment on Brian's face. "A baby?" he'd said, eventually. "A *baby*?" Not a holiday. Not a car. A baby.

Preferably a girl, she'd told him. If that could be managed.

The receptionist interrupted her reverie. "Mrs. Stanford? Dr. Orme will see you now," she called from her desk.

Dr. Orme, Jane soon discovered, was young. Barely out of medical school, probably. Young, fair-haired, with pale, freckled hands and almost invisible eyelashes. "What can I do for you today, Mrs. . . . erm . . . Stanford?" He looked down at her notes, flipping through them for clues.

"I'm not ill," she told him. "There's nothing wrong with me. I've come for . . . advice."

"Advice?" His head came up.

Jane took a deep breath. It was too late to chicken out now. "I want to have a baby," she said.

He stared at her; was that, she wondered, a look of surprise, or of disbelief? "And you want to know whether I think that's a good idea?" he asked.

184

"No." She was not interested in this young man's opinion; the advice she required was of a more practical nature. "I need to know what to do."

Biting his lip, he looked down again at her notes. "I see that you have . . . is it two sons? Evidently you've figured that part out for yourself."

Oh, ho ho, thought Jane. A real wit. Refusing to rise to the bait, she explained. "Medically, I mean. I understand that folic acid is a good idea?"

"Before conception? Yes, that is what we recommend. And for the first twelve weeks as well. It prevents spina bifida."

"Are there other things like that? It's been quite a few years since my last pregnancy," she admitted. "I know that medicine has moved on since then."

Dr. Orme opened a drawer and rummaged round, finally producing a leaflet. "This is the latest NHS advice," he said. "No drinking, if possible. And no smoking."

"Not a problem."

"And there are food issues, as well," he explained. "Foods to avoid: raw eggs, tuna, soft cheeses, pâté. It's all in here." He shoved the leaflet across the desk towards her. "And caffeine intake should be limited."

Jane took it and put it in her handbag. "I have another . . . question."

"Yes?"

"I'm hoping to have a girl. Are there any new . . . techniques . . . to make that more likely?"

Now he definitely looked surprised. "Not that I know of, Mrs. Stanford. Unless you're willing to spend a

185

great deal of money and undergo some fairly unpleasant procedures. Perhaps you should consider adopting or fostering instead? At your age —"

There it was, on the table. "I'm not that old," Jane said tartly. "Certainly not too old to have a baby. Lots of women in their forties have babies. It's not like we're Sarah and Abraham, after all!"

She'd used that same line on Brian, who had smiled wryly at the reference. Dr. Orme, though, gave her a puzzled look. He was, she reminded herself, very young, and young people these days just didn't know their Bible stories. "Sarah and Abraham?" he echoed.

"Never mind," said Jane. "The point is, I'm not too old to have a baby. Everything is still . . . working."

He shook his head. "That's not really the issue, Mrs. Stanford. Are you aware of the risks of pregnancy for women over, say, thirty-five? There have been studies recently, as more and more women delay having families. All sorts of problems and risks have emerged — difficulties conceiving, ectopic pregnancies, foetal abnormalities, miscarriage. Not to mention genetic anomalies like Down's Syndrome."

"I know. I know." She *did* know. She'd read about the studies, seen the reports on the news. And in case she'd forgotten it, Brian had been all too happy to refresh her memory. But it didn't matter. She was determined. She wanted a baby, and she would have one.

The inquest had been the formality everyone expected: it had been opened, the barest of known facts had been entered, and then the Coroner had adjourned it until some future date.

When they came out of the courtroom, the press were waiting, cameras at the ready. Neville should have been expecting it — after all, this was the first access they'd had to the bereaved, pregnant widow. And the morning papers had printed the blurry still of the CCTV footage which the police had supplied to them, showing the bloke in the hoodie, so the story was still on the boil as far as the press were concerned. Automatically Neville stepped in front of Rachel to shield her from the cameras.

"Mrs. Norton!" shouted a reporter. "Do you have anything to say about your husband's murder? About the yob who killed him?"

"Mrs. Norton is too upset to speak to you," Neville stated firmly. "I'm sure you understand."

"Inspector Stewart, have there been any further breaks in the case?" someone else asked. "Now that you have a picture of the killer?"

Thinking quickly, Neville decided to take advantage of the opportunity; he hoped that while he was talking to the press, Yolanda and Sid could get Rachel out of there and away from them.

"Well," he said deliberately, "we have asked the public for their help in identifying the man in the photo, of course. And we are planning to stage a re-enactment of the crime on Friday morning. A week after the murder."

The distraction worked; they asked him a few more questions, he spun out his answers as long as he could, and when he finally left the building with the press on his heels, Yolanda and Rachel had gone.

Cowley, though, was waiting for him outside, with the inevitable cigarette. "They got a taxi," he said. "Rachel was pretty shook up."

"I'm not surprised."

"I was afraid she was going to have the kid right on the spot."

Cowley shook his head. "God, she's bloody huge. When my sister had her baby —"

Not *that* again. Neville cut him off. "Yes, Sid. I've heard all about your sister's baby," he reminded him. "More than once."

"Okay. Okay."

Additional distraction seemed called for. "Is there anything else I need to know? About the case?"

Cowley studied the glowing tip of his cigarette before answering. "The computer boffins have finished with Trevor's machine. Danny Duffy stopped by to see me yesterday afternoon. After you'd gone home."

Was that meant to be some sort of veiled criticism, Sid's way of getting even after being prevented from rehashing the details of his sister's pregnancy and labour? Neville decided to let it go. "And what did he say?"

"He said that they hadn't found anything. Just business stuff, like Rachel said. Accounts, proposals, project management, e-mails to clients. That sort of rubbish. No girlfriend on the side or nothing. At least not that he sent e-mails to."

"But," said Neville, "it's all moot at this point anyway. Since the CCTV footage turned up. You were right about it being a random crime. About the iPod."

"Yeah, Guv. Seems I was right." Cowley took a long drag on his cigarette, smiling in satisfaction.

"But you can wipe that smirk off your face, Sid. Until we've found the bloke in the hoodie. Preferably clutching the iPod in his hot little hand."

They didn't, Neville reflected, seem any nearer to doing that than they'd been at the start.

Mark had really enjoyed his evening out with Callie the night before. He'd taken her to a nice Italian restaurant off Piccadilly, where they'd had a good meal.

Just not as good, he thought ruefully, as they would have had at La Venezia. Callie would love Mamma's ravioli.

It was silly that he couldn't take her there. And high time that he did something about it.

Determined to talk to his sister, he left work a bit early and, instead of going back to his flat, took a detour to her house. Serena was almost always at home at that time of the day, between the end of lunch and the beginning of dinner at the restaurant; Mark knew that she liked to be there when Chiara came in from school. After all, Chiara was only twelve, and though quite capable of looking after herself, she was rather young to be left on her own.

It was Chiara who opened the door to him. "Uncle Marco!" she squealed in a most undignified way, and threw herself into his arms, knocking the breath out of him and nearly bowling him over.

"Hey. Hey." He hugged the compact little body to him. She had grown taller of late, but she still seemed a child to him.

Eventually she let go of him and stepped aside to let him into the house. "Is Mum expecting you?" she asked. "'Cause she's not here."

"Not here?" Marco automatically went through to the kitchen, almost as though he would find that Chiara was mistaken and Serena would be there presiding over the coffee pot.

"No. When I got home from school, she wasn't here." There was a slight worried note in her voice.

"Did she leave a note?"

"Oh, yes." Chiara picked it up from the kitchen table and handed it to him. "It just says that she had to go out. And that she'd left sandwiches for my tea."

This seemed most uncharacteristic, but hardly alarming.

"I haven't eaten them yet. Want one?" Chiara went to the refrigerator and brought out a plate of sandwiches. "There's plenty here, Uncle Marco. Mozzarella and tomato."

Mark put the kettle on, then settled down with her at the table, where they quickly devoured the sandwiches.

"I'm glad you've come, Uncle Marco," Chiara said candidly. "Did Mum ask you to call round? To keep an eye on me or something?"

"No, it was just good luck. I was hoping to have a word with your mum. About . . . something."

Unconsciously she played with a strand of her long black hair, twisting it round her finger. Mark had known her all her life, and knew that Chiara only fiddled with her hair when she was upset or unsettled. Maybe it was the pressure of the school nativity play that had her wound up. "Is everything going okay?" he asked. "With the play and everything?"

"Oh, the play is fine," she said dismissively. "I've learned my lines. All of them."

"Even the soliloquy?"

"Even that." Chiara shrugged. "It will be fine." She was still twisting her hair.

Maybe, then, it was the uncertainty over Angelina — the new boyfriend, the fact that she might not make it home in time for the play. "How's Angelina doing?" he asked.

"Fine, I suppose. I talked to her on Sunday night, when she rang. She's got a boyfriend, did you know?" Chiara grinned. "His name is Li. L - I, not L - E - E. He's Chinese." She added, "I'm not sure whether that's really his first name, or his surname. I think the Chinese do it the wrong way round for some reason."

"I don't suppose your dad is very happy about that," Mark said, probing. "About the boyfriend, I mean."

She shrugged again. "No. But then Dad wouldn't like any boyfriend that Angelina brought home."

That, thought Mark, was a very wise and insightful statement. Perhaps Chiara was more grown up than he was giving her credit for. "How about you?" he asked. "Do you have a boyfriend yet?"

Chiara wrinkled her nose in distaste. "No way! Boys are gross."

Not *that* grown up, then. "Gross?"

"No offence," she added. "But then, you're not a boy. Not any longer."

No, he wasn't a boy any longer. Mark might have given up at that point, had Chiara not done the one thing which indicated she was really agitated: she conveyed the bit of twisted hair to her mouth and started chewing on the end of it.

Mark abandoned subtlety; he leaned across the table and touched her arm. "Hey, *bambina*, is everything okay?"

Her face crumpled and she squeezed her eyes shut. "No," she said softly. "No, I don't think it is."

"What's wrong? Tell Uncle Marco."

"I'm not sure." Her voice was almost a whisper, which wasn't like Chiara at all. "But I just have the feeling that something is . . . wrong. Really wrong."

"Because your mum isn't here?" he guessed.

"Partly that. And last night there was something going on."

"Something? Like what?" Mark asked sharply.

"Like . . . a fight, I think. An argument." Chiara gulped, as though she were on the brink of tears. "It was late. I was in bed. Asleep. And it woke me up. They were yelling. Really yelling at each other."

"Your mum and dad?"

She nodded miserably. "Mum and Dad bicker sometimes. Like over Angelina's boyfriend. But this was different, Uncle Marco. They were yelling."

"Did you hear what they were saying?"

"No." She shook her head. "But it was loud. And . . . I think Mum was . . . crying." At that point Chiara lost it; her own tears overflowed.

Alex Hamilton didn't just miss her mum and her best friend Kirsty: she also missed her Granny. She hadn't seen Granny in weeks — only a couple of times since Granny had moved to London, and then for no more than a few minutes. When they'd lived in Gartenbridge, in those long-ago days when she hadn't known how happy she was, she'd seen Granny nearly every day. During school holidays and on Saturdays, when Mum was working in her bookshop, she'd practically lived at Granny and Granddad's house. Granny had fed her, baked her favourite shortbread, read books to her, taught her to pick out some tunes on her piano, played board games with her, let her walk Macduff. She loved her Granny.

But whenever she mentioned her to Dad or Jilly, they shrugged. "Granny's very busy," they'd say. "Now that she's living in London, she doesn't have much free time."

It had only just occurred to her: she could ring Granny.

Yesterday, after school, she'd called Directory Enquiries and got her number. Excitedly she'd tried it, only to be disappointed by a recorded message on the other end. Not available. Leave a message.

She'd left a message. Granny hadn't rung back.

Today she had an even more compelling reason to talk to her grandmother.

At school she'd had an encounter with her step-cousins, the odious Beatrice and Georgina. Usually she managed to avoid them, but today they'd caught her off her guard. She'd been sitting alone at a table in the dining hall, daydreaming about Jack, when they'd sneaked up behind her.

Their chosen taunts and torments had been as usual: all about her mother.

It upset Alex, and it made her feel guilty. She'd been so busy thinking about Jack that she hadn't given that much thought to her mum and how much she missed her.

And could it be true, those horrible things they said about Mum? Was her mother dead? Alex had no positive proof that she wasn't.

Granny, she'd said to herself. Granny will know. Granny will tell me the truth.

This time she was in luck: Granny answered the phone on the second ring.

"Alex!" said Granny, sounding delighted. "How are you, lovie? It's been way too long since I've seen my wee lass."

Alex couldn't help herself. "I left a message yesterday. You didn't ring me back."

"But I did! Jilly said you were too busy to come to the phone."

Oh, the treachery of it! Alex was speechless for a few seconds, overwhelmed by hatred for Jilly and her whole horrible family. "She's a liar! Jilly's a rotten liar!"

Granny didn't say anything, so Alex went on. "Granny, can I ask you something?"

"Of course."

"My mum." The words came out almost on a sob. "Tell me the truth. Is my mum dead?"

"Dead?" Granny sounded shocked. "Oh, lassie. Of course she's not."

"You'd tell me if she was?"

"I'd tell you," promised Granny.

"Then why," Alex demanded, "hasn't she written to me? Or e-mailed me? Or come to see me? Or anything? My mum loves me. If she was alive, how could she just . . . ignore me like that? If she's not dead, then where is she?"

"Oh, Alex, lassie." There was a long silence, then Granny spoke slowly, as if she were choosing her words with special care. "Your mother is alive. But she's . . . not well."

"She's dying?" It came out as an anguished cry.

"No, no. She isn't well . . . in her head." Granny took a deep breath. "You and your dad — well, you were her whole life. She loves you both so much. And when she lost you . . . she just . . . couldn't cope."

"Are you saying that Mum is crazy?" Alex asked baldly.

"She's . . . not well," repeated Granny. "But she's being well looked after."

"She's in a crazy house." As Alex put it into words, she knew it was true. If she wasn't dead, what other reason could there be for her mum not to contact her?

"They don't call it that, of course. It's a sort of private hospital."

Alex's world reeled. "Have you seen her? Talked to her?"

There was another long pause. "I tried to. She's not allowed to have visitors. But I do keep in touch with . . . her condition. The doctors think she might be getting a wee bit better."

Alex groaned. "Why didn't Dad tell me? Jilly always tried to make me think that I was with them because Mum didn't want me. I knew that couldn't be true. But why didn't Dad tell me the truth?"

She knew the answer, really. It was because Dad wouldn't do anything Jilly didn't want him to. And Jilly didn't want her to know where her mother was.

"I can't answer that," said Granny.

"But you *can* tell me where she is!" Alex realised. "I could write her a letter! Oh, tell me, Granny! Where is my mum?"

Usually, after Evening Prayer, Callie was anxious to get back to her flat — to see Bella and give her a quick walk, then to put her feet up and have a cup of tea. But now, with Peter in residence, she dreaded what she'd find.

Bella came to the door to meet her as usual, wagging her whole body with pleasure. Callie crouched down and stroked her, looking round for Peter.

"Hi, Sis," he called. "I'm in the kitchen."

What was he up to? With a last pat for Bella, she straightened up and went through to see.

196

Peter was standing by the counter, grinning, pointing to an unfamiliar black-and-chrome contraption on the work surface. "Look, Sis!" he said. "Look what I've bought you!"

"What is it?" she asked blankly.

"What is it? Why, it's only the latest and most wonderful gadget!"

It wasn't immediately evident to Callie what the gadget was meant to do. "Is it a fancy tin-opener?" she guessed.

"Oh, Sis." He shook his head reproachfully. "Can't you see?"

"Well, no," she admitted.

Peter opened a box next to the contraption. "What would you like? Tea? Or coffee? Espresso, cappuccino, filter coffee? Decaf or regular? Or maybe hot chocolate?"

"Tea, I suppose," Callie said, still mystified.

"Okay." he selected something from the box and showed it to her; it was a sort of capsule. "See, Sis? You pop this in here. Like this. Then you put your mug here. Very important, that. Then you push this button. And in a few seconds . . ." With a grand, theatrical gesture he pointed to the machine as it spewed out a stream of brown liquid into the mug. "Voilà! Fresh tea, made to order!"

"But . . . why?" What, Callie wondered, was the matter with boiling a kettle? Why did you need a machine that took up half the available work surface, just to make a cup of tea?

"It's easy. It's fast. You can have any sort of hot drink you fancy, with no effort." He displayed the box of metallic capsules. "Just pop one of these into the machine, and before you know it, your drink is ready." Peter looked at her expectantly. "Well, Sis? Isn't it brilliant?"

"It's . . . very nice."

His face fell, just like a small child whose gift had been rejected. "I thought you'd like it," he said. "I wanted to do something to thank you for putting up with me, and I thought you'd like it."

"I *do* like it." Touched, Callie made an effort to sound enthusiastic. "It's a lovely surprise, Peter. Really. I love it."

He was, she thought, awfully sweet. A nuisance as a house-guest, but her brother was awfully sweet. Callie felt ashamed of herself for resenting his intrusion into her life. What sort of a priest would she make, if she couldn't even tolerate her own beloved brother for a few days?

Yolanda made a hot milky drink for Rachel, to settle her before bedtime, and took it upstairs to Rachel's bedroom. She raised her hand to tap on the door, which was cracked open, then paused as she heard a murmured voice on the other side.

"I e-mailed you," said Rachel, softly. "Didn't you get it?"

She must be on her mobile phone, Yolanda realised.

What she ought to do was to knock loudly, wait a few seconds, then push the door open and go in.

But instead she waited, and listened.

"I know. I know," Rachel said, in a hushed voice that was half impatient, half tender. "It's hard for me, too. But we can't see each other. Not now. Maybe not for a while." There was a pause. "I know. But you mustn't ring. It's too dangerous. She never leaves me alone. Not for more than a few minutes. I can barely go to the loo without her wanting to go with me. She means well, but —"

Yolanda didn't move; she felt that she couldn't have moved if she'd wanted to.

"Yes," murmured Rachel. "You know that I love you, too. We just have to be patient, that's all."

CHAPTER
TEN

Alex didn't get much sleep that night. Her mother was alive; her mother wasn't well. All of her suppressed emotion about her mother's absence from her life had been stirred up into a turmoil of love and longing.

Granny, in the end, wouldn't tell her exactly where Mum was. But she'd gleaned some clues, both from what Granny had said and from what she'd been unable to deny. She was in Scotland. Not the Highlands, and not in Edinburgh. Somewhere in the Borders area, in some sort of private clinic.

If there was one thing Alex was able to do, it was to find information on the internet. And the internet didn't sleep.

Through the night, in her darkened room, she trawled electronic waters in search of clues; by the time she finally slipped into bed, unable to keep her eyes open a moment longer, she had a little list of possibilities.

If Alex got little sleep, Yolanda got none. In the room next to Rachel's she was tense and wakeful, her mind going round and round in dazed circles.

It was obvious that she had to do something. But what should she do? Should she confront Rachel? Or go straight to Neville Stewart?

Maybe, she told herself, she was overreacting.

Perhaps there was an innocent explanation for what she'd overheard, and it hadn't meant what she thought it meant. In that case, she owed Rachel the opportunity to explain.

But to talk to Rachel first presented two difficulties. First of all, Rachel was in a very delicate physical state. Any sort of excitement or agitation — above and beyond what she'd already been through — could bring on premature labour. And if her worst suspicions were true, it would show Rachel her hand, give her an opportunity to take some sort of action which could compromise the investigation.

Besides, her efforts to think of a possible innocent explanation had produced absolutely nothing credible. And she had tried very hard. Yolanda had come to be very fond of Rachel over the past days, beyond just her natural protective and nurturing instincts. She admired Rachel's stoicism and bravery; she liked her as a person.

But what if that stoicism, that bravery, had an entirely different significance? What if they meant that she really didn't care about Trevor's death? That she was, in fact, relieved to be rid of him?

Or even something more sinister . . .

Yolanda shied clear of taking that last step. It was difficult enough for her to get her head round the fact that Rachel loved someone other than Trevor. Someone whose existence Yolanda had neither known about nor suspected . . .

It was then that she remembered the phone call she'd intercepted, early that first morning. A whispered voice, asking "Rache?"

She ought to tell Neville Stewart. Now. But how could she betray a poor, helpless woman who could give birth at any moment? If confronting Rachel herself involved the risk of bringing on a premature birth, how much more so would the inevitable consequences of informing the officers in charge of the case?

She was, Yolanda reminded herself sternly, a police officer. That was her job, her calling. And it was the basis on which she was here in this house. Not as a midwife, not as a friend and companion to Rachel. As a police officer, with a duty to uphold the law. Her next course of action shouldn't even be an issue: it should be a foregone conclusion.

Then an idea came to her — one which would, in any case, buy her a few hours of time. She would talk to Eli. Eli was wise and experienced. She thought she could probably guess what he would say, but she would put the facts before him and see.

Mark was troubled with a profound unease.

Chiara was not, he knew, a fanciful child, quick to make something out of nothing. No, if Chiara was worried that something in her family was wrong, he was prepared to believe her.

Serena and Joe shouting at one other? Yelling, as Chiara had put it?

He couldn't imagine Serena yelling at anyone, for any reason. She was the most placid, the most unruffled of people. Mark thought back over all the years of his life and couldn't remember a single instance of Serena losing her temper. Even his brazen schoolboy efforts to tease her into betraying some sort of emotion, when she was a teenager beginning to be interested in Joe, had been lamentable failures. Serena just couldn't be drawn into an outward display of feelings.

His sister's unflappability was one of the touchstones of his own existence.

Mark had wanted to confide in Callie when he went round to see her later that evening, but was constrained by Peter's presence. He was distracted, though — enough so that Callie noticed. She walked out with him to say goodbye in privacy.

"Are you okay, Marco?" she asked. "You seemed . . . not quite with us tonight."

He shook his head. "I have something on my mind. Sorry."

"Work?" Callie guessed.

"No. Family." Mark grimaced.

"Not *my* family? Not Peter." She sounded apprehensive. "I know he was going on a bit about that coffee machine —"

Quickly he reassured her. "No, not Peter. Of course not. No, it's *la mia famiglia*, as usual."

"Anything you can tell me about?" Callie suggested diffidently. "I'm a pretty good listener."

Grateful for the offer, and sorely tempted to take her up on it on the spot, Mark hugged her. "You're a *wonderful* listener, *cara mia*." He kissed her on the nose. "And I *will* tell you. When I've managed to get my own head round it. Soon."

But how was he going to get his head round it, without talking to Serena?

On his way to work, Neville stopped at the newsagents on the corner to pick up the morning papers: with all those reporters and photographers haunting the inquest, there was sure to be something about the case.

It hadn't made the front page of any paper except the *Globe*. They'd been lucky enough to snap a photo of Rachel in the instant before Neville got between her and the cameras, and they'd made the most of it.

TRAGIC RACHEL, screamed the headline.

"Oh, hell," Neville muttered. He paid for the papers with a five pound note, shoved his change in his pocket, and went across the street to his favourite greasy spoon caff to have a quick browse.

"Coffee," he ordered automatically, knowing it would be blessedly strong.

The *Globe*'s story was, of course, written by Lilith Noone, his old nemesis; at times it seemed to Neville that she had been put on the earth especially to plague him, though he knew that she did not confine her efforts to him alone. She had, as usual, put her finger on the one thing guaranteed to get him in hot water with Detective Superintendent Evans. Skipping over the preliminaries about poor tragic Rachel, he went to the end.

204

"It has been nearly a week since the murder of dad-to-be Trevor Norton. The police have CCTV footage of the killer, just seconds before he committed the evil crime that will deprive a child forever of its father, and all for the sake of an iPod. Why have they not yet caught this monster, before he kills again? These lawless yobs must not be allowed to make our streets no-go zones for decent people!"

On Thursday mornings, Callie always went to the vicarage for a staff meeting with Brian — to compare diaries, make forward plans, and discuss the events of the past week. While she didn't at all mind the meetings themselves, she inevitably found herself dreading the moment when Jane Stanford opened the door to her.

The fact of the matter was that Jane didn't like her. Callie was as sure of that fact as she was baffled as to the reasons. Marco said it was because Jane was jealous of her, but she didn't see why that should be so: she had absolutely no interest in stealing Jane's husband. Brian was perfectly acceptable as a colleague and boss; she couldn't, though, imagine any circumstances in which she would fancy him. Even if she were desperate, even if she didn't have a gorgeous and very fanciable man in her life already, she would never find Brian even marginally attractive as a man. So why should Jane Stanford dislike her so?

The dislike was usually manifested as an icy politeness. That was preferable to the occasional alternative, a spiteful sniping. On a few occasions Jane had even gone out of her way to discomfit Callie. So it was no surprise that Callie didn't look forward to their encounters.

She drew a deep breath before ringing the bell, bracing herself, wondering — not for the first time — why Brian never came to the door himself.

The person on the other side of the door, though, was neither Jane nor Brian. It was a young man with Jane's dark hair and Brian's slightly weak chin. One of the twins, home from Oxford for the Christmas holidays, she realised instantly.

"Oh, hello. Charlie, is it? Or Simon?"

The young man grinned at her. "Right the first time. I'm Charlie. We're identical, but these days it's easy to tell us apart. My brother is the one who's currently joined at the hip with his girlfriend. You won't see him without her."

"Oh — I didn't know he had a girlfriend. Is she visiting, then?"

Charlie jerked his head in the direction of the stairs. "Upstairs. They're in his room. Snogging, no doubt. At least they have the decency not to do it in public, and frighten the horses."

What, Callie couldn't help wondering, did Jane make of that? Jane was very proprietorial when it came to her boys; Callie had never met them before now, but it was clear from everything Jane ever said about her sons that she took a very active interest in their lives.

"You must be the curate," Charlie said. "Dad's expecting you." He looked her up and down appraisingly. "He didn't tell me you were pretty."

Callie felt herself blushing. Ridiculous, at her age.

"But I suppose," Charlie added, "he wouldn't dare say that, in front of Mum."

"I need to go out for an hour or so. Will you be all right, or shall I get someone else to come and stay while I'm gone?" Yolanda tried not to be hurt by the fleeting expression of relief on Rachel's face. It reminded her of the one thing she hadn't really allowed her to think about: the wounding things Rachel had said about her. "She never leaves me alone . . ." And that, after she had put her own life on hold for nearly a week!

"I'll be all right," Rachel said.

Yolanda handed her a bit of paper. "Here's my mobile number, in case of emergency."

"I'll be all right," repeated Rachel.

Yesterday Yolanda would have found it very difficult to leave her, even for a few minutes. There was still a small tug of regret, the irrational feeling that she was abandoning her duty.

Still, she discovered that in spite of everything, she was looking forward to seeing her husband. She'd been away from home for five nights, and that was way too long for her. Yolanda and Eli had always been close, in the way that many childless couples are; the fact that they now had a career in common had brought them even nearer together.

They had arranged to meet during his lunch hour, at a comfortable cafe not far from the police station; it was a favourite haunt of theirs, where they'd often eaten together as and when their schedules permitted. Eli was already there, at their preferred table in the corner. He rose to greet her, enveloping her in a bear hug that left Yolanda in no doubt that he was glad to see her.

"Hey, doll," he said. "I've missed you."

"And I've missed *you*."

Oh, it was good to be with him again. They smiled at each other across the table, wordlessly, until the waitress came to take their order.

"Ham sandwich," said Eli, without looking at the menu. "And a bowl of chips."

"Jacket potato, with tuna and sweetcorn," Yolanda decided.

When the waitress had left, Eli reached over and took her hand, squeezing it. "Sure is great to see you, doll. To what do I owe the pleasure, exactly?"

"Oh, sweetie." She suddenly found that there was a large lump in her throat. "Something's happened. I wanted to talk to you before . . . well, before I did anything about it. To get your advice."

"Tell me," said Eli, adding, "I've seen the papers, if that's any help."

"Papers?" Yolanda was startled.

"Newspapers," he amplified. "Yesterday, that bit about you. Not, if you don't mind me saying it, the most tactful thing you've ever done." Eli grinned at her. "Every word of it true, of course, but not the way to win Evans' heart."

"I just said what I thought."

Eli continued, "And today. Front page of the *Globe*."

"Today? What have I done *today*?"

"Not you," he reassured her. "There was a photo of Rachel, after the inquest. I could see you behind her. The story was all the usual rubbish about yobs and the police not doing their job to make the streets safe."

"Oh, Evans will love that." Yolanda gave a wry grin. "But that's not what I need to talk to you about."

"Well, go ahead, then." Again he squeezed her hand.

She recounted to him, as nearly as she could recall it, the one-sided conversation she'd overheard. "I just don't know what to make of it," she finished.

Eli was frowning. "She loves someone. Not her husband, unless he was ringing from the other side."

"Or unless . . ." That had given Yolanda a new idea. For a moment she sat silently, trying to work it out. "What if Trevor isn't really dead after all?"

"Not dead? But his body was pulled out of the canal," Eli reminded her.

"A body was pulled out of the canal. She's the one who identified him."

He ran his hand over his smoothly shaved head. "Oh. I see what you mean."

"We only have her word for it that the body was Trevor's." Yolanda spoke with increasing excitement. "He wasn't carrying any ID, remember. Jogging. Very convenient."

The waitress put their food in front of them.

"Ta," said Eli, giving her a smile.

Hoping he wouldn't notice, Yolanda reached across the table and grabbed a chip.

"Hey! Those are mine!" Eli put his hands round the bowl in a protective gesture.

"Yeah, but what's yours is mine. That's what marriage is about." The chip was hot; gingerly she nibbled at it, still turning over the new possibilities in her mind. "Okay. Say Trevor needs to disappear for some reason. Say he's involved in some business deal that's gone wrong. Or say he's on the ropes financially — has over-extended himself with the business and has creditors he can't pay."

"Yeeees . . ." Eli nodded, encouraging her to go on, as he squirted tomato ketchup on his chips.

"If it all gets to be too much for him and he just does a runner, he leaves a pregnant wife who has to sort everything out. If she's a partner in the business, she may even be financially liable. That's not very fair on Rachel. Especially if he loves her."

"So," said Eli, "he fakes his own death?"

"Exactly. And she's in on it. She reports him missing, says he's gone out jogging. In the meantime, he's gone into hiding. Everyone thinks he's dead. He can lie low for a long time. Eventually, when no one is paying any attention to her any longer, Rachel can go off and join him, somewhere else, and they can make a new start."

Eli took a bite of his sandwich, chewed it and swallowed before he spoke. "Plausible, I must say. Possible. But it just leaves one little question unanswered."

"I know." Yolanda forked up some of her potato. "What do I do about it?"

"That wasn't the question I had in mind." He quirked his eyebrows at her. "I was thinking more about the body in the canal. If it wasn't Trevor Norton, who the hell was it?"

Knowing that Serena would be tied up at the restaurant, Mark waited until after lunch to ring her on her mobile. "I was wondering if I could come and see you," he suggested. Whatever the problem was, it certainly wasn't anything they could talk about over the phone.

Serena sounded tense. "I'm busy this afternoon, Marco. I need to spend some time taking inventory."

"Inventory?" Of her life? That sounded serious.

"At the restaurant," she amplified. "With all of these Christmas parties, we're running low on quite a few things, and I'll need to place some orders before Christmas if we don't want to run out."

"Oh, I see." Relieved, Mark nevertheless didn't give up. "Could you use some help?"

"Don't you have to work?"

"As a matter of fact," he said, "I'm rather at a loose end this afternoon. I was supposed to be going to court with someone, and the hearing has been rescheduled at the last minute. So I could come and give you a hand."

"All right," his sister replied, sounding grateful. "That would be great."

So, a little while later, the two of them were alone in the storeroom of La Venezia. Mark was counting, and Serena was writing the numbers down.

"How about loo rolls?" she asked.

"Twenty-seven. That's two packets of twelve, and three spare ones."

"Oh, Lord." Serena sighed. "That won't last us more than a couple of days, at the rate we're going through loo paper. I'll have to run to the cash-and-carry and stock up. I don't know when I'm going to do that."

She sounded so uncharacteristically forlorn that Mark turned to her, seeing his opening. "Look, Serena," he said gently. "Is everything okay?"

Serena looked away from him. "These Christmas parties. We're so busy. I suppose it's getting to me." She swallowed hard, and Mark noticed with dismay that there were tears running down her cheeks. He couldn't remember ever having seen his sister cry.

"It's not just the Christmas parties, is it?" he suggested, moving closer to her. "There must be something else."

"Bloody loo rolls!" The words exploded from her, then as if they contained and dissipated all her resistance, she hunched over and sobbed aloud.

"Serena!" Mark put his arm round her shoulders. "What's the matter?"

"I . . . just . . . can't . . . cope!" she wailed.

"Tell me. Tell me what's wrong."

"I . . . can't."

Mark remembered an earlier conversation. "Is it Angelina?" he suggested. "Something to do with the boyfriend?" His imagination raced ahead. "Does she want to marry him? Is she . . . pregnant?" That would explain a great deal.

212

"No. No." Serena shook her head violently. "Not Angelina."

"And Chiara's okay?"

"She's fine."

Maybe Serena was ill, he thought with a hollow feeling in his gut. Women's problems. Cancer, even. He couldn't imagine his sister being unwell: apart from all those miscarriages, which she'd borne with her customary stoicism, and a cold or two, she'd never been ill.

But why, if she were unwell, would she be shouting at Joe?

Mark wasn't sure he wanted to go there.

His sister's marriage, like that of his parents, had always been a shining example to him. It was perhaps one reason why he hadn't yet married: living with two such close and loving relationships as exemplars of the matrimonial state, he was not in a hurry to rush into something that would be any less satisfying.

Yet he had to ask; he had to know.

"Joe?" he said.

Serena fumbled in her pocket, then, not finding a tissue, grabbed a red paper serviette from a nearby stack and pressed it to her face.

"Is something wrong with Joe?" Mark pursued.

"Joe!" The name came out in an anguished, hiccoughing sob.

Mark hazarded a guess. Of all the possibilities, for him it was the least difficult to handle. "Is he . . . sick?"

His sister shook her head, slowly at first and then picking up momentum.

"Then —"

Her words were muffled in the serviette, but Mark understood them all too well. "He's having an affair," Serena choked.

Yolanda pulled a chair up next to Neville's desk. She sat down, crossed then uncrossed her legs, and cleared her throat.

"Yes?" Neville said with as much patience as he could muster.

He wasn't feeling very patient. Evans had summoned him to his big corner office and let him know in no uncertain terms that he wasn't very impressed with the progress of the investigation, not least with the way that Lilith Noone now seemed to have the bit between her teeth on this one. That old familiar song: why aren't the police doing their job? The last time she'd sung that tune, the chorus had been racism; now it was yobbishness. Neville had to hand it to her — she sure knew how to pick her little ditties to fit in with the public mood.

"I'm not sure how to tell you this," said Yolanda, fiddling with one of her braids.

Neville's gut twitched. "Tell me what?"

"I've been wondering whether we've been barking up entirely the wrong tree with this case."

By now he knew for certain that he didn't want to hear what she was going to tell him. The trouble was, he respected her as a police officer; he knew she was neither stupid nor fanciful. "Yes?" he repeated, apprehensively this time.

214

"I know this sounds mad, but hear me out."

Neville sighed. "Okay."

"Is it possible that . . . well, that the body in the canal was someone other than Trevor Norton?"

His head jerked up. "His wife ID-ed him," he said sharply. "You were with her. Remember?"

"My point exactly."

Neville stared at her. "Maybe I'm being thick, but I don't have a clue what you're talking about."

She didn't meet his eyes. "What if Rachel Norton wasn't telling the truth? What if the body wasn't her husband at all, but someone else?"

"Why the hell would she do that?"

"Maybe because she wanted us to think that he was dead," Yolanda stated. "Maybe he needed to . . . disappear. For some reason."

"Oh." Neville was silent for a moment, as his brain kicked into another gear. What if they *had* been looking at this the wrong way round all along? It wouldn't be the first time. "Yes . . ." he said at last. "Yes, I see what you're getting at. But why?"

"If he had debts, or was in trouble of some kind," she prompted. "There are all kinds of reasons why people need to disappear."

He shook his head. "No, I mean *why* would you think this, all of a sudden? Has something happened? I mean, do you have some reason to think that this case is anything other than straightforward? Other than what it looks like? Yobbism, random crime, whatever?"

"Well, yes," Yolanda said slowly. "I'm not mad, Neville. I didn't come up with this out of the blue."

215

"Tell me."

"It was something I overheard."

Neville felt suddenly alert, his brain firing on all cylinders. As she recounted the conversation, he was way ahead of her.

"'We just have to be patient, that's all.' That's what she said," Yolanda finished.

"So you think that Trevor has done a runner, is laying low somewhere until it's safe for him and Rachel to be together again? And she's in on all this with him?"

"It's possible," she said. "It fits with what she said."

"It *does* raise a few other questions, though," Neville pointed out.

"I know," she admitted. "Like whose body did she ID?"

If you started questioning that, Neville realised, it opened a huge can of worms. Was it merely a coincidence that a body was pulled out of the canal which matched the description of her missing husband? Or had it all been some sort of massive misdirection on her part, with a more sinister and complex operation behind it? Had Trevor, in fact, murdered an innocent jogger — one who looked a bit like himself — to provide himself with an escape mechanism? "The CCTV footage!" he recalled suddenly. The cameras didn't lie. There were two men in those shots, even if the poor weather conditions rendered them unrecognisable.

"I've thought of that," Yolanda said. "What if Trevor was the guy in the hoodie, and not the jogger at all?"

"Bloody hell." He closed his eyes, overwhelmed by the possibilities. Topsy-turvy. That's what this was. Trevor, a murderer rather than a victim? Rachel, a liar?

As if echoing his thoughts, Yolanda said, "Whatever interpretation you put on it, what I overheard means she's a damned good actress. She sure had me — had all of us — convinced with that grieving wife routine. What a bunch of idiots she must have taken us for."

Neville recognised the bitterness in her voice and wondered about it in passing.

"Idiots." He snapped his fingers. "That's exactly what we are! We're forgetting something!"

"What?"

"We still have the body! Or at least the Coroner does." Neville grinned, suddenly jubilant. "The camera may or may not lie, but DNA pretty damn well tells the truth."

Yolanda nodded. "Yessss . . ."

"So all we've got to do now is get hold of a bit of Trevor's DNA, and we're away."

She stood up. "I suppose that means me."

"Too right it does." He made a broad sweeping gesture with both hands. "Off you go. Back to Rachel's. Grab a toothbrush, a hairbrush, whatever. I'll send Sid round a bit later, and you can hand over the goods. Just try not to raise her suspicions — I wouldn't want her to think we'd rumbled her."

Maybe, thought Neville, this was just the break they needed. Not exactly the one he'd been hoping for, but sometimes police work was like that.

CHAPTER
ELEVEN

Mark had known Joe as long as Serena had, if not as intimately; like his sister, he'd thought he knew him.

Eventually Serena managed to tell him the details, or as much as she'd discovered.

She'd found a note — a love letter, really — in Joe's pocket when she'd taken his jacket to the dry cleaner. For a few days she'd pondered it, then she'd confronted her husband. Faced with the evidence, he'd admitted everything. Yes, he was having an affair. With one of his graduate students, a girl — a young woman — called Samantha Winters. It didn't mean, Joe told her, that he didn't still love her. He was committed to his marriage, to his wife and his daughters. This was just one of those things.

Serena had tried to accept that, she confided to her brother, even if she didn't understand it. She was trying not to be angry. But it was hard. So hard. The stability of her marriage was something she'd always taken for granted. That, and the fact that she and Joe both viewed marriage in the same way: as a life-long commitment made before God, as exclusive as "forsaking all others" implied. Now it seemed that Joe was inclined to take a broader view of it.

218

"He says he still loves me," she wept. "But how can he, Marco? If he's doing that. I just don't understand."

Mark didn't know what to say, didn't feel he was equipped to answer adequately for one of his sex. He listened to her outpouring of pain, soothed her with sympathy and love, and supervised as she pulled herself together to face Chiara's return from school and an evening at the restaurant, during which she would have to continue to present a calm face to the customers and — more importantly — to her parents. Mamma and Papa must never know, must never even suspect. That much was evident to both Serena and Mark.

By the time he left her, he was seething. Usually the most reasonable of men, Mark was incensed on his sister's behalf, his bewilderment crystallised into anger. How dare Joe treat her like that, after so many years of marriage?

He stood on the pavement for a moment, watching the pedestrians in their heedless progress, the cars inching along through traffic, trying to reorientate himself after his world had been turned upside-down.

What now?

In his rage, Mark's first instinct was to go to Joe's office and confront him: to scream at him, to punch him in the face and call him every name he could think of. Then break every bone in his treacherous body and tear him limb from limb.

His second, more rational, impulse was to go to Callie, to throw himself into her arms, hold her close and pour the story out to her as Serena had poured it out to him, to take comfort from her sensible and

219

compassionate view of life. To let her soothe his anger from him.

But what if Callie wasn't there? And what about Peter? For a moment he'd forgotten about Peter, now ever-present in Callie's flat.

He had no right, really, to impose on Callie. This was a family matter. *His* family. He needed to deal with it, not pass it on to her.

He *would* see Joe. He'd try not to beat the crap out of him, but he needed an explanation. For himself, as much as for Serena.

Joe's office, at the university, wasn't far from the restaurant. Mark walked it in ten minutes — briskly, as the temperature seemed to be dropping — during which he began to have doubts about the wisdom of this mission. Would Serena want him to do this, or would she be upset for Joe to know that she'd confided in her brother? He stood for a moment at the door of the building, watching the students coming and going. Unprepossessing boys in tattered jeans and anoraks, rucksack-toting girls looking impossibly young. Was *this* one Samantha Winters? Or that one?

It was too cold to stand around for very long so he followed a gaggle of half a dozen students into the building, then hesitated again, trying to remember the location of Joe's office; he'd been there once or twice on family errands, but had little reason to visit him here over the years. There was a board near the front door, which he consulted. Second floor.

Maybe Joe wasn't in his office, Mark told himself as he climbed the stairs: he might be lecturing, or even at home. He might be in the middle of a tutorial. By the time he reached the door, he was almost hoping for an excuse to avoid this confrontation.

He rapped on the door with his knuckles; there was an immediate response. "Come in," called Joe's familiar voice.

Joe was behind his desk, pen in hand, with a stack of exercise books in front of him; he looked up as the door opened. "Oh, Marco. Hi." He sounded surprised: was he expecting someone else? "End of term," he went on with a grimace, indicating the exercise books. "I hate marking anyway, but the end of term is the worst."

"I've just been to see Serena," Mark said baldly. He was in no mood for friendly chat or any other preliminaries.

"Oh," said Joe, putting down his pen.

"She's upset," Mark said. It wasn't what he'd planned to say, but it was what came out as he struggled to control a rising swell of fury. How could Joe just sit there when he was ruining his family's life?

Joe raised his eyebrows. "Yes, I believe she is. She's made that fairly clear." His voice was mild, with a hint of irony.

Swallowing hard, Mark clenched his fists in his jacket pockets, then the words burst out of him. "How could you do it, Joe? She's your wife! Doesn't that mean anything to you?"

"It means a great deal to me. It always has." He shook his head. "Surely you're not that naïve, Marco. These things happen, especially in a position like this. It almost goes with the job."

Mark stared at him as the words and their implication sank in. "Does this mean . . .?" he asked slowly. "This isn't the first time, is it?"

"You're not going to get me to answer that," Joe smirked. "Let's just say I'm sorry that Serena has become involved."

"You're sorry you got caught, you mean."

Joe inclined his head. "I never wanted to hurt her. You must understand that."

"Not hurt her? You've ruined her life!"

"She'll get over it," Joe stated, picking up his pen and fiddling with it. "She'll have to. What else is she going to do? Leave me? I don't think so. That's not an option. 'For better or for worse,' remember? And she'd die rather than have your parents find out. So," he added, "nothing is going to change. Not really."

He was right: Serena would never leave him, no matter what he did to her. "Except that she'll never be able to trust you again," Mark said with bitterness. "You've betrayed her, and she'll have to live with that knowledge."

"As I said, I'm sorry about that. I love Serena, and I never wanted to hurt her."

"You *love* Serena? You can say that, after what you've done?" Without waiting for an answer, Mark went on, "What about this . . . this girl? Don't you love her?"

"Oh, Marco. Marco." Joe shook his head wearily, as though he were tiring of the conversation. "You sound just like your sister. Why do women have to go on so about love?"

222

Stung by the condescending tone, Mark retorted, "Because love is everything. It's what holds us together, what keeps families going —"

"You *are* naïve."

The door flew open and a young woman rushed in, burbling breathlessly. "Darling, I have some good news. Those theatre tickets I was trying to get —" She stopped abruptly as she realised that Joe wasn't alone. "Oh." She looked at Mark, then her head swivelled back to Joe. "Am I interrupting something?"

She was a wispy sort of blonde, and she was so very young. Scarcely older, Mark realised, than Angelina.

"It's not a good time, Sam," Joe said without looking at her.

But Mark couldn't bear it any longer. There was nothing more to be said, and never in his life had he been more tempted to exercise physical violence; he knew that if he stayed for one more second, he wouldn't be responsible for his actions. Shoving his hands more deeply in his pockets to keep them from going for Joe's throat, he spun round and left the room.

Going back to Rachel Norton's house, knowing what she now knew, was one of the most difficult things Yolanda had ever been called upon to do as a police officer. No longer could she take Rachel at face value; whatever the truth about the body in the canal, and about the person at the other end of that telephone call, Rachel had gone to great lengths to conceal something from her. And she had to pretend not to know that, to continue to treat Rachel as she always had.

With a blast of cold air the clouds had come in, and to Yolanda's eyes they looked like snow clouds. Quickly she let herself into the house with the key Rachel had given her, careful to make enough noise with the door to alert Rachel that she was there. "I'm back," she called out for good measure, unwrapping her scarf and shedding her coat.

There wasn't any sign of Rachel; eventually Yolanda found her upstairs in her bedroom, stretched out on the bed and looking rather done-in.

"Oh — you're back," Rachel said groggily.

Yolanda realised that she'd been gone far longer than she'd originally intended or indicated. "Sorry. Sorry it's taken me so long," she apologised. "Are you okay, lovie? Can I get you something?"

"I'd love a cup of tea." She struggled into a sitting position with some difficulty.

"I'll be back with it in a few minutes," Yolanda promised. "You don't need to get up."

To her relief, Rachel obeyed and didn't follow her to the kitchen. Automatically she filled the kettle and switched it on, glancing at the clock in the gathering gloom. Just gone three, and already it was dark enough in the kitchen to need the lights on. Yolanda had been in London for most of her life, but she had never truly become accustomed to the brutally short days of the British winter.

She could do with a cup of tea herself. Retrieving the teapot from the draining board, she popped a couple of bags in, then fetched the milk from the fridge.

224

Rachel liked her tea weak, so Yolanda poured a cup for her and left the rest in the pot to brew to her own taste. Carefully she carried the cup upstairs. "Here you are, lovie," she said, putting it on the bedside table.

"Thanks." Rachel smiled her gratitude.

Yolanda went back downstairs and poured herself a mug of tea. Hot and strong — just what she needed. She sipped it appreciatively as she drew the curtains, put on a few more lights, and puzzled over her course of action.

As a matter of urgency, she had to get her hands on something with Trevor's DNA. And as Neville Stewart had suggested, she had to do it without arousing Rachel's suspicions. That might not be easy: with Rachel in the bedroom, her access to the ensuite bathroom, the most likely place to find Trevor's toothbrush, was problematical. And would she even know which toothbrush was his?

The empty evidence bag was in her pocket; Sid Cowley was waiting for her call. She had to do something, and soon.

Alex didn't linger on her way home from school. Apart from the fact that it was too cold to hang about, she was in a hurry to get home. During maths, the last period of the day, instead of listening to the boring teacher she'd been plotting out what she could do to find her mum. It all depended, she decided, on her ability to sound like a grown-up on the phone.

She practised as she climbed the stairs to the flat, lowering the pitch of her voice and speaking in a considered way. "Good afternoon," she attempted, turning her key in the door. It didn't sound all that convincing, she decided, dropping her bag inside the door as usual, but she had to try.

"I'm home," she called in her normal voice, not as a greeting but by way of testing the waters to see if anyone was there.

No reply, thank goodness. That meant Jilly was out, and Alex would have the flat to herself.

She didn't bother with food today, grabbing the cordless phone, then going straight to her room and her computer. After typing in her password, she brought up the screen with the list of care facilities she'd compiled.

Start at the beginning, Alex told herself. She punched in the number for a residential care home in Jedburgh.

"Hellooo?" A woman answered after three rings, and what nearly derailed Alex from her purpose was the unexpected wave of nostalgia and longing at hearing the Scottish accent. She clutched the phone and swallowed.

"Hellooo?" repeated the woman.

Alex recovered herself and lowered her chin, which at least psychologically helped her to speak in a passably deep voice. "Good afternoon," she said. "Would it be possible to speak to one of your . . . um . . . residents?" Were they called residents, or patients? Alex wondered, adding, "Mrs. Harriet Hamilton."

"There's noo one of that name here," was the reply. "I'm sorry."

"Oh. Sorry to have bothered you."

Well, Alex told herself philosophically, she couldn't expect success on the very first try. At least the woman hadn't denounced her as an impostor. She went to the second number on the list.

Everything had changed for Neville. This case, which had from the beginning seemed to him like a cut-and-dried bore, was suddenly interesting. Turned on its head.

Not just a random opportunistic crime, then, but something cunningly planned and executed.

He sat at his desk for a long time after Yolanda left, just thinking through the possibilities before he talked to Sid about it, scribbling a few notes on a bit of paper as he brainstormed.

A murder. A real murder. Cold-blooded and calculated, though if he were right about the way it had happened, the choice of victim had an element of randomness involved. Someone not unlike Trevor in build and appearance; someone similar enough that Rachel's identification of the body wouldn't be questioned, but not a specific person.

It was strange; it was unlikely. It would have required cunning and more than a fair bit of luck.

Okay, thought Neville. Say Trevor killed some poor sod, shoved him in the canal, and then did a runner.

Who? he wrote.

That one word didn't just pose one question: it raised quite a few.

Not just the little matter of who the body belonged to, but a host of allied puzzles. For instance, if the body

227

wasn't Trevor's, but some other bloke's, then why had no one else been reported missing? Why hadn't some other worried wife or girlfriend been on the phone?

It would be worth checking that out, to make sure there weren't outstanding missing person reports at other stations.

And the CCTV footage would have to be looked at again. Looked at in a new light, with a different interpretation. Would it be possible for the wonks and computer geeks to enhance the images at all, to get a better look at the two men involved? It had just been assumed that the jogger was Trevor Norton; that hadn't been in question at that point. Might they be able to get a better look at him if they tried?

That sent Neville's thoughts down the path of Trevor's computer. Again, the data which had been retrieved from his machine had been taken at face value. Business stuff. Accounts, appointments. That's what the geeks had said. Nothing of a suspicious personal nature.

But what if that business stuff revealed some sort of financial trouble or some serious impropriety? If you looked at it a different way, would it tell them something new and unexpected? Something important?

Computer, Neville wrote, followed by *Telephone*.

Those mysterious calls to Rachel: the one Yolanda had just overheard, and the one she'd intercepted a few days ago. Whether they had been made to a land-line or a mobile, they should be traceable. It might take time to get the phone records, but eventually they ought to be able to track down the source of those calls.

Maybe he was barking up the wrong tree, Neville told himself. Perhaps this was the wild goose chase to end all wild goose chases.

Maybe. If so, though, it still gave him something to do, something to think about. A new direction to take. And that couldn't be bad, even if it led him nowhere in the end.

He pushed back from his desk and went to look for Sid Cowley.

It had been a couple of days since Alex had heard anything from Kirsty. That hadn't worried her too much, especially as she'd had other things to think about.

She had just crossed another possibility off her list when her computer pinged to notify her that she had incoming e-mail.

Jack, she thought with an odd flutter in her stomach. But it was a message from Kirsty, who had of late — since the escalation of her regrettable association with Ewan Fraser — adopted the strange all-caps style which had originated with text messaging and made teenagers' communication all but incomprehensible to anyone else.

JUST HAD 2 TEL U!!!!!! U KNOW THE XMAS DISCO?!?!!??? EWAN HAS ASKED ME 2 GO WITH HIM!!!!!!! OMG LOL. THIS IS SO 2TALY COOL!!!!!!! LOL

Alex had become fairly adept at translating, though she had vowed to herself that she wouldn't sink to that level in her own communication. She quickly grasped the fact that Kirsty was going to the school's Christmas disco with the objectionable Ewan. And that she was happy about it.

A year ago, things had been so different, Alex recalled. She and Kirsty had laughed together about the girls who tried so hard to get boys to notice them, and who set such stock in the Christmas disco. *They wouldn't be caught dead there*, they'd agreed. Least of all with Ewan Fraser, she added to herself, picturing him in her mind. Either she had been very wrong about him, or he had changed beyond recognition.

Or maybe Kirsty had gone blind, and hadn't bothered to tell her.

When Callie got home from her afternoon calls in the parish, rubbing her hands together to warm them, the flat was empty: no Peter, no Bella. He'd got off his backside at last and taken the dog for a walk, then, she concluded gratefully. She could use the time to work on her next sermon. First she made herself a warming cup of tea — the traditional way, with a guilty sideways glance at the shiny new machine — and carried it through to her study, turning the thermostat up a notch as she passed it.

But no sooner had she sat down at her computer and pulled up the file than the phone rang.

"Callie?" said her mother's voice, on a querulous note.

Oh, Lord. Mum. "Hello, Mum," she replied with as much cheerfulness as she could muster as she quickly calculated how long it had been since she'd talked to her mother. She and Peter had been to see her last Friday; she certainly hadn't rung her since then.

"I just wondered if everything was all right," Laura Anson said. "Since I hadn't heard anything from you."

Guilt, guilt, guilt. How did her mother do it?

"Oh, I'm fine." Callie's voice was unnaturally hearty; it was a tone she often adopted with her mother, as a defence mechanism against sounding too apologetic.

"I haven't heard anything from Peter, either," her mother went on. "And he's not answering his phone."

"Have you tried his mobile?" suggested Callie.

"You know I hate those things. And they're so expensive to ring. Have *you* talked to him?"

Now there was a loaded question, if ever there was one. "As a matter of fact, he's staying with me at the moment," Callie said neutrally.

"With *you*?"

"He's had a problem at the flat, and needed a place to stay for a few days."

"Oh," said her mother, investing that single syllable with a wealth of meaning.

Knowing her mother as she did, Callie picked one unspoken question at random and went with it. "I'm sure he didn't want to put you out. He comes and goes at odd hours, you know. The life of a musician . . ."

Her mother gave a loud, disapproving sniff. Peter's choice of career was a source of ongoing pain to her; she had wanted him to follow his father into the Civil

Service, and she never missed a chance to mention her disappointment. On the other hand, her way of dealing with Peter's homosexuality was to ignore it. She went on, "Well, I'm hoping that he'll be able to come round one evening next week. My friend Ida's daughter is home from university, and I think she'd suit Peter very well. She's a bit young for him, of course, but she's reading medicine, so she'll have a good, steady career. It's about time he settled down."

Callie had long since given up trying to point out the folly — and the utter futility — of trying to pair Peter up with eligible girls. "I'll tell him to ring you, shall I?" she suggested.

"He's not there, then?"

"Not at the moment. He's out with Bella."

"Bella?" Her mother asked sharply.

"My dog," Callie clarified.

"Oh. I'd forgotten you had a dog."

That reminded Callie that her mother had not yet been to visit her flat; she seemed always to have an excuse. "Listen, Mum," she said on impulse. "Why don't you come round here tomorrow? It's my day off. Peter will be here, and I could make lunch. You could meet Bella, and see where I live. I could even take you round the church."

"Oh, no," her mother said promptly. "That wouldn't be possible. I have a bridge afternoon tomorrow. It will have to be some other time."

Well, thought Callie, who had regretted her gesture as soon as the words were out of her mouth, at least that let her — and Peter — off the hook for tomorrow.

232

She wouldn't have to spend her precious day off trekking across town to Kensington for a tedious maternal visit. Maybe she could do some Christmas shopping instead: it wasn't that long till Christmas, and it was high time she got to grips with it. "Some other time," she echoed, hoping she didn't sound as relieved as she felt.

"Will you get that brother of yours to ring me? As soon as possible?"

"Yes, I'll tell him."

"Maybe you'd better not tell him why," Laura Anson said, adding petulantly, "He doesn't seem to appreciate all I do for him — how I put myself out to find the right girl for him. Since he doesn't seem capable of doing it for himself."

There wasn't really an adequate answer for that, reflected Callie. With impeccable timing, the doorbell rang. Not Peter: he had his own key. "There's someone at the door, Mum," she said. "I'd better go. Talk to you soon."

Yolanda needed Trevor's toothbrush, and she needed it as soon as possible. While she drank a second cup of tea she thought about how to obtain it, and in the end decided that the straightforward approach was the best one; after all, Rachel had no idea of her suspicions, and would have no reason to think that this was anything other than routine.

She went upstairs and tapped on the bedroom door, hoping that Rachel wasn't asleep.

"Come in," called Rachel, leaning over to slip something under the bed as Yolanda pushed the door open.

"Sorry to bother you again, lovie. But they tell me they need to do some more tests, and wondered whether they could have Trevor's toothbrush." She kept her voice matter-of-fact, brisk.

Rachel closed her eyes briefly, as if in pain, then replied with equal briskness, "Sure. Not a problem. Do you want me to get it for you?"

"No need for you to get up." Yolanda went through to the ensuite. "Just tell me what colour it is."

"It's the red one. With Homer on the handle."

With that description, it wasn't hard to find, stuck in the tooth mug next to a more sedate blue one. Carefully Yolanda slipped it into the evidence bag.

"This is the one?" She went back through and showed it to Rachel.

"Yes." Rachel grimaced. "I gave it to him last Christmas, as a joke. It's all worn out, but he won't . . . wouldn't . . . let me throw it out and get him a new one." The words ended on a stifled sob. "He loved that daft Homer Simpson toothbrush."

"Oh, poor lovie," Yolanda said impulsively. *It's an act*, she reminded herself. *Just an act.* But Rachel mustn't be allowed to suspect that she knew it. She pocketed the toothbrush, then came round the bed to hand Rachel a tissue.

"Thanks," sniffed Rachel, wiping tears from her face. "I'm just being silly. Over an old toothbrush. Sorry."

234

Mark had lost track of the time. It was dark; it was very cold. He had walked for a while in Gordon Square, then he'd got on a bus, though with no conscious destination in mind. The bus had taken him to Oxford Street, where he'd disembarked and spent some more time walking. The pavements were packed with Christmas shoppers laden with carrier bags, rushing past windows replete with tempting goodies and glitzy holiday displays. Mark pushed his way through the crowds, vaguely wondering why everyone put themselves through this each year. He was as guilty as the rest; he hadn't yet started thinking about buying Christmas gifts.

He turned off Oxford Street, away from the lights and the people. He kept walking; at some point he was remotely aware that the frosty black sky had begun to dispense a few desultory flakes of snow.

Eventually he realised he was in Bayswater. He had at no point made a conscious decision to go to Callie, but his feet were taking him there.

To Callie. He turned, then turned again, into the road that would bring him to her door. The snow was falling in a more determined way; his feet left a trail on the pavement.

Up the stairs to the flat. Ring the bell.

And then Callie was there, opening the door. "Marco! You're covered with snow! Where on earth have you been? You must be freezing."

Tongue-tied, he stood and looked at her. So normal, and just the same as she'd been before his world had turned itself upside down.

She drew him in, taking his icy hands between her warm ones. "Oh, Marco," she said.

Mark leaned over and kissed her lightly; her lips were as warm as her hands.

"You're so cold," she gasped. "I wish I had a fire going, but come over here by the radiator." She rubbed his numb hands briskly as she steered him along.

Still he hadn't spoken.

"You should have something hot to drink," Callie stated. "What would you like? Coffee? Tea?"

"Coffee. Black."

Callie flashed him a wry smile. "I can do that. Or I could do it any number of exotic ways, with my magical new machine." She released his hands. "You stay there and warm up. I'll be back in a minute."

And she was, with a steaming mug which she held out to him, then helped him wrap his fingers round.

The first sip was scalding, wonderful, going down his throat like fire. Mouth, throat, stomach — all felt better. Why hadn't he realised how cold he was? It hadn't even occurred to him that he was cold, until he'd been drawn into the warmth of the flat. Was that how people died of hypothermia?

"Now," she said when he'd had a few mouthfuls of the coffee. "Now tell me what's going on. Why have you turned up here, looking like the abominable snowman?" She reached up and brushed a shower of now-melted droplets from his hair.

Till that moment, he hadn't been sure he wanted to tell her. Now he was more than sure: but where to begin?

236

Just then the door flew open. A black and white dog — currently more white than black — tumbled in, followed by Peter. "God, Callie," he said, as both he and Bella shook themselves, dislodging a flurry of flakes. "Did you know it's snowing out there? Like the clappers! Bella's gone mad." He stopped, looking at the two of them, then made an apologetic face. "Oops. I haven't interrupted anything, have I?"

CHAPTER
TWELVE

It was almost inevitable: that night Rachel went into labour. This time there was no doubt about it, especially for one as experienced as Yolanda in these matters.

Yolanda was sleeping — more soundly than she would have expected — when Rachel cried out from the room next door. She woke instantly, tuned in to such sounds and knowing instinctively what they meant.

In a few seconds she was at Rachel's side. Rachel was struggling to get out of bed, and there was no pretence now in the emotion she conveyed. "I think . . . I think my water's broken," she gasped. "And . . . ooooh." She doubled up in agony.

"It's okay, lovie." Yolanda put an arm round her shoulders.

After a long moment of struggling through the contraction, Rachel went limp, her face sheened with sweat. "It's really happening, isn't it?" she whispered, gripping Yolanda's hand. "I'm having the baby."

There was no point beating about the bush or denying the obvious. "Yes, it looks like it. But I'm here, and it's going to be all right."

★ ★ ★

238

Almost always, Neville's preferred tipple was Guinness; it was only when he was suffering from a particularly severe bout of Celtic melancholy that he drank Irish whiskey.

Tonight was one of those nights. Unable to sleep, he had left his bed, fetched a bottle and glass, and taken up a seat by the window, where he could watch the snow drifting down in fat, silent flakes. There was something hypnotic about the inexorable snow, just as there was something anaesthetic to be found in the bottle, the glass. Once upon a time there would have been cigarettes as well, but it had now been several years since he'd quit; never had he regretted that decision more. If he'd had a packet of fags in the flat, he would have lit one up.

Neville knew that he should be feeling elated. Things were happening; the case was on the verge of a major breakthrough. They had Trevor's toothbrush, and the lab would be pulling out all the stops to work on a DNA match.

He had no reason to be depressed. But depressed he was: profoundly depressed, doubting himself and his own abilities.

Yes, the murder of the jogger — whoever he might have been — was nearly wrapped up. But not through Neville's skills, superior instincts, or even his hard work. Most of it had been blind luck, and any good police work that came into it had been achieved by Yolanda, not by him.

Was he past it? Had he been at this game too long?

Inspector Neville Stewart. Where did he go from here? The rank of Chief Inspector had virtually been eliminated, and he'd certainly never make Superintendent. He wasn't enough of a brown-noser, not willing to suck up to the right people just for the sake of career advancement. He'd made it to Inspector on merit and hard work but those qualities would take him no further.

Was it time to chuck the whole thing in? Do something completely different? Sell insurance, perhaps, or get himself some qualifications to repair cars or fix computers?

He'd always wanted to be a policeman; he'd never even imagined himself doing anything else. Maybe it was time to start thinking about it.

He poured himself another finger of whiskey and watched the snow. The snow reminded him that it was winter, nearly Christmas, and the year was almost over — and that reminded him that next year he would turn forty. Forty! Once that had seemed impossibly old, the end of any sort of real life.

Forty. Christ Almighty. Over the hill. Past it.

At the bottom of his melancholy, of course, was the inescapable thought of Triona. He'd been trying to not to think of her. Trying for days, for weeks. Telling himself that he didn't need her in his life. Didn't need the aggro, the complications.

Neville took a sip of his whiskey, then a gulp to drain the glass, then slammed the glass down on the table beside the bottle. Damn it, Willow had been right. He *did* need Triona. Bloody hell — he *loved* her. There. He'd admitted it to himself.

"You'll never be happy without her," Willow had said. And he wasn't. He was miserable.

Blindly he reached for the telephone, but stopped himself before he punched in her number. It was the middle of the night, for God's sake. Triona wouldn't thank him for ringing her now.

But if he waited till morning, till he was sober, he might change his mind.

Neville got up and went to his computer. He used it rarely, not being much of a one for e-mail; if anything, he mostly kept it around because the odd game of solitaire sometimes relaxed him when work schedules meant that recourse to the bottle wasn't an option.

He called up his e-mail program: no messages. Thank God for that. Opening a new message, he typed with two efficient fingers. "Hi Triona, I need to talk to you. I think we should talk. Give me a ring and maybe we can get together. N."

That should do. It wasn't committing him to anything irrevocable. He hesitated for only a second before hitting the "send" icon.

Unusually for a first baby, this one showed signs of making an appearance fairly quickly. Timing the contractions, Yolanda judged that they shouldn't wait too long before going to the hospital. She rang for a taxi and started putting together a few things in a holdall.

"There's no one you want me to call? A friend or relative?" The question was perfunctory; she knew what the answer would be, but she watched Rachel's face as she shook her head.

"No one. But you'll come with me?"

"Yes, of course I will."

"And you'll stay with me?" gulped Rachel. "When . . . when it happens? You won't leave me?"

"If that's what you want."

"Yes. Yes, I do. Very much."

In spite of herself, Yolanda was touched. She told herself that she needed to maintain some professional objectivity — both as a midwife and a police officer — but she was finding it difficult. In spite of everything, in spite of the lies and the deception and the overheard hurtful words, she cared about Rachel Norton. Whatever Rachel had done — and they didn't yet know exactly what that was — it had been for love. What woman hadn't done foolish things in the name of love?

Rachel clung to her in the taxi, as it inched through the still-falling snow, and during the admissions procedure at the hospital. And when, before too long, Rachel went into the delivery room, Yolanda was at her side, holding her hand.

Jane Stanford left an oblivious Brian asleep in bed and crept to her favourite window on the landing, where in the dim orange glow of the street lamp she watched the snow's silent descent. Already it blanketed everything in sight: grass, trees, pavement, road, parked cars and church alike. No cars were on the move at this hour, spoiling the snow's perfection with tire marks. It was truly a winter wonderland, almost magical in its silent whiteness.

But Jane wasn't thinking about the snow. Nor was she thinking about the subject which had obsessed her for the last several days: her desire for a baby, and Brian's strange inability to understand why this was so important to her. She hadn't yet managed to convince him that it was a good idea, to make him see that their out-of-the-blue legacy was God's answer to her prayers. No: in his more sensible moments Brian was still rather favouring a down-payment on a cottage near Brighton or Hove or Eastbourne, when his fancies didn't tempt him to splash out on a cruise or a posh sports car.

Instead, Jane was thinking about the unexpected events of the evening. Reverting to childhood, Charlie had dashed out into the snow and gleefully attempted to build a snowman. But Simon had looked at the snow and shaken his head with a worried frown.

"It's not going to be very good for travelling if this keeps up," he'd said.

"Travelling? But we're not going anywhere," countered Jane.

"Ellie and I are. Tomorrow. I'm sure we told you, Mum."

Then he'd broken the news, as if she must already have known. As if it wouldn't make any difference to her, one way or the other.

He and Ellie were leaving in the morning, to go to her parents'. The Dickinsons lived in a village in Northamptonshire, and would meet Simon and Ellie off the train at Kettering. They'd be there through

Christmas, and would come back to London for the New Year.

Casually, just like that. Simon would not be at home for Christmas. For the first time in his life, he wouldn't be at home with the family.

Christmas wouldn't be the same. Not this year, and not ever again. Jane knew it with a certainty which alarmed and distressed her. Sick at heart, she wrapped her arms round her body, leaned her forehead against the cold windowpane, and watched the snow falling.

It took Frances a bit longer than usual to get to the hospital that morning, with the snow and the resultant traffic chaos. She went to her office first, to shed her coat and check her telephone voice mail and her computer for messages.

Nothing urgent, thank goodness. And no post of any importance, either. She was about to lock her handbag away and start off on her rounds when there was a tentative tap on her office door.

"Come in?" Frances looked up to see Triona pushing the door open. "Oh! I wasn't expecting you," she said, adding quickly, "Not that I'm not delighted to see you."

Triona gave a self-deprecating grimace. "I hope I'm not bothering you."

"Not at all."

"Mind if I take my coat off?"

"Be my guest." Frances gestured to the coat stand where she'd hung her own outerwear.

Triona complied. "Sorry to drop in on you like this. I tried to send you an e-mail to warn you, but my computer's totally buggered up at the moment. I think it must have a virus." She made a face. "I hate technology anyway."

Still unclear whether there was a particular reason for the visit, Frances pointed to a chair. "Did you want to sit down? Can I get you a coffee or something?"

"No time for that. Didn't I say?" Triona glanced at her watch. "I have an appointment for a scan. Ultrasound. I've been to see my GP, and she thought it was a good idea to have one early on. Since I'm over thirty — ancient, you know. I just wondered whether you'd be free to come with me — to hold my hand and all that."

Whatever else Frances had to do, it could wait. "Yes, of course," she said immediately, gratified to be asked.

Neville struggled in to work, a bit the worse for the late-night whiskey and cursing the snow. But he didn't have the leisure to sit at his desk and drink black coffee: things started happening almost immediately.

First was the call from the lab, where they'd been working through the night. "Just wanted to confirm the DNA results for you," said the technician. "It's a match."

"A match?" Startled, Neville almost dropped his coffee cup. This wasn't at all what he'd expected to hear. "Are you trying to tell me that our dead bloke *is* Trevor Norton?"

"I'm telling you," said the patient voice, "that the toothbrush belonged to the man in the mortuary. It's a definite match. 99.9 percent definite."

So it *was* Trevor Norton. Putting the phone down with a belated word of thanks, Neville rearranged his thinking. The dead bloke was Trevor Norton. Unless Rachel had given them the wrong toothbrush, and that seemed way too fantastical to believe. Especially if you went with the theory that Trevor had murdered a random stranger. How would they have got hold of his toothbrush?

So Trevor was dead, and they were back to square one. Yolanda's speculations were nothing more than that, with no basis in fact.

Trevor Norton was dead. Yet what about Rachel and that phone call?

Neville needed to talk to Sid Cowley. But a quick look round indicated that Sid wasn't in yet. After a few minutes, Neville reached him on his mobile. "I'm stuck in traffic," Cowley groaned. "Some wanker's gone and blocked the intersection. Skidded halfway across, and now nothing's moving."

"Well, get here as soon as you can." Then Neville tried reaching Yolanda, first on her mobile — which a tinny voice informed him was not available — and then at Rachel's house. No luck.

Where the hell was she, and why had she switched off her phone at such a critical time?

Rachel's delivery, though the birth was more than a week early, was quite straightforward. Yolanda, who had attended hundreds of births, coached her through it expertly, careful not to step on the attending doctor's toes.

Just after ten in the morning she laid a tiny but healthy baby in Rachel's arms. "It's a girl," she said. "A beautiful girl."

"Trevor was so sure it was a boy." Rachel sounded on the edge of tears.

"What do men know?" The cynical words were out before Yolanda had a chance to consider their possible impact, but Rachel didn't seem to notice.

"So much hair," Rachel murmured.

Yolanda had already taken note of it: a head of copious black hair. Jet black, raven's wing black.

Mark usually preferred taking a bus to work; this morning, in view of the traffic problems above ground, he decided to go for the Tube instead.

He wasn't the only one to make that decision: habitual drivers, cyclists, bus-riders and even walkers poured down the escalators and crammed themselves into already-full carriages.

Cheek by jowl with far too much humanity, hanging onto a few inches of a metal pole, Mark let his thoughts wander back to the pathways they'd been following, back to the day before.

Peter's untimely entrance had prevented him from telling Callie what had happened; he was still carrying the burden of Serena's pain and his own anger, unrevealed and unshared.

The revelation of Joe's infidelity triggered feelings in Mark that he'd been managing to keep submerged for weeks: conflicts and uncertainty about that wonderful and terrible entity, *la famiglia* Lombardi, about his place in it and his responsibility for maintaining its equilibrium. Why did he feel that the onus was on him not to rock the boat? Why did he think that if he acknowledged to them — to himself — how important Callie had become to him, the world would come crashing down round all their ears?

There was something he needed to do. Something he should have done many weeks ago. He'd put it off far too long, and now he resolved to put it off no longer, whatever the consequences. Today. It would happen today.

Once Rachel was settled on the maternity ward, Yolanda excused herself to look for a telephone. "I need to let them know where I am," she explained to Rachel.

Exhausted but radiant in the glow of motherhood, Rachel only nodded.

Unlike most of mobile phone-dominated London, where pay phones were an endangered species, the hospital, as a mobile-free zone, was well equipped with pay phones.

Well equipped, Yolanda told herself, except when you were in a hurry. Not surprisingly, the phones near the maternity ward were in great demand. She got into a queue behind several young men and one new granny.

The men, proud and voluble new fathers, were bad enough, but the granny was the worst. She made three calls, one after the other; Yolanda was right behind her and able to hear every word. The phone calls were roughly the same: detailed descriptions of the labour, followed by rapturous paeans of praise to the baby, surely the most wonderful baby ever born. Finally there was speculation on the baby's name. "Sal wants Benjamin, but she says Nige won't have it. Says it sounds too much like a poncy git, does Nige. Nige is sure he's gonna be a footballer, in't he? Says he may as well be called Wayne. He's got a little football jersey for him, to take him home from hospital in, has Nige. Cutest thing you ever seen."

In other circumstances Yolanda might have found it mildly amusing, even after the second repetition, but impatience was getting the better of her. "Come *on*," she muttered under her breath, looking at her watch. They *were* going to be wondering what had happened to her.

At long last the gran finished her final recitation of the name dilemma and flounced off without a backwards glance. Yolanda lunged for the phone and rang Neville Stewart's number.

"Where the hell are you? And where have you been?" he demanded. "I've been trying to reach you all morning. You're not at the Nortons' and your mobile's switched off!"

"Yes. I know. Sorry."

"Where are you?" Neville repeated.

"Hospital," she said tersely. "Rachel's just had the baby."

"Oh." There was silence on the other end of the phone as he digested this information.

"It's a girl, in case you're interested. Small but healthy. Mother and baby are doing well."

"Never mind about that. You need to get here to the station. Right away. There are some things you need to know about. The DNA and all that. We have to decide where we're going from here."

"I was wrong about Trevor being alive, wasn't I?" she guessed.

"You sure were. A million miles off."

"Then . . . well, never mind. But I don't really feel comfortable leaving Rachel here on her own," Yolanda said. "Not even now. Especially not now."

Neville laughed. "I don't suppose she's going anywhere for a while, but don't leave her alone. Find someone who can sit with her and keep an eye on her until . . . well, we'll have to talk about that."

"Like who? Can't you send an officer?" Yolanda suggested. "A PC?"

"I don't think that's necessary," he said. "Find a nurse. A chaplain. Tell them it's important. And it shouldn't be for long."

More easily said than done, Yolanda reflected as she hung up the phone, glancing over her shoulder at the impatient young man who was next in the queue. Everyone in this hospital had a job to do. Did Neville Stewart seriously think there were nurses hanging about, waiting to be called upon to do the police's job for them?

Then, like an answer to an unspoken prayer, she spotted a woman in a dog collar, walking down the corridor.

Two minutes later she was back at Rachel's bedside. "Rachel, lovie, I need to . . . be away for a little while."

Rachel turned her head and smiled dreamily. "That's all right. I'll be fine."

"This is Frances." Yolanda introduced the woman who followed behind her. "She's a chaplain. Frances is going to stay with you while I'm away."

"But I'm not religious."

"It doesn't matter. She's just going to . . . keep you company. You don't have to talk to her or anything."

Rachel shrugged, too tired to argue.

Mark waited till late morning to ring Callie; it was, he knew, her day off, and perhaps she was having a lie-in. But it was Peter who answered.

"She's not here," Peter announced. "She's gone off to do some Christmas shopping. Left me to look after the dog," he added plaintively. "I had to take her out in the snow."

"The snow didn't put Callie off?"

"It's stopped coming down now, and it's melting already. She shouldn't have any trouble — traffic seems to be moving pretty well, and the buses are running. Try her on her mobile," suggested Peter.

Mark followed that advice, and reached Callie on the third ring.

"I'm in Oxford Street," Callie confirmed. "It's actually a good time to be shopping. The snow has kept quite a few people away."

"About tonight," said Mark, then stopped to take a deep breath.

"If you can't make it, don't worry."

"That's not it." He'd made his mind up; now he may as well get on with it. "I wondered whether you'd . . . come out to dinner with me."

"Of course, Marco, if that's what you'd like to do."

"I want to take you to La Venezia."

Now there was a pause on Callie's end of the phone. "Okay."

"But first we need to talk," he went on. "There are some things I need to explain to you before we go there. So if we meet up for a drink beforehand?"

"Yes, that's fine. I take it," Callie added wryly, "that Peter isn't included in this invitation?"

Mark laughed. "You've got it in one."

Frances pulled a chair up beside Rachel's bed. She wasn't at all sure what she was doing here: the black woman who'd identified herself as a police officer had given her an explanation which was sketchy at best, but her urgency had been evident. "It's very important that she shouldn't be left alone," she'd said. "I hope I won't be away very long. If it looks like I can't get back right away, I'll send a PC to take over from you."

It appeared to Frances as though Rachel was on the verge of sleep. "You don't have to talk or anything," she said. "I'll just sit here."

Rachel nodded drowsily and almost immediately drifted off. A few minutes later, a nurse brought a tiny dark-haired baby to the bed and roused Rachel. "Time for a feed, dear," she announced. "Baby's hungry."

Taking the baby from the nurse, Rachel's ineptitude was evident. "First time, is it, dear?" clucked the nurse.

252

"Never mind. I'll give you a bit of help and show you what to do. It's as easy as falling off a log, really. Nothing to it. Baby knows what to do, you'll see."

She kept up the encouraging chatter through the feeding session. Frances wondered whether she ought to withdraw, out of delicacy, but recalled the injunction of the woman Yolanda Fish not to leave Rachel, even for a moment.

"Would you like to keep baby with you for a bit, dear?" asked the nurse, when the feed was accomplished to her satisfaction. "You don't have to, mind. I can take her away if you'd prefer to have a sleep."

"Oh, yes, please. I'd love to keep her." Rachel tightened her arms round the baby.

"Well, then. Let's get her settled." The nurse made sure that Rachel was decently covered, then arranged the baby in the crook of her arm. "Perhaps baby's daddy will be visiting later?" she suggested coyly, with a wink in Frances' direction.

Rachel bit her lip. "I don't think so."

"Oh, well. Never mind. I'll fetch her presently."

Once the nurse had gone, Frances leaned over and inspected the baby. "She's beautiful, isn't she?"

"The most beautiful thing I've ever seen." Rachel's voice was soft, almost indistinct with emotion. "I never imagined . . . well, I just couldn't imagine her at all. Not as a real person or anything. But she's . . ." Choking on tears, she stroked the baby's cheek with one tender, tentative finger.

"I know exactly what you mean," said Frances. "It was the same with my daughter. You carry a baby for nine months, and you think you're ready, but nothing prepares you for what it feels like to hold her in your arms."

Rachel twisted her head and looked at Frances, as if she were seeing her for the first time. "You have a daughter?"

"Yes, just the one. Heather, she's called. She's nearly twenty-five now — I can't believe it. Seems like just last week that I was holding her like that."

Rachel's eyes travelled to Frances' dog collar. "Are you really a priest?"

That, thought Frances, was a loaded question in some quarters: there were any number of traditionalist male priests who didn't believe that her ordination was lawful or valid. But this young woman, of course, wasn't interested in the ontological or theological niceties. She smiled wryly and gave a simple answer. "Yes, I am."

"Can I talk to you? As . . . a priest, I mean?"

"Yes, of course." Frances nodded.

Now Rachel looked away, almost shyly, and whispered her next question. "Is it true that you won't . . . can't . . . tell anyone else what I say to you?"

"Anything you tell me is just between us." And God, Frances added to herself.

"I'm not religious," Rachel repeated, as if she'd heard the unspoken words. "I don't go to church or anything."

"That doesn't matter. I'm here for anyone who needs me," Frances assured her.

Rachel was silent for a moment, bending her face over her baby's downy dark head; tears dropped from her eyes onto the baby's cheek. When she finally spoke, her voice was almost non-existent, a thready whisper. "I've done something terrible. Something really, really terrible."

CHAPTER
THIRTEEN

The three girls stood behind Alex in the food queue and spoke in deliberately loud voices, so she couldn't fail to hear every word.

"Sad, isn't it?" said Beatrice, Alex's step-cousin. "She's flat-chested enough to be a boy."

"Maybe she *is* a boy," Georgina contributed.

"That would explain a lot," said Beatrice's best friend, Sophie.

"Yeah, like why she doesn't have a boyfriend. Although she's so ugly that no boy would look at her twice. Not unless she put a bag over her head," added Beatrice. "And then there's that brace on her teeth. Who would want to snog a mouth full of metal like that?"

Georgina and Sophie giggled hysterically as Alex spun round to confront them. She'd tried to ignore them; she'd told herself that it wasn't worth it to rise to their bait. But she'd had enough.

"Are you talking about *me*?" she demanded furiously.

Beatrice folded her arms across her own rather well-endowed chest. "I don't see any other ugly, flat-chested girls around here. So if the shoe fits . . ."

Alex wasn't sure whether to punch her or to cry. She resisted the impulse to do either. "As a matter of fact," she said coldly, "I do too have a boyfriend."

"In Scotland, I suppose," Beatrice sneered. "Very convenient. What's he called, then? Nessie?"

"Her boyfriend's the Loch Ness Monster!" Georgina taunted.

"He's called Jack! And he lives in London!" Without stopping to ask herself whether it was wise, Alex reached for the chain round her neck and pulled the locket out from under her uniform. "Here's his photo!" she announced, opening the locket.

Beatrice leaned over and scrutinised the tiny photo. "That's what you say. You probably cut it out of a magazine or something."

"I did not!"

"Let me see," Georgina demanded, grabbing for the locket. "Who's this other photo, then? Is that you?"

"It's my mother. When she was my age."

Alex's tone of voice should have warned them to go no further, but they were oblivious.

"Oh, your ugly mother. She's just as ugly as you. No wonder your dad left her." Georgina tugged at the locket chain; it was old and delicate, and it snapped, leaving the locket in her hand.

"Give me that!" Alex grabbed for it, but Georgina was quicker.

She closed her fist round it tightly and held it above her head. Although she was a year younger than Alex, she was taller and had longer arms. "Make me!"

"It's mine! It's mine!" There was a weight in Alex's chest; she almost had to struggle to breathe. Her most treasured possession in all the world, clutched just out of reach in the hand of that unspeakably awful girl . . . She sobbed in frustration and anger. "Give it to me!"

"Oh, she's a cry-baby," mocked Sophie. "Honestly, Beatrice. I'd never admit that that loser was related to me."

"She's *not* related to me," Beatrice retorted, turning on her friend. "Just because my Aunt Jilly was stupid enough to marry her father, that doesn't make her any relation of *mine*."

Alex grabbed a hank of Georgina's long blonde hair and, in her fury, pulled hard. "Give me my locket!"

Georgina screamed. Loudly. Heads turned, and an instant later one of the teachers was beside them. "What on earth is going on here?" she demanded.

Neville sat at his desk while Yolanda paced back and forth.

"So," said Yolanda. "Trevor Norton is really dead."

"As a doornail," Neville confirmed. "It's definitely his body in the mortuary. A DNA match."

"And Rachel . . ."

"She's playing at something. We know that. But we don't know what." Neville shook his head. "And it may not have anything at all to do with his murder. At the end of the day, Yolanda, we may find out that he *was* killed by a yob. For his iPod. Full stop, end of story. Just like Sid always said."

If only, thought Yolanda, it were that cut and dried. Yet there was something about that scenario that just didn't feel right to her.

"So where do we go from here?"

"I'm not sure where *I'm* going from here," said Neville. "Back to square one, I suppose. But I know where you're going. Home."

She stopped pacing. "Home? You must be joking."

"Listen to me, Yolanda." Neville's voice was firm as he enumerated his points on his fingers. "You're a Family Liaison Officer, not a detective. You've worked bloody hard for the past week. Rachel Norton is in hospital — she's not going anywhere for a day or two. There's nothing for you to do at the moment. So just go home."

"Well," Yolanda admitted with some reluctance, "they're not likely to release her before the end of the weekend, especially with the baby being that bit early."

"My point exactly." Neville smirked at her. "Go home, Yolanda. Shag your husband, sleep in your own bed. And don't come back until Monday. That," he added, "is an order."

Alex sat in the Headmistress' office, her heart pounding painfully. She'd never been in trouble before. She'd never fitted in at this dreadful posh school, but she'd been careful not to draw attention to herself in such a way as to warrant the personal notice of the Headmistress.

She made an effort to relax, leaning back in the hard chair, feigning nonchalance. The Headmistress was talking; Alex was listening only intermittently. "Disgraceful behaviour," she heard. ". . . common street children."

The Headmistress leaned over her desk, opened a file, and consulted it for a moment. "Your father will be very disappointed in you," she said, glaring at Alex over the tops of her half-moon glasses. "Now, do you have anything to say for yourself, young lady?"

Alex could guess what was expected of her. "I'm sorry," she said docilely, but it was only a preliminary, so she could get on to the next — the important — bit. "And could I please have my locket back? That . . . Georgina. She still has it. I want it back."

Frances had been the recipient of a good many hospital-bed revelations over the years, but she found Rachel's one of the strangest she'd ever heard — and one of the most moving.

In a voice that was at times little more than a whisper, emotional but not hysterical, Rachel recounted the story of a marriage gone sour almost as soon as it had begun, a rekindled romance, and the almost inevitable tragedy when it became impossible to hold the two things together.

Things had been fine for the first few years, as long as Rachel and Trevor were just living together. He'd been a bit controlling, a bit jealous of her friendships with her workmates. When they were married, though, it got much worse: he didn't want her spending any time with anyone but him. Then he'd bought the house in

Paddington and started his own business, and effectively cut them off from anyone else and from their old life.

Rachel had chafed a bit, but she was a fairly docile — even passive — soul, and it wasn't part of her nature to confront him openly.

Then one day she'd been playing round on her laptop, surfing the internet, and had stumbled across findagain.co.uk.

She'd registered for the service, but the first approach had come from the other side: from a young man who had, for a brief period, been her boyfriend at school. Their relationship had been doomed from the start, that first time. Abdul Mahmoud was the child of first-generation Pakistani immigrants, and his parents had been even more opposed to the romance than hers. Her parents hadn't much liked the colour of his skin; his, as devout Muslims, had considered her an infidel. They were both very young and had allowed themselves to be parted.

But Rachel had never quite forgotten Abdul, cherishing a flickering memory of sweet, stolen kisses in deserted school corridors and a few furtive dates, tentative fumblings in the back row of the cinema. When Trevor was being particularly difficult she would sometimes allow herself to remember Abdul, would dare to imagine how it might have been if they'd defied their parents and built a life together.

When he'd contacted her by e-mail, she'd been elated — and terrified. Elated at the thought of seeing

Abdul again, yet terrified that Trevor would find out, terrified that things would get out of control.

Trevor hadn't found out. But after a few weeks of e-mails — dozens a day, in both directions — Rachel and Abdul had met up again, and things had indeed got very much out of control.

She and Trevor had been trying for a baby. It was one reason they'd got married: Trevor had badly wanted a child, and had wanted to make her his wife before that happened.

When she found out she was pregnant, though, she was not at all sure whose baby it was.

In other circumstances it might not have mattered; she might have got away with it. But she and Trevor were both fair, and Abdul was not. Rachel knew enough about genetics from her GCSE biology course to know that if Abdul was the father, the baby would not have the blonde hair that Trevor was expecting.

The more she thought about it, the more frightened Rachel became. As soon as the baby was born, Trevor would know. And Trevor would kill her.

She'd had no doubt that he would. He loved her so utterly, so possessively; he was so sure of her. Presented with irrefutable evidence of another man in her life, he would kill her.

And more than that: he might harm her baby. Her childhood history of parental abuse, so long pushed into the back of her mind, resurfaced. She spoke to Frances of her controlling, abusive father — the man, ironically, she had fled into Trevor's arms to escape.

History threatened to repeat itself; Trevor had become her father, and her baby's safety was at risk.

So, as the birth drew inevitably nearer, their actions were born out of desperation.

The plans had been carefully laid, over several weeks.

Trevor was a creature of habit; that was one thing in their favour. He went out running at the same time every day, summer or winter, rain or shine. He followed the same path along the canal. So all Abdul had to do was to wait for him in a secluded spot — a spot not overlooked by CCTV cameras.

There were several abortive attempts, when their plans had been foiled by an inconvenient passer-by. Eventually, though, the circumstances were perfect: a day of foul weather, of heavy and persistent rain, discouraging all but the most fanatical jogger.

In the end it had all been absurdly easy. The unexpected blow to the head, the shove into the canal. Taking the iPod had been Abdul's idea, on the spur of the moment. He reasoned — correctly, as it happened — that the theft would obscure the true motivation for the murder.

Rachel made no excuses for her behaviour, and took full responsibility for it; that in itself was unusual in Frances' experience, and she found herself respecting Rachel for it. During her long hospital chaplaincy, Frances had discovered that, even in extremity, most people found someone else to blame for their misdeeds and their failures. "I wouldn't have done it if my husband hadn't . . ." or "If only my wife had given me more encouragement, I could have . . ." or "My children always kept me from . . ."

"It was a terrible thing to do," she said. "But I had to do it. For myself, for my baby. It was my idea to kill him. I was so scared about what would happen when he found out, and I couldn't think of any other way out of it. Abdul may have been the one who killed him, but we planned it together all the way. I'm as guilty as he is."

When she finished, Rachel was quiet for a moment. Frances, too, was silent; she felt that the soothing noises which she usually made at such moments would be not only inadequate but inappropriate in these circumstances. Eventually Rachel struggled into a sitting position, reached to the bedside table for a fresh tissue, and dabbed at her eyes. Then she spoke with determination. "I want you to ring him for me. Now," she said.

"Abdul, you mean?"

"He needs to see his daughter. He needs to be here with me."

"The police," said Frances, remembering the urgency with which Yolanda Fish had recruited her to sit with Rachel. "Do they suspect? Do they know?"

Rachel shook her head. "They don't know. Maybe they suspect. I think they might. But you can't tell them. You promised you wouldn't. You promised you wouldn't tell *anyone*."

"No," said Frances. "I won't."

"You have to ring Abdul. I love him," stated Rachel. "He loves me. We've done something very bad because of that. But we still have each other, and our daughter, and we need to . . . to be together, whatever happens."

So in spite of her promise to Yolanda that she wouldn't leave Rachel alone for even a moment, she wrote the number on a slip of paper and went to join the queue for the pay phones.

Alex took her time going home from school. The snow had mostly melted into a dirty slush; Alex dawdled along, looking for shady spots where the snow remained, kicking at it with her good school shoes, not caring whether she ruined them or not.

The Headmistress had tried to ring her father at work, but he'd been in a meeting. That was one good thing. He would have been so cross — not just disappointed in her for fighting at school, but annoyed to be interrupted at his precious job. Alex knew better than to do that ever; even dumb Jilly knew better and wouldn't dare bother him when he was working. Alex had tried to tell the Headmistress, but she hadn't listened. She'd just gone ahead and tried to ring him.

At least she hadn't rung Jilly. Not that Jilly would care. Not that Alex cared whether Jilly cared or not. "Jilly, Jilly, very silly," she chanted under her breath, kicking over a diminutive snowman that someone had created in a front garden. Then she tried a new version: "Silly Jilly, very frilly."

That kept her going all the way to the door of the flat. She unlocked it, dumped her rucksack, shed her coat, and headed towards the kitchen in search of food; the incident in the school dinner queue meant that she'd missed out entirely on anything to eat, and her stomach was beginning to remind her of the fact.

265

She needed more than a banana or a packet of crisps; maybe there was a ready meal in the fridge that wasn't too gross. Alex pulled open the stainless steel door and rummaged till she found some macaroni cheese, then took it to the microwave and bunged it in.

"Just what do you think you're playing at?" said a furious voice behind her; Alex spun round, her heart thudding, to confront a frowning Jilly.

That, Alex knew, meant that it was serious. Alex frowned often, or at least whenever she felt like it, and so did her dad, but Jilly didn't believe in frowning; it caused wrinkles, she frequently reminded them.

Alex looked down at her wet shoes, and then at the trail of damp footprints she'd left across the kitchen. Jilly wouldn't like that at all. Well, too bad, she thought defiantly.

Jilly, though, had more important things on her mind. It transpired that she had been out shopping with her sister Melanie when the call from the Headmistress had come through on Melanie's mobile. Melanie's two daughters had been involved in a scuffle, and with none other than Alex. "Fighting at school," she said with a moue of distaste. "How . . . common. And how dare you pick on your own cousins? It's outrageous!"

"They're not my cousins," Alex pointed out furiously. "They're no relation to me, thank goodness. And I didn't pick on them! They started it."

"I very much doubt that," Jilly stated. "They're . . . young ladies. They've been brought up properly. They know how to behave. *They* didn't grow up running wild."

"And I did? Is that what you're saying?"

"Your mother, too busy with that shop of hers to look after her own family! Neglecting her husband and child, leaving you to be raised by that mad old woman!"

Alex's eyes widened with shock; she felt as if she'd been socked in the stomach, as if all the air had suddenly been sucked out of the room. Was that what Jilly really believed? Is that what Dad had told her?

She drew in a lungful of air. "My mother did not neglect me!" she shouted. "How could you say that? And my Granny is not mad!"

Jilly folded her arms across her chest and went on, ignoring Alex's outburst. "And as for that nonsense you told the girls about you having a boyfriend — well, it's just ridiculous. Don't you know better than to tell lies?"

"I don't tell lies," Alex snarled through gritted teeth.

"Oh, come on. Look at you! A boyfriend? Don't make me laugh." With a flick of her head, Jilly tossed her artfully coiffed blonde hair.

Once upon a time, not long after her father had married Jilly, Alex had made a deliberate promise to herself not to be drawn into any fights, verbal or otherwise, with her new stepmother. Up till now she'd managed to keep that promise by detaching herself mentally and emotionally, by reminding herself that Jilly wasn't very bright and it would be an unequal battle in any case.

Never had she been so badly tempted to ignore the little voice in her head which reminded her that it was time to walk away. She wanted to scream at Jilly. She wanted to hurt her, with words and with the sort of thing that even stupid Jilly would understand: to pull her perfect blonde hair, to dig fingernails into her perfect pink skin.

With a huge effort of will and a deep breath, Alex clamped her mouth shut, balled her hands into fists at her side, turned her back on Jilly, and headed for her bedroom.

"Where do you think you're going?" Jilly demanded to her retreating back. "I want to know about this locket that started all the fuss. Why haven't I ever seen a locket?"

Alex ignored her. She reached the door of her room, marched in and slammed the door behind her. Unfortunately there was no lock, so she dragged the chair from her desk up to the door and jammed the back of it under the knob. Just in case.

The chain of her locket was broken; it would have to be mended or replaced. For now she had it tucked safe in the breast pocket of her blazer. She sat down on the edge of the bed and touched it where it nestled against her heart, caressing it through the fabric. She would *not* show it to Jilly. Never in a million years. Not even to her father. It was hers; it was private. Her biggest mistake today had been to show it to those horrible girls.

Her mother. Her dear, beautiful, funny, wonderful mother. And Jack. With a quick glance at the door to make sure that Jilly was making no attempt to breach its defences Alex reached into her pocket, pulled the locket out, and opened it. Mum. And Jack.

She kissed the photos, one after the other, snapped the locket shut and tucked it under her pillow.

After a moment she crossed to her desk. As the chair was otherwise employed, she knelt down on the floor in front of her computer and touched the keyboard. The computer asked for her password; she typed it in, then went straight to her mail program.

There was only one new e-mail, and it was from Jack. "Get 2gether" was the subject line. Her heart thudding, Alex opened it.

"Hey Sasha!" it said. "I want 2 C U!! Lets get 2gether. 2night okay???!? Paddington Station under the clock. I'll B there at 5!!! U wear something red!! Me 2!! xoxoxoxox Jack."

Although she didn't have that many people on her Christmas list, Callie was finding her shopping expedition to be exhausting. The Oxford Street crowds had picked up as the day wore on; by tea time it was dark and her carrier bags were weighing her down.

With relief she spotted an empty table at a coffee shop in the middle of a large departmental store. The table hadn't been cleaned yet but at least she wouldn't have to share it with anyone else; she needed the extra chair for her bags, and she wasn't in the mood for polite chit-chat with some friendly stranger.

"A pot of tea, please," she said to the harried waitress who materialised to take her order. "Ordinary tea."

"Anything to eat?"

The thought of a toasted teacake tempted her — she hadn't had lunch — but she reminded herself that she was going out for dinner. "No, thanks," she said.

While she waited for her tea, she poked round in her bags and took inventory. Had she managed to remember everyone?

Frances had been the easiest to buy for, as usual. She didn't pamper herself enough, in Callie's opinion, so Callie always bought her some extravagant toiletries: this year it was bath bombs in assorted exotic flavours, all of which smelled good enough to eat.

After that it grew more difficult. Well as she knew her brother, choosing something Peter would like — and didn't already have — was always a challenge. Keeping in mind his new-found enthusiasm for all things Italian, she'd settled on a large and very heavy book on Italian cookery, and now wished she'd waited to buy it until she was on her way home.

She'd enjoyed buying something for Bella, even though Bella wouldn't know Christmas from any other day. A chew toy which promised to keep her occupied when she was home on her own was supplemented with a little bag of doggie chocolate drops; both should make Bella happy.

And then there was Brian. A bottle seemed the safest bet for him — but a bottle of what? From her observation of his habits, Callie didn't think that Brian was much of a spirit drinker, and wine was a bit predictable. Callie remembered that her father had been fond of Tio Pepe sherry, so she tracked it down in

270

Selfridges' food hall, and picked out a nice box of chocolates for Jane while she was there.

Her mother had perennially been the most difficult person to buy for. Callie knew, without a doubt, that anything she selected for her mother would be unsatisfactory in some way: wrong size, wrong colour, wrong style. Furthermore, Laura Anson wouldn't hesitate to let her know in what way the gift had fallen short. The safest thing was to buy it — whatever it was — at a chain store where it could be easily returned. As far as Callie was aware, her mother had never kept one of her gifts. It was an exercise in futility. So why did she bother? Habit, she supposed. And a little challenge to herself: one day, maybe her mother would open a Christmas present and say, "Oh, Callie! It's just perfect — I love it!" instead of saying, "I've always loathed this shade of blue" or "This is way too big for me, dear. I'd swim in it!" Playing it safe, Callie selected a dressing gown in a colour very similar to one she'd seen her mother wearing. It was soft and appealingly cuddly, but Callie was sure that her mother would be able to find fault with it in some way. Maybe, when the inevitable happened, she wouldn't bother to return it: she'd just keep it for herself and give her mother the money to buy something else.

At least she didn't have to worry about buying anything for Adam this year. She should, Callie reflected, be thankful for small mercies. But there was the very fraught question of Marco.

She'd been thinking about it for a long time. She needed to get him something — almost certainly he'd

271

give her a gift of some sort, and she must reciprocate. But what? How intimate, how costly should it be? She could scarcely give him a box of handkerchiefs, yet she couldn't presume to buy him an item of clothing or something more personal.

In the end she settled on a gift that seemed a perfect compromise. She'd stumbled on it while choosing Peter's cookery book, and had fallen on it with a cry of joy. It was a lavish, large-format book of photographs of Venice. He would, she was certain, love it. She couldn't wait to see his face when he opened it, as he paged through its slick pages of glorious and evocative photos.

Pouring out her tea and waiting for it to cool, that image of Marco's face brought back the preoccupation that her mind had been circling around for hours: Marco's phone call, with its sudden suggestion of dinner at La Venezia, and the hint of revelations to be made. Significant revelations, at that. "Things I need to explain," he'd said.

What sort of things did he need to explain? And did she really want to hear them? Although she was curious about his family, and had often wondered about his reticence in talking about them, this development seemed to signal a new phase in their relationship, and Callie wasn't entirely sure that she was ready to go there.

She'd had to assimilate so many changes to her life recently, with the new job following right on the heels of her parting from Adam. And, by and large, the relationship with Marco was fine just as it was. Why did it have to change? Falling in love with Adam, taking step after step down the road of commitment to him, had brought her only heartache.

Peter was the one who fell in love at the drop of a hat. Callie knew herself to be more cautious, and she had been badly burned — not that long ago.

And yet . . .

Yet she did enjoy Marco's company. More than that: there was a strong chemistry between them. Marco was handsome and sexy; his kisses gave her flutters in all the right places. And it wasn't just physical, either. From the first time they'd met she'd found him easy to talk to, like someone she'd known all her life. She could relax and be herself with him: no pretence, no games. That was a rare and wonderful thing.

And, she reminded herself, she wasn't getting any younger. She was thirty. Not a great age in this day and time, but sooner or later the alarm on her biological clock was going to go off, big-time.

Why did life have to be so complicated? Was she being overly cautious, looking for excuses to keep Marco at arm's length? Recently hurt, new job and new situation, innate wariness. Were they just excuses for fear? Was she no more than a coward, unable to cope with growth and change?

She took a gulp of the tea before it had cooled sufficiently, and gasped as it burned all the way down her throat. Get a grip, Callie, she told herself. Just look at this evening as a chance to get away from Peter, and don't sweat it. As the Italians would say, *che serà, serà*.

CHAPTER
FOURTEEN

Wear something red.

Alex rummaged through the clothes in her wardrobe, trying to ignore the butterflies in her stomach. Red wasn't really her colour. It drew too much attention to her, when all she wanted to do was fade into the background.

Her mother loved red. Red suited Mum, brought out her dark colouring and resonated with her vibrant personality.

Alex preferred brown or black or navy.

Then she remembered the jumper that Granny had knitted for her, last Christmas. Scarlet, it was. A cheerful lipstick red. She'd put it on a couple of times, to make Granny happy, but since moving to London she hadn't worn it even once.

She thought perhaps she'd seen it recently, in the bottom of her chest of drawers. Kneeling on the floor, she rummaged through the untidy drawer, pulling out and dropping on the floor other similarly unworn items of clothing till she unearthed the red jumper. Alex unbuttoned her school blouse, added it to the discards on the floor, and pulled the jumper over her head, inspecting herself in the mirror.

Not very good. The jumper was tight — she *had* grown in the past year — and only emphasised the flatness of her chest. No room for concealment, for suggesting that a voluptuous figure lurked somewhere within. For a moment, regarding herself in the mirror, she considered what she might do to remedy the situation.

Frilly Jilly, she thought. Brainless though Jilly might be, if there was one commodity she didn't lack, it was cleavage. Presumably she had a drawerful of frilly bras to emphasise the fact.

If Jilly was in her bedroom, it was a lost cause.

But luck was with Alex. The door to the master bedroom was open, and she could hear that Jilly was in the adjoining ensuite, running a bath. Quietly, on tiptoes, she slipped into the bedroom and started opening drawers at random.

There was a drawer full of knickers — mere scraps of lace. Alex held one pair up to inspect it; for reasons she didn't quite understand, it made her uncomfortable, and her face burned with embarassment. "Gross," she said out loud, dropping the knickers and shoving the drawer shut.

The next drawer yielded nothing but a pile of envelopes. Alex was about to push it back in when she saw that the one on top was addressed to her. "Miss Alexandra Hamilton," it said, along with the address.

Alex pulled it out and looked at it. The letter had been through the post, but it was unopened. Beneath it was another, also with her name and address.

A whole stack of letters! Unopened letters, for her. In Jilly's drawer! Alex scooped them out, just as the cordless phone on the bedside table rang.

Would Jilly cut her bath short to answer the phone? Alex couldn't take any chances.

She dashed back to her own room, abandoning the idea of borrowed cleavage.

Jack would have to take her as she was. If he didn't like that, there was nothing she could do about it now.

"You're going out?" Peter, lounging on the sofa with a mug of coffee resting on his stomach, raised his eyebrows in mild surprise. "You didn't say so this morning. Not that it matters," he added. "I'm out this evening as well. A gig. Playing for some Christmas party."

"Marco rang earlier." Callie kept her voice deliberately calm. "He wants to take me to La Venezia for dinner."

"Oh!" That brought Peter into a sudden sitting position as hot coffee slopped all over him and the sofa. "Oh, bugger. I didn't mean to do that."

Callie sprinted to the kitchen for a cloth, which she applied to the sofa as Peter dabbed at himself with his handkerchief. "Are you okay?"

"Only a few second-degree burns. I'll live."

"You haven't done your shirt any good, either," she pointed out. "Take it off and I'll put it in the washing machine before it sets."

"Seriously, Sis." Obediently Peter unbuttoned his shirt. "He's taking you to La Venezia! At last. He wants you to meet his family?"

276

"He didn't say," she admitted.

"That must be what it's about. Oh, this is brilliant!"

Callie's mouth twisted as she reached for the shirt. "I'm glad you think so. I'm not so sure. Now that it's come down to it, I don't know that I *want* to meet his family."

"How many times do I have to tell you, Sis? Go with the flow. And hold on to Marco with both hands. He's a keeper. A vast improvement over what's-his-name."

"Adam," she supplied wearily.

Peter shrugged. "Whatever. He's history. You care about Marco, don't you?"

"Of course. But . . ."

"Then go with it. Meet the family. See what happens. And," he added with a wink, "if nothing else, you'll get a jolly good meal out of it. Trust me on that one."

Alex was dying examine the letters, but there wasn't time. She wasn't sure how long it would take to get to Paddington Station, or how much it would cost. She didn't want to be late, and she didn't want to be caught short of cash.

Her father had always been generous with pocket money, and Alex's needs were minimal — a few packets of crisps and bars of chocolate each week. So she had a stash of ten-pound notes in the bottom of her sock drawer. She went to it now and stuffed a handful of notes into the pocket of her jeans: better to be safe than sorry.

Alex put her head out of her bedroom and crept into the sitting room. She could hear Jilly on the phone in the master bedroom: probably talking to her sister, telling her how unrepentant and uncooperative Alex had been.

Too bad.

Alex grabbed her coat from the chair where she'd dropped it, shoved the bundle of letters into one of its deep pockets, opened the front door of the flat, slipped through, and pulled it shut quietly behind her. Jilly would be none the wiser — not for hours, if at all. Jilly always left her alone when she was in her room. Her dad usually stuck his head in to say hello when he got back from work, but that was a long way off. She'd probably be home by then, and with any luck she could sneak back in without ever having been missed.

Outside it was dark, and getting colder again. Alex headed for the St. John's Wood tube station, her breath preceding her in a frozen cloud. She couldn't walk too fast; the pavements were now slick with re-freezing moisture and her trainers had a tendency to slip, so she had to lift her feet carefully and try not to rush. That didn't come easily to her; at one point she picked up speed, skidded and took a tumble onto the pavement.

"Be careful, little girl," admonished an old man who'd seen it happen, giving her a hand to help her to her feet.

"Thanks." Alex flashed him a smile and continued, a bit more cautiously.

A couple of tourists — middle-aged, hung about with cameras, as unmistakable as if they'd been wearing signs — were emerging from the tube station as Alex drew near. "Abbey Road?" said one of them to Alex in a broad American accent.

Alex pointed. "That way," she said. It wasn't the first time she'd been asked, out and about in St. John's Wood, but she never had understood what all the fuss was about. The Beatles had been famous about a hundred years ago. Even before her dad was born.

She'd never been in the tube station before, had never ridden on the tube. On the rare occasions she'd been out with her father and Jilly, they'd gone in his car or taken a taxi. But how hard could it be? Lots of people did it every day. There was a ticket machine; she fed a ten-pound note into it, only to have it spit back out at her. "No change" said the digital read-out. So Alex went to the ticket window and shoved her money through the opening. "Paddington. Return," she requested in a firm voice, trying to sound authoritative.

With her tickets and her change she received confirmation that her efforts hadn't been too successful. "Change at Baker Street," said the ticket woman kindly. "Bakerloo, Circle or Hammersmith and City."

"Thanks."

Through the ticket barrier, down the escalator, on to the train. Not too crowded, going in towards town. At Baker Street, though, rush hour had begun in earnest, and once she'd found her way through the maze of tunnels to the Bakerloo Line, Alex had to shove her way into a packed carriage.

She'd already decided that she didn't like the tube. Too many people, too close together. No personal space, and there were evidently people in the world — in London, even — who didn't have a daily bath. Alex clung to an upright pole, trying not to breathe too deeply, hoping not to get trampled. Maybe she'd take a taxi home, in spite of the fact that she had a return ticket.

She almost missed her stop at Paddington, fighting her way between immobile pairs of legs to the carriage doors just before they slammed shut. "Excuse me. Excuse me," she repeated breathlessly till she achieved the platform.

Now. Where was the clock? Jack had assumed that she would know where to find it.

Not here. Not on this platform. She waited a minute, until the train had pulled out and people began filing up the platform in anticipation of the next one.

"Excuse me," she said to a kind-looking older woman. "Could you tell me where the clock is?"

"Oh, you want the time?" The woman looked at her wrist. "It's just gone five, dear."

She was late, then. "No, I want the clock. I'm meeting someone there." Surely Jack would wait for her. Surely. Surely.

"The clock?" The woman glanced round. "Oh, you must mean the big clock. In the mainline rail station. Up the escalator. You can't miss it."

"Thanks," said Alex over her shoulder, already following the "Way Out" sign.

Down the corridor, up the escalator, through the ticket barrier. Alex hadn't known she'd need the ticket again at this end; fortunately she hadn't thrown it away, but there was a momentary delay as she scrabbled in her pockets for it.

The mainline station was massive, cluttered with shops and eateries like a self-contained town. People strode through it rapidly, from train to tube and from tube to train. A few paused to buy a newspaper or a sandwich. Some checked the giant boards which displayed train information: arrivals, departures, destinations, platform numbers, times. Changing every few seconds.

And there — there in the middle — was the clock. The big clock.

Alex stopped and took a deep breath.

The clock read ten past five.

Neville had sent Yolanda home; now he could hardly wait to follow her example. It was Friday evening, for God's sake, and he was sick to death of this case. A week of slogging away, and they were no farther on than they'd been. He wanted to go home, switch on something mindless on the telly, eat a takeaway curry, then drink himself into a state of numbness. He was scheduled to have the weekend off, which meant that he could drink as much as he bloody well wanted to.

Drinking. Triona. So much had been happening that he hadn't been able to spare a thought for her. For the e-mail he'd sent her, and the reply she would surely have sent by now.

He turned to the computer on his desk, opening the e-mail program.

Lots of junk. Spam, and other rubbish. People wanting to sell him something.

Nothing from Triona. Nothing.

Jack had said he'd be wearing red. A red jacket, a red hat, a red scarf, a red jumper like her?

Alex scanned the people in the vicinity of the clock. There was a woman wearing red leather gloves, a girl with a red rucksack on her back. Both seemed to be just passing through, on their way to somewhere else.

He's gone, she said to herself, a wave of desolation engulfing her. Gone, gone, gone. She'd endured the wretched tube journey, come all this way, and it was too late. He hadn't waited for her.

Tears pricked at her eyes.

"Sasha?" said a voice from behind her.

Alex spun round, all smiles now; no one but Jack knew her by her *nom de plume*.

But the person who had spoken to her wasn't the handsome boy she knew so well from the oft-kissed photo in her locket. This was a man. An *old* man, older than her dad. Fatter than her dad. Balder than her dad. Though he was wearing a red baseball cap, she could see that he didn't have much hair at all.

"Sasha?" he repeated, grinning. His teeth were bad.

"You're not Jack." She didn't realise she'd said it aloud — vehemently — until he nodded his head.

"I'm Jack, all right. If you're gonna get upset with me because I don't look a lot like my photo . . . Well, Sasha, you don't look much like yours, either." He

282

grinned again — those horrible teeth — and took a step towards her. "I won't complain if you don't."

"No." Alex didn't take her eyes from him, stepping back blindly. He continued to advance.

"I won't hurt you," he said. "Come on, Sasha. Let's go and get a burger. We can have a good time together."

"No."

He reached a hand towards her, touched her cheek.

Only then did she turn and run through the crowded terminus, as if for her very life. She saw a narrow opening between two people pulling suitcases and squeezed between them, sprinting towards the exit. "Sasha!" she heard him shout; she didn't look back.

Frances usually took the bus home to Notting Hill, but today she decided to walk. The buses were crowded, and though it was cold as darkness descended, she felt she needed the fresh air. Towards the end of the afternoon the hospital had seemed stifling to her, overheated and airless.

She wished, as she walked briskly along the pavement, that Leo weren't so far away. Some of his down-to-earth advice would be welcome, as would one of his comforting bear-hugs.

Well, Frances reminded herself, husbands were good for supplying those things as well. With any luck, Graham would be at home.

He was in his study, scribbling away at his desk.

"Do you have time for a chat?" Frances asked, putting her head round the door.

Graham laid his pen down straightaway. "Always." He peered at her over the top of his glasses. "Sweetheart, you look frozen! Your face is redder than your hair!"

"I'm a bit cold," she admitted.

He went to her and cupped her cheeks in his warm hands. "You need a cup of tea," he announced. "Let's put the kettle on."

Frances followed her husband to the kitchen and allowed him to fuss about with the tea, while she stripped her gloves off and warmed her hands on the radiator.

Graham had been a priest for a good many more years than Frances had. Though she knew she wasn't free to share Rachel's story with him, there was no harm in drawing on his experience to help her in dealing with it. "Darling," she began. "Can I ask your advice?" Without waiting for a reply she went on, "Something happened today. Someone told me something . . . important."

He stopped what he was doing and turned to look at her.

"Important?"

It was the way Graham said the word, raising his eyebrows, that made her defensive. "Oh, I know. Everything that everyone tells me is important. To them. To other people as well, sometimes. But this was more than that." How much could she safely say? "This has bearing on . . . on a police matter. On a criminal investigation."

284

He opened a cupboard and reached for two mugs. "So you have some information which would help the police — something they don't know." It was a statement rather than a question.

Frances nodded.

"Is anyone's life in danger?"

"No. Not now."

"And you promised this ... person ... that you wouldn't tell anyone?" he surmised.

"As a priest. I gave my word."

"Then I think you know the answer, Fran." Graham poured boiling water into the tea pot. "It's hard. One of the hardest things we're called to as priests."

"To hold people's secrets for them," she said.

"When it would be so much easier — and so much better for everyone concerned — to pass them on." He sat down abruptly at the kitchen table and sighed. "There's something ... I never was able to tell even *you* about this, Fran. It happened a long time ago, but I still think about it."

"What?"

Graham closed his eyes, as if in pain. "One of my parishioners — not in this parish — told me about a ... compulsion he had. Something that did him no good, and was positively bad for his wife. A few months later she ended up in hospital. She almost died. If she *had* died ... well, to this day I don't know how I would have lived with myself."

Frances resisted the temptation to figure out which of his former parishioners he was talking about. "Did you ever think about telling the police?"

"That," said Graham, "wasn't an option. I knew it then, and you know it now. There's only one thing you can do."

She didn't need to ask, but she did. "What's that?"

"Pray, Fran," he said. "Pray for them, and for yourself."

Angus Hamilton wasn't really an impulsive sort of man, though he sometimes liked to think of himself that way. After all, he'd married Jilly; he'd left the town where he'd lived all his life and moved to London. What he failed to understand about himself was that the chief motivator in all he did, impulsive or not, was the need to be in control.

That was really why he went home early on Friday afternoon. If anything, he usually left the office quite late on a Friday, after everyone else had gone, wanting to make sure that everything was in order for the next week.

But on this particular Friday, one of his underlings came to him with a request. "Do you mind if I leave a bit early, Mr. Hamilton? The traffic's foul, and I don't want to miss my little boy's school Christmas concert tonight. He's playing a solo."

Angus Hamilton said no, for no particular reason except that he could. Then, as if to emphasise his exalted position as Chief Financial Officer, conferring on him the rights and privileges denied to others, he decided that perhaps he would try to beat the rush hour traffic himself, and leave an hour before his accustomed time.

He took the lift down to the underground executive car park; on the way he tried to ring Jilly, to let her know he'd be early and to ask her to ring his favourite restaurant to book a table for dinner. But the line was engaged, so instead he rang the restaurant himself.

"We're very busy tonight, Mr. Hamilton. Coming up to Christmas, you know. Fully booked, all evening. But I'm sure we'll be able to do something for you. Squeeze you in."

Something wasn't good enough. "I would like my usual table," he insisted.

"Consider it done, Mr. Hamilton."

He gave a grunt of satisfaction. That was all right, then. It was as well he hadn't left it to Jilly, he reflected. She might have been fobbed off with some inferior table, necessitating an unpleasant scene on their arrival.

He had booked the table for three people, in the hopes that Alex would condescend to go with them. That was by no means assured; the lass had grown so stubborn these days, and was as like as not to refuse flat out. She used to be so biddable, such a sunny little thing, but teenage stroppiness had set in early in her case, and he never knew what would set her off.

No, that wasn't quite true. What set her off, more times than not, was Jilly.

Unconsciously he reached into his pocket for an indigestion tablet.

His job was demanding, yes, but by far the biggest source of stress in Angus Hamilton's life was the tension between his wife and his daughter.

He hadn't really expected Alex to react to a new stepmother with joy and rapture. Nor had he any illusions about Jilly's maternal instincts — she'd never pretended to have any. Yet he hadn't really been prepared for the problems the new set-up would engender. Alex and Jilly: their dislike was mutual, characterised by contempt on the one side, and indifference on the other. Alex despised Jilly and didn't bother to hide it; Jilly wasn't the least bit interested in Alex, finding her presence a burden. "She's not my child," she was fond of reminding him whenever Alex was being difficult about something.

Jilly would have been far happier, he knew, if he hadn't insisted on having Alex with them. But she was his daughter; it was out of the question that she should have been allowed to stay in Scotland with her mentally and emotionally unstable mother. Or *his* mother, for that matter, who had offered to keep Alex when the move to London was first mooted. Alex was his flesh and blood; she belonged with him.

As much as he loved anyone other than himself, he loved Alex.

Mark looked at his watch as he pulled his jacket on. "I'm out of here," he said to no one in particular.

He wanted to go home, have a shower, and change into something a bit smarter before he met Callie. They had arranged to meet at a wine bar in the West End for a drink, then go on to La Venezia from there.

But when he was halfway home, squashed in a packed Central Line carriage, he realised that he hadn't made any arrangements for their dinner. Any other time of the year it wouldn't be a problem; at the moment, though, with all of those blooming Christmas parties . . .

Having made up his mind to do this, he was desperate that it should go well, should happen according to plan.

Once he was over ground and assured of a clear signal, he pulled out his mobile and rang the restaurant. As he'd hoped, Serena answered.

"I know I'm asking for a big favour," he said, "but I really, really need a table tonight."

"A table? Marco, you must be joking."

"It's important. I wouldn't ask you if it wasn't," he wheedled in his best little-brother voice.

Serena sighed. "I don't suppose you're going to tell me what this is all about?"

"It's a surprise."

"Oh. Great. Remember, Marco — Mamma doesn't like surprises."

That was certainly true, Mark acknowledged to himself. For a moment he was in danger of losing his nerve. He could take Callie somewhere else for dinner, and do this another time. After Christmas, when things had settled down on all fronts.

No. It had been put off long enough.

"I'll deal with Mamma," he said with more conviction than he felt. "Just find me a table, okay? Remember, you owe me one, after I came in and worked last weekend."

"That's true," she admitted. "I'll see what I can do. But it will have to be late. Not before nine."

It would have to do. "Okay. Nine o'clock."

"Or a bit after. A table for . . . please don't say six."

"Two," said Mark firmly. "A table for two."

Angus Hamilton put his car in the garage behind the flat, then let himself in with his key. "Jilly?" he called.

She was definitely at home; he could hear her voice in another room. Still on the phone, then. Jilly seemed to spend hours on the phone with her sister, her mother and her girlfriends. What they had to talk about he had no idea, since as far as he could determine they usually spent mornings together at the gym and the hairdresser, and afternoons together in the shops.

He followed the sound of her voice to the bedroom, where she was sprawled — alluringly, he thought — on the bed, cordless phone to her ear. For just a moment he entertained the notion of cancelling the dinner reservation and having an early night in. Starting now.

Then he remembered the inconvenience of Alex. Well, she could entertain herself in her room, playing with that expensive computer he'd bought her. She usually did anyway, finding the computer better company than her parents.

Jilly smiled up at him. "I have to go now, Mel," she said into the phone. "Angus is home. I'll ring you later."

Angus loosened his tie. Jilly really did look lovely: silky blonde hair against the pale blue satin of the bedspread, a fine pink cashmere sweater emphasising rather than concealing her curves.

But she was sitting up, putting the phone on the bedside table, arranging her clothing. "You're home early," she observed.

"I've booked a table for tonight. Chez Antoine. I fancied going out for a meal."

"Well, I hope you weren't planning to take Alex with us," Jilly said with the raised-eyebrow, wide-eyed expression she generally substituted for the face-damaging frown. "Your daughter is in disgrace, as far as I'm concerned."

His heart sank; against all expectation, he'd been hoping for a pleasant evening, a relaxing weekend. "What has she done?"

Jilly flicked her hair. "Only started a totally humiliating fight at school. With Beatrice and Georgina, no less! The Headmistress rang Mel! I've spent the afternoon on the phone, apologising to my own sister for your daughter's bad behaviour. I mean, I'm sure she did it just to get at me."

Angus' first instinct was to defend his daughter. He had seen Jilly's young nieces in action, Sunday after Sunday, and was under no illusion that they were blameless in whatever had happened. To make allegations to that effect, though, would be counter-productive. He needed to talk to Alex, to get her side of the story, to determine what had really happened before taking any action. "Where is she now?" he asked.

"In her room. Sulking. She can stay there all weekend, as far as I'm concerned."

Angus turned and started for the door.

Jilly raised her voice. "I suppose you're going to go and tell her it's all right. Well, it's *not* all right. Not as far as I'm concerned."

"I'm going to ask her what happened," he said, as reasonably as he could manage.

"And you'll believe whatever she tells you. Your precious daughter," Jilly sneered. "Never mind Melanie, and Beatrice and Georgina. Never mind *me*."

Angus chewed on another indigestion tablet on his way to Alex's room. He knocked softly on the door. "Alex? Alex, lassie? Can I come in?"

There was no reply.

"Listen, lassie. I know there's more than one side to every story. I'd like to hear what you have to say." He debated whether he should mention Jilly at that point, and decided against it.

After a long moment of silence, he tried one last time. "Alex, lassie, if you don't open the door, I'm going to do it myself. We need to talk."

Still there was silence on the other side of the door. He turned the knob and pushed the door inwards.

Alex's bedroom was the usual tip: bed unmade, school uniform discarded in a heap, clothes strewn on the floor. Jilly refused to set foot in Alex's room; even the cleaning lady hadn't touched it in days, and it showed.

Angus looked to the left; he looked to the right. He looked at her desk, with its glowing computer screen and its piles of books and papers.

292

Everything much the same as the last time he'd seen it. Everything, except that Alex wasn't there.

He peeked into the wardrobe, just to make certain that she wasn't hiding in there to alarm him.

"Jilly," he called, going back out into the corridor. "Alex isn't in her room."

She came out of the bedroom, shrugging. "Have you checked the loo? And the kitchen?"

Angus went from room to room. There was no trace of her.

"Maybe she sneaked out while I was on the phone," suggested Jilly. "Just to spite me."

"Is her coat here?" he demanded. "Surely she wouldn't go out without her coat, on a day like this."

Jilly looked over towards the chair which served as the usual receptacle for Alex's coat. "It was on that chair earlier," she admitted. "She does it to annoy me. Usually I hang it up, but today I just decided I wouldn't. I'm not that girl's nursemaid, you know."

"Then she's gone!"

Jilly shrugged again. "She's just playing up, looking for attention. She'll come back as soon as she's had enough of her little game."

Angus' heart hammered, the bile rose up in his throat, and his imagination conjured up a terrible picture: a vision of Alex's broken body, lying somewhere on the streets of London, abandoned and alone.

He made an effort to keep his voice calm. "Alex is gone," he said. "My wee lassie. And I'm calling the police."

CHAPTER
FIFTEEN

Time to go home. At last. Neville gave Sid Cowley a
few instructions for keeping the Trevor Norton
investigation ticking over during the weekend, then
went back to his office just long enough to get his
jacket. He checked his e-mail one last time before
shutting the computer down: still nothing from Triona.
And no messages on his voice mail or his mobile.
Maybe she would have rung his home number and left
a message there.

Detective Superintendent Evans was bearing down
the corridor towards him as he shut his office door.
Evans didn't often stray from his expansive corner
office; it must be something important to bring him out
like this.

"Oh, Stewart. Glad I caught you," Evans said, fixing
him with his close-set eyes.

That, thought Neville apprehensively, did not sound
like something he wanted to hear. "Sir?"

"What's the latest on the Norton case?"

"We're still . . . working on it, Sir." Neville tried to
think of something positive to say, something that
would distract Evans from the fact that they were no
closer to solving the murder than they'd been a week

earlier. "Mrs. Norton's had her baby," was all he could come up with.

"Girl or boy?"

Neville thought for a moment. "Girl, I think DC Fish said."

Evans frowned, and belatedly Neville remembered that Yolanda Fish's indiscretions with the press — in the form of Lilith Noone — had landed her in Evans' bad books. He tried to make amends on her behalf. "DC Fish has been excellent, Sir," he said. "A great asset."

"Good. Good."

"Well, have a good weekend, Sir." Neville turned to go.

"Just one minute, Stewart. I have something else to talk to you about. Something important."

Neville suppressed a sigh of weariness. "Actually, Sir, I was on my way home. For the weekend."

But Evans stood his ground. "That can wait, Stewart. I need you to look into something that's just come up."

I'm bloody knackered, Neville wanted to shout into his ugly mug. I've just spent a week on a dead-end murder case, and I want to go home. "Sir?" he said.

"Little girl missing. Well, not so little, I suppose," he amended. "She's twelve. Almost a teenager. Still, she's missing. Left home some time this afternoon and hasn't come back. I'd like you to go round and see her parents. St. John's Wood."

No, no, no, Neville's brain screamed. I want to go home. "She hasn't been missing for long, Sir," he pointed out. "She's probably just gone round to see a friend. Or sneaked out to meet a boyfriend. They start young these days, Sir. I believe."

Evans shook his head impatiently. "I'd like you to deal with it, Stewart."

He did *not* want to do this. How far could he push Evans? "But, Sir. I have the weekend off," he dared to say, in his desperation. "Couldn't you send DS Cowley? Or someone else? She'll probably turn up in an hour or two anyway."

"Detective Inspector Stewart." Evans drew his bristly caterpillar brows together in displeasure. "Do I have to spell this out to you? I want *you* to do it. Not Cowley, not anyone else."

"Sir."

Evans lowered his voice. "I need a man with a bit of discretion. A bit of *nous*. Not some lout who will go in and upset people."

Flattery, thought Neville wearily, in no mood to accept it with good grace.

"Mr. Hamilton, the girl's father. He's an important man. Rich." Evans gave a confidential wink. "He plays golf with the Assistant Commissioner, for God's sake. He didn't ring 999 like normal people, Stewart. He rang the Assistant Commissioner. At home. Now do you see why I can't send Cowley in there?"

Neville was struck with a sudden inspiration. "If it's that important and sensitive, Sir, perhaps *you* — "

"Out of the question," Evans interrupted crisply. "It's my son's christening this weekend. The wife's

296

family, descending from all over. Big dinner party this evening."

Ah. Neville hoped his smile didn't give away what he was thinking. The lovely Denise. The second Mrs. Evans. Not overly endowed with brains but making up for it elsewhere. Erstwhile secretary, now trophy wife. Mother of the latest Evans sprog.

Poor little devil, with — if photos were to be believed — the massive Evans chin already terrifyingly in evidence.

"I have faith in you, Stewart. And, as you say, it will probably be all over before you even get there," Evans added, with what he seemed to think was a reassuring smile. He clapped Neville on the shoulder. "What I *will* do, Stewart, is let you have my home number. So you can keep me informed."

Neville gave up.

In spite of her feigned nonchalance for Peter's benefit, Callie was nervous about the evening ahead; she had dressed with as much care as she had on the first occasion she'd gone out with Mark. In all likelihood she would be meeting at least some members of his family, so jeans just wouldn't do. Nothing in her wardrobe seemed quite right, but eventually she'd settled on her best pair of black trousers and a claret-coloured velvet shirt, accessorised with a rich-looking silk scarf woven in jewel tones. Her coat looked a bit shabby, she decided at the last minute, but it was too cold to go out without it, so the best she could hope for was that no one would notice. At least she had some smart black boots to wear.

The wine bar was new to Callie, who tended not to venture into the West End very often. She found it with no difficulty, though. Mark was waiting outside.

"*Cara mia!* You look smashing," he greeted her.

She lifted her face for a public, social kiss in the form of a peck on the cheek. "You're not looking too bad yourself, Marco." That was an understatement: he was wearing a tie, which was rare for him, and a freshly-ironed shirt. His face was smooth from a recent shave and a faint scent of spicy aftershave wafted towards Callie, sending her pulses racing unexpectedly. For just an instant she wished that they were alone together.

The wine bar was buzzing with post-work Friday night drinkers, but most of them were in transit to somewhere else, so it wasn't long before they were able to claim a table with a reasonable amount of privacy. "You sit," said Mark. "I'll get some wine. Is red okay?"

"Fine." She looked down at her shirt. "At least I'm wearing the right colour in case I spill it."

He came back with a bottle and two glasses.

"A whole bottle?" Callie queried. "Is someone else joining us?"

Mark shook his head. "I'm afraid we have rather a long time to drink it. We can't get a table at La Venezia until after nine. I hope you don't mind."

"I don't have any other plans. Except," she added, "that I'm on early duty for Morning Prayer tomorrow. Brian's day off."

298

"I'll have you home well before that," Mark assured her, with a rather strained laugh.

He seemed, Callie thought, as nervous as she felt. What on earth was this all about? His twitchiness only increased her own apprehension.

Mark poured two full glasses. "*Cin cin*," he said, clinking rims.

"What, exactly, does that mean?" She'd often wondered, never asked.

"It's just the Italian equivalent of 'cheers'. I thought it was appropriate for Italian wine."

Callie took a sip. She was no connoisseur, especially of Italian wines, but she could tell by the complexity of the flavour that this was no bottle of plonk; he'd obviously spared no expense. "Mmm. Nice."

"Glad you like it."

They sat silently for a moment, sipping, then both spoke at once.

"Listen, Callie —"

"Marco, I —"

They laughed, which eased the unaccustomed tension between them by a fraction.

"Okay," said Callie. "You first."

"No, you."

"Well, I just . . . I wondered what this was about, is all. Does it have anything to do with last night? I mean, you were about to tell me something when Peter made his entrance and interrupted us."

"That's what started it, anyway."

"Does it," she asked with a flash of intuition, "have anything to do with your family?"

"My family!" Mark let out his breath in a huge, gusty sigh. "*Esattamente, cara mia.*"

Neville had dealt with his share of odd situations in the course of his job; this struck him from the beginning as one of the oddest.

It was immediately evident to him that the man and his wife were not, so to speak, singing from the same hymn sheet.

The man, Angus Hamilton, was tense, agitated. His manner was abrupt, his tone of voice demanding — the strong Scottish burr notwithstanding.

His wife, whom he introduced as Jilly, was as cool as ice — the ice that clinked in the glass she held in a relaxed hand.

"Could I get you something to drink, Inspector?" she asked, holding up her glass. "Gin and tonic? Or aren't you allowed to drink on duty?"

"No, thank you, Mrs. Hamilton."

"Or would you like a coffee?"

Neville thought about it for a second and decided that he would, but by the time he'd opened his mouth to say so, Angus Hamilton pre-empted him with an impatient gesture. "Just leave it, Jilly. The Inspector has more important things on his mind."

Like getting home to that six-pack, Neville thought longingly.

"My daughter," said Angus Hamilton, coming straight to the point. "Alex. What are you going to do to find her?"

"Well, Mr. Hamilton, I'd like to ask you and your wife a few questions. That will help us in our . . . investigations."

Angus Hamilton gestured towards the sofa; Neville interpreted that as an invitation to sit. Hamilton took the chair opposite him, sitting well forward, his elbows on his knees, his hands clasped together.

Mrs. Hamilton, meanwhile, draped herself rather languidly beside Neville on the sofa. He was sorry about that: she was, he'd already decided, rather delicious to look at. Easy on the eye, to say the least. And he couldn't see her without turning his head in a rather obvious manner. He concentrated his attention on Angus Hamilton, meeting his eyes. "Now," he said. "What time did Alex leave the flat?"

"I wasn't here at the time. You'll have to ask my wife that question."

Neville turned and beheld the delectable Jilly Hamilton, half-smile on her glossy pink lips. "Do you have any idea what time your daughter went out?" he repeated.

Now Jilly Hamilton grimaced. "She's *not* my daughter."

Ah. That explained a great deal. Apart from anything else, Jilly Hamilton didn't look as if she was even close to being old enough to have a twelve-year-old daughter. He wouldn't have thought she was more than a few years over twenty, at the most. Probably nearer to twenty than twenty-five, if his well-educated eye was right.

And Angus Hamilton? Not all that old, either, for all that his hairline was receding. Early thirties, perhaps?

Older than *she* was, though. Second wife, evidently.

All this went through his head in the time it took Angus Hamilton to say, "Never you mind about that, Jilly. Tell the inspector what happened. *All* of it."

"Oh, all right." She shrugged her shoulders, moving her cashmere-clad chest in a rather distracting way. "We had a . . . disagreement. All right? Me and Alex. Right after she got home from school. Then she went off to her room to sulk, and I . . . well, I was on the phone. In the other room. I didn't see her go out."

"Can you give me an approximate time, Mrs. Hamilton?" Neville hoped she would shrug again, and she didn't disappoint him.

"I suppose it was between, oh, say, four and six?"

"You can't be more specific than that?"

"No. Sorry."

"Alex often spends time in her room," Angus Hamilton stated, perhaps afraid that Neville would think his wife was neglectful. "She's very . . . studious. A serious lass. Wouldn't you agree, Jilly?"

Neville glanced at Jilly in time to see rolled eyes. "Dead serious," she affirmed, and it didn't sound like a compliment. "Not interested in girlie things at all. Not like her cousins."

It was time, Neville decided, to get out his notebook. He opened to a blank page. "Her cousins?"

"Step-cousins, really," she corrected herself. "Beatrice and Georgina. My sister's girls. Melanie's quite a few years older than me," she added, as if an explanation were necessary. "And she was married young. So her girls are about Alex's age. I'd hoped they would be great friends. I mean, they're so close in age, at the same school, and they just live a bit up the road." Jilly pointed vaguely towards the window. "But she's so different from them. They're proper girlie girls. Like I was. Clothes, makeup, boyfriends. Pop groups. Not computers and books, like Alex."

Neville picked one word out of her rambling monologue. "Boyfriends?"

"Beatrice and Georgina have loads." She gave him a smug smile. "Just like I did at their age."

"But Alex? Does she have any boyfriends?"

"Oh, that's a laugh." Jilly produced a tinkly, artificial giggle. "Not a chance, Inspector." She hesitated, looking sideways at her husband. "As a matter of fact, that's sort of what the whole argument was about. I mean, her saying she did when she didn't."

He frowned. "You didn't tell me that."

"Please, Mrs. Hamilton," said Neville, thoroughly confused. "Could you explain?"

"Well, it was silly, really." That alluring shrug again. "According to Beatrice and Georgina, Alex insisted that she had a boyfriend. She said he was called Jack, and lived in London. She said she had a photo of him in some old locket she was wearing."

"Her grandmother's locket!" Angus Hamilton said, sitting up straighter. "Must have been. I didn't know she still had it."

Jilly continued. "Her cousins said they asked to see it, and she showed them some picture she'd obviously

303

cut out of a magazine or something. I mean, did she really think they'd believe her?"

"Did it ever occur to you that she might have been telling the truth?" Neville asked, looking back and forth between the two of them. "It's possible, isn't it?"

"Alex is very young for that sort of thing," her father stated. "I know that some lassies of her age are interested in boys. But my Alex is young for her age, if you know what I mean. Give her a year or two — but not now."

Neville decided it was time to move on; having written down *Jack?*, he flipped over to an empty page in his notebook. "All right. No boyfriends, then. But what about girlfriends? Other girls at her school, or in the neighbourhood? Any girls who would come home from school with her, or drop over in the evenings to study or watch television?" That comprised the sum total of Neville's vague concept of pre-teen female friendship.

"No, nothing like that," Jilly said. "She doesn't have any friends."

"She's a solitary sort of lass," Angus Hamilton added. "Though she had a good friend in Scotland. Kirsty, I think she was called. Alex wasn't happy about leaving her."

"Anyone else she's close to? Family?"

"Alex loves her granny," Angus Hamilton said, almost grudgingly. "But she doesn't see her very often. Not any more."

"Not since we moved to London," Jilly added.

Grandmother in Scotland, Neville wrote in his notebook. He'd get the address later, if necessary. "Has

Alex ever done this sort of thing before?" he went on. "I mean, gone out without telling anyone?" He looked at Angus Hamilton, whose eyes were fixed on his wife, so Neville shifted his gaze accordingly.

She gave a dismissive shrug. "All of the time. I mean, Alex comes and goes as she pleases. She's a free agent. We're not her keepers. *I'm* certainly not."

Something else occurred to Neville. "I suppose I should have asked straightaway. Does Alex have a mobile phone?"

"I offered to buy her a mobile," Angus Hamilton stated. "Any one she fancied. She said she didn't want one."

"She just couldn't be like everyone else," Jilly added tartly. "What girl doesn't have a mobile these days? It's perverse."

That was it, then, Neville realised. He was clearly wasting his time here. The stepmother didn't give a damn where the girl was or what she did, and this wasn't the first time Alex had wandered off — only, perhaps, the first time her father had become involved, and only because he'd come home from work early that night. Who knew how often the kid had gone out when he wasn't aware of it? "I suppose I'd better have a look at her room," Neville said, snapping the notebook shut.

Angus Hamilton nodded. "Of course, Inspector. But I'll warn you: it isn't very tidy."

"It's a disgraceful tip," Jilly whispered to him, out of her husband's hearing.

Neville himself was no exemplar of domestic tidiness, but even he found Alex's room a bit daunting.

It was as if she had gone out of her way to create chaos out of order. Perhaps, he thought, recalling the immaculate state of the rest of the flat, she was doing just that. As an act of defiance.

He stood in the door, trying to process everything he saw, just in case he should need to investigate further. He realised that ever since he had arrived at the Hamiltons' flat, he'd been listening with half an ear for the door to open, expecting Alex to return at any moment. Now that he understood the reason for her departure — a row, and an unpleasant one at that, with an unsympathetic stepmother — he was more than ever convinced that her absence was only temporary. Once she'd cooled off, once she'd blown off steam, when she knew her father would be home, she'd be back. She would appeal to her father, hoping he'd take her side and she could score some sort of points off her stepmother.

In one way, Neville did not envy Angus Hamilton: caught between two determined females who doubtless hated each other's guts.

In another way, he envied him very much. To have the delicious Jilly in his bed every night . . .

He didn't dare to allow his thoughts to wander down that particular road. That would be fatal.

Picking his way through the clothing on the floor, Neville crossed to the desk. Perhaps, he thought, she'd left a note there, explaining where she'd gone.

Nothing of that sort was immediately evident.

The computer, then?

He pressed a key at random; the screen saver disappeared and in its place was a box asking for a password to be entered.

It was way too soon to be invading a young girl's privacy like this. If she came back — *when* she came back — she would probably be furious that her father had let a policeman tromp round her room.

Neville picked his way back out again. "Mr. Hamilton," he said, and it wasn't just the vision of the six-pack that motivated him. "Here's the way I see it. No one has come into your flat and abducted your daughter. She's gone out of her own free will, and there's no reason to think she won't come home soon." He proffered a card. "My mobile number. Please ring me as soon as she's back."

"Inspector." Angus Hamilton ignored the card, staring into Neville's face with an expression as cold as his voice. "It's not good enough. We're talking about a child here. My Alex is twelve years old. She's been missing since this afternoon. It's now . . ." He dropped his eyes long enough to consult his Rolex. "It's now nearly eight p.m. If that's the best advice you can offer me, be assured that I will be on the phone to the Assistant Commissioner as soon as you're out of that door. I *will not* be fobbed off."

"Where do I begin?" Mark sighed. "I suppose I'd better start with what I was going to tell you yesterday."

The wine was already beginning to go to Callie's head; she remembered that she hadn't had lunch and

307

had forgone that tempting teacake. "All right," she said.

"My brother-in-law. Joe."

"Married to your sister?"

"Right." He nodded. "They've been married for ever. More than twenty years. I've known Joe even longer than that. Since I was a kid. Joe . . . well, let's say I've had a shock."

He was looking down into his wine glass, not meeting her eyes. Callie touched his hand. "Tell me, Marco."

"I've always thought they had a great marriage. Two girls. They would have liked more kids, but Serena's had problems with her pregnancies. Like Mamma."

That was news to Callie; she admitted to herself that she'd wondered why, in this seemingly traditional Italian family, Marco had only one sibling.

"They've always been, like, the perfect couple, in my mind. Devoted to each other and the family. But now . . ." He shook his head. "Everything's turned upside down. I found out that Joe's been . . . playing around."

"Maybe you've got the wrong end of the stick," she offered. "Things aren't always what they seem."

He looked up. "You don't understand, *cara mia*. He's admitted it. To Serena, to me. He's been having it off with one of his students."

Betrayal. With her own recent history, it struck at Callie's heart. Poor Serena, she thought. "Well, if he's sorry . . ." she began.

"But he's not!" Mark stated furiously. "He's absolutely unrepentant. He laughed at me for taking it seriously. And he as much as admitted that it wasn't the first time. And it won't be the last, either."

"But Serena . . ."

"He said that Serena will just have to live with it. That's the worst thing of all." He paused, breathing deeply. "No, the worst thing is that she *will*. She'll live with it. Put up with it. Send him off to work every day, with the knowledge that he might be shagging one of his students on the sofa in his office while she's . . . oh, I don't know. Ironing his shirts. Putting someone's credit card through the machine at the restaurant. Helping Chiara with her homework. All the while pretending that nothing's wrong. That their marriage is perfect. Pretending to their girls. Pretending to Mamma and Papa. Pretending to *herself*. God, Callie. I can't stand it."

"Oh, Marco." She didn't know what else to say.

He gulped at his wine. "I wanted to kill him," he said, more quietly. "For the first time, I understood what drives people to murder. To crimes of passion, as it were. I suppose it's a useful thing for a policeman to learn." He gave a short, ironic laugh. "And this was at second hand. On behalf of my sister, not even for myself. I can't imagine what it must feel like to be *her*. To be the one betrayed."

Callie didn't have to imagine; she knew. She hadn't actually ever wanted to kill Adam. Not consciously. But if he'd just happened to fall under a bus . . .

Belatedly Mark met her eyes, and must have seen the stricken look there. "Oh, Callie. I'm so sorry. I didn't mean . . ."

"Never mind," she said briskly. "That's all in the past. But Serena . . . you're going to have to help her through it, Marco. At least she'll have you to talk to. She won't have to go through it alone."

Neville withdrew to the Hamiltons' kitchen, pulled out his mobile, and rang Detective Superintendent Evans' home number.

Not surprisingly, Evans didn't actually answer the phone himself. It was the lovely Denise who picked up the call. Mrs. Evans number two. He recognised her voice instantly: slightly nasal, a bit common. Essex.

"Mrs. Evans, this is Neville Stewart. DI Stewart. I need to speak to your husband urgently."

"It's not a convenient time," she said. He couldn't tell from her tone of voice whether she knew who he was or not — whether she remembered him specifically, as one of the hordes of young policemen who had unsuccessfully tried their luck with the lovely Denise when she was nothing more exalted than Detective Superintendent Evans' secretary. His extremely, awesomely well-endowed secretary. If Helen of Troy's face had launched a thousand ships, Denise's chest might have done something similar in another day and time. But Denise had held out for the big prize — if prize he was — and had won it. Neville supposed she was in it for the long-term pay-off. Putting up with Evans now, and bearing his children, might not seem that wonderful — especially if the children all ended up looking like him; eventually, though, he would end up with a gong. A knighthood, and she'd be Lady Evans. Wouldn't Denise's Essex relations be proud?

"It's urgent," Neville repeated. "He gave me this number, and told me to use it."

"But we're just sitting down to dinner," the lovely Denise protested. "I'm dishing up the soup right now."

"Could you please tell him that Mr. Hamilton is going to ring the Assistant Commissioner again?" he requested, adding, "I'll hold."

"Oh, all right, then," she said grudgingly. "I'll tell him."

A moment later Evans was on the phone. "What's this about the Assistant Commissioner?"

"Hamilton's playing hard ball, Sir," Neville said tersely. "He says he won't be fobbed off."

"Were you trying to fob him off?" demanded Evans. "I thought I told you to get it sorted."

Neville drew in a deep breath. "Sir. It's the sort of thing that happens every day. The girl has a row with her stepmother and walks out. It's not the first time it's happened, either — according to the stepmother, the kid comes and goes as she pleases. Maybe she's staying away longer than usual because of the row. She's taken her coat, so she won't freeze to death. She's probably gone to a school friend's house. Or she's wandering round the shops, eating chips. Hating her stepmother. She'll come back when she gets bored or fed up. I'd stake my life on it."

"I wouldn't do anything that rash, Stewart," Evans growled. "Mind, I'm sure you're right. But that's not the point, is it?"

"I suppose not," he admitted.

"This Hamilton isn't going to be happy until his precious daughter is home safe and sound."

"That's it in a nutshell, Sir."

"In the meantime, he has to believe that we're taking it very seriously. That we're doing something, in actual fact. Whether we are or not."

Neville wasn't sure what Evans was getting at. "So what are you telling me to do, Sir? Just sit here and make soothing noises until the shops close, the girl gets tired and comes home?" The idea didn't appeal, even with Mrs. Hamilton as eye candy.

"Ring the station and get them to alert uniformed," Evans said crisply. "They can be keeping an eye out for the girl, in the neighbourhood and round the West End. Ask Hamilton for a photo. And if you don't want to be there all night," he added, "which I suspect you don't, then get an FLO over there to hold their hands. That's what Family Liaison Officers are for. DC Fish, maybe? You said she'd been doing a good job in this Norton business."

"That's just the point, Sir. I sent her home. Told her to take the weekend off."

"Well, find someone else, then. There are other FLOs. I'm sure you can find one who won't squawk too much about being hauled out on a Friday night. Just make sure it's someone civilised. Like I said before.

Someone who won't ruffle Hamilton's feathers too much."

"Bugger," Neville muttered as Evans rang off.

Who the hell could he ring?

Mark Lombardi, said a voice in his head.

He and Mark were mates. Drinking buddies, fellow bachelors. He couldn't do this to Mark.

For a long moment he looked at his mobile phone, inert in his hand.

Mark Lombardi. Presentable, personable. Discreet. Just what Evans demanded, what this situation required.

The number was in his phone's directory. Mark's mobile, in case he wanted to ring him for a spur-of-the-moment get-together at the pub. He wouldn't even have to look it up, or ring the station to get it.

"Sorry, mate," he said under his breath as he pushed the button. "It's either you or me."

"Anyway," said Mark, having refilled their wine glasses, "all of this business with Joe has got me thinking. About all kinds of things. About the family. *La famiglia.*"

"Yes?"

"The thing you have to understand about my family . . ." he said earnestly. "They're Italian."

Callie wanted to laugh but didn't. "Well, yes. I rather guessed that."

"I mean, *really* Italian. Or really Venetian, to be more precise. I was born here, in London, and so was Serena.

313

But my parents, *i genitori*, were both born in Venice, and their parents and grandparents, going back forever. They've lived in London for more than forty years, but they're not Londoners. They never will be. They'll always be Venetians who just happen to live somewhere else."

"Lots of people in London come from somewhere else," she pointed out, not sure what he was getting at. "Most of them become Londoners, sooner or later."

"Not my parents," he stated. "Not in a million years. And they don't understand what it's like for me. They think I'm as Italian as they are."

Now Callie *was* confused. "But . . . aren't you?"

"Genetically, anyway. And culturally, in a lot of ways. Being born to Italian parents has shaped me in ways I probably will never really understand. The language, the Church . . ."

Ah, thought Callie. The Church. Was that what this was all about?

"But I'm a Londoner, too," he went on. "I've grown up in a multicultural city. An *English* city, as well. Eating fish and chips, drinking English ale. When I can't get Italian wine or Peroni beer," he added with a self-deprecating grin.

Callie raised her glass, smiling, and he did the same.

"And when it comes to relationships . . ." Mark tailed off, looking away from her and into his glass.

Callie stopped smiling.

"All my life I've tried to do what my parents wanted me to do. What I thought would make them happy. Serena, too. Yes, she loved Joe when she married him.

She still does. But what if she'd felt free to fall in love with someone else? Someone who wasn't Italian? Maybe her life would have been completely different."

"And maybe not," she felt compelled to say. "Or not necessarily any better."

"But she never felt she had the choice. And neither did I. 'A nice Italian girl.' That's what my parents have been waiting for me to find, all these years. I haven't found one. And I've never found anyone that I felt strongly enough about to risk my parents' displeasure."

Callie swallowed. Hard.

"What I'm saying," Mark continued, looking up at her at last with tears in his eyes, "is that this is what tonight's all about. I want you to meet my family. I want them to meet *you*."

"Marco . . ."

His phone bleated.

Mark groaned. "Not *now*."

He pulled it out of his pocket and looked at the display. "Neville Stewart," he said. "I suppose I'd better answer it."

CHAPTER
SIXTEEN

"It's really not a good time, Neville," Mark said, when Neville had provided a terse explanation of the situation. "I'm in the middle of ... something important. And I have dinner reservations for later."

"My sympathies, mate." He didn't sound very sorry. "The thing is, this bloke has connections. And Evans doesn't want to take any chances. There's pressure from higher up. The Assistant Commissioner, no less."

Mark tried again. "I've drunk half a bottle of wine. Even if I had a car here, I can't drive."

"The Jubilee Line. Straight to St. John's Wood. You're in the West End? You can change at Baker Street. I'll hang on till you get here."

He couldn't believe it. To have reached this point . . .

Ending the call with a savage punch of his finger, Mark looked up at Callie. "I'm so, so sorry," he said. "I'll put you in a taxi."

Callie gave him a wry smile. "I think I can find my own way home, Marco." She was already pulling her coat on, gathering up her handbag and her gloves.

"Neville says it can't be helped," he floundered, wanting to delay their parting, desperate that the evening shouldn't end on this note. Nothing resolved, not even a response from her about the admission — the declaration, even — that he'd been working himself up to for so many weeks.

"This would be Neville Stewart, I assume?" There was, Mark thought, a tiny edge to her voice. Though it was something they didn't really talk about, he knew that she had no great love for DI Stewart, having met him only in rather adverse circumstances.

Mark nodded. "It's not Neville's decision," he added lamely. "Pressure from higher up, he said."

"Well, if it can't be helped, it can't be helped." Callie gave a pragmatic shrug, then, seeming to take pity on him, said, "My job can be like that, too. Only my Higher Authority is a bit different from yours."

In spite of himself, he laughed. "Yes, the Assistant Commissioner only *thinks* he's God."

They'd reached the street. The parting of the ways. "You're sure you'll be okay getting home from here?"

"No problem."

"I'll ring you," he said. "As soon as I can. I'll let you know what's going on."

"Take care of yourself, Marco."

By the time Alex had stopped running, she had no idea where she was.

Not that she would have known anyway: London was a mystery to her, a puzzling monstrosity. She knew her way round St. John's Wood, just about. The flat, her school, and places in between. But not these streets.

She might as well be in a foreign country. Kebab shops, curry houses, redolent with exotic smells.

How far had she run? How long had she walked? Alex had no idea. She looked at her watch: it was past six o'clock.

She walked some more. It was the best way to keep warm. Once she'd stopped running, once her heart had slowed from its frantic pounding to something like a normal beat, she had realised how cold it was. If she slowed down, if she stopped, she would freeze. Keep moving.

Busy commercial streets gave way to quiet residential ones, all equally strange. Then she was back in the bustle again. Posher shops this time. People a bit better dressed. Rushing about, laden with bags of Christmas shopping.

And there, at the corner, directing traffic, was a policeman. He was wearing one of those yellowy fluorescent jackets over his uniform, but he was surely a policeman.

Alex paused.

Callie decided to be extravagant and take a taxi home. She could have used the tube, of course, but the Friday night merrymakers were already out in force and she knew it would be unbearably crowded with exotically dressed young people looking for a good time. Besides, she justified to herself, it would be a cold walk from Paddington to Bayswater.

It wasn't until she'd paid the taxi driver, gone up the steps to her flat, let herself into its welcoming warmth, and received Bella's rapturous greeting that she realised she hadn't had anything to eat. No lunch, no teacake, no dinner. Nothing but a few nuts at the wine bar. And the wine, which, unimpeded by food, had gone straight to her head and made her feel more than a bit tipsy.

With Peter in residence, there wasn't likely to be much left unscoffed in the kitchen; he seemed to think that living there gave him the right to eat whatever he could lay his hands on. Callie opened a cupboard and found a packet of breadsticks which Peter had somehow overlooked, and the fridge yielded up a plastic pot of olives, only slightly withered with age. After shedding her coat, she sat at the table and devoured them with her fingers. Crunchy breadsticks, slithery olives. When they were gone, Callie licked the salty oil from her fingers.

Still hungry, she explored the freezer compartment. There was a tub of ice cream: Ben and Jerry's Cherry Garcia. Peter's favourite; he must have bought it. Well, too bad. If he felt free to help himself to her food, Callie wasn't going to suffer undue qualms of guilt about eating his ice cream. Maybe he wouldn't even notice if she only ate a bit of it.

Prying the top off, she saw that it was already half empty. She fetched a spoon and scooped out one bite, then another. Before she knew it she'd emptied the carton, scraping the last bits of chocolate from the sides.

Callie shivered as she hid the evidence in the bin, under the bread-stick wrapper, the olive pot and an empty juice carton. In spite of the warmth of the flat compared to the outdoors, the ice cream had chilled her from the inside out. She went to her bedroom and took her boots off, sliding her feet into her pink fluffy slippers, then she pulled on her old, shabby dressing gown over her clothes. It was dilapidated, and she knew it looked silly, but it was comfortingly cosy. Besides, there was no one but Bella to see her.

A hot drink. That would sort her out. Might help her to think straight as well as warm her up.

The least she could do was use Peter's fancy machine. She popped in a capsule for hot chocolate and a minute later the drink was ready.

Nice, comforting hot chocolate. She took it through to the sitting room and curled up on the sofa, where Bella joined her almost immediately, snuggling next to her. Callie stroked the silky ears with her free hand. Bella was such a comfort, such a wonderful companion.

Did she *need* comforting? Callie asked herself.

Yes, she'd been stood up. Or, more accurately, abandoned. Yes, she'd prepared herself for something she sensed was important. Crucial, even. And that critical moment in her life had been interrupted.

"I want you to meet my family." What, exactly, did that mean? Marco had seemed to be investing it with an importance beyond the face value of the words.

Now that the moment had passed, would it ever come back again?

Was she disappointed? Or was she actually relieved?

Caressing her dog's soft ears, Callie wasn't sure.

Neville and Mark had a quiet consultation in the corridor just outside the Hamiltons' flat. A handover, Neville told himself with satisfaction. Mark could see

320

this one through from now on. The girl would come home, then they could wash their hands of this business.

"The wife is a piece of work," he told Mark. "She doesn't seem to care about the kid at all. It's not her kid," he added at Mark's puzzled look.

"Oh. She's a stepmother, then?"

"That's right. Wicked as they come, I don't doubt." He grinned. "All she seems to care about is herself. I suppose the best that kid can hope for from her is benign neglect."

Mark's expression changed to one of alarm. "You don't suspect that she's had anything to do with the girl's disappearance?"

"Good Lord, no. Nothing sinister like that. Quite frankly, from what I've seen here tonight, she couldn't be bothered."

"What about the father?" Mark pursued, lowering his voice.

"He does seem to care about the kid," Neville admitted. "But not to the extent of spending much time with her, from what I could see."

"Doesn't sound like much of a family to me," said Mark; Neville couldn't tell from his expression whether he thought this was a good thing or a bad thing.

"You'll see for yourself, soon enough. I suppose it's about time for you to get in there." Time for me to go home, Neville added to himself.

"What, exactly, do you want me to do?"

"Oh, the usual thing." Neville shrugged. "Hand-holding, soothing noises."

Mark looked distinctly put out. "Is that really what you think my job is all about?"

Put my foot it it now, Neville said to himself ruefully. "Not at all, mate," he back-pedalled. "Just one of your many talents. But it's what *this* job is about. I have no doubt in my mind that the kid will be home any minute. Cold and tired, most likely. The stepmother will be royally pissed off at her for wrecking their evening," he added. "She'll probably tear a strip off her, if she can be bothered. The dad will be relieved, though he probably won't show it. He'll give her a hard time as well, make her wish she'd stayed away. Poor kid."

Mark didn't seem convinced. "We'll see."

"Ring me in the morning and tell me if I'm right." Neville pushed the flat door open. "Okay, mate. It's show time." He ushered Mark into the sitting room. "Mr. and Mrs. Hamilton, I'd like you to meet Detective Sergeant Mark Lombardi, one of our finest Family Liaison Officers. He'll be looking after you until Alex comes home."

It would have been so easy just to have gone up to that policeman, to tell him she was lost and wanted to go home. He would have made a phone call, probably taken her home in his panda car, and that would have been that. In no time she would have been tucked up in bed with Buster. With any luck, Dad wouldn't even be home from work yet and Jilly wouldn't have noticed she was gone. At the worst — if she'd been missed — Dad would be a bit worried and Jilly would shout at her for worrying him.

Alex came very, very close to approaching the policeman. She stepped up to the kerb and looked at him. The words were on her lips: "Can you help me to get home?"

That's when it came to her.

Home: what a joke.

St. John's Wood wasn't home. No way. It was the place she lived, for now. Where her stuff was, but it wasn't home. Not by any stretch of the imagination.

Scotland was home. Always. No matter what happened.

And Mum was in Scotland.

Alex turned her back on the policeman and walked away.

Investigating Alex's disappearance and whereabouts was not Mark's job, and he knew it. As the Family Liaison Officer, his role was quite a different one: to support the family and keep them informed. He might not have appreciated Neville's dismissive "hand-holding, soothing noises," but at times that's what it boiled down to. That, and cups of tea. Mark was very good at making tea.

"Could I get some tea for you, Mrs. Hamilton?" he suggested.

"Tea." Jilly Hamilton rolled her eyes. "You could make me another gin and tonic, if you really wanted to be useful."

Angus Hamilton also waved away his offer of tea. He was pacing: back and forth, up and down, clenching and unclenching his fists. "I just don't know where that lass has got to," he muttered. "Does she not think we'd be worried sick?"

To Mark's eyes, Jilly Hamilton didn't seem worried sick: she seemed bored. While her husband paced, she examined her fingernails, as a group and singly. They were painted a deep coral pink, each one meticulously shaped to match its fellows. As far as Mark knew, neither his mother nor his sister had ever had a manicure in their lives, but he was able to recognise an expensive professional manicure when he saw one. No chips, no flaws. Perfection. Yet Jilly examined each one minutely, pushing gently at her cuticles, running a fingertip over each nail as though checking for any irregularity or roughness.

"Do you like the colour?" she said to Mark idly, stretching out both hands to show him.

"Very nice."

"It's a bit darker than I usually have. But this morning I thought, why not? If I don't like it, I can have something different tomorrow." She held them up against the paler pink of her sweater. "I don't know. Maybe they *are* too dark. Angus, sweetie, what do you think?"

Angus Hamilton made an impatient noise at the back of his throat, but said nothing. She subsided into silent contemplation of the digits in question.

Hungry. Not just hungry: she was starving. Ravenous.

Alex's lunch had been interrupted before it happened, and so had her attempt to eat something

324

after school. Now her stomach rumbled, reminding her that it needed feeding.

She had money in her pocket, so that wasn't a problem.

Stopping, she looked round and saw the golden arches of McDonald's hanging from a shop front on the other side of the street.

Unlike most girls of her age, Alex was not a frequenter of McDonald's. She'd been to one exactly once, a long time ago. Her mother had taken her to Aberdeen on a shopping expedition, and they'd had lunch at McDonald's. "I have a secret fondness for McDonald's," her mother had confessed to her. "When I was a student in Edinburgh, I used to live on Big Macs."

A Big Mac. That's what she'd have: the very name reminded her of Scotland, and of her mother.

She pushed the door open and stepped into the bright, warm restaurant. It was full of people: family groups, small gangs of teenagers, a raucous children's birthday party. She looked round self-consciously, aware of being on her own, but no one paid her any attention.

Alex got into the queue to order, reading the menu. By the time she'd reached the counter, she'd decided what to say. "A Big Mac Meal," she declared firmly.

"What drink?" asked the bored, acne-afflicted youth at the till.

Her mother hadn't usually given her fizzy drinks, but when they'd gone to McDonald's, she'd been allowed to have a Coke as a special treat with her Happy Meal. "Coke," she stated.

The youth took her ten-pound note and gave her a handful of change. Alex shoved the change in her pocket, and a few seconds later was presented with a tray.

"Where should I sit?" she asked the youth.

He looked surprised. "Anywhere ya want."

Alex carried the tray to a table by the window. That way she could look out at the shoppers bustling by, or she could watch the people in the restaurant.

She stuffed a few chips into her mouth, took a slurp of the Coke, then turned her attention to the main attraction. Alex opened the yellow carton, lifted the Big Mac out, and stretching her mouth wide open, bit into it. It was heaven: never in her life had anything tasted so delicious to her. Pale orange sauce dribbled out onto her coat.

Alex scrubbed at the stain with a paper serviette. And it was then, when she noticed the bulge in her coat pocket, that she remembered the envelopes.

Neville pushed open the door of his flat and wrinkled his nose in involuntary disgust. The place stank of whiskey and misery.

The central heating was on a timer and it had been set to come on hours before, in anticipation of an earlier return, so the flat was stuffy as well. Coming in out of the cold, Neville had expected to find the warmth comforting; instead it seemed stifling. He opened a window and drew in a bracing breath of icy air. "That's better," he muttered.

The phone. Surely she would have left a message.

There was no message.

And there was but a mere dribble of whiskey left in the bottom of the bottle.

Well, he had his Guinness. Six cans, and the off-license just round the corner in case of emergency. If he were feeling more sociable he would have gone to the pub for the real thing, on draught and freshly pulled, but the last thing he wanted right now was to be with other people. Convivial strangers, drinking buddies: he didn't need that.

Drinking buddies. As he popped the tab on his first can and poured it with exquisite care into a glass, Neville spared a passing thought for Mark Lombardi, and not without a pang of guilt. He shouldn't have done that to him. Not really. Mark was too nice a bloke; those wretched Hamiltons would chew him up and spit him out.

The envelopes. Alex pulled the bundle from her coat pocket and looked at them for a minute, thumbing through the stack. Her name and address were printed on each one in a neat though nondescript hand. And the stamps: they were Scottish stamps.

Most of the letters, it appeared to Alex, had never been opened, though there were a few at the bottom of the pile which had been slit across the top.

She started with that one, slipping a folded sheet of paper out of the envelope.

With a jolt that was almost physical, she recognised her mother's handwriting. It was distinctive: bold, yet legible.

My dearest Alex, she read, then had to stop as tears filled her eyes.

It was intolerable, Angus Hamilton said to himself. He had clearly been fobbed off with a police officer who wasn't up to the job.

"I'm not an investigating officer," DS Lombardi explained. As if that was any sort of excuse. Why hadn't they sent a proper detective? The Assistant Commissioner would be hearing about this.

"You're a detective sergeant, are you not?" he demanded. "Well, how about doing some detecting?"

"What, exactly, is it that you want me to do?"

Angus glared at him. "Something. Anything. Her room, for starters. Alex's room. Can you not search it for clues?"

"I suppose I could take a look," the policeman said hesitantly.

"Then get on with it, man." Angus led the way to the closed door and flung it open.

DS Lombardi spent a moment just surveying the mess within. Indicating the heaps of clothing on the floor, he said, "Do you know what she was wearing when she went out?"

"My wife didn't see her. So no. We don't know. Her coat isn't here, so she must've worn it, but apart from that, no."

"Is that her school uniform?"

Blazer and skirt on the floor. "It is," Angus acknowledged.

"So she wasn't wearing her uniform."

"I should think that's bloody obvious."

The sergeant pointed at the teddy bear in the middle of the unmade bed. "And she didn't take her teddy with her."

Angus snorted. "She's twelve years old, man. Not a wee bairn. She hasn't taken Buster out with her since she was two."

DS Lombardi picked his way through the disaster zone that was Alex's room. "That's a nice computer," he said. "Looks pretty state-of-the-art."

"It's what Alex wanted," Angus said smugly. "So I bought it for her. She fancies being a graphic designer one day."

"Is it all right if I touch it?"

"As long as you don't break it."

The policeman pressed a key and the black screen sprang to colourful life. Superimposed on the picture — Angus recognised the Highland landscape, just outside Gartenbridge — was a log-in box. *Enter password*, it said.

"I don't suppose you know her password?"

Angus shook his head, scowling. "Now what would be the point of that?" Was the man a blethering idiot, or was he just pretending to be one?

At least, though, this one wasn't drooling over Jilly the way the other one had been. The DI's eyes had been out on stalks when he'd looked at her.

Much good it would do him.

Alex went into the loo at McDonald's and wiped her face with a paper towel. She was afraid that she'd made a public spectacle of herself just now, crying in public like that.

But she couldn't have helped it if she'd wanted to. All of those letters from her mum. She'd read each one, crying like a baby.

Her mother had been writing to her every week, for months and months. Every letter was there: letters telling her how much she missed her, how much she loved her. How she longed for them to be together again, never to be separated.

"Why don't you write to me?" her mother asked over and over again. "I think about my darling little girl every minute of every day, and I long to hear from you."

Mum was afraid that Alex had stopped loving her — as if that could ever happen.

But the letters hadn't reached her. All along they'd been piling up in Jilly's drawer.

Jilly! Hateful, horrible Jilly. Alex had known that Jilly was bad news, but even she hadn't ever thought her capable of such a wicked act. Intercepting Alex's letters, hiding them from her, letting her think that her mum had forgotten about her. Or worse.

She never wanted to see Jilly again, as long as she lived.

And what was more, she now knew where her mother was. The address was on each of the letters: Lochside, Kelso, Roxburghshire, TD5 8JT.

That was where she was going. She would find Mum, and nothing would ever separate them again.

Alex went into one of the cubicles; while she was there she took the money out of her pocket and counted it. If she was going to get to Scotland — and she *was* going to Scotland — she would have to be very careful with her money.

She had three ten-pound notes, a five-pound note, and six pounds thirty-one pence in change. Just over forty pounds.

Would it be enough?

Probably not.

How could she get some more cash?

There was at least a hundred pounds in her sock drawer. If she could somehow get to that . . .

But that was out of the question. She couldn't go back there. Not now. Jilly might have missed her; Dad might even be home from work. The chances of sneaking in undetected weren't good. And besides, she never wanted to see that flat again. Not ever.

Her greatest regret was that she'd left Buster behind.

Unconsciously her hand went to her neck, as it so often did, to fondle her locket.

It wasn't there.

Oh, no.

Her heart thudded unpleasantly, then she remembered. The chain was broken, and she'd tucked it under her pillow.

Did she dare to go back? One minute, or two at most, was all it would take. Money, Buster, locket. Could she take the risk?

Jane Stanford had a job to do: in her universe, a very important job.

Sunday afternoon the church would be holding the Christingle service, that annual pre-Christmas service for children at which each child would be given a decorated orange — a Christingle. Tomorrow morning the Mothers' Union would be gathering to make the Christingles. That would involve a sort of assembly-line procedure in which each orange, representing the world, would be wrapped round the centre with a length of red ribbon, then acquire a candle on top, and finally be stabbed with four cocktail sticks on which were threaded various small sweets and dried fruit.

Through years of experience, Jane had found that the whole procedure went much more smoothly when advance preparations were made. The spool of ribbon needed to be cut into segments of the appropriate length, and the cocktail sticks could have the raisins and sweets stuck on them. Most tedious of all was the cutting up of kitchen foil into squares to act as wax catchers for the candles.

Years ago, when the boys were young, it had been a family affair. She and Brian had cut up the ribbon and foil while Simon and Charlie enthusiastically — even gleefully — impaled sweets and raisins, managing to eat quite a few of them in the process. Jane cherished those memories, and had secretly hoped that this year she might revive that tradition — might even use it to draw Ellie into the family, since

332

it seemed inevitable that the girl was destined to be a part of their lives.

But Simon and Ellie were gone — departed that morning for Northamptonshire. Brian had sloped off to his study to work on his Christingle sermon, which to Jane seemed unnecessary since he said the same thing every year, and even Charlie had deserted her. "There's a good film on the telly tonight, Mum," he'd said. "Why don't we do the Christingle stuff in front of the telly?"

That, though, was not part of the tradition. So Jane sat alone in the unheated dining room, shivering as she snipped lengths of ribbon, pricking her fingers on sharp cocktail sticks. Abandoned, desolate.

Simon had gone, and all the life of the house seemed to have departed with him. Oddly enough, it was much worse than after the boys had gone off to university. Then Jane knew they'd be back home for Christmas; there was something to look forward to. Yes, Simon and Ellie were returning in time for the New Year, but it just wasn't the same. There was such an air of finality about this departure. It signalled the end of an era, somehow. The end of their family unit.

By the time Jane had finished and cleaned up the detritus, Charlie's film was over and he was nowhere in evidence. Automatically she tidied the sitting room, fluffing the squashed cushions, picking up a discarded newspaper and retrieving the old knitted throw from the floor where Charlie had left it. He'd also left a dirty coffee mug, and Jane knew that there would be another in Brian's study. She sighed. What was it about men that gave them some sort of touching faith that mugs, if left for long enough, would find their own way to the kitchen?

Brian was no longer in his study, and when Jane eventually made her way to the bedroom, she found him propped up in bed reading a battered paperback thriller, bought for ten pence at the last church jumble sale. He closed it and put it on the bedside table when she came in.

"Don't let me disturb you," she said shortly.

Brian patted her side of the bed. "Janey, I think we need to talk."

Jane didn't want to talk; she didn't expect Brian to understand how she felt about Simon's departure, and trying to explain would be useless. Reluctantly she sat down.

"About this . . . well, what you said about having a baby."

She drew in a quick breath. This was the first time Brian had mentioned it since that first night, early in the week, when she'd told him that was what she wanted more than anything. To say he'd been astonished would be an understatement; he'd practically laughed in her face. Once he'd got over the initial shock and realised she was serious, he'd trotted out all the arguments and clichés she'd expected: too old, too set in their ways, potentially dangerous to her health. None of her carefully prepared counter-arguments had swayed him in the least, and since then she'd assumed that the subject was dead. "Yes?" Jane said.

"Well, I've been thinking about it," Brian admitted. "Quite a lot over the last few days. I don't think I was very . . . tactful. But I was just so surprised, Janey."

"I'm not too old," she stated, not looking at him, picking at a loose thread on the duvet cover. "Lots of women my age have babies these days."

"I never dreamed you felt that way," he confessed. "I thought the boys were . . . enough for you."

Jane shook her head. "It doesn't have anything to do with the boys." This was only half true, and she knew it, but she continued. "I've wanted it for years. Wished desperately that it was possible. But financially it was out of the question. Just not an option." She was the one who'd always paid the bills, and knew better than Brian how true that was.

"Well, Janey, I've been thinking, and if it's what you really want —"

She turned to him, her eyes welling with unexpected tears. "More than anything."

"Then hadn't you better come here?"

Brian opened his arms, and she went into them.

Granny!

The word came into Alex's head, along with a picture of a beloved face, and her face split in a smile.

There was no need to go back to the flat to retrieve more money.

Granny had lots of money, and she would give her some. Granny would help her get to Scotland. Maybe Granny would even go with her. Take her to her mother.

And Granny would understand why she couldn't go back to the flat. Granny didn't like Jilly any more than Alex herself did; she'd never said so, exactly, but she didn't have to. Alex had seen the disapproval on Granny's face whenever she and Jilly were in the same room.

Which wasn't very often. Maybe, thought Alex suddenly, with a flash of grown-up insight, that was why they rarely saw Granny. Even stupid silly-billy Jilly wasn't thick enough not to notice her mother-in-law's contempt for her.

It was another thing to hate Jilly for: the fact that she hardly ever got to see Granny any more, even though Granny was living in London too. Yet another thing to add to the long list of reasons to hate Jilly.

Yes, Granny would help her to get away from Jilly. The trouble was, Alex wasn't exactly sure where Granny lived. She'd only been there a few times, and never on her own. Bayswater: that was all she knew. Not even the address. Just Bayswater.

Well, she'd find Bayswater. Wasn't there a tube stop there? She could take the tube to Bayswater, and once she was there, she'd probably recognise Granny's block of flats. Bayswater couldn't be that big, could it? If she had to, she could stop someone and ask them where Granny lived. Mrs. Morag Hamilton: surely anyone in Bayswater could point her in the right direction, just as anyone in Gartenbridge could have done in the old days.

Alex shoved the forty-odd pounds back in her jeans pocket and sauntered out of the loo, out of

McDonald's, onto the street to look for the nearest tube station.

Mark had dealt with tough customers before. After all, as statistics on inter-family violence bore out, there was always a strong likelihood in dealing with the families of murder victims that he was also dealing with the murderer.

Never, though, had he come up against anyone quite like Angus Hamilton.

Hamilton wasn't just rude. He was demanding, peremptory. Downright insulting, when it came down to it. He treated Mark as an ignorant underling, someone who was there expressly to do his bidding and nothing else.

Mark didn't envy the people who worked for Angus Hamilton.

"How many officers are out looking for Alex?" Hamilton demanded.

"I'm not sure, Mr. Hamilton," Mark prevaricated.

"Well, find out. Ring the station. Is that not what telephones are for?"

Mark walked a few steps away from the Hamiltons — Mrs. Hamilton now buffing her nails with a tool which looked to be made for that purpose; her husband resuming his pacing the length of the sitting room — and turned his back on them to make the call. As he expected, no one could tell him much. Yes, they were aware of the missing girl. Uniformed officers throughout London had been alerted to keep their eyes open for her. But no one had seen her or anyone matching her description.

Angus Hamilton stopped pacing and smacked his forehead with an open hand. "*I'm* the blethering idiot," he announced. "Why did I not think of it? Why did *you* not think of it, for that matter?"

Mark turned round. "What's that, Mr. Hamilton?"

"The hospitals, man! Ring them *now*. All of them. Ask them if they've had a young lassie admitted. On her own. Been in an accident or such like. Get on with it, man!"

Something in his voice reached Mark then, through the layers of his own defensiveness at being treated like a brainless underling and his disappointment at the ruin of his evening. Alex Hamilton, the missing girl, was twelve years old. Exactly the same age as his niece Chiara. Chiara was growing up — he'd observed it himself — but she was still a little girl. Defenseless, trusting, naive. Not street-smart. If Chiara were missing . . .

Serena would be beside herself. Joe would be out there himself looking for her. He would be threatening to dismember anyone who laid a finger on her. Pressurising the police, just as Angus Hamilton was doing.

Mark's heart softened. Yes, Angus Hamilton was a rude, objectionable man. But they were on the same side. They both wanted to find a little girl who was missing from home. From now on he would remember that.

338

Callie was still on the sofa with Bella, watching a mindless — and as far as she could tell, pointless — film on the television when Peter let himself in, well past midnight.

"Oh, Sis! I wasn't expecting to see you here," he said. "I thought you'd still be out on the town. Charming look, by the way," he grinned, indicating the threadbare dressing gown over the velvet shirt.

"Thanks. Actually, today I bought a dressing gown for Mum for Christmas. I'm hoping she'll hate it, so I can keep it for myself."

"Well, I suspect you're on to a winner." He dropped his leather jacket on the nearest chair. "When has she ever liked anything you gave her?"

"Just about as often as she's liked anything *you* gave her," Callie pointed out.

"That's our Mum. At least she doesn't play favourites."

She made a wry face. "That's some consolation, I suppose."

"Anyway, what are you doing back already?" Peter didn't pause for a reply, continuing to fire questions at her. "How did it go? How was the restaurant? And how was Marco's family? Ready to welcome you with open arms?"

"Don't ask," Callie said, in what she hoped was a firm voice. "Really. I mean it. Don't ask."

CHAPTER
SEVENTEEN

Things really started to happen shortly after midnight, when Angus Hamilton rang the Assistant Commissioner, rousing him from his virtuous bed. The Assistant Commissioner in turn disturbed the ongoing familial festivities at the Evans home, and Evans immediately rang Neville Stewart.

As it happened, when the phone went, Neville wasn't nearly as intoxicated as he might have been. For some reason the first Guinness had sent him into a sound, dreamless sleep, right there on the sofa; only the persistent ringing of the mobile in his pocket penetrated that sleep and brought him round to almost sober consciousness.

"Oh, God," he said, fumbling for the phone, realising in some part of his brain that he was more disorientated than drunk. He had no idea what time it was, or how long he'd been sleeping.

"I don't care what you're doing or who you're with," Evans said, in tones that brooked no argument. "I want you back at that flat in twenty minutes. Thirty, tops. Take Cowley with you, if you must. But keep him on a short lead."

"Yes, Sir."

"I mean it, Stewart. I don't want anybody upsetting Angus Hamilton. No funny business. Of any kind whatsoever."

Neville wondered whether Evans had some inkling of the attractions of Mrs. Hamilton — attractions of the sort which were sure to appeal to the red-blooded Sid Cowley — or whether he was speaking in general terms. Sid wasn't exactly renowned for tact or impeccable manners. "Yes, Sir," he repeated.

Cowley hadn't been drinking at all; unlike Neville, he wasn't scheduled to have the day off on Saturday. So he collected Neville by car and they set off for St. John's Wood.

On the way, Neville filled him in about the situation — and about why they had been called out in the middle of the night to deal with it. "This is a kid-gloves job," he warned Cowley. "Evans was insistent. The Hamilton bloke knows the Assistant Commissioner. So we're to be on our best behaviour."

"Guv." Cowley turned his head briefly from his concentration on the icy road, shooting a quick, reproachful look at Neville. "When am I ever not on my best behaviour?"

Neville snorted. "Oh, please, Sid. Give me a break."

"Maybe he meant *you*, Guv," Cowley suggested smugly.

Ignoring that remark, Neville continued. "The main thing I want to tell you before we get there is that you're not to start drooling too obviously when you see Mrs. Hamilton. That's about the worst thing you could do."

341

Cowley looked interested. "Worth drooling over, is she, Guv?"

"God, yes. Younger than him by, oh, maybe ten years. Blonde. Great body." He thought about how else he might describe her, remembering that delicious shrug she was so good at, consciously or not. The thing about Jilly Hamilton, though, was that she wasn't just some cheap, flirtatious, curvaceous blonde. She was rich. Posh. Polished, in every sense of the word. St. John's Wood, through and through. Born to it. He couldn't put it into words that Cowley would understand, so he just said, "But she's not for the likes of you or me, Sid. Not only is she a married woman, she's way out of our league. And don't you forget it."

Sid Cowley managed to get himself on the wrong side of Jilly Hamilton almost immediately, within just a few seconds of their arrival. "Mind if I smoke?" he said to no one in particular, pulling out a packet of fags.

"Yes, I do mind," Jilly Hamilton countered sharply. "This is a non-smoking home. Once it gets in the curtains, you can never get it out. Surely you know that . . . Sergeant, is it?" She glared at him until he put the packet back in his pocket.

It was the most emotion Neville had yet seen her express over anything. Well, well, he thought. Jilly Hamilton *does* care about something after all. Even if it's only her curtains.

In the hours Neville had been away, Mark might have been able to tell him that Jilly's demeanour had gone from indifferent to bored, and now she had moved

342

on to sulky. She obviously, Neville thought, was unused to not being the centre of attention.

While Neville consulted with Angus Hamilton about the steps which were now being taken or would shortly come into play in the search for Alex, Jilly crossed and re-crossed her legs, got up and moved round the room, ostentatiously consulted her delicate Rolex, and finally announced, "I'm going to bed. There isn't any reason for me to stay up, is there?"

Angus broke off what he was saying and looked at her, his brows drawn together. "Do you really think you can sleep?"

She shrugged. "If she comes home, she comes home. If she doesn't . . . well, there isn't anything I can do about it either way, is there?"

By Saturday morning, the police were well and truly mobilised in their search for the missing girl. Although it was obviously too late to get anything in the morning papers, her photo had been released to the press and the Assistant Commissioner himself had scheduled a press conference. By lunchtime it would be the lead story in news bulletins, at least in London, and the public would be made aware that anyone who had seen a girl fitting Alex Hamilton's description should ring the Metropolitan Police on a special number.

Though the Hamiltons' flat was not itself regarded as a crime scene, SOCOs had visited it and given Alex's room in particular a thorough inspection, retrieving DNA samples and taking away her computer. Danny Duffy had been called in, forcing him to turn back on the motorway en-route to a Christmas shopping trip at Bluewater with his girlfriend. The girlfriend, it was understood by everyone at the station, was not amused.

When Alex woke early on Saturday morning, cramped and chilled, it took her some time to remember where she was.

Her search for her Granny had not been a successful one. She'd found Bayswater, all right, but it was a bigger place than she'd expected, sprawling into Paddington on one side and Notting Hill on another. Not a village like Gartenbridge: just part of London. In the dark nothing looked familiar to her; she didn't recognise Granny's block of flats or even any landmarks.

By that time of night she'd even had problems finding anyone to ask about Granny. The streets of the residential areas were virtually deserted; eventually she'd found a 24-hour convenience store and enquired of the young dark-skinned man behind the till whether he knew Mrs. Morag Hamilton. He stared at her as if she'd come from another planet, and shook his head, spreading his hands in a universal gesture of helplessness. He probably, she realised, didn't understand her. Either her Scottish accent was unfamiliar to him, or he didn't actually speak English.

So she'd continued to wander, feeling more and more cold and weary. All she wanted now was to find a warm place and sleep.

Eventually she'd spotted her chance, and had taken it. A car pulled up to an empty spot on the kerb and a

344

woman got out, then let herself into a block of flats — council flats, probably — with a key. Alex hurried to catch her up and slipped in behind her, into a draughty passageway. The woman nodded at her, unconcerned, and continued on her way.

The passageway itself was chilly and unpromising, but surely something better would present itself. Alex went down to the end of it, where she found a small, unlocked room: a laundry room, evidently for the communal use of the flats' residents. It held several industrial-sized washing machines and tumble dryers, all with coin slots. The walls were concrete; so was the floor. It was damp and clammy, and smelt of dirty clothes and pungent washing powder. The lighting, which consisted of a single bare bulb dangling from the ceiling, seemed to be permanently on, casting grim shadows into the corners. Not exactly a congenial spot, but as welcome to Alex at that moment as a room at the Ritz.

And she was in luck. One of the tumble dryers was in operation, throwing off a fair amount of heat. Alex opened it and pulled out an armful of towels, nearly dry and so hot they almost burned her hands. She spread them on the concrete floor in between two of the machines, curled up with her back propped against the warm one, and promptly fell asleep.

She woke up once in the middle of the night, cold and cramped. The dryer had shut itself off and the room no longer held any of its lingering warmth. Alex tried to go back to sleep with no success; eventually she got up, rooted in the dryer till she found a sheet to cover herself with, and when even that didn't work she sacrificed one of her precious pound coins for another hour of heat from the dryer. After that she slept till morning, uncomfortable but warm enough.

Yolanda hadn't realised how tired she was, how worn out by the stresses of the past week. She'd gone home, on Neville's orders, and had virtually fallen into bed, not even waking up when Eli joined her at some point on Friday night. She didn't wake up, in fact, until Eli wafted a mug of black coffee under her nose on Saturday morning.

"Hey, doll," he said when she'd half-opened her eyes. "Thought you might need this."

"Mmmm." She rubbed her eyes and sat up, taking the cup from him.

"You slept well?"

Yolanda nodded. "Did I ever." She'd seldom before reflected on what a delightful luxury it was to sleep in one's own bed.

Eli perched on the edge of the bed. He was, she saw to her disappointment, already dressed for work. "Do you want to tell me what's going on?" he asked. "I've got five minutes before I have to leave."

"Rachel had her baby. A girl. The DNA results came back, and I was wrong about Trevor still being alive." She sighed and took a tentative sip of the coffee. "Which means that we still don't know who killed him, or whether Rachel was involved in any way. They'll obviously keep an eye on her, but at this point there's nothing to go on. And she's in hospital for a day or two, so there's nothing for me to do."

"Except catch up on your sleep," Eli stated. "And get reacquainted with your husband, who was beginning to forget what you looked like." He leaned over and gave her a squeeze.

She stroked his cheek. "I wish you didn't have to work today."

"So do I, doll," said Eli. "So do I."

Callie had her usual Saturday morning rush to get to Morning Prayer, exacerbated by Peter deciding to get up early for a change and take a long shower. Why today, of all days? she asked herself in frustration. Any other day he'd still be sound asleep on the pull-out sofa, grumbling that she'd woken him with her noisy ablutions.

Now he was the one abluting, and he didn't seem inclined to stop any time soon. He was singing in the shower: always a bad sign. He only did that when he was in it for the long haul. Tunes from Broadway musicals were his favourite. "If ever I would leave you . . ." he was warbling, in his fine tenor voice.

"I wish you would," Callie muttered, feeling distinctly uncharitable. She stood outside of the bathroom door for a moment, finally resorting to banging on it. Peter, in full flow, didn't miss a note; evidently enchanted by the sound of his own voice, he hadn't even heard her. "Oh no, not in springtime, summer, winter or fall . . ."

If he was still here in the springtime, she would slit her wrists. Giving up, Callie sprinted back to the bedroom and pulled on her clericals and her cassock, then gave her hair a quick brush and put on a bit of lip gloss. She'd have to shower when she got back.

As she ran for the door, Peter emerged from the bathroom in his towelling dressing gown, looking angelically pink and clean, and incredibly young, his wet hair ruffled round his face. "Oh, hi, Sis. Going somewhere?"

"Morning Prayer. As usual," she snapped over her shoulder, then pelted down the stairs. She knew it was the wrong mood in which to approach an act of worship, but at this point she was beyond caring.

When she got home some thirty minutes later, Peter was waiting for her with a freshly-brewed cup of coffee. "Sis, I'm sorry about the shower," he said contritely. "I just wasn't thinking, I suppose. I thought I was being so virtuous, getting up early. And instead I buggered up your day."

He looked so woebegone and penitent that Callie nearly burst out laughing; it just wasn't possible to stay angry with Peter for long. Annoying as he was, he was also the most charming man she'd ever met. Genuinely so: there was no calculation or guile in him. He could be thoughtless, it was true, but he was also capable of the most touching sensitivity.

"It doesn't matter," she said. "There were only three people at Morning Prayer, and none of them complained about my personal hygiene."

Peter laughed. "Well, drink this coffee, then you can take your shower. I've already given Bella a short walk, so you won't have to worry about that. You'll have the flat to yourself — I'm off in a minute."

For a wild, joyous instant she thought he meant he was leaving for good. "Where are you going?"

"You put me to shame by doing your Christmas shopping yesterday. So I thought I'd head to Sloane Square and get mine done."

"Sloane Square? Not Oxford Street?"

He shrugged. "Too many people in Oxford Street. And the shops are better in Sloane Square." He added, "And then I'll drop in to see Mum. I'll be the good son. Maybe it will take the heat off you for a few days."

"Oh, bless you." She really was grateful: looking at her diary the day before, she didn't see how she was going to manage to fit in a visit to her mother before Christmas.

"I have my uses," he grinned. "Even if I'm a royal pain in the tush most of the time."

She couldn't dispute either part of his statement. Callie flopped down on the sofa, which — miracle of miracles — he'd already closed up, and gulped at the coffee.

"What are you up to for the rest of the day?" Peter asked as he wound a striped cashmere scarf round his neck.

"Ugh." She pulled a face. "Making Christingles with the Mothers' Union this morning. I can hardly wait."

Peter stopped winding. "What the hell are Christingles? Wait — don't tell me. Let me imagine something really exotic and kinky." He winked at her.

Callie laughed. "Oh, would that it were so. I'll put it this way: it almost makes me wish I were going with you to see Mum."

"Now *that* is alarming."

"It wouldn't be so bad if it wasn't for Jane," she admitted. "Most of the people in the MU are really nice. But Jane is so . . . bossy. So proprietorial, like she owns the Mothers' Union. She always manages to put me in the wrong. And she seems to enjoy showing me up. I've never understood why she dislikes me so much."

"Oh, Sis." Peter zipped up his leather jacket. "You still have a lot to learn, don't you?" Suddenly he sounded knowing, wise, like an older brother rather than a younger one. "You seeing Marco tonight?" he added, heading for the stairs.

"I'm not sure," she said.

She *wasn't* sure. They had no advance plans; he hadn't rung. Well, she'd worry about that later. Now it was time for a shower and the Mothers' Union.

Before leaving St. John's Wood for the station, Neville took Mark to the kitchen of the flat for a quiet word. "How is it going?" he asked.

Mark lifted his shoulders helplessly. "Well, *she's* not helping, of course. She's like a spoiled brat. And you were right: she doesn't care a fig about Alex. Everything has to be about *her*."

Ah, the delightful Jilly was right on form, then.

"I feel so sorry for *him*," Mark went on. "He's such a take-charge bloke. Used to being in control, getting his own way. And there's not a blessed thing he can do, but

350

wait and hope. And pray, I suppose, if he's that way inclined. Which I somehow doubt."

"And boss the police about," Neville added tartly. "I'm surprised you've managed to forget that, mate. It almost sounds like you're on his side."

Mark shook his head, startling Neville with his vehemence. "We're on the same side, Nev. We all want to find Alex. I'm surprised you've forgotten *that*."

"But he's so bloody arrogant . . ."

"The man's child is missing. She's twelve years old. Just a kid. A little girl." Mark had tears in his eyes. "The same age as my niece. He's going through hell right now, so cut him a bit of slack, all right? He may not be the world's best dad, but he loves Alex."

Feeling suitably chastened, Neville left the kitchen and collected Sid Cowley. "I'll be in touch," he said to Angus Hamilton, making an effort to remind himself of the man's difficult position. "I'll keep you informed. As soon as we have any information at all, I'll ring you."

"Thank you, Inspector," said Angus Hamilton through clenched teeth.

"We'll see ourselves out," Neville stated to no one in particular.

Cowley reached for his fags and lighter as soon as they were out of the door. "Arrogant poncy sod," he said conversationally.

"And the lovely Mrs. Hamilton? What did you think?"

The sergeant paused long enough to light his cigarette and take a long, thoughtful draw. "She's a stuck-up cow," he pronounced. "A selfish bitch. 'Non-smoking home,' my arse."

Neville chuckled. "That's what I like about you, Sid. You're so tolerant."

"But dead fanciable, for all that," Cowley added, leering. With his hands he sketched exaggerated curves in the air.

"And," said Neville, "you're so predictable."

Alex knew that the trains to Scotland went from King's Cross station. What she didn't know was how to get to King's Cross from Bayswater.

She could take a taxi, but she was reluctant to spend any of her dwindling cash. If she was lucky, she might have just about enough money to get her to Scotland. So no taxi. It would have to be the Underground.

Somehow, by trial and error, she found her way back to the Bayswater tube station. There she pored over the complicated map, like a heap of tangled electrical wires or a bowl of multicoloured spaghetti. With her finger she traced the lines: the yellow one went all the way from Bayswater to King's Cross. She checked the colour key at the bottom; the yellow one was the Circle Line. Simple enough.

All right. She could do this.

She had to part with one pound and fifty pence into the machine, but she reminded herself that the taxi would have cost much more.

Alex put the ticket into the slot at the ticket barrier and passed through, following the signs *District and Circle* to the platform. No one paid any attention to her as she stood on the platform. "The next train . . ."

woofed the tannoy, followed by an incomprehensible list of destinations.

Most everyone got on the train, and Alex followed.

It was crowded. The penultimate Saturday before Christmas: shoppers, tourists and all the rest. Alex wedged herself into a tiny space by the door and held onto the back of the seat beside her.

Neville was resigned to the fact that although he was the Chief Investigating Officer in the case of Alex Hamilton, Evans wasn't about to leave him alone to get on with it. He supposed he ought to be thankful that the Assistant Commissioner didn't have him on speed dial as well. It was all chain-of-command stuff; everything came to him through Evans, his immediate boss.

"Family?" Evans demanded during one of his calls, taking time out from the in-laws. "I understand that Mrs. Hamilton isn't the girl's mother. Do we know where her mother is? And what about any other family?"

"I'm not sure about the mother, Sir. I can ask." Neville opened his notebook and flipped through it. "The only thing I have is that there's a grandmother in Scotland."

"Get her address," Evans ordered. "And the mother as well."

"Maybe she's dead."

"And maybe she's not. Find out."

"Yes, Sir."

Instead of ringing Angus Hamilton, Neville took the coward's way out and rang Mark. He explained what he needed. "Can you find out?" he requested. "Ring me back."

He drummed his fingers on his scarred desk for what seemed like an age, until the phone bleeped. "Yes?"

Mark sounded puzzled. "The mother seems to be in some sort of institution. A care home, he called it. She's had some type of breakdown."

"Breakdown?"

"Mental, I assume. Mrs. Hamilton — Jilly — said she — the other Mrs. Hamilton, the first one — had gone 'round the twist' when he left her."

"Good God," Neville muttered. "I'd dance a jig and thank my lucky stars."

"But it's the grandmother that surprised me," Mark went on.

"What about her?"

"It's his mother. Angus' mother. Morag Hamilton, she's called. You said she was in Scotland. But he says she lives in London. Bayswater."

"The devil she does." Neville wanted to swear; somehow he managed to hold his tongue. Evans was definitely not going to be amused by this little slip-up. For all they knew, the girl might have gone to her grandmother's house yesterday afternoon. That was the first place they should have looked; it might have saved them all a great deal of aggro. Though, Neville told himself, if she had done, surely the grandmother would have rung her son, or taken the girl home?

"Do you want the address? I have the phone number as well."

Neville scribbled them down. "Thanks, Mark. I'll send someone over there right away."

★ ★ ★

354

To Callie's astonishment, Jane smiled at her when she came into the church hall. "Ready to learn all about Christingles?" Jane greeted her.

"I don't know a thing about them," admitted Callie, disarmed out of the customary defensiveness she felt where Jane was concerned.

Jane had laid the various components out on long folding tables: trays of oranges, boxes of stubby white candles, heaps of red ribbons and squares of foil, decorated cocktail sticks.

Some members of the Mothers' Union were already there, and others arrived within the next few minutes, standing round the tables.

Morag Hamilton was one of the later arrivals. She headed for a spot next to Callie, who smiled warmly at her. She hadn't seen Morag for a few days, and had intended to call on her at some point during the weekend to see how she was getting on.

"I'm glad you've come," Callie greeted her. "I hoped you would. I meant to ring you and remind you about this, but yesterday was my day off."

"Well, it's a chance to get out of the flat and meet people."

"Any news from the hospital?" queried Callie.

Morag shook her head. "Still no appointment. I suppose it could be weeks."

"You'll let me know when you hear, won't you?"

"Aye. I will."

Jane was looking at the clock, clearly impatient to begin. Knowing how jealously Jane guarded Brian's Saturday days off as sacrosanct family time, Callie was a bit surprised that Jane was there at all, especially with her sons at home. She supposed — perhaps uncharitable, but true — that Jane couldn't bear not to be in charge of this enterprise, and it couldn't really be done at any other time. The Christingle service was always held on the third Sunday of Advent, and the oranges wouldn't keep if they were done any earlier than the day before that.

"For those of you who are new to this," Jane said in her official vicar's wife voice, looking towards Callie and Morag Hamilton, "perhaps a bit of history about Christingle and what we're doing here today would be in order." She smiled at everyone else. "If the rest of you could just bear with me for a minute."

White and grey heads nodded. Callie nodded as well, to indicate her appreciation at being granted special consideration.

"The Christingle service is of Moravian origin, and dates back to the mid-seventeen hundreds in Germany," Jane explained. "It has always been intended for children — a way of demonstrating, at Christmas time, the light of Christ coming into the world. The Church of England began holding Christingle services in 1968, sponsored by the Church of England Children's Society. It's always one of the most popular and best-attended services of the year."

Jane held up an orange. "I'll demonstrate how we make a Christingle. We'll do it in assembly-line fashion, passing them along the tables — that's the most efficient way. But here's the whole process."

356

She took a sharp knife from the table in front of her. "The orange represents the world," she said, cutting a deep cross in the top of it. "I'm preparing it now to receive its candle. But first it needs its red ribbon. The ribbon symbolises the blood of Christ, given in sacrifice for the world and all its people." She wrapped a pre-cut length of ribbon round the centre of the orange, securing it with sellotape.

"Now it will be passed on to the person with the kitchen foil." Jane held up a small square of foil. "The foil is a safety feature, rather than a symbol. It helps to catch the wax from the lit candle. A piece of it is placed over the cross at the top, then the candle is inserted through the centre of the foil." She demonstrated this move, pushing the candle down firmly into place. "I don't need to tell you that the candle represents the light of Christ in the world."

"Finally," she went on, "we have the cocktail sticks. They have raisins and sweets on them, representing the fruits of the earth. We used to use nuts as well," Jane added. "But that is discouraged these days, because so many children have nut allergies. And I've read that the Moravians used to use goose quills instead of cocktail sticks, but goose quills are in rather short supply these days." She laughed. "Each Christingle gets four of these cocktail sticks stuck round the candle, like this." She positioned them carefully, then held up the finished product so everyone could see it. "At the end of the assembly line, I'll take the Christingles and put them in the boxes, ready for tomorrow."

There was a smattering of applause, then the women began arranging themselves at chairs round the tables, probably, thought Callie, each taking up the task they'd done for years on end. Maybe since 1968, in some cases.

"Callie, why don't you sit here?" Jane suggested. "You can put candles in. Is that all right?"

"Yes, fine."

"And Mrs. Hamilton, isn't it? If you come here next to Callie, you can place the foil squares on and pass them on to her."

Obviously, Callie realised, the newcomers were given the simplest jobs — they were not to be trusted with knives or cocktail sticks or anything else that could inflict injury.

"I'm pretty good at candles," Callie whispered to Morag. "Though it could be a bit tricky to get them in straight, so they don't tip over or fall out or drip wax."

Morag smiled. "It's a charming custom, isn't it? I've never seen it in Scotland. I imagine the bairns really enjoy it."

"Why don't you bring your granddaughter to the service?" Callie suggested impulsively. "Alex. She'd like it, wouldn't she?"

Morag looked away, her eyes shadowed. "She'd love it. But they'd never allow it. I'm sure of it."

The tube train pulled into a station. "Edgware Road. This service terminates here. All change," announced an amplified voice.

Obediently everyone shuffled off the train. Everyone but Alex, who remained tucked into her little space.

358

Edgware Road? But she wanted to go to King's Cross. This train was supposed to take her there.

Then other people started getting on, and before she knew it the train was going back in the other direction. The way she'd come, towards Bayswater.

"Paddington," came the announcement a few minutes later. "Change here for Circle Line and Bakerloo Line services, the Hammersmith and City lines, and mainline rail services."

"Excuse me." Alex pushed her way out of the door.

She'd made a mistake, she realised as soon as she looked at the map. She'd got on one of the green-line trains, which only went as far as Edgware Road, when she'd needed to get on a yellow one. Circle Line. That's what she wanted.

Alex saw that there was an illuminated board overhead, showing the next three trains. The second one said *Circle Line, 6 mins*. She'd make very sure she got on the right train this time. Not the first one; she must wait for the second one.

Neville could imagine it quite clearly in his mind: Sid Cowley, lighting up a fag and lounging against the wall. Taking his own sweet time before ringing.

"She's not here, Guv," Cowley said. "I've tried the bell. I've waited for five minutes. If she's here, she's not answering."

"Neighbours?" Neville suggested.

"I talked to the old bloke across the corridor. Hardly knows her, he said. Only by sight. She hasn't been here long, and she keeps herself to herself."

"Anyone else?" Someone, he thought, might have seen the girl yesterday afternoon.

"No one else about. Nearly Christmas, innit?"

"Well, never mind, then, Sid. I'll just have to ring her." He hadn't wanted to do that; he'd preferred to have the news broken to her in person that her granddaughter was missing, even if it were done by the less-than-tactful Sid Cowley. If she wasn't at home, he'd just have to hope that she had an answerphone or a call minder service.

There was indeed an answerphone. "Please leave a message," said a cultured female Scots voice.

"My name is DI Stewart, from the Metropolitan Police CID. Please don't be alarmed, but could you please give me a ring at your earliest convenience, Mrs. Hamilton?" Neville left his mobile number, hoping she'd pick the message up before she found out about her granddaughter's disappearance in some other way.

His mind was almost immediately occupied by a more pressing matter: a call from Danny Duffy, the computer boffin.

"Guv," said Danny, "could you come to the computer lab? I need some advice."

Maybe the whizz kid had found something, Neville told himself with rising excitement. Though he couldn't imagine what it might be. Had the girl left a message for her father on the computer, telling him where she was going?

It was a beautiful, expensive-looking computer, a white slab with a large flat screen, putting to shame the other shabby machines in the lab. Danny was hunched over it, tapping the keys; he looked up as Neville came in.

"Ah, Guv."

"You've found something?"

"Well, no." Danny lifted his hands, palms up, an empty-handed gesture of defeat.

"Then what am I doing here?"

"It's a little girl who owns this computer?" Danny asked.

"Twelve years old," confirmed Neville, still not at all sure what this was about.

"That figures. Kids — they're much more computer-savvy than adults."

Neville remembered pressing a key on Alex's computer, seeing the password prompt. "But this computer *does* have a password."

"Exactly. And she's done it cleverly, as well. No way round it, by re-booting or holding down an option key or anything like that. It's iron-clad. You've got to know the password to get in, or the whole thing locks down. I'll hand it to the kid — she's done it properly."

"But that doesn't help us," stated Neville.

"We're buggered," Danny said cheerfully. "Unless maybe her mum or dad knows the password? Or can guess it?"

"Guess it?"

"That's the thing with kids," said Danny. "They may be technologically clued-in, but their password is usually something pretty easy. Their name, sometimes. Most often the name of a pet. Like Fluffy or Spot."

"Her name is Alex."

Danny tapped the name in, then shook his head. "No go."

Neville pulled his phone out and rang Angus Hamilton.

"Yes?" came the reply after just one ring.

As quickly as he could, Neville explained the call. "Mr. Hamilton, sorry to bother you. But we're trying to get into Alex's computer, and we need her password. Any idea what it is?"

"Like I said to your colleague, DS Lombardi, the whole point of a password is that it's secret," Angus Hamilton stated. "She certainly hasn't told me what it is."

"Does Alex have any sort of pet?" This, Neville knew, was a long shot: he couldn't imagine Jilly allowing any creature with fur, feathers or even fins into her immaculate flat.

"No."

"Not even a goldfish?"

"No."

"Has she *ever* had a pet? In Scotland, perhaps?"

"No." This time there was a thoughtful pause on the other end of the phone. "But her granny had a wee dog. Dead now. Alex loved that dog. She cried when he died."

"And what was the dog's name?" Neville asked.

"Macduff."

"M-A-C-D-U-F-F?" Neville spelt it out, looking at Danny with a nod.

"Aye," Angus Hamilton confirmed.

Danny's fingers moved on the keys; he shook his head disappointedly.

362

That was no good, then, but Neville wasn't ready to give up. "How about friends? Did you say she had a friend called Kirsty?"

"Aye, that's right."

Danny tried it, then shrugged.

"Any other ideas?"

Neville heard a voice in the background. "Mr. Hamilton, could I speak to DI Stewart?"

The phone was evidently handed over, because the next voice he heard was Mark's. "How about Buster?" Mark said.

"Buster?"

"Her teddy bear. According to her dad, she loves that bear."

Danny was already tapping it in; he lifted his head, grinning from ear to ear. "Buster?" he said. "Bingo."

"Bayswater. Change here for the District Line," said the tannoy.

Bayswater? How could it be Bayswater? That's where she'd come from, not where she was going.

Alex scrambled out of the train as the light dawned. Circle Line. That meant it went in a circle, all the way round. She'd somehow ended up going the wrong way — probably because she'd come back from Edgware Road and was on the other side of the tracks. There must be another platform.

She surveyed the signage. Yes, the eastbound platform was on the other side, over the bridge. Eastbound, towards King's Cross.

"Piece of cake, now that we're in," said Danny smugly, as if he was the one who'd come up with the password.

Full marks to Mark, Neville said to himself. Clever bloke.

"I always look at the e-mails first," Danny went on. "These days, that's where everything's happening. If there's nothing interesting there, I can check her web browser. See what sites she's visited and what she's bookmarked."

With a few deft taps of the keys, Danny had the e-mail program open; Neville stood behind him where he could view the screen.

Danny pointed with his finger. "Here's the list. The last e-mail she opened came in yesterday afternoon. From Jack."

Jack? The phantom boyfriend? Jilly had been so insistent that there was no boyfriend, that Jack was a figment of Alex's imagination . . .

"The subject line is 'Getting 2gether'. 2-gether. Get it?" He clicked to open the message.

"Oh, crikey," said Danny, reading it aloud, translating from text-ese. " 'Hey Sasha! I want to see you! Let's get together. Tonight, okay? Paddington Station under the clock. I'll be there at five! You wear something red! Me too.' "

"Oh. My. God," said Neville, adding for good measure, from somewhere out of his distant past, "Jesus, Mary and Joseph."

"No," grinned Danny. "Jack."

CHAPTER
EIGHTEEN

King's Cross — at last!

Alex got off the tube train with a real sense of accomplishment. She'd made it! She felt as if she were halfway to Scotland already.

King's Cross station seemed vast, cavernous, yet swarming with people. It appeared that a great many people were escaping from London today — dragging suitcases, hefting backpacks. Going home for Christmas already?

That, Alex realised with a great swelling of joy in her breast, was precisely what she was doing. Going home for Christmas. She would find her mother and they would be together. For Christmas and always. Together in Scotland. Home!

She had to queue for the ticket machine, and when she finally got there and punched all the right buttons — child, single, Edinburgh — she was dismayed. The fare was in excess of forty-six pounds, and she had less than forty pounds in her pocket. Not enough. Close, but not enough.

If she hadn't got this far, and with such effort, she might have given up at that point.

But her mother was was waiting for her. Longing to see her, as Alex was desperate to be reunited with her. Alex struggled against tears of frustration and disappointment, resisting any admission of failure. She would *not* give up. She couldn't. Not now.

Abandoning the ticket machine, she headed for the platforms to see whether there were the same sort of barriers in place that the tube had, the sort which required you to put a ticket in the slot before you could get through.

But, she discovered, that was not the case. Ticket-checking at the platforms was manual, done by one or two fairly lackadaisical guards. Stern signs advised travellers that travelling without a ticket was a criminal offence, punishable by a stiff fine, and warned that tickets would be checked on board.

Well, she would just have to risk it.

She walked along until she found the next Edinburgh train, due to leave in about a quarter of an hour. Alex stood close to the entrance to the platform, waiting and watching.

A large family group approached the platform: mother, father, a gaggle of three or four children. Alex sidled up close to them; the father waved a fistful of tickets in the direction of the guard, and the guard in turn waved them all through. Alex casually attached herself to them, and in an instant she was on the platform. Safe. So far.

She followed them into a carriage, just in case anyone was watching. There she discovered that most of the seats had little printed tickets in the headrests, indicating that they were reserved for particular people. The family had evidently booked two facing rows, on either side of the aisle; while they stowed their baggage and settled themselves into their seats, Alex checked the reservation tickets. They were booked for various segments of the journey, some all the way from King's Cross to Edinburgh, and others to or from Peterborough or York, or another point along the line. Alex found a pair of them, in the row behind the family, booked from Doncaster to Edinburgh. She slipped into the window seat; that would be okay for at least part of the way. When they got to Doncaster, if not before, she'd have to move.

Neville took a deep breath. A very deep breath. "There are more e-mails from this Jack, I assume?"

"Oh, lots." Danny pointed to the in-box list, then to a folder labelled *Jack*. "In fact, he seems to be about the only person she writes to, apart from someone called Kirsty."

"Her best friend in Scotland." Those should be pretty harmless, though it was possible that Alex might have confided in her best friend about Jack, so they were potentially useful as well. "Can you print them out for me? Everything. All of them."

"No problem," said Danny. "Anything else you need, Guv?"

Neville sighed. "I don't suppose that machine can tell you who Jack is, and where we might find him?"

"Oh, it probably can." Danny patted the top of the computer with a self-satisfied smirk.

"How can it do that?"

"Well, it should be a fairly simple thing to trace the e-mail address he uses, through the ISP. Internet Service Provider," he amplified at Neville's blank look. "They'll have registration details. We'll track him down, all right."

"Can't people open anonymous accounts? Or use false information?"

"Possible," Danny admitted. "False information, certainly. But e-mails leave trails. Not a lot of people know that. Every computer has a unique address, and leaves a unique footprint. So eventually we'll find him."

Eventually might not be good enough. A lurch in Neville's stomach reminded him that a little girl was out there somewhere, possibly not with a teenage boy but with a man who had set up a meeting, intending her harm. "Wear something red" — bloody hell. Was that what a boyfriend would say?

And he, Neville, had discounted the danger she might be in, just because her stepmother couldn't believe she might have a boyfriend.

Jilly Hamilton might, potentially, have a lot to answer for. But so might he.

He didn't look forward to telling Evans.

Evans, hell. Evans was a piece of cake compared to his other dilemma. How on earth was he going to tell Angus Hamilton?

Yolanda spent most of the morning tidying up the house. At least she called it tidying in her own mind, though it was more like industrial cleaning. Eli, she reflected, had many sterling characteristics, and she loved him dearly, but she had always recognised that cleanliness was not one of his priorities.

A week's worth of washing-up awaited her in the kitchen, filling the sink and spilling onto the work surfaces. It was like an archaeological excavation, revealing a history of meals consumed: crusty baked beans, dried egg yolk, bacon grease. Lots of fry-ups, then; that was Eli's main culinary speciality, though his expertise didn't extend to cleaning up after himself. There was additional evidence of ready meals and takeaways, including a plate so badly stained with curry remnants that Yolanda gave up and binned it as irretrievable.

She didn't mind the cleaning up, though she sighed and rolled her eyes at each additional piece of evidence that Eli hadn't lifted a finger for a week. In a funny way, it was soothing work, distracting her from thoughts of Rachel and the unsatisfactory state of the investigation. She enjoyed making order out of chaos, in her home as in her job.

When she moved to the bathroom, Yolanda sighed yet again. Eli had been trimming his moustache over the basin, she inferred from the scattering of little black hairs on the porcelain.

Black hairs. There was something about black hair that had been niggling at the back of her mind.

She suddenly remembered: Rachel cradling her baby. A tiny girl with black, black hair.

Blonde Rachel and her black-haired baby. What was wrong with that picture?

Callie had switched off her mobile during the Christingle-making session; she turned it back on as she went up the stairs to her flat and saw that she had a message from Marco.

"Hey, Callie, I'm really sorry about last night," he said. "Really, really sorry. And I don't know yet whether I'll be free tonight to see you. This case I've been called in on — well, it's a difficult one. A girl has gone missing. I'll tell you more about it later. *Ciao, cara mia.*"

She slipped the phone back in her pocket and looked at her watch. At their staff meeting on Thursday, Brian had asked her to do the hospital visits on Saturday, so she'd need to get on with that. With all of the cold weather, it seemed that quite a few of their parishioners, particularly the elderly, had succumbed to nasty bugs and were in need of a bit of pastoral comfort. At the back of her mind was the thought — the hope — that she might be able to meet up with Frances for a quick bite of lunch or at least a cup of coffee in the hospital cafe.

First, though, she ought to have enough time for a brisk walk round the park with Bella. Peter said he'd taken her out earlier, but it couldn't have been for much longer than a few minutes.

Bella was more than willing. The sight of her lead sent her into even greater ecstasies than the sight of Callie herself had done. Callie clipped the lead onto Bella's collar, then wrapped herself up in a warm scarf, hat and gloves while Bella wriggled with impatience at the door.

They were halfway round their customary route on the fringes of Hyde Park when Callie's phone rang in her pocket. "Oh, blast," she muttered, tucking Bella's lead between her knees and pulling her gloves off with her teeth while fumbling for the phone. "This had better be important."

"Callie?" said Morag Hamilton's voice, sounding tremulous and upset.

"Morag!"

"I'm so sorry to bother you. But something . . . dreadful . . . has happened."

"Oh, Morag. What is it?" Callie's mind leapt to all sorts of possibilities and scenarios. Mugging? An accident? It had been less than thirty minutes since she'd seen her.

"I've just been on the phone with the police. My granddaughter — my wee Alex — has gone missing. There's nothing I can do. But . . ."

"I'll be there," Callie said instantly. "I'll be with you just as soon as I can. In a few minutes."

Bella was looking at her expectantly.

"Do you mind if I bring Bella?" Callie asked. "I'm in the park, and can get to you sooner if I don't have to take her home first."

"No, I don't mind. Of course I don't."

Callie shoved the phone back in her pocket, pulled on her gloves, and took up the end of the lead. "Come on, girl," she urged. "Let's run!"

The train had stopped at Peterborough, where a few people got out and a few more got on. Now they were passing through flat, frozen fields, some still with a covering of snow. Alex sat by the window, watching the landscape as it flashed by.

In the space between the seats she could see the family, and at the moment they were more interesting than the scenery. The youngest child was fussing; the dad was trying to distract it with a colouring book. The mother reached up to the overhead luggage rack and hauled down a cool-bag, which she began to unpack on the table between the facing rows of seats. A flask, some cups, small cartons of juice which she passed out to the children, helping where necessary to puncture the tops with the little bendy straws.

A refreshment trolley was headed their way down the centre aisle. "Sandwiches?" said a perky young woman in a striped shirt. "Snacks, hot and cold beverages?"

"We've brought our own," said the mother smugly, continuing to unpack her bag.

The trolley paused at Alex's row. "Sandwiches? Snacks, hot and cold beverages?"

Alex looked with longing at the packets of crisps, the chocolate bars, the biscuits. McDonald's and her Big Mac were a distant memory. Her mouth watered. She could murder a bag of salt and vinegar crisps right now, or a Mars bar. "No, thank you," she said bravely.

The mother distributed wrapped packets of home-made sandwiches and bags of crisps to her brood while the dad poured something steaming and brown out of the flask into the cups.

Alex could see the little boy — around seven or eight, she guessed — in the aisle seat of the row in front of her. He looked suspicious as he began to peel the cling film from his sandwiches. "What sort are they?" he asked.

"They're tuna and cucumber," said his mother. "Your favourite."

"They're *not* my favourite. I *hate* cucumber. You know I hate cucumber."

His mother frowned. "You didn't hate cucumber last week, Henry."

"But I hate it now. It's slimy and horrible."

"Then take the cucumber out," suggested his mother, turning her attention to another of her children, the one directly in front of Alex, and thus hidden from her view except in the reflection in the window.

Henry tore open his bag of crisps — a green bag, salt and vinegar, Alex noticed with a pang — and crunched them loudly. "Mmm," he said. "Salt and vinegar. Yummy."

"Gross," said the oldest of the children, on the other side of the aisle. "They make your lips shrivel up."

Alex got her money out and put it on the tray table attached to the seat-back in front of her, counting it yet again. Thirty-eight pounds, eighty-one pence. Maybe, just maybe, she could afford to spend a bit of it and buy a packet of crisps. If she could catch up the trolley at the back of the carriage . . .

While his mother's attention was occupied elsewhere, Henry leaned round the seat and caught Alex's eye, staring at the money on the tray table. Then he stretched his arm through the gap and dropped his whole packet of sandwiches on the empty seat next to her, turning back round before his mother noticed his sleight of hand.

Alex looked at them lying there for a long moment before she touched them. Food! Tuna and cucumber wasn't exactly her favourite either, but this was like a gift. It *was* a gift. Not to be scorned, but to be accepted thankfully.

At any minute Henry's mother might discover the mysterious disappearance of his sandwiches and decide to investigate. Hastily Alex unwrapped the cling film and devoured them with single-minded intensity. When she'd finished, and tucked the tightly-wrapped ball of cling film into her pocket to hide the evidence, Henry turned round yet again, for just an instant, and favoured her with a solemn wink.

While Danny got on with his arcane work, as mysterious and opaque to Neville as brain surgery or nuclear physics, Neville tackled the challenge facing him head-on. He knew that he didn't have the luxury of waiting, mulling it over, getting round to it in his own time. No: Alex was still missing, and this information was by far the most potentially valuable thing they had going for them. The Assistant Commissioner needed to be in possession of all the facts; his would be the decision about how much of this would be made available to the press. The press: their greatest friends, their biggest enemies. A two-edged sword.

He rang Evans' home number, and was surprised to be told, by the lovely Denise, that her husband was not there; he had, it would seem, departed not long since for the police station.

Neville went upstairs, towards Evans' corner office, and found the door standing open.

"Come in, Stewart," Evans called out, the phone in his hand. "I've just arrived. Organising some coffee. Want some?"

He'd been drinking coffee all morning, it seemed, but another cup couldn't hurt. "Yes, Sir. That would be good."

Evans ordered an underling to bring some to his office, then put the phone down. "Looking for me, were you, Stewart?"

"I wasn't expecting you to be in today," Neville said. "With the family get-together and all."

Evans chuckled. "To tell you the truth, Stewart, the in-laws were getting on my nerves a bit," he confided. "You've never been married, have you, Stewart?"

"No, Sir. I haven't had the . . . pleasure."

"Well, if you had done, you'd understand. Believe me. Fine in small doses, families, but they can be a bit much at times. Denise's — Mrs. Evans' — father. What a know-it-all! And her mother never stops talking."

Evans must have served, and partaken of, a few very nice bottles of wine last night, Neville reflected. He'd never seen him quite so confidential, or so mellow. Long may it last, he thought fervently.

In a few minutes the coffee arrived: two cups with proper saucers, along with a large plate of sandwiches. "Help yourself," invited Evans, so Neville took a triangle of ham-and-pickle and finished it off in one bite.

He could delay no longer. While Evans gulped at his coffee, he plunged into what he had to say. "The girl's computer, Sir. There was an e-mail. From someone called Jack. Arranging to meet her yesterday evening at Paddington Station."

"Good God." Evans choked on the coffee, spluttered, then quickly recovered himself. "And what do we know about this Jack?" he demanded.

"She described him as her boyfriend. To her step-cousins. But I don't think she'd met him before, Sir. He told her to wear something red, so I believe this was their first meeting."

"Bloody hell."

"It could be quite innocent, of course." If only. "But —"

Evans was right there with him. "But he could be some bent paedophile. That's what you're thinking, isn't it?"

"Yes, Sir."

There, it was out. On the table. The worst-case scenario.

"The computer chaps . . ."

"They're on to it," Neville assured him. "Printing out all of the e-mails for me. Trying to track him down electronically. I don't understand it, but Danny assures me it can be done. He says they'll find him."

"Good." Evans had put his coffee down and was picking up the phone. "I'll ring the AC. He needs to know about this straightaway. You go back to the computer lab and read those e-mails. All of them. You can précis them for me. Call in the CCTV footage from all round Paddington for the relevant time yesterday, and see if that shows anything. You might also check to see whether any promising calls have come in since it's gone out on the news. Probably not, but you never know."

Neville hesitated. "Sir, about Alex's father . . ."

Evans shot him a knowing look. "I'll ring him myself," he said, waving Neville out of the office.

Like a condemned man reprieved at the very last moment, Neville headed back towards the computer lab, smiling in spite of himself.

"She's been gone since yesterday afternoon," Morag said, the panic in her voice mingled with bitterness. "No one thought to let me know."

Given what she'd heard about Morag's son and his wife, Callie wasn't surprised.

"I had to hear it from a policeman. Angus *still* hasn't rung me."

Callie could see that Morag was badly shaken, even in shock. She hadn't taken Callie's coat or offered to make tea. "Shall I make some tea?" Callie suggested. Morag could use it: the best remedy for shock.

"Aye. All right."

She left Bella behind with Morag in the sitting room; by the time she returned with the tea, the dog was on the sofa and Morag was cuddling her, as if receiving silent comfort. "I do miss my Macduff," Morag said.

Callie understood, without being told, how much else was behind those words. Macduff, Morag's Cairn terrier, represented a whole way of life, now gone forever. Home, husband, family. Community. All gone, and in their place, a solitary existence in cruelly impersonal London.

"Would you like me to ring your son?" she offered as she poured the tea.

"No. It wouldn't do any good." Morag bent her face over Bella's black-and-white head.

"Did that policeman say why she'd left? Do they know? Did she just disappear from home?"

"Jilly." This time there was no masking the bitterness in Morag's voice. "She had a row with Jilly, he said. That woman is . . . she's a monster. A selfish monster. I've tried to get on with her, for Angus' sake. For Alex's sake. The truth of it is that when she turned up at that dinner party, it was the worst day of all our lives."

Callie was inclined to agree with her, but didn't see what would be gained by saying so.

"Tickets, please!" announced a uniformed man, coming through from the forward carriage, brandishing a paper punch. "All tickets and rail cards!"

Alex's heart thudded.

He was still half a carriage away from her, but if she got up and walked out now, everyone would notice. She would have to wait for her moment.

The first row was straightforward: tickets proffered, examined, punched and returned. But then there was a bit of a diversion. "Could I see your rail card, please, ma'am?" requested the ticket man of a rather corpulent woman in a bright blue coat.

378

She fumbled in her handbag. "I don't seem to have it," she said.

The ticket man frowned, scrutinising her more closely. "This is a rail card fare," he pointed out. "It states very clearly on the ticket that you must be in possession of a valid rail card."

"I do have one. I must have left it at home."

Alex didn't wait to hear any more; she scooted out of her seat and strolled, inconspicuously as possible, towards the toilet at the back end of the carriage.

No one looked at her as she went by, and no one watched as she locked herself in.

She had plenty of time to look at herself in the mirror: not a very pretty sight, she admitted. She looked like she'd slept rough, which she had. Of course her hair wasn't very tidy at the best of times; that horrible frizz resisted all attempts to style it. Alex combed at it with her fingers and wet it down with a splash of water from the tap, then she moistened a paper towel and attempted to wash her face. She brushed her coat down with her hands, picking off a few bits of lint from the laundry. There: almost respectable. Allowing a few more minutes — just to be on the safe side — eventually she crept out and returned to her seat, as though she had every right in the world to be sitting in it.

She didn't feel triumphant; she felt sick.

What would her mother say if she knew that she was a fare dodger? A common criminal, or just as good as. She'd seen the sign about the things that could happen to you if you boarded a train without a valid ticket. Mum would be ashamed of her. So would Granny.

Alex reminded herself, fiercely, that it was all in a good cause. She had to get to Mum. She had to. No matter what it took.

"Now approaching Doncaster," came an announcement on the tannoy. "Next stop Doncaster. Change here for Grimsby, Selby, Hull and Wakefield."

Doncaster! Alex had to vacate her seat, and fast. She should have done it long ago. Turning round, she surveyed the situation.

Two rows behind her, a woman was beginning to collect her bags and struggle into her coat. Her companion was also stirring. Maybe she was in luck!

Indeed, the couple made their way down the aisle before the train had reached Doncaster station, and Alex was able to ascertain from the little tickets that their seats had been reserved only from King's Cross to Doncaster. That meant she ought to be safe in those seats all the way to Edinburgh. She waited till the train pulled into the station and the doors opened, then she made her move.

After Doncaster the scenery opened up as they entered into the Vale of York; coming into York station she had a fleeting view of the cathedral, white and majestic, the ornate curlicues of the window tracery reminding her of a heart.

York. They must be at least halfway to Edinburgh.

The countryside was more interesting after York, and Alex forgot about the family, now three rows ahead of her.

Just before they reached Durham, though, she heard Henry's voice, unmistakable, loud and penetrating. "Mum, I have to go to the loo."

"Oh, all right. But be careful, Henry."

Alex didn't look at him as he went by; she was fascinated by the remarkable sight of Durham Cathedral, rearing high above the train on a bluff, looking as though it had grown up in an organic way out of the cliff. Surely no one could have built it like that.

A few moments later, when they'd left Durham behind them, he slid into the seat next to her and spoke more quietly than she'd imagined him capable of. "You don't have a ticket, do you?" he whispered.

"What do you mean?" she bluffed, also in a whisper.

"I saw you. You got on the train with us. And you went to the loo when the ticket man came round. You thought nobody saw you, but I saw you. You don't have a ticket."

"So what?"

"Don't worry," Henry said with an exaggerated wink. "I won't tell."

Alex let out a deep breath she hadn't realised she was holding. "Thanks."

"If you give me twenty pounds."

"What?" she hissed.

"Twenty pounds. You have more than that. I saw it."

"But that's . . . that's blackmail!"

"Whatever." He gave a little shrug. "It's up to you. Give me twenty pounds, or I'll tell my mum. I'll find the ticket man and tell him. They'll take you to gaol. Is that what you want?"

Alex would have liked to strangle him. Instead she reached in her pocket, peeled off two ten-pound notes from her already diminished bankroll, and slapped them on the tray table.

Henry snatched them up. "Thanks," he said. "You won't regret it. Your secret's safe with me." Then he was gone.

What stupid television programme did he get that from? Alex wondered. Mirrored in the window, two fat tears slid from the corners of her eyes. Angrily she dashed them away. She hadn't cried yet, and she wasn't going to cry now. Crying would get her nowhere.

Neville collected a stack of e-mail printouts from the computer lab and returned with them to his desk. Before he started reading them, he followed Evans' suggestion and made a phone call to check on the hot-line. Probably not much had come through yet; Alex's photo would have been shown on the telly's midday news bulletins, but it wouldn't be until it appeared in the papers that they would expect to get much response.

"We've had a few calls," he was told. "The usual nutters, of course. They're always the first ones to ring. One bloke swears he saw her at a chippy in Kilburn, a bit after four yesterday afternoon. I'm more inclined to believe the old chap who says he saw her in St. John's Wood High Street at about the same time. He says she wasn't watching where she was going, and she slipped and fell on the ice. He helped her up, he says, and told her to be more careful."

"That sounds about right," Neville acknowledged, though it didn't actually help them much.

"The most interesting one," she went on, "was from a woman who was going through Paddington Station last night, rushing to catch a train at a quarter past five."

"Oh?" Neville sat up straighter; the Paddington connection had not yet been made public, so there was a good chance that this one was authentic.

"She says that a girl who looked like Alex pushed past her, running. She took a good look at her, she said, because she was annoyed at the girl's bad manners — didn't stop or even excuse herself, after she'd knocked the woman's suitcase over. Our caller ended up missing her train by a few seconds, and blamed the girl."

"The girl was running?" he repeated, swallowing round a sudden lump in his throat.

"Yes, and someone was running after her, calling 'Sasha'. An older man. Overweight, balding. He didn't stop, either."

"Did she say whether this man caught the girl?"

"The woman didn't hang about to find out. She was running for her own train, wasn't she?"

Neville put the phone down, and cradled his head between his hands. "Oh, God," he groaned. "Christ Almighty."

At least, he told himself, she'd had the sense to run. Maybe — just maybe — she'd got away.

And there should be CCTV footage from Paddington which could help them to determine that. He picked the phone back up and sent an officer to collect it.

At some point the penny had dropped for Callie: "a girl has gone missing," Marco had said in his message. That girl must be Morag's granddaughter.

Leaving Morag with Bella for a few minutes, she slipped back into the kitchen and used her mobile to ring Marco.

"Can you talk?" she said when he answered.

"Well, it isn't really a very good time. Did you get my message? I'm involved in a difficult case. Would it be all right if we talked tonight?"

"It's why I'm ringing, really," she explained quickly. "Your case. The girl who's missing. Alex Hamilton, is it?"

"That's right. You've seen the news, then?"

The news: she hadn't even thought about that. She'd have to turn it on and see what they said, although that might upset Morag. "No. I'm with her grandmother. She's a member of my congregation. I've got to know her a bit recently, since she's moved to London."

"The grandmother!"

"I was just wondering if you could tell me anything that I could pass on to her. Anything helpful. She heard about it from the police, Marco," she added, her voice shaky with emotion. "Her son hasn't even rung her, and she says that it wouldn't do any good to ring him."

"She's probably right," Marco acknowledged quietly. "He wouldn't want her here."

"Well, can you tell me anything? What's the situation?"

He lowered his voice even further. "Listen, *cara mia*. Give me a couple of minutes. I'll ring you back."

From that she understood that he wasn't really free to talk. She busied herself by tidying the kitchen, washing up the tea mugs and rinsing the pot in readiness for the next inevitable round of tea-making.

When he rang back as promised, he spoke in a more normal tone of voice, though it echoed a bit. "I'm in the loo," he explained. "For privacy."

He confirmed to her what Morag had already heard: Alex had walked out of the flat at some point in the afternoon, after a row with her stepmother.

"Her stepmother sounds like a nightmare," Callie said. "Or is Morag just prejudiced against her? Is Jilly really as bad as Morag says?"

"Probably worse. I think she's probably the most self-absorbed person I've ever met. And shallow with it." He added, "Thank goodness she's gone."

"Gone!"

"Oh, not for good." Marco gave a mirthless laugh. "Jilly just couldn't cope with not being the centre of attention. This morning she packed a bag and said she was going to her parents', until all this was resolved. I certainly wasn't sorry to see her go."

"What about *him*?" Callie asked. "Angus? What do you make of him?"

"At first I didn't like him at all," Marco admitted. "Yes, I know he's under a lot of pressure, but I don't in general deal well with people who have to be in control. And he patronised me dreadfully."

Callie felt indignant on his behalf. "But you're there to help him."

"Not in the sort of specific way he was looking for. I couldn't just wave a magic wand and bring his daughter home. I have to say, though, he's treated me with more respect since I figured out the password to Alex's computer." He chuckled.

"Now you've lost me. Computer? Password?"

"It's a long story, *cara mia*. I'll tell you all about it some time."

"I don't suppose I'll see you tonight?" Callie asked, surprised at how disappointed she was at that prospect.

"Possibly not. Depends on what happens this afternoon."

"I suppose Alex might walk in any minute? Or be found somewhere, safe and sound?" That, thought Callie, seemed unlikely: the longer the girl was away, the less chance there was of a rapid happy ending to the story. That was the unarticulated fear which, she knew, gripped Morag at the moment. Alex had been missing overnight, not just for an hour or two. How could that be explained away?

"So what shall I tell Morag?" Callie asked. "I want to be as helpful as possible."

There was a pause on the other end of the phone, as if Marco were weighing his words. "If you want to be helpful, *cara mia*, just stay with her. Keep her out of our hair, and out of Angus' hair. We've got enough to cope with here without an hysterical granny added into the mix."

"Morag isn't hysterical," Callie protested. "She's concerned — of course she is. And worried sick. But she's not the hysterical type."

"Then," Marco said, "just do whatever you have to do to keep her occupied."

The train stopped at Newcastle, with its high bridges over the Tyne, then Berwick-upon-Tweed, right on the edge of the sea. A moment later they were across the border.

Scotland!

Alex wished she could open the train window and breathe in the air of her homeland. But these trains were not designed with window-opening in mind. She had to content herself with feasting her eyes instead, gazing at the gentle hills of the Borders, beautiful even in the icy grip of winter. Not spectacular like her own Highlands, she thought, yet beautiful in their own dignified, understated way.

Scotland: the country of her birth, the land of her ancestors. Blue-painted Picts, warlike Celts, stretching back beyond recorded history. She couldn't have articulated, nor did she fully understand, the pull the country exerted on her, the grip it had on her heart. Yet Alex knew that, in spite of everything, she was happier now than she had been in months — since that black day when she'd been taken across the border into England, all the way to alien London.

She was home.

CHAPTER
NINETEEN

The e-mails were profoundly depressing. Neville, reading through them, felt almost suicidal.

Such a lonely girl Alex was. Isolated.

Kirsty, it was clear to see, had moved on. She had new friends, new interests. A boyfriend, even.

Alex, on the other hand, had not moved on. She lived entirely in the past, clinging to memories of a close friendship which had run its course, unnurtured by proximity.

And then Jack had come along. Jack, with his easy familiarity and ready compliments. Jack's friendship, proffered by e-mail, had been grabbed by her like a lifeline.

She had constructed a fantasy world round him, round their relationship. "Sasha" — the name she used to sign her e-mails, and by which Jack addressed her. That had baffled him at first, but as he read the e-mails Neville quickly came to understand that Sasha was the fantasy Alex: older, sophisticated, knowing. She'd tried so hard to sound grown up, worldly-wise.

He had no doubt, though, that Jack would not have been fooled for a minute. Jack must have known full well that Sasha was not sixteen. Not, as she wanted him to believe, experienced in the ways of the world and of men. Alex's naivety, her innocence, shone through her e-mails. Any fool could have seen it.

Jack, then, knew that she was really just a little girl.

And he had taken advantage of her loneliness, her need for human contact. He had flattered her, complimented her, offered her emotional intimacy and the chance to confide in him. Led her down a path with inevitable consequences.

Grooming. Wasn't that the word they used now for what internet paedophiles did to lay the groundwork for eventual face-to-face contact with their victims? It was calculated, gradual, carefully judged. Don't rush things; don't scare them off. Just make them trust you. Make them . . . love you.

Neville slammed his fist down on the printouts. It was disgusting. Sickening. The worst sort of exploitation. And the mind boggled at where it might actually lead.

Where *was* Alex Hamilton? Was she with this sicko, right now?

He was going to catch this piece of scum, Neville vowed to himself.

His phone rang.

"Hey, Guv," said Danny Duffy. "This bloke wasn't as clever as he thought. He could have used a Hotmail account, or something that would have made it harder to track him down. But he's used a regular ISP, and they've given me his details. His real name isn't Jack, of course," he added.

"Tell me." Neville was already halfway out of his chair.

"He's called Lee Bicknell. Lives in Camden Town. Off Chalk Farm Road."

"I'm on my way."

Waverley Station, Edinburgh.

Alex had been to Edinburgh several times. Once she'd been on a school trip, on a coach, but the other times she'd come by train from Aviemore into Waverley Station. With Mum and Dad, once that she could remember, when they'd stayed in a hotel for several days and done all the sights. Mum had been at university in Edinburgh; she loved the city and wanted to show it off. Then there had been a few day trips with Mum alone, and one time with Granny and Granddad, who had taken her to Jenners to see the Christmas decorations and Father Christmas.

So it was a sense of familiarity that greeted her as she stepped off the train. She was so excited that she almost forgot to be cautious about the guards at the end of the platform.

They *were* actually checking tickets, she realised with alarm.

Looking round quickly, she saw Henry's family a bit behind her, just getting off the train; it had evidently taken them a while to gather their possessions and their children together. Alex lingered till they passed, then once again attached herself to them.

Henry gave her a knowing look; she returned a malevolent glare, and once she was safely through the barriers, she stuck her tongue out at him — the hateful little toad — and peeled off in a different direction.

Now.

She was in Edinburgh, but she still had to get to Kelso. Alex had a vague idea of where it was, somewhere in the Borders area that they'd just passed through. Not too far from Berwick, from Melrose.

Perhaps there would be a train. Though, she reminded herself, she was now down to eighteen pounds, eighty-one pence.

A bus, then?

She came out of the station, following the signs for the Tourist Information centre. That would be her best bet for getting her bearings, planning the next step.

Neville knew he could have justified sending someone else to bring in Jack, also known as Lee Bicknell. There were plenty of things for him to do at the station, not least briefing Evans on the contents of the e-mails. But he was beginning to take this one very personally, and he reasoned that the e-mails were less important now that they knew who they were after.

First he rang Danny Duffy back. "Good work," he said belatedly. "But don't think it means you can go home just yet. Or head off on that shopping trip, a few hours late."

"I hate shopping anyway," Danny said cheerfully. "What's up?"

"I hope we'll have something else for you to take a look at this afternoon. And the CCTV footage from Paddington ought to be with you soon as well."

"No problem, Guv."

Then he collected Sid Cowley — "I'll explain on the way," he said — and set off by car across London.

Traffic was bad. "Bloody Christmas shoppers," Cowley kept reminding him, like a broken record. And he wasn't very familiar with this part of town. Way off his patch. Fortunately Cowley was a pretty good navigator.

"I always figured that if I couldn't make it as a cop," Cowley confessed after he'd got them out of a fairly nasty tailback by directing Neville round some side streets, "I could drive a taxi."

"You never cease to amaze me, Sid," conceded Neville.

The house was a small mid-terrace Victorian, red brick, wedged between one which had been pebble-dashed and another with fake stone cladding.

"Let's get this over with," Neville said, pulling the car up in front. He was, he acknowledged to himself, looking forward to it.

The man who opened the door to them was short, chubby, balding. Late thirties, early forties. His nervous smile revealed bad teeth. "Can I help you?" he asked, looking back and forth between the two of them.

Neville showed his warrant card. "Mr. Bicknell? Lee Bicknell?"

The man nodded. Another nervous smile, this one even less convincing.

"I'm Detective Inspector Stewart, and this is Detective Sergeant Cowley. Is it all right if we come in and have a word?"

392

"Well . . ."

"Thank you." Neville virtually pushed past him, through the narrow corridor and into the tiny front room. The lounge: two chairs and a telly.

"I don't know what this is all about," Lee Bicknell said, his voice breathy, finishing almost on a squeak.

"We're about to tell you." Neville narrowed his eyes. "Mr. Bicknell, do you know a girl called Alex Hamilton?"

"Uh . . . no."

"How about someone called Sasha?"

There was an unmistakable intake of breath, and the answer came too quickly, too firmly. "No."

"Mr. Bicknell, is it all right if we take a look round your house?"

He spread his hands out defensively. "But I haven't done anything wrong!"

Neville smiled. "Then you won't have anything to hide, will you?" He nodded at Cowley, who was already on his way out into the corridor.

It was a basic two-up-two-down house, with another small room — furnished as a dining room — behind the one they'd been in and a diminutive galley kitchen at the back, leading out into a paved yard with a washing line. A few bedraggled containers round the edges of the yard, containing dead plants, seemed to constitute the garden.

"See, there's nothing here," the man said triumphantly.

"Upstairs?" suggested Cowley.

They retraced their steps, with Bicknell following them closely, making little noises of protest. The steep, narrow stairs to the first floor were almost impassable, with more than half their width taken up with a stair-lift. Neville, who was pretty fit himself, didn't know how the chubby Bicknell could squeeze himself through that space.

Two rooms upstairs, plus a bathroom tucked behind the stairs. The door of the back room was open; Neville led the way into it.

It was neat as the proverbial pin, he observed. Bed — a single bed — made, the spread pulled up and tucked round the pillow. The bedside table dust-free; an old wardrobe crammed in the corner. Ugly patterned carpet, but it bore the marks of a recent hoovering.

Either this man was a clean-freak, or he was hiding something.

Neville had a quick look in the wardrobe, which held nothing but a few shirts and pairs of trousers, then turned and went towards the closed door of the front room.

"That's Mother's room," squeaked Lee Bicknell, clearly agitated.

That explained the stairlift. "We'll try not to disturb her," promised Neville. "Is she ill?"

"Actually, she's . . . passed. Last year."

"Then she won't mind, will she?" contributed Cowley, pushing the door open. "Guv, here's the computer," he said over his shoulder.

"That's . . . that's mine." Bicknell shoved his way past Cowley into the room — an old-fashioned room, slightly larger than the back bedroom, dominated by a bed with a candlewick spread — and stood protectively in front of the computer. Sitting incongruously on what was evidently his mother's dressing table, it was a new-looking machine with a large flat screen. The better, thought Neville cynically, to view downloaded images on — downloaded images, he had no doubt, of a particularly nasty sort.

"Mind if we take a look, Mr. Bicknell?" he asked.

"No! I mean, yes. I do mind." The man drew himself up to his full height and stared them down. "This is private property. My own private property, and you have no right."

Neville and Sid Cowley looked at each other as Neville spoke. "Mr. Bicknell, we have good reason to believe that this computer contains evidence relevant to a criminal matter which we're investigating. That gives us the right to take it with us. And we'd like to ask you to come with us, as well. We have some things we'd like to discuss with you, back at the station."

"Helping us with our enquiries, like," Cowley added.

The man's eyes widened; his pupils dilated. "Are you arresting me?"

"We're asking you to come with us," Neville repeated. "If you refuse, we might feel that arrest is the only option."

His shoulders sagged; he lowered his head. "All right. I'll come."

But Neville wasn't quite finished. "One more question before we go, Mr. Bicknell," he said. "Does this house have a cellar?"

"No. No cellar. You've seen everything."

"I'll check to make sure," volunteered Cowley as he unplugged the computer, detached its internet connection, and hefted it in his arms.

It was soon ascertained that Lee Bicknell was telling the truth, at least in one matter: there was no cellar, no loft to speak of. Not even a garden shed. Nowhere to hide a stack of dirty magazines, let alone a little girl. A *live* little girl, anyway.

Neville wasn't sure whether he was relieved or disappointed. Maybe, he told himself, it meant that she'd got away.

The alternative didn't bear thinking about.

The woman at the counter in the Tourist Information centre had a lovely, warm Edinburgh accent and a smile to match. "Buses to Kelso?" she said in response to Alex's question. "Couldna be easier, lassie. Walk straight along this street," at which she pointed in the proper direction, "and you'll be in Waterloo Place. The calling point for the Borders buses is right there on the street. It's marked. There are several buses a day — I'll give you a timetable." Efficiently she riffled through a file and pulled one out, handing it across the counter.

"Do you have any idea what the fare might be?" Alex asked, trying not to betray her apprehension.

"For a child? Two or three pounds, I imagine."

That was all right, then. It would even give her enough money to get something to eat before she caught the bus. Impulsively she asked, "Is there a McDonald's near here?"

"Oh, aye. Just round the corner. Right here in the Princes Mall, as a matter of fact." Again the woman pointed in the general direction.

Alex found the McDonald's with no trouble. This time she knew what she wanted, without even having to look at the menu board. "A Big Mac Meal," she stated confidently, handing over her last five-pound note. Now there was just a ten-pound note and some change in her pocket.

It was worth it, she decided when she bit into it. Her Mum's favourite. She might even be sitting in the very seat Mum had sat in, when she ate at McDonald's in her student days.

Neville escorted Lee Bicknell to an interview room while Cowley carried the computer to Danny in the lab.

But even by the time Cowley returned, Bicknell wasn't ready to answer any questions. "I don't have anything to say," he stated, after Neville had turned on the tape recorder and said the appropriate preliminary words into it. "I don't know what you're talking about."

"Sasha. Tell us about Sasha."

"I don't know anyone called Sasha."

Neville leaned across the table; it was time to cut the crap. "We have your e-mails, mate. Jack to Sasha, Sasha to Jack. She kept them all. And we have your computer. Even if you erased those e-mails, our boy Danny will find them. He's brilliant that way."

Bicknell remained stubborn. "My name is Lee, not Jack. And I don't know any Sasha."

"What did you do with her?" Cowley put in. "With Sasha?"

"I don't know what you're talking about. What am I supposed to have done? Tell me that."

"You know bloody well what you've done," Neville snapped. "And so do we. Tell us where she is, and save us all a lot of trouble."

He folded his hands in front of him. "I'm allowed to have a solicitor, aren't I?"

"Of course you can have a solicitor. You're here voluntarily, anyway," Neville reminded him. "You haven't been arrested or charged with anything. Yet."

"Oh, yeah. Voluntarily. Ha ha." Now Bicknell crossed his arms across his chest. "I'd like to see a solicitor before I answer any more questions."

"Fine." Neville said the appropriate words to terminate the interview. "Did you have one in mind, or will you need some help finding one?"

"If you're trying to imply that . . . that I've been arrested before, then you're wrong." Bicknell's defensiveness was becoming more pronounced by the minute. "I tell you, I'm an innocent man. I haven't done anything."

"We'll see about that," Neville said. "Sid, could you help this gentleman? I have other things to do with my time."

Alex finished her Big Mac with a satisfied sigh. It had tasted, she decided, even better than the English one.

She paid a quick visit to the loo, then was ready to go and catch the bus. Now that she was so close to her goal — to her mum — she was anxious that it should happen as quickly as possible. By this evening she and Mum would be together, and nothing could tear them apart again. Not Dad, and certainly not Jilly. She was almost there.

It was dark outside, and getting even colder. But it wasn't far to the bus. She walked along Princes Street to Waterloo Place confidently.

Here was the calling point. It was, as the nice woman had said, well marked with a sign, though no one else was waiting there.

Alex stood for about a quarter of an hour, feeling the cold more intensely with each passing minute. Surely it wouldn't be long: weren't buses supposed to come along every ten minutes or so? She stomped her feet, clapped her hands together.

Then she remembered that the nice woman had given her a timetable.

Yes, she'd put it in her pocket.

Under the light of a nearby street lamp she opened it up. Monday to Friday? No, this was Saturday, she reminded herself.

The buses which went all the way to Kelso on a Saturday left at nine and eleven fifty-five in the morning.

She had missed the last bus by hours.

Bitter, bitter disappointment rose in her throat like bile.

Well, she told herself sternly, if she had to wait till tomorrow morning for the next bus, then she'd just have to wait. Last night she'd slept rough; she could do it again. Surely she could find a warm place in Edinburgh to spend the night — if nothing else, a secluded corner of Waverley Station. Then she'd be close by to catch the early bus tomorrow morning, and be with her mum by well before lunch time.

She ran her finger down the timetable to the Sunday buses.

Two through buses again. But this time they were at five past three and twenty-five past five. In the afternoon.

Nearly twenty-four hours from now.

It was just too much. The tears she'd so heroically resisted till now welled up and would not be stemmed.

She fumbled in her pocket for a tissue; not finding one, she wiped her eyes on her coat sleeve. But still the tears flowed. Alex sobbed, gulped, sobbed some more. She was so close — had come so far — and now this had happened. Twenty-four more hours!

A car paused at the kerb and the window was wound down. "Are ye all right, lassie?" said a man's voice.

Unrelenting cheerfulness: it was one of the things Neville had come to appreciate about Danny Duffy — and perhaps resent a bit as well. Danny smiled through the most horrific revelations, able to take pleasure in his abilities to uncover them.

"Some of the worst pictures I've ever seen, Guv," he said, beaming. "Really nasty stuff. And there aren't just a few. There are thousands. Do you want to take a look?"

"No, thank you."

400

Danny went on, undeterred. "I suspected I'd find something like this when his ISP told me he had an account for the highest-speed broadband available. You don't pay for that sort of speed if you're just sending a few e-mails, Guv. It means massive downloading."

"Girls?" Neville guessed, not bothering to hide his revulsion.

"Well, yes." Danny nodded. "But the thing is, Guv, they're very specific. From what I've seen, anyway. Not *little* girls. Not teenagers. Girls of that sort of in-between age. Eleven, twelve, thirteen — that kind of thing."

"Like Alex," said Neville.

"Like Alex. Or Sasha, as he knew her." Danny shook his head. "And another thing, Guv. Alex — Sasha — isn't the only one he's been e-mailing, using the name of Jack. There are lots of them. Charlotte, Jennifer, Mandy, Kylie. Others."

"Sounds like we have enough there to lock him up for a while," Neville said with grim satisfaction. The trouble was, they wouldn't lock him up for long enough. If he got himself a moderately decent lawyer, he'd be able to wriggle out of it with some minimal sentence. Maybe four years for the downloaded stuff, of which he'd only end up serving two years. The next thing they knew he'd be out, e-mailing a new crop of pre-teen girls.

For a fleeting moment, Neville fantasised about leaving Lee Bicknell alone with Angus Hamilton for five minutes.

"Thanks, Danny," he added. "You've been brilliant."

Danny's grin was even wider than usual. "I can't take that much credit for it, Guv. Honestly. I just turned the machine on and walked right in. Wouldn't you have thought the bloke would have protected his porn with a password?"

The man smiled at Alex, his teeth flashing in the light of the street lamp as he leaned across the car to the window on the passenger side. "Are ye all right?" he repeated.

He looked, she thought immediately, like her granddad. Very like him, from his sandy hair to his tweed jacket. And his voice was like Granddad's as well. That lovely country burr.

"The bus," she sobbed. "It won't come till tomorrow afternoon."

"You've missed your bus, lassie? Where is it ye were wanting to go?"

"Kelso. To find my mum." The tears just wouldn't stop; she wiped at her face with her sleeve.

He rolled the window down further and a handkerchief appeared in his hand. "Here, lassie. Take this. It's clean, I promise."

Alex leaned over and accepted it. "Thank you."

"Do you want to tell me what's happened?"

She *did* want to tell him, she realised. He was looking at her with such concern. Just like Granddad had done, when she'd skinned her knee.

But the words refused to come. There was only one overriding thought in her head. "My mum," she sobbed. "I want my mum."

"Your mum's in Kelso, ye say?"

She nodded, pressing the handkerchief to her face and finding that it carried a faint scent of pipe tobacco, a smell she'd always associated with Granddad.

"Well, isn't that a stroke of luck! That's exactly where I'm going."

"Oh!" she gasped.

"Come on, lassie — what are ye waiting for?" he said as the passenger door swung open. "Get in."

Sid Cowley rang Neville to say that the solicitor had conferred with his client, who was now prepared to make a statement. "A bit late for that, sunshine," Neville muttered.

On his way back to the interview rooms, he looked at the clock. It was nearly half-past six, which meant that Alex's photo would have appeared on the six o'clock news by now. He decided that a detour to check on phone calls to the hotline might be in order.

"Not a great deal that seems promising," admitted the man who was now staffing the phone. "The only plausible one was a woman who works at St. John's Wood tube station. Says she sold a ticket to a little girl on her own who looked like Alex. Maybe half-past four yesterday afternoon."

"Thanks," said Neville, disappointed.

Yes, it was good to know that Alex had, as they suspected, taken the tube to Paddington. What he really wanted, he admitted to himself, was to hear from someone who had seen Alex after, say, quarter-past five. After she had run from Jack — Lee Bicknell.

Someone who could confirm that she had escaped from him. That — to put it bluntly — she was still alive. Until they'd seen something from the CCTV, that was the best they could hope for.

Well, if Bicknell was ready to talk, all might soon become clear.

The interview room had been set up and everything was in readiness. Neville nodded at the solicitor, a pale middle-aged man with a badly-fitting set of dentures.

"My client is ready to make a statement," he told Neville.

"All right. Let's hear what he has to say." Neville turned to Lee Bicknell.

Bicknell had a sheen of sweat on his forehead and he focused his eyes on a point somewhere over Neville's shoulder. "Okay. I admit that I didn't tell you the whole truth before. I . . . um, yes. I arranged to meet Sasha. At Paddington Station. Just to have a chat, like."

Sure, thought Neville, but he didn't interrupt.

"I saw her. But she ran away from me. Maybe because . . . I didn't look exactly like the photo I'd sent her. A bit older." He stopped.

"And?" said Neville. "What then?"

Bicknell spread his hands. "Nothing. She ran away. I ran after her for a bit, but I didn't get very far. I'm not as fit as I used to be," he admitted.

Neville just looked at him. It was plausible; he hoped it was true.

"I'm telling the truth. I'll sign a statement, then I'd like to go home."

"Not so fast, sunshine," Neville said, with a smile that didn't reach his eyes.

"What do you mean?"

"My client has been fully co-operative and has made a statement," the solicitor interposed. "His presence here has been on a purely voluntary basis. You can't force him to stay if he wants to go home."

"Well, let's change that, shall we?" Neville looked at Cowley, then at Bicknell, ignoring the solicitor. "Mr. Bicknell, I'm arresting you and holding you on a charge of possession of indecent images of children. You do not have to say anything. But it may harm your defence if you do not mention, when questioned, something you may later rely on in court. Anything you do say may be given in evidence. And that," he added, "ought to do for starters."

Yolanda's home had been restored to order; she'd prepared an extravagant supper for Eli on his return from work. They'd enjoyed the first part of the evening lingering over the meal with a bottle of wine. Now they were snuggled up together on the sofa, watching a DVD of an old film, allowing the anticipation to build for the next stage of the evening.

The phone rang. "Can you leave it?" Eli suggested, tightening his arm round Yolanda's shoulder.

"It could be important," Yolanda reminded him. She pulled away from him with some reluctance and reached for the phone.

"Hello?" Yolanda recognised Rachel's voice.

"Lovie! Are you all right?"

"Fine. I'm feeling fine. A bit sore, but . . ."

"And the baby?"

There was a noticeable softening of her voice. "Oh, she's lovely. Just gorgeous." Rachel paused. "I have a favour to ask."

"Yes? I'll do anything I can, of course." Yolanda turned her head to avoid Eli's accusing glare.

Rachel went on to explain that she and the baby were to be sent home from hospital the next day, and she'd come away in such a hurry that she didn't have any warm things for her daughter: the fleecy baby-gro with the hood, the warm blanket. "Do you think you could get them and bring them to me?" she requested. "You have a key, and you know where to find the things. I know it's a lot to ask . . ."

"Not a problem," said Yolanda. "I'll be there as soon as I can."

"Have you forgotten," Eli said, scowling, as she put the phone down, "the things that woman said about you? That you never left her alone? She's abused your good nature for a week, and now you're going to let her take advantage of you some more. Are you crazy, woman?"

"It's for the baby's sake," Yolanda said. She was already putting on her coat.

Callie and Morag had played Scrabble for the better part of the afternoon, with Bella snuggled up next to Morag in her armchair as if she knew she needed the comfort of a warm body. It had been a real struggle on Callie's part to keep Morag's mind off the matter closest to her heart; deliberately she avoided suggesting that they turn on the radio or the television. If and when Alex was found, Marco would ring them — of that Callie was certain. For now, she was doing her bit to provide a distraction.

Inevitably, though, Morag kept returning to the subject. "Poor wee Alex," she would sigh. "I wish I knew where she was."

"I'm sure she's fine," Callie reassured her, though she was by no means certain of the fact. "If she had a row with Jilly, she probably wouldn't want to go back home very soon."

"She should have come to me," Morag stated. "I just don't know where else she might have gone."

Bella stirred, then jumped down and trotted over to Callie, looking up at her with a supplicating gaze.

"I think she wants to go outside," Callie guessed.

"That's right," said Morag, more to the dog than to Callie. "Go to your mummy. She'll look after you, lassie."

Then Morag's eyes widened; her mouth went into a round O.

"That's it," said Morag, her voice strong with conviction. "Alex will have gone to Scotland. To look for her mother."

Eli had offered to come with her, but Yolanda preferred to go to Rachel's house on her own. She let herself in with the key, then went straight upstairs to the nursery and fetched the baby's warm things from the chest of drawers.

The black-haired baby.

Yolanda knew that there was a photo of Trevor and Rachel's wedding hanging on the wall in the master bedroom. To refresh her memory, she went through and looked at it.

Yes, Trevor was every bit as fair as Rachel. If anything, his hair was lighter than hers, an almost Scandinavian blond.

She sat down on the edge of the bed, thinking.

Biology hadn't really been her best subject at school, but in her years as a midwife she had learned a good deal about genetics in action. And she didn't recall that she had ever, with all of the infants she'd delivered, seen two blond parents with a black-haired baby.

The baby-gro slid off her lap onto the floor. Yolanda leaned down to retrieve it, and saw the corner of a laptop computer protruding from under the bed.

A laptop?

Yolanda had stayed in the house for a week, and didn't remember having seen a laptop. Surely if there had been one, DI Stewart would have taken it away to be looked at in the lab? By Danny Duffy and the computer whizz kids?

Her mind flashed back to just a couple of days before, when Rachel had been surprised by her sudden entrance into the bedroom, and had shoved something under the bed.

It was none of her business, Yolanda told herself. Not her job. She should go to the hospital, as she'd promised Rachel, and deliver the baby's things.

★   ★   ★

"I'm certain of it," Morag stated. "Sure as sure. Alex has gone to look for her mum. For Harriet."

"But how would she know where to go?" Callie asked. "She doesn't know where Harriet is, does she?"

"Weeeell . . ." Morag got up and went to the array of photos on the piano; she picked up one of Alex and caressed the frame abstractedly. "I don't think I told you. I spoke to wee Alex on the phone a few days ago."

"You said she'd rung and left a message," Callie recalled.

"It was after that. She rang again. She asked me about her mother — asked me if her mother was dead."

Callie was startled. "Dead?"

"That's what she thought, apparently. She was terrified that her mother was dead. So I told her . . ." Morag looked off into the distance.

"What did you tell her?" Callie prompted after a moment of silence.

Morag gave a sharp shake of her head, as if recalling herself to the present. "I told her that her mother wasn't well. That she was in a care home in the Borders area. I didn't give her the address." She rubbed her forehead. "Maybe I shouldn't have told her that much. If I was even a wee bit responsible for her running away from home . . . oh, Callie. I'd not forgive myself. Not ever."

"I'll ring Marco," Callie decided. "If you have her mother's address . . ."

"Oh, no." Morag shook her head. "No, I can't let Angus know that I told Alex anything. He'd blame me. I blame *myself*."

Callie hadn't met Angus Hamilton, but she'd heard enough about him to believe that Morag was probably accurate in her assessment of his reactions. "If she's looking for her mother, though, surely the police need to know that."

Morag narrowed her eyes and her face took on an expression which told Callie that, stubborn as Angus Hamilton was, he had in some measure come by that stubbornness honestly. "No," Morag said. "No police, and no Angus. I'm going to find her myself."

The nursing sister on the maternity ward wasn't very happy about Yolanda's visit. "It's past visiting hours," she pointed out. "Only dads are allowed to come this late."

Yolanda resorted to showing the nurse her police ID, which mollified the woman enough to let her in. "Official business, then? I suppose that's all right," the nurse murmured, standing aside.

Rachel was drowsing in bed, holding her baby in the crook of her arm.

"Oh, she's such a darling," said Yolanda as she approached the bed. "Have you settled on a name for her yet?"

Rachel shook her head. "Trevor was so sure it would be a boy. We talked about boys' names all the time, but didn't get round to choosing a girl's name. I just don't know what to call her." She raised the baby up. "Would you like to hold her?"

That was exactly what Yolanda had been yearning to do. She put her carrier bag down and accepted the precious bundle, crooning over the tiny black head.

410

"Oh," said Rachel in a surprised voice, a moment later.

Yolanda looked up and followed Rachel's gaze to the door.

A young man was coming in, smiling at the nursing sister, smiling at Rachel, smiling at Yolanda and positively beaming at the baby.

A young man with dusky skin and very, very black hair.

"Hey, Rache," he said. "I didn't know you had another visitor."

He held out his arms for the baby; automatically Yolanda transferred the little bundle. "I just couldn't stay away," he added.

Rachel looked more than a bit discomfited. "Um, Yolanda," she said quickly. "This is my . . . um . . . friend. Abdul."

Callie couldn't believe her ears. "You're going to *Scotland*?"

"Aye," said Morag. "Right now."

"But *how*?" protested Callie. "It's late. The trains . . ."

"Trains? I never said anything about trains."

"Then how on earth will you get there?"

Morag was already moving, opening a drawer in her bureau. "By car, of course."

"But you don't have a car."

"And why would you think that, lassie?" Morag pulled a keyring out of the drawer and shook it in Callie's face. "You don't think I moved into this ugly

411

block of flats because I liked the architecture, do you? I bought this flat because it came with a lock-up garage. And that's where my car is."

"Your car?" Callie echoed stupidly.

"Aye. The Flying Scot, she's called. I couldn't bear to give her up when I came to London."

Morag went into the kitchen and switched the kettle on. "I'll make a thermos of coffee. It's going to be a long night, and I can't count on finding motorway caffs when I need them."

If you couldn't beat them, Callie told herself, you may as well join them. "And I'll make some sandwiches," she said. "I'm coming with you."

It was no great distance from the hospital to Rachel's house. Telling herself that she was overstepping her job description, Yolanda nevertheless retraced her steps to the Victorian semi near the canal and let herself back in.

The laptop was where she'd left it, sticking out from under the bed. Yolanda hesitated for no more than a few seconds before pulling it out.

She hadn't properly thought through what she was going to do with it. Strictly speaking, she knew that she should ring Neville Stewart and allow him to deal with the matter. But it was too late at night for that; if he wasn't at home, sleeping in his own bed, he ought to be.

And that, Yolanda decided, was where she should be as well. In her own bed, with her own husband.

The laptop would wait until morning. In the meantime, though, she was going to take it home with her. For safekeeping, she told herself.

The Flying Scot, Callie discovered when they got to the lock-up garage, was an ancient Morris Minor estate wagon, with wood on the sides and tartan plaid seat covers. "Are you sure this car will run?" she asked doubtfully.

Morag gave a decisive nod. "She took Donald on his rounds all over the Highlands for years and years. Reliable as they come." She patted the car's bonnet.

"Where, exactly, are we going?" Callie asked as she lifted Bella into the back of the car.

"I told you, lassie. You don't have to come."

"I'm not letting you go by yourself." That much was certain: it was the least she could do.

She tried not to think about what Marco would say when he found out. Yes, he'd instructed her to stay with Morag and keep her out of everyone's hair. But she was sure he didn't mean that she was to accompany Morag on a wild goose chase to Scotland. He'd probably be furious with her, and she wouldn't blame him.

And then there was Brian. This was, Callie reminded herself, Saturday night. She would be missing the morning services, and she'd almost certainly miss the Christingle service as well. Never mind Brian: Jane would be incandescent if she missed the Christingle.

Well, it couldn't be helped. She was going, and that was that. It was too late to contact Brian; she'd have to ring in the morning.

"We're going," said Morag, "to Kelso. In the Borders, so it's not so very far. Only six or seven hours. Depending on how fast I can convince the old girl to go."

Driving six or seven hours in the middle of the night to Scotland in a Morris Minor that was probably older than Callie herself? She must, Callie told herself, be mad.

When she got home, Yolanda couldn't resist taking just a little peek at the laptop. Eli was in the bath — she could hear him splashing about — so she set it up on the dining table and opened the lid.

There was no password protection, and the e-mail programme was already open. Yolanda scrolled through the list of e-mails, reading one or two of the most recent ones. From Abdul. To Abdul.

"Hey, doll." Eli emerged from the bathroom wearing no more than a towel wrapped round his waist. "You're home, then. About time."

She looked up from the laptop. "Eli, I've found something. Rachel —"

"Never mind about Rachel." He closed the lid of the laptop and took Yolanda's hand. "Come on, doll. We've got other fish to fry."

CHAPTER
TWENTY

"So," said Morag when they'd left the London conurbation and were headed up the A1. "Talk to me, lassie. Tell me about yourself. Ever since we met, I'm the one who seems to have done all the talking. Now it's your turn."

And so Callie talked. She started with her family: her difficult mother, her beloved father's death, Peter's homosexuality. Eventually she told Morag about Adam and the broken engagement; finally, several hours into the trip, she got round to the subject of Marco.

"He sounds a lovely young man," Morag said.

"Oh, he is."

Perhaps she didn't sound very convinced, because Morag gave her a searching look. "But?"

"But." Callie sighed. "But I'm just not sure I'm ready for another relationship like that. Like I had with Adam. Maybe I never will be." There — she'd said it. It was something she'd never before articulated, even to herself. "I have a job I love. Not just a job — a vocation. Being a priest — which is what I'll be in less than a year — can be your whole life, something that will take all the hours I can possibly give to it. Will I

415

have the energy for a relationship as well? I don't know."

"With all due respect," said Morag, "I just don't accept that. You're still a human being, Callie lass. Not superwoman. Not a hermit, either. You still need love and support. It's not good to be alone. Not good for anyone. Believe me. I've had it both ways, and alone is . . . lonely."

"But relationships complicate your life." She was thinking about Morag's son. About the complications his new marriage had caused for so many people, not least for his mother . . .

"And enrich it." Morag kept her eyes on the road. "Lass, I know there must be a temptation for you to think that God — and the Church — will be enough for you. Enough to fill in those spaces in your life. And Bella," she added with a smile, glancing over her shoulder at the back seat.

Grudgingly Callie nodded. That *was* what she thought. Though perhaps she wouldn't have put it quite like that . . .

"If you go down that route, lass, you'll only be living half a life. And you'll never know what you've missed out on." She smiled, almost to herself. "I had nearly forty years with my Donald. Not enough years, mind you, and not all of them were wonderful. I'd be the first to admit that. But you have to be prepared to take the rough with the smooth, and the smooth makes it all worthwhile. I would not trade the time I had with my Donald for . . . for anything. I'm just so thankful for the years we had."

416

Callie thought about the contrast between Morag and her own mother: about her mother's embittered widowhood, and how she'd never forgiven her husband for dying on her. How much healthier Morag's attitude was, in spite of what she'd been through. Perhaps, Callie admitted to herself, her mother's negativity had influenced her more than she'd ever realised.

One thing she knew for sure: she didn't want to turn into her mother.

"I'm not trying to tell you how to live your life, lass," Morag said, almost apologetically. "I hope you don't think I'm interfering."

"Not at all."

Morag's voice became brisk. "I think we'd better look for a place to pull off the road, Callie lass. Time for coffee and sandwiches. And I suspect that wee Bella wouldn't mind stretching her legs."

It took quite some time for the sound of the telephone to penetrate Neville's dreams — unpleasant dreams, full of formless horror which evaporated as soon as he struggled to consciousness, leaving behind only a nasty aftertaste.

His eyes were still closed; he wasn't entirely sure where he was. The phone was ringing somewhere near his right ear and he fumbled for it for a moment.

"DI Stewart," he managed to say into the receiver, in a voice which creaked and croaked.

He was, in fact, in his office, at his desk, where he'd been for most of the night. At some point, exhausted beyond all reason, unable to keep his eyes open for another moment, he must have put his head down on his desk and fallen asleep.

It was still dark. What time was it? Neville pried his eyes open and squinted at his watch. Just a bit past seven.

"Oh, you're still there," said the voice of Detective Superintendent Evans. "Good."

Neville wasn't sure what was good about it. Every muscle ached from the unnatural position in which he'd been sleeping; his head hurt. He longed to be at home in his bed, away from all of this, sleeping the sleep of the just. Instead he was still here, and Alex Hamilton was still missing. Unless Evans knew something he didn't know . . .

"Nothing new?" Evans asked.

"Uh . . . no."

"Well, Stewart, I just wanted to let you know that I'm not going to be available for a few hours. The christening, you know. I'll be in church," Evans explained, adding, "I'll leave my phone on vibrate. Just in case there's a major breakthrough. Like you've found the girl."

Or her body, Neville said to himself.

"But for God's sake, Stewart, don't you dare ring me for anything less than that."

"Yes, Sir."

Neville leaned back in the chair and closed his eyes. Someone, he thought, must be in there behind his eyes, pushing on them from the back. He couldn't recall the last time he'd had a headache like this. Caffeine poisoning from those endless cups of coffee which he'd

418

poured down his throat in the last twenty-four hours? He hadn't had any alcohol; that much he knew.

The nasty taste in his mouth was more than metaphorical: his mouth tasted like an ashtray.

"Oh, God," he groaned, remembering.

He, the smug ex-smoker, self-righteous and fanatical about it, occasionally to the point of obnoxiousness, at some point during the long night had cadged a fag from Cowley. What's more, he had smoked it, all the way down to the end. And he had enjoyed every toxic puff.

Now he was going to have to pay the price. The headache, for starters. And Cowley would never let him live it down. Never.

"But Guv," he'd protested when Neville had asked him for it. "Smoking is a filthy habit. As you tell me every single day. And it kills you."

"Just shut up and give me the bloody fag," he'd insisted. Then he'd smoked it, defying Cowley's superior sneer.

Cowley. Speak of the devil. In he strolled, looking as seedy as Neville felt. Unshaven, a bit grimy round the edges. "Hey, Guv," he smirked. "How are you feeling this morning? A bit ropey?" He took a packet out of his pocket and shook it in Neville's direction. "Want another fag, then? Hair of the dog, so to speak?"

"Go to hell," Neville muttered.

Morag and Callie had made it nearly as far as Newcastle when the Flying Scot decided she'd gone far enough. That wasn't too surprising: after all, she'd been sitting in a garage for months, undriven.

It happened in the wee hours of the morning, when they pulled into the forecourt of a roadside Little Chef. The Little Chef was closed for the night but it seemed a convenient place to have their sandwiches and coffee, as well as give Bella some water and an opportunity to relieve herself.

All had been fine up to that point. Though their progress hadn't been speedy, the Flying Scot had moved steadily in the right direction. But when they got back in the car and Morag turned the key in the ignition, there was an ominous grinding noise rather than the sound of the engine starting up.

"Oh, dear," said Morag. "What do you suppose is wrong?"

Callie, who had lived in London for most of her life and had never even got round to getting a driving license, was not the best person to ask. "I wouldn't have a clue," she admitted.

Morag tried again, with no more success; if anything, the noise sounded worse. "It might be the battery," she ventured. "It's not turning over."

"Maybe," said Callie, "it wasn't a good idea to leave the lights on when we got out."

The third try was also a failure. Morag took the key out of the ignition.

"Now what?" Callie asked. "Can we call the AA or something? I have my mobile."

Morag sighed. "I'm afraid my membership has lapsed," she confessed. "Donald always took care of that, and I just never got round to renewing it."

"Well." Callie considered their environs. "There *is* a garage next door. But of course they're not open."

"They're sure to be in a few hours," Morag said philosophically. "Look at it this way, Callie lass — this gives us a chance for a few hours of kip. We can't very well fetch up at Lochside at five in the morning, in any case."

So Callie had curled up on the back seat with Bella. The seat had a definite doggy pong, which Callie deduced was more to do with the late Macduff than with Bella. It didn't prevent her from closing her eyes and falling into a deep sleep.

Neville went down the hall to the loo to splash some cold water on his face. Afterwards he sought out more coffee. It tasted stale, but he didn't care: maybe it would help to wash that lingering tang of ashtray out of his mouth.

The interview with Lee Bicknell had been a waste of time. It had gone on for hours; they'd tried every trick in the book to get something out of him, but Bicknell had steadfastly insisted that he hadn't seen Alex Hamilton — Sasha — after the moment she'd run from him at Paddington Station. Nothing would shake his story.

Neville had been pinning his hopes on the CCTV cameras. Another wash-out. Yes, one camera had picked up Alex, coming up from the tube and heading towards the mainline terminal. The discovery of that had provided a momentary boost.

It was short-lived, though. The camera which might have helped them, the one pointing to that critical spot under the clock, had malfunctioned. And the one which covered the exit door — the door through which Alex had run, if Bicknell was telling the truth — had run out of tape.

So all they had was that one image. Alex, smiling, going to meet someone she thought of as her boyfriend.

Neville had looked at her hopeful smile and found it haunting. More than that: profoundly disturbing. A few seconds after that, the smiling girl had disappeared from the face of the earth.

It was at that point he'd cadged the fag.

Yes, the SOCOs had gone in to Bicknell's house at some point during the night. Tearing the place apart, looking for any evidence whatever that Alex had been there. Fibres, hairs, traces of blood: if she'd been at the house in Camden Town, alive or dead, they would know it. Eventually. They'd impounded his car — an old Skoda, it was — and it would be undergoing a similar fate.

Until those tests were complete, though, Lee Bicknell was still very much in the picture. And he was admitting nothing.

"Guv!" Cowley caught him up at the coffee machine. "Yolanda Fish is on the phone."

"Yolanda Fish?" He looked at Sid blankly. "But she's off-duty. At home. What does she want?"

"She said she had to talk to you. About Rachel Norton." Cowley added, "She said it was important."

"That's all I need right now," Neville muttered sourly, but he took the call.

Yolanda was apologetic but insistent. "It *is* important. I found a laptop in Rachel's bedroom. And there are some things on it that you need to know about."

"What were you doing in Rachel's bedroom?" Neville demanded. "You're supposed to be at home. Shagging your husband, remember? That's what I told you to do."

"Never mind that." With admirable brevity and conciseness, Yolanda told Neville what she had discovered.

Five minutes later, Neville put the phone down and turned to Cowley, who was hovering close by, unashamedly listening to every word on Neville's side of the conversation.

"Well," he said, shaking his head. "Well, well."

"Tell me!"

"Seems our Rachel has a lover! And it's a short step from that to a motive for Trevor's murder."

"Bloody hell," said Cowley.

"And that gives us a clear indication of the murderer, as well. We've got a ways to go to prove it, but I think we'd be justified in arresting Rachel as an accessory, at the very least. With any luck she'll finger the bloke, and we'll be home free."

Cowley grinned. "Arrest her now?"

"As soon as she's ready to leave hospital." Neville waved at the phone. "Give them a ring, will you, Sid?

Ask them to let us know when she's going to be released."

"It's your battery, all right." A nice young man with a Geordie accent confirmed Morag's diagnosis.

"But I don't understand," Morag said. "She got us this far. All the way from London."

"The battery must have been pretty low, though. As long as you kept going it was all right. But when you stopped — you didn't leave your lights on, did you?"

"I'm afraid we did."

The young man shook his head. "Well, it's not the end of the world. How long have you ladies been here?"

Callie looked at her watch. What time had it been when they'd stopped? "I'm not sure. A few hours."

"We had a kip," Morag added.

"Well, I'll soon get you back on the road," he said cheerfully. "I can give you a jump. How far are you going?"

"Kelso," said Morag.

"Oh, that should be fine. But before you think about going any further than that, you ought to look into getting a new battery."

Neville sent a PC round to Yolanda's house to collect Rachel's laptop, then indulged in another mug of coffee before Cowley reappeared. "Guv, another phone call."

"Phone call?"

"To the hotline," Cowley expanded. "I think you need to talk to this woman, Guv. She says Alex Hamilton is in Scotland."

424

"Scotland? Bloody hell." Neville frowned sceptically. They'd had dozens of calls from all over the country, including the Channel Islands, reporting sightings of the missing girl. Why should this one be any different?

"Talk to her, Guv," Cowley repeated. "I have a hunch about this one."

So Neville rang the woman, who had given the number of an Edinburgh hotel.

"They left a newspaper outside of the door this morning," she said. "Complimentary."

"Yes?" Neville tried not to sound impatient.

"The little girl. The girl who's missing. There was a photo. I thought she looked a bit familiar."

You and a few hundred other people, Neville said to himself.

"My son Henry," she went on. "When he saw the photo, he went all quiet. That's not like Henry. Not really. You'd understand if you knew him."

Fortunately, thought Neville, he had been spared that pleasure.

"Then, after a while, he told me. That girl was on the train with us yesterday. The train from King's Cross to Edinburgh. She got on with us, he said. She was sitting behind us. And she got off when we did."

Neville tried not to let himself get excited. Why should he believe Henry? No doubt the kid was just looking for attention.

His mother must have had the same reservations about his motivation. "Finally," said the woman, "I got the whole story out of him. He didn't want to tell me. Said it was a secret, that he'd vowed not to tell."

"A secret?"

"He noticed that she — the girl — got on with us. I mean, she pretended she was part of our family. Then she went to the toilet when the ticket collector came into the carriage. Henry figured out that she didn't have a ticket. So he . . . well, he blackmailed her. Told her he'd keep her secret, if she gave him twenty pounds. He showed me the money. Two ten-pound notes. Now *that*," she added, sounding exasperated and a tiny bit proud, "is like Henry. If you knew him, you'd understand. He's telling the truth."

Thank you, Henry, Neville said to himself with rising elation. You miserable little toe-rag of a blackmailing grass. Then, when he'd finished the call — had, in fact, spoken to Henry himself and been convinced that he was indeed telling the truth — he turned to Cowley with a grin which was simultaneously relieved, jubilant and bemused. "Scotland!" he said. "Bloody hell, Sid. The kid's in Scotland!"

Within a few minutes they had received confirmation of this from what they considered a more reliable source: the woman at the Edinburgh Tourist Information office, who had seen the photo in the morning paper and was unshakeably certain that the missing girl had been in on Saturday afternoon, asking for information about buses to Kelso, in the Borders area. She had also, the woman added, sought directions to the nearest McDonald's.

"Kelso? The Borders?" said Neville with a frown. "Why there?" He had only the vaguest of ideas where the Borders were, but it didn't sound like they were anywhere close to the Highlands, and that was where he would have expected her to go. To her old home, to her best friend Kirsty.

"What about the mum?" Cowley suggested.

"The mum! She's in some sort of care home, isn't she?"

Cowley got out his notebook and flipped through. "Here it is, Guv," he announced. "Lochside, Kelso."

"Sid, you're bloody brilliant!" Neville could almost have hugged him at that moment. "Let's get on to the police up there. We'll have her in no time."

When they were back on the road, and nearly to the Scottish border, Callie got out her mobile and rang Brian. He didn't seem bothered — or even particularly surprised — to hear that she wouldn't be at church that morning because she was en route to Scotland. "I'll manage just fine," he said.

That was a relief.

She ought, she knew, to ring Marco and tell him what they were doing. But what if he were really angry with her? She'd prefer to tell him face to face; she'd leave it for a bit and see what happened.

And then there was Peter. She'd rung him on his mobile on Saturday afternoon to let him know that she and Bella were with Morag. He would have expected her to be home last night, though, and was probably worrying about her absence. Callie looked at her watch: it was still way too early to ring Peter. His regular

Saturday night gig meant that he rarely surfaced much before noon on Sunday.

It had been the road signs which had made Alex uneasy. At first it was fine. The nice man who looked and sounded so much like Granddad had driven out of Edinburgh and headed south, towards Lauder and Jedburgh. At some point they'd swung off on a smaller road signposted to Gordon and Kelso, so that was fine as well.

Then they'd got to Gordon, where they turned, and suddenly there was no further mention of Kelso on the signs.

"Where are we going?" Alex had asked. "Isn't Kelso the other way?"

"Just a bit of a detour," he said, turning his head to smile at her. "Don't worry, lassie. I'll get you to Kelso. I'll look after you." Then he took one hand off the wheel and reached over to stroke her hair. It was the lightest of touches, and the briefest, but she jumped as though she'd had an electric shock.

A few minutes later he'd pulled into a petrol station along the side of the road. "Just running a bit low," he said. "I'll fill up, and I'll get you a bag of sweeties, shall I?"

"No, thank you," she said stiffly. Her mother had told her never to take sweets from strangers. Not even ones who looked and sounded like Granddad. She'd also told her never to get into cars with strangers. Why hadn't she remembered that an hour ago?

428

He got out of the car and used the petrol pump, then went towards the little shop to pay.

As soon as he was inside, Alex opened the car door and jumped out. She didn't know where she was, but she knew that she couldn't stay in that car any longer.

Instinctively she headed away from the car, away from the petrol station, looking for cover.

A few houses straggled along the side of the road. Cottages, really. Holiday lets, probably, and this wasn't the holiday season. At any rate, there were no lights on in any of them to indicate that they were inhabited.

Away from the lights of the petrol station, it was very dark. Well, thought Alex, that might not be a bad thing. If she couldn't see very much, then neither could he, and at that moment she knew with certainty that she didn't want him to see her. Not even if he reminded her of Granddad.

Fuelled by adrenaline, she headed for the nearest of the cottages and circled round to the back of it. Stumbling over some shrubbery, she bumped — literally — into a dilapidated sort of shed, half falling down. An old garden shed or perhaps a wood store, she thought.

Its door was hanging off the hinges. Alex pulled the door open and slipped inside, tripping over something on the floor. A pile of split logs, she perceived by feel. Carefully she eased her way round the logs and pressed herself into the corner of the shed, gasping for breath.

Just a minute later she heard him. "Lassie!" he called. "Where are you, lassie?"

There were wide gaps between some of the boards; within a few seconds she could see a light through the gaps. A torch! He had a torch, its beam swinging round as it drew closer.

Why hadn't she opened the glove box and looked for a torch? Now he had the advantage. And he would find her.

Alex held her breath and kept herself very still, conscious of the sound of her pounding heart. Surely he would be able to hear her heart.

The torch was getting closer now. It glanced off the side of the shed. His voice was closer as well. "Lassie? Lassie?"

The noise of her heart was deafening, filling the tiny shed.

Involuntarily she screwed her eyes shut, waiting for the worst.

And then he tripped over the shrubbery. Over the clamour of her heart she heard it: the stumble, the involuntary curse.

Alex's eyes flew open and she saw that it was dark again. He must have dropped the torch. She could hear him scrabbling about for it, cursing under his breath in a continuous stream of words. Some of them were words she'd never heard before, but she could tell that they were bad.

Then . . . silence.

She held her breath; she strained her ears. The next sound she heard was the car engine starting, and then it moved away.

Still Alex didn't move. Perhaps it was a trick, and he'd be back. Waiting for her to come out.

Eventually, though, her legs grew cramped and her arm went to sleep. She crawled out of her hiding place, stretched her limbs painfully, and started walking.

CHAPTER
TWENTY-ONE

The first phone call Neville made was to the Roxburghshire police, who promised their co-operation and assured him that they were as good as on the way.

Then he contemplated the phone, steeling himself for ringing Angus Hamilton. He hadn't had any direct contact with Hamilton since that first night; everything had gone either through Evans or the Assistant Commissioner. But Evans was unavailable and Neville wasn't about to skip up the chain of command to the AC. They'd promised to keep Angus Hamilton informed, and this was a major breakthrough.

"Mr. Hamilton, we have reliable information that Alex is in Scotland," he said.

There was a huge sigh on the other end of the phone: pure relief, Neville interpreted. "Tell me," Hamilton demanded. "Where? How do you know?"

"She was seen in Edinburgh yesterday afternoon. Some time between half-past three and four. I've spoken to a reliable witness."

Inevitably, Hamilton immediately jumped on the aspect of the situation that Neville was most uneasy about. "Yesterday afternoon? But where is she now? That was hours ago, man."

"We're not sure where she is now," he said reluctantly. "There was some indication that she was planning to go to Kelso."

"Kelso!"

"I've talked to the police up there," he assured him. "They're on their way to —"

"To Lochside! So am I. I'll use the company jet and I'll probably get there before they do."

Neville wasn't at all surprised that, thwarted and constrained up till now, Angus Hamilton was ready to take action at the earliest possible opportunity; he had no doubt that Hamilton was already halfway out of the door. "If you could just wait a minute, Mr. Hamilton," he said quickly. "I think it would be best if we waited to hear from them. And if you're going to make your own arrangements to go to Scotland, perhaps one of our officers could accompany you."

"I'll take DS Lombardi, of course."

"That's fine," said Neville. "But I was thinking of one of the investigating officers as well."

An investigating officer. Was he going to have to do it himself? Neville sincerely hoped not: a trip to Scotland, in the company of Angus Hamilton, was not high on his wish list.

Cowley hovered at his elbow, and as soon as he'd procured Angus Hamilton's agreement to proceed no further than putting the pilot on standby, the sergeant spoke. "Can I go to Scotland, Guv?" he said, to Neville's amazement.

"Scotland? Why on earth would you want to go to bloody Scotland?"

Sid Cowley gave him a sheepish grin. "Well, Guv, you know I'm signed up with findagain.co.uk? That first girl I made contact with was a wash-out, you remember, but this week I've been emailing someone in Edinburgh. A girl from the year below me at school. Really hot. I figure if I can get up to Scotland, I'm in with a chance."

Neville shook his head, bemused. He should have known it would be something like that, though he could hardly imagine how Sid could think that if he was there on official business he would have an opportunity to pursue his own private passions. But why not? If Sid wanted to go, so much the better. "Findagain.co.uk?" he couldn't help saying. "After everything that's happened, I would have thought you'd have bloody learned your lesson."

Alex felt as though she'd been walking all night. Maybe she had been. It wasn't quite light yet, though there was a glimmer of brightness on the horizon. Morning couldn't be too far away.

She hoped that Kelso wasn't far away, either. Alex knew she was on the right road; the last signpost she'd passed had said that Kelso was three miles, and that had been a while ago. Alex had never been to Kelso, and didn't know where to begin to look for Lochside. That wasn't, she knew, a very specific address — apart from the clue in its name about proximity to water. She followed the road into the town and discovered that the most prominent body of water was in fact a river. There

434

were signs to the Abbey, to Floors Castle, but nothing to do with a loch.

It was Sunday morning, she realised, and most of the shops were closed. Then she spotted a board on the pavement in front of a newsagents which indicated that it was open.

The man at the till was busy sorting out Sunday papers and scarcely glanced at Alex as she put a chocolate bar on the counter. "That'll be 35p," he said, holding out his hand for the coins.

"Could you please tell me where I could find Lochside?" Alex asked.

He scratched his head. "Oh, that'll be that place for daft people. Outside of town. Artificial lake, not a proper loch. Don't suppose the dafties know the difference, mind you." He pointed. "Out towards Eden Water, it is. About a mile. Off the road."

She thought she'd seen a sign for Eden Water. "Thank you," she said, taking her chocolate bar.

The man raised his head and looked at her properly, then glanced at the pile of newspapers on the counter. "Hey, aren't you the lassie they're looking for?"

Her heart lurched. "No, I don't think so," she said calmly, walking out of the shop.

In case he was watching, she resisted the temptation to break into a run. She was too tired for that, anyway.

After all the distance she'd travelled, the last mile seemed to be the hardest. It was uphill; the angle of the winter sun was cruel, blinding her so that she had nearly passed the discreet sign to Lochside before she realised what it said. And "off the road" was an understatement: the drive, frozen underfoot, seemed nearly as long as the road out of town.

At last, though, she was there. It was a large stone house sitting behind the sweep of a circular drive, the water behind.

A car pulled up behind her and stopped; a door opened.

At last Neville went home. Cowley had gone to Scotland, Evans was doubtless enjoying the extended christening festivities, and the Assistant Commissioner was getting ready for his next press conference.

He didn't even want to think about how many hours it had been since he'd slept in his bed. Far too many. He wouldn't need drink to put him to sleep, and all the coffee in the world wouldn't keep him awake.

Neville didn't even bother to undress; he just threw himself down on the bed and was out like a light.

Then it was like a rerun of early that morning: the phone, ringing and ringing.

He struggled to consciousness. "Bloody hell," he muttered as he reached for it. Was he never going to be allowed to sleep? This was worse than a nightmare.

It was someone at the station. "We've had a call from the hospital regarding Rachel Norton," he said. "She's about to be released, with her baby. They said she could go home, but that you wanted to be notified. What would you like them to do?"

Neville didn't hesitate. This was his case; it had been since the moment they pulled Trevor Norton's body out of the canal, and he was going to see it through to the end. It was his duty. His job. "Tell them to keep her there until I arrive. Tell them I'll be there as soon as I can."

"Alex, lassie!"

Alex spun round at the sound of the familiar voice. "Granny!"

There was Granny's funny old car, the Flying Scot, and Granny was getting out of it, running towards her, scooping her up into her arms. "Oh, wee Alex! It's that glad I am to see you, lass." Granny cried. There were tears on her cheeks, running down her face.

Alex discovered that there were tears on her own face as well. Granny! She said it, over and over again. "Granny, Granny, Granny."

And Granny was saying her name. "Alex, Alex." Crying, hugging, their tears mingling on each other's cheeks.

Once the initial surprise was over, it seemed natural and right to Alex that Granny should be here.

But then there were other people there as well. Police cars appeared out of nowhere; policemen surrounded them. All talking at once, to each other and on mobile phones.

"She's safe," Alex heard one of them say. "We've got her."

Frances Cherry was wrapping Christmas presents on the dining room table with a sense of real anticipation. Only a couple of days before her daughter Heather came home, for the first time in over a year. Never mind that Heather had married an aged hippy whom Frances and Graham had yet to meet; never mind that the newlyweds were strict vegans and turkey was off the menu. She was going to see Heather, and it was going to be a good Christmas.

Advent Three. The penultimate Sunday before Christmas. At Graham's church that morning they'd sung her favourite Advent hymn, "Lo, he comes with clouds descending". She hummed it to herself now as she snipped ribbon and fashioned it into a bow.

When the phone rang, she ignored it. Probably one of Graham's parishioners, anyway. He'd pick it up on the phone in his study.

"Fran," Graham called a minute later. "It's for you."

She went out into the entrance hall and grabbed the receiver. "Frances Cherry speaking."

"I'm sorry to bother you," said a hesitant voice: hesitant, yet clearly distressed.

It was Rachel Norton, who had just been informed that she and her baby were ready to be released from hospital. "But they're not going to let me go home," she said tearfully. "They said that the police were coming. I think maybe they're going to arrest me. I don't know what's going to happen to my baby."

There was no question of what Frances' response would be. "Would you like me to come and stay with you until they arrive? I can be there in a quarter of an hour."

"I wouldn't want to ask that. Not on your day off."

"You're not asking. I'm offering. I'm leaving now."

So the police had found out somehow, or at least they had reason for strong suspicions. Frances hoped that Rachel didn't think she'd told them.

She was already reaching for the coat draped over the banister, calling out to Graham, "I have to go to the hospital. I'll give you a ring when I know how long I'm likely to be."

Callie had remained in the car when Morag ran to embrace Alex; now that the police had arrived, she got out and went to stand at Morag's side.

A woman police officer was trying to steer Alex towards one of the police cars. Alex, though, was ignoring her, focusing her attention on Morag.

"I have to see Mum," she said fiercely. "You understand, don't you, Granny? I've come all this way. Ever such a long way. I have to see her. I'm not going anywhere till I've seen her."

Alex was, Callie observed, a bit the worse for wear. Her frizzy hair was wild, uncombed, and her coat was filthy, with bits of wood and dead leaves clinging to it. But her spirit was unquenched as she stood her ground. Callie found herself admiring the girl enormously, rooting for her to get her dearest wish.

Morag put a protective arm round Alex's shoulder and faced the police woman. "Officer," she said, "I'm going to take Alex inside, and ask whether it's possible for her to see her mother."

Her authoritative voice carried the day; the police woman backed off and Morag marched through the front door of Lochside, holding Alex's hand.

Callie, not sure what else to do, followed, nodding at the policewoman. The policewoman made no effort to stop her, perhaps, Callie realised, because she was wearing a dog collar. Callie stood by Morag and watched as she spoke to the receptionist, who in turn called a doctor.

The doctor arrived in person a few minutes later. Dr. Farnsworth was a woman: late middle-aged with a kindly face, in spite of the bags under her eyes and a harassed expression. She looked at Alex, who stared back at her without flinching, then at Morag, and finally at Callie, her eyes travelling down from face to dog collar. Pressing her lips together, Dr. Farnsworth beckoned Morag and Callie and drew them aside, away from Alex's hearing.

"I've spoken to you on the phone, haven't I?" she addressed Morag.

Morag nodded. "That's right. I try to keep up with my daughter-in-law's condition. But I haven't talked to you for — oh, a few weeks, I suppose."

"Mrs. Hamilton has been making good progress," said the doctor quietly. "Very good progress indeed. I'm very encouraged." She smiled — a professional sort of smile. "I don't want to get too technical, but the treatment we've been using seems to be effective. She's far more responsive than she was, even a few weeks ago. The depression isn't nearly as severe and debilitating as it was at first. But she does miss her daughter, most dreadfully. And she's been asking for her more frequently."

"Then Alex can see her?" Morag asked.

"I'm inclined to think that at this stage in Mrs. Hamilton's treatment, it could be very beneficial." This time Dr. Farnsworth's smile reached her eyes, and she glanced over at where Alex stood, her arms folded across her chest in defiance. "And I'm sure it would do Alex a world of good as well."

Frances didn't have much time with Rachel before the police arrived — just a few minutes to sit next to her on the bed, to say a handful of reassuring words, sounding far more positive than she felt. She'd been there; she knew how terrifying the experience was, whatever its outcome. Being arrested was not something she would wish on her worst enemy.

"Will they take my baby away?" Rachel asked, choked with emotion.

Frances shook her head. "No, I'm sure they won't."

"Not even if I . . . if I get sent to prison?"

"Not even then." Frances knew one or two prison chaplains, so she could speak with some authority. "If you're sent to prison, they'll let you take the baby. They'd put you in a women's prison, with a special baby unit. Don't worry about that."

Alex held onto her granny's hand tightly. Now that she had nearly achieved her goal, and was about to see her mum, she was assailed by just a flicker of doubt. What if Mum had changed? What if she didn't recognise Alex, or was reluctant to see her? What if they didn't have anything to say to each other?

"I'll be with you," Granny said, as if reading her mind. "The doctor says your mother is eager to see you."

Someone opened a door; Granny led her to it, then released her hand.

Mum. Just the same, just as beautiful. Smiling and laughing and crying all at the same time. Rushing forward to meet Alex halfway, arms outstretched.

Alex threw herself into her mother's arms.

While Morag took Alex to see her mother, Callie stepped outside to use her phone. It should be safe now to ring Peter.

First she tried her own flat, reasoning that Peter would be there, and probably quite concerned about her absence.

There was no reply, so she rang Peter's mobile.

He answered after a couple of rings. "Oh, hi, Sis," he said breezily. "Hope you haven't been too worried about me. I suppose I should have rung."

"Worried about *you*? Why should I be?"

"Since I didn't come home last night. I thought maybe you'd be worried."

She didn't need to explain her own whereabouts, Callie realised. "So where *are* you, then?"

"Well, you remember Jason?"

"Jason, who ran off with a chorus boy?" She wasn't likely to forget him, she reflected. Not after Peter had cried on her shoulder for what seemed like days when Jason left him. Jason had been one of the longest-lived of Peter's relationships; his departure had hit Peter hard.

Peter chuckled. "He's lived to regret that. Anyway, Sis, he turned up at the club last night. He bought me a drink between sets. And . . . well, we're back together," he announced triumphantly. "He said it was the biggest mistake of his life, walking out on me like that."

She didn't remind Peter that he'd declared he wouldn't have Jason back if he were the last man on earth. "That's great," she said loyally. "I'm so glad for you."

"I don't think I ever stopped loving him," Peter confided. "And you can be glad for yourself, as well. He has a little flat in Chelsea and I'm moving in with him, so I'll come by later and collect my stuff, then I'll be out of your hair from now on. I know it hasn't been easy, having me round underfoot."

"Oh, no, Peter. Don't say that," she protested. "As you once said, what are families for? I'll miss you."

As Callie pressed the button to end the call, she realised that she meant it.

Bella would miss him too.

Bella! She'd been left in the car when they'd encountered Alex in the drive. Guiltily Callie went towards the car to check on her.

The police were still there, standing about, evidently not quite sure what to do. The woman officer who'd tried to move the immovable Alex was on her mobile, probably seeking further instructions.

Another car was approaching up the drive: a sleek black limousine. It drew up behind the police cars and stopped.

The first person to get out was a man whom Callie recognised immediately from his photo: Angus Hamilton. Short, powerfully built, receding hairline. He was followed by someone she'd met before, in other circumstances — a youngish, blond policeman whom she seemed to remember was called Sid.

Then someone else got out of the other side of the limousine, and Callie's heart constricted.

Marco. It was Marco.

He saw her at almost the same instant that she spotted him. Of the two, he was the far more surprised: his jaw dropped; his eyes widened. "Callie," he said. "What on earth are you doing here?"

Inevitably, it was Neville Stewart who came into Rachel's room, followed by a WPC. He looked dead tired, Frances observed with an unexpected rush of sympathy. In fact, he looked worse than that: unshaven, unkempt, as though he'd slept in his clothes.

She'd heard on the radio that the little girl had been found, safe and sound. He'd probably been involved in looking for her. "They've found Alex Hamilton?" she said to him, hoping to buy a few more seconds of freedom for Rachel.

"Thank God. Yes." He ran his hands through his hair, causing it to stand straight up. "Her father is on his way to bring her home."

He really wasn't such a bad person, she said to herself. Not like some of those policemen you saw on the television, in those programmes that Graham loved so much.

Then she remembered what he'd done to Triona.

Impulsively, not stopping to consider the finer points of professional ethics, she stood up and faced him. "Could I have a word with you, Inspector? Alone?"

He looked startled; perhaps he thought she was going to try to intervene on Rachel's behalf.

"It's a personal matter," she added.

"Well . . . all right." He nodded to the WPC, then followed Frances to a small waiting room.

Frances didn't beat about the bush, afraid that she would lose her nerve if she didn't come straight to the point. "It's about Triona."

Immediately he looked defensive, crossing his arms across his chest. "What about her?"

"I think you should ring her. Talk to her." There — she'd said it.

He pressed his lips together. "Forgive me, Reverend Cherry, but that's not any of your business." Interfering cow, his expression said.

Frances didn't back down. Too late for that. "She's my friend. I've known her for a long time. I care about her."

"What has she been saying to you about me, then?" he frowned.

Now she'd have to tread carefully. "Just that the two of you . . . weren't exactly seeing eye-to-eye. I think you need to talk." You're both so stubborn, she wanted to say. Each as bad as the other.

Neville hesitated. "For your information," he said at last, "I've e-mailed her and said just that — that we needed to talk. But she hasn't even bothered to reply. I think you're blaming the wrong person here."

Triona's complaints about her computer came back to her. "But her computer's not working!" Frances blurted. "She won't have had your e-mail."

"Oh." He passed a hand over his bloodshot eyes, bewildered, as though it were taking him an age to absorb that information.

"Ring her," Frances repeated. "As soon as you can, after you've had some sleep."

"You know," he said, a slow smile creasing his unshaven face, "I think I will."

This was not the time or place to talk to Marco, Callie realised. She made a sketchy gesture of apology in his direction, then followed Angus Hamilton, who — after a brief word with the policewoman on the scene — was striding through the doors of Lochside in a very determined manner. "Where is she?" he demanded to no one in particular. "Where is wee Alex?"

The receptionist shrugged. "I'm not sure, sir."

"I'm her father," Angus Hamilton shouted. "And I want her, now!"

A quick phone call was made, and it wasn't long before Dr. Farnsworth reappeared. "Can I help you?" she said.

"My daughter is here. I've come to take her home." He tapped his foot impatiently.

"She's with her mother at the moment," the doctor told him. "Would you like a cup of tea or coffee while you're waiting?"

"With her mother?" he roared. "What idiot allowed that to happen?"

"As a matter of fact," said Dr. Farnsworth in a quiet voice, "I did. I thought it would be good for both of them. When Alex has had a chance to catch up with her mother, and they've had a good chat, I'll tell her you're here."

Angus Hamilton paced the length of the reception area for at least a quarter of an hour, ignoring everyone around him. Callie didn't dare to speak to Marco, nor did she want to leave, so she slipped into a chair as inconspicuously as she could manage. The other policeman went outside, fumbling with a packet of cigarettes as he went, but Marco remained. He sat down on the other side of the room from Callie, his eyes swivelling between her and Angus Hamilton.

Morag was the one who broke the spell. She appeared in the doorway from the corridor, stopping Angus Hamilton in his tracks.

"Mother!"

"Hello, Angus," she said calmly.

"I should have known you'd be behind this."

"Behind what? I'm here for the same reason you are, Angus," Morag stated. "Because of wee Alex."

He glowered at his mother. "Did you put her up to running away? Has she been with you all this time?"

"Don't be ridiculous," she snapped. "If anyone's responsible, it's that wife of yours."

His nostrils flared. "And don't you bring Jilly into this! You've turned Alex against her. Can you deny it?"

"I've scarcely seen wee Alex for months. How could I have done any such thing?"

"And you won't be seeing her for quite some time, if I have anything to say about it." Angus Hamilton turned back to the reception desk and banged his fist on it. "I want my daughter. *Now.* What do I have to do to make myself clear? I'm taking her home right now."

"No."

Everyone turned to the source of the quiet voice which had uttered that one word with such force.

Alex stepped out from behind her grandmother. "No, Dad," she said again. "I'm not going back with you."

"Alex, lassie!" He took a step towards her; she moved back.

"I'm not going back to Jilly. Jilly is . . . horrible. I hate her, and I'm not going back."

He frowned, then spoke in an unnaturally wheedling voice. "I'll allow, lass, that Jilly's not always the easiest person to live with. But she cares about you. And she'll try harder. We both will. I promise."

"She does *not* care about me. She never has, and she never will." Alex reached into her coat pocket. "Jilly is a liar. She's hateful." She drew out a bundle of letters and waved them at him with a defiant scowl. "These letters

448

from Mum. Jilly hid them from me. She let me think that my mother didn't care about me any more."

"I'm sure that's not true." He reached out his hand for the letters.

Alex threw them at his feet. "Oh, it's true, all right. I found them in Jilly's drawer."

"No." But he reached down and collected them from the floor, then opened one to look at it. For the first time, he appeared shaken. "Jilly hid them from you?"

Alex folded her arms across her chest. "I'm not going back."

"You have no choice," Angus said, though in a much more subdued voice. "Where else would you live?"

"With me." Morag took a step forward and put her arm round Alex's shoulder. "I'll look after her, just like I did for all those years."

Angus stared at his mother. "But where?"

"I still have the house in Gartenbridge," Morag stated.

"I thought you'd sold it!"

She shook her head. "There was no need to do that," she said. "Not with the money your father left when he died. And I decided I might be glad of a bolt-hole at some point."

"Alex belongs with her parents," Angus stated, but with a great deal less conviction this time.

"You may be her father, but Jilly is *not* her parent. And when Harriet is better," Morag added, "she'll come and live with us as well. Dr. Farnsworth seems to think that could happen quite soon."

★　★　★

Callie caught up with Marco before it was time for him to depart in the limousine with Angus Hamilton. "Listen, Marco," she said. "I'm really sorry I didn't ring you and tell you about this. I was afraid you'd be . . . angry."

He grinned at her. "I suppose I should be. Maybe I would be, if it had turned out differently. But I *did* tell you to stay with the grandmother, and you were following instructions."

She let out a deep breath, not aware till that moment of how worried she'd been.

"*Cara mia*, I think we need to . . . talk," Marco said. "I wanted to apologise for the other night. I was wrong, and I'm really sorry."

Wrong that he'd almost — she was sure — told her that he cared for her? Callie's mouth went dry. "Oh, you don't need to apologise," she managed.

"I should never have invited you to go to the restaurant. That wasn't fair to you, or to my family. Thank goodness it didn't happen."

"What do you mean?" Her eyes welled with unbidden tears — ridiculous.

"It wasn't fair to spring you on each other like that. I was just too eager. I wanted to get it over with, get it all out in the open. But I need to talk to them first and prepare them a bit. Like I talked to you." His words tumbled over each other.

Prepare them for *what*? "And then . . ."

"Then I'll introduce you to them properly. As the woman I love."

"Oh," Callie said. She looked down at her feet.

450

"I'll do it soon. This week." Marco took both her hands in his; her stomach performed an alarming flip-flop. "Listen, Callie. Are you free on Thursday? My niece Chiara has the lead role in her school nativity play. As the Virgin Mary. With a specially written soliloquy, no less."

She gave a nervous giggle.

"Will you come with me? Come and meet my family?"

Callie didn't hesitate — not even for a second. "Yes," she said, raising her eyes to his face. "Yes, Marco. I'd like that very much."

Also available in ISIS Large Print:

No Suspicious Circumstances

The Mulgray Twins

It can be tough working undercover for HM Revenue & Customs, but DJ Smith has more than a little help from her trained sniffer cat, Gorgonzola, a moth-eaten Persian with gourmet tastes and a mind of her own.

This first investigation finds DJ and Gorgonzola on the trail of a heroin smuggling ring operation in and around Edinburgh. Their first port of call is the White Heather Hotel, owned by the formidable Morag Mackenzie.

Beneath the innocent surface of the country house hotel eddies a sinister undercurrent. One death follows another. Who among the guests specialises in making murder look like accident? As sea mists gather, the killer awaits a chance to strike. A deadly game of cat and mouse is played — but who will survive to fight another day?

ISBN 978-0-7531-7978-9 (hb)
ISBN 978-0-7531-7979-6 (pb)

Tremor of Demons

Frederic Lindsay

Racked by fears for his daughter and her young son, at odds with his detective sergeant, and haunted by the worry that he is losing his grip, DI Jim Meldrum has to draw on all his resources of integrity and courage as he seeks to find the connection between the death of a one-time pentecostal minister and a call-girl. A darkly compelling psychological murder mystery, layered through with conspiracies and a sinister religious undertone.

ISBN 978-0-7531-7910-9 (hb)
ISBN 978-0-7531-7911-6 (pb)

Little Face

Sophie Hannah

Fascinating and original . . . beautifully written . . .
oustandingly chilling   **Spectator**

Alice's baby is two weeks old when she leaves the house
without her for the first time. On her eager return, she
finds the front door open, her husband asleep on their
bed upstairs. She rushes into their baby's room and
screams. "This isn't our baby! Where's our baby?"
David, her increasingly hostile husband swears she
must either be mad or lying, and the DNA test is going
to take a week.

One week later, before the test has been taken, Alice
and the baby have disappeared. Run away, abducted,
murdered? The police who dismissed her baby swap
story must find out and, as they do, they find dark
incidents in David's past — like the murder of his
ex-wife . . .

ISBN 978-0-7531-7822-5 (hb)
ISBN 978-0-7531-7823-2 (pb)

The Mallorca Connection

Peter Kerr

A rare combination of suspense and humour, with a real twist in the tale.

Peter Kerr writes with a combination of nice observation and gentle humour **Sunday Times**

Bob Burns is an old-fashioned kind of Scottish sleuth, more interested in catching villains than creeping to get promotion. So, when his enquiries into a brutal and bizarre murder are blocked by his bosses, should he risk losing his career by carrying on his investigations?

Encouraged by an attractive, though maverick, forensic scientist and assisted by a keener-than-bright young constable, Bob does it his way. The trail leads the trio from Scotland to Mallorca, where intrigue and mayhem mingle with the crowds at a fishermen's fiesta.

ISBN 978-0-7531-7844-7 (hb)
ISBN 978-0-7531-7845-4 (pb)